STRAIGHT TO HELL
BY
DAVID LOWRIE

10 9 8 7 6 5 4 3 2 1
FIRST PRINTING, 2020

ISBN **9798619853711**

BLACK DOG GAMEBOOKS

BLACKDOGGAMEBOOKS@GMAIL.COM

The Hellscape Volume 1:

Straight to Hell

Words and pictures

By

David Lowrie

BLACK DOG GAMEBOOKS

Playing a gamebook

The chances are that if you have bought this book, then you will probably know what a gamebook is. If so, then please feel free to move on straight away to the next section.

If by some chance you haven't played a gamebook before, then it's basically interactive fiction. Most books are sequential. You start at page 1 and read page 2, 3 etc. until you get to the final page and then the end. Then each time you re-read it, the book and the story are the same.

In a gamebook, however, you make choices which indicate which way the story goes. The book is divided up into numbered sections. You start at section 1. You read the text, and you are given the option of turning left or turning right. If you turn left you will be told to turn to a new section, let's say 142. If you decide to turn right, then you are told to go to section 347. Therefore, the choices you make will determine which route you take through the book. I would say that you are the hero in your own story, but let's see, shall we?

As well as that, you also create a character with different attributes. In this book, there are things like fighting skill, endurance and agility. Your fighting skill helps you when you meet beings you may have to fight. Your endurance is how healthy or close to death you are, as you can easily die in this book - probably many times in many different but equally gruesome ways. If your endurance gets to zero, then unless told otherwise, you are dead, and your adventure will end. This means you will have to start the book again – and maybe try a different route, or just be luckier.

Things like fights and tests are determined by rolling various dice and adding them to different attributes. For this book, you will need 2 6-sided dice (called d6) and a set of dice used in Dungeons and Dragons (d4, d8, d 10, d12 and d20). If you don't have these, don't worry. They are cheap on the internet or via board game shops, or there are loads of free apps you can download instead. So if you are told to roll 2d6 – you roll two 6-sided dice and add the numbers together.

As well as random encounters using dice, there are also some puzzles to solve and clues you will have to collect, and even some items that will help or hinder you in your quest.

As well as dice, you will also need a pencil (not a pen!), an eraser and paper (probably lots of paper) to keep track of your attributes, which will change over time. There is an adventure sheet at the back of this book which you can write on, or ideally photocopy so you can use them again and again.

I would also recommend using blank paper to draw a map, or a route through the book, as there may be times when the path is not clear, and mapping where you have already been will help you immensely.

Of course, this being your gamebook now (as hopefully, you have bought it from me) then you can ignore the dice rolling etc. and just read it and try to find your way through without worrying about dying. It's entirely up to you.

So, whichever way you choose, I hope you enjoy your time playing this book. This is my first gamebook, and so there may be errors or mistakes. If you do find any, then please let me know via my Facebook pages:

THE HELLSCAPE GAMEBOOK SERIES

Or email:

Blackdoggamebooks@gmail.com

Any feedback would be very appreciated. If you get stuck, drop me a line, and I will give you a hand (if you deserve it!)

A Word of Warning

Where you are going is not a nice place. Not nice at all. And there is a very strong chance you will die horribly on a number of occasions. Please note, some of the images and text in this book may not be to everyone's taste, and may upset those who don't like horror-themed books. I try not to use bad language, as I think there are far more fun ways to visualise things than via swearing, but some of the descriptions you may find unsettling or unnecessarily bloody. There are over 50 different ways (each one of them horrid) to die in this book. They are not for the squeamish.

My apologies if you do get upset – but the clue is sort of in the title that it's not going to be, to quote William Goldman, a "kissing book."

Your characters statistics

Throughout your adventure, you have a series of stats that will determine how good you are at fighting, how lucky you are, how long you can keep going for, and how quick you are. Each of these need to be generated by rolling dice and recording them on the Adventure sheet at the back of the book. These attributes will change over time – normally for the worst!

Strength: Roll 1d6 and add 6. **STRENGTH** is important in combat, as it helps you hurt your opponents. However, it is also useful at other times. Your **STRENGTH** can never exceed your initial value unless you are told otherwise.

Fighting Skill: Roll 1d6 and add 6. This is mainly used in combat. It is how proficient you are with arms and in hand to hand combat. There may be weapons or other items that will enhance (or decrease) your **FIGHTING SKILL**. Your **FIGHTING SKILL** can go above its original value with some additions.

Agility: Roll 1d6 and add 6. **AGILITY** is useful in lots of ways. In combat, it helps you defend against **ATTACKS**. In pursuits or other times, it can help you escape from enemies. It can also help you dodge traps due to your speed of movement. It can never exceed its original value.

Endurance: This is the ability of your human form to resist any wounds inflicted upon it. To find out your **ENDURANCE**, roll 2d6 and add 12. If your endurance gets to 0 during a game, your physical form is dead, and your adventure is (most likely) over. There may be times when this does not apply, but you will be told in the text.

Fitness: To find out your **FITNESS**, roll 1d6 and add 6 to the score.

Fitness is your ability to keep on running, moving or fighting despite your all too human body getting tired. If you are in a fight, the longer it goes on, then the more fitness has to do with it – as you get tired and so are less able to attack and defend effectively. Fitness will go down by a point after each round of a fight or pursuit. However, this is only temporary, and it will return back to full levels by one point each subsequent paragraph. So if you go into a second fight soon after a first, you will be less able to fight.

Intelligence: This is the ability to think and reason. The higher your **INTELLIGENCE**, the more likely that you may be able to escape traps, outwit enemies and work out the logical puzzles. Roll 1d6 and add 6.

Fortune: This is the most random of characteristics. Sometimes pure chance will decide your fate. You have no fortune statistic as such, but there will be times when a roll of a die will be all that's between you and eternal damnation. Some items you find may help (or hinder) your fortune so be careful when deciding what you want to take with you.

Faith: This is a very important score. As you journey through this world, things that you see and do will affect your belief in good, as well as your mental strength to fight the evil around you. At times in your adventure, you will be told to **TEST YOUR FAITH**. If you fail, you will lose **FAITH** points. There will be decisions you have to make, and making the right (or wrong) decision can also increase or decrease your **FAITH** score.

Your **FAITH** starts at 13.

Very Important! Please note this down - If your **FAITH** falls to 0, then you have to turn to reference 13 immediately.

Making "Test your" rolls

There will possibly be many times when you are told to test an attribute. Unless instructed otherwise, the normal thing to do is roll 2d6 and compare this to the attribute you are testing.

If you roll less than or equal to your current score in that attribute, you pass. If you roll higher, you fail and have to face the consequences. The act of rolling 2d6 may be the difference between life and death!

For example, if you **TEST YOUR FORTUNE**, roll 2d6 and compare that to your current **FORTUNE** score. If it is less than or equal to your current score, then you pass.

Combat

COMBAT is often avoidable, but sometimes inevitable. To get through this ordeal, there will be times when strength, arms or an iron fist are the only way you can proceed. There are two types of combat in this book: Simple or Advanced.

Simple combat

This type of combat is aimed at those who either haven't played many gamebooks or just want to have a quick playthrough. This is the same as a lot of gamebooks, in that you and your enemy both have **a FIGHTING SKILL (FS)**. You roll 2d6 for your character and add the result to your **FIGHTING SKILL**. Now roll 2d6 again and this time add the resulting number to your opponent's **FIGHTING SKILL**. The one with the higher total has hurt the other, who loses 2 **ENDURANCE** points. You continue until you or your opponent has 0 **ENDURANCE** – and so is dead or defeated.

Dice needed: Simple combat only requires the use of 2d6 – and if you have this book, then it would be hoped that at the bare minimum you own a set of 2d6!

Advanced combat

The aim of this is to make combat more realistic. In simple combat, you still have the same fighting skill whether your **ENDURANCE** is 20 or 2. In reality, the more injured you are, the poorer your fighting skill would be. Also, the longer the fight went on, the more tired you would become, again affecting your ability. Also, if you happen to go from one fight straight to another, you would still be tired, and this would affect your ability to fight effectively. Thus **FITNESS** is also an issue.

Therefore each attack and defence round you have to work out your **ATTACK STRENGTH (AS)** via a combination of your current **FIGHTING SKILL** and **FITNESS**, and then add on random dice rolls. You will then have to compare this to your opponent's **DEFENCE ABILITY (DA)**, which is based upon their **AGILITY** and **FITNESS**.

Finally, not every successful blow in combat inflicts the same amount of injury to the opponent. Therefore, each time either your attack or your opponent's attack is successful, you must work out how much damage, if any, is inflicted.

Dice needed: As advanced combat is more random, then you will need more than just 2d6. A complete set of gaming dice is recommended. Advanced combat is more brutal, and not fair, and so you may see that one bad dice roll can put you at a serious disadvantage (or advantage).

Attack Strength: When fighting, you must add your current **FIGHTING SKILL (FS)** to your **FITNESS (F).** Now roll 2d6. This is your **ATTACK STRENGTH (AS)** for that round.

Defence Ability: In each round of combat, you will attack your enemy and they will attack you back. To work out your **DEFENCE ABILITY (DA),** add your current **AGILITY (AG)** to your **FITNESS (F)**. Now roll 2d6. This is your **DEFENCE ABILITY (DA).**

Combat has various stages per round.

1: First attack: Unless told otherwise in the text, you have to determine who has the advantage of attacking first. In order to do this, roll 1d10 for you and your combatant, and add this to your respective **FIGHTING SKILL (FS)**. The highest total gets to **ATTACK FIRST**. Once this has been determined, you will always fight during that combat in the same order.

2. You attack first: Assuming you win the first attack, you now roll your **AS**. Now roll your opponent's **DA**. Whichever is highest wins. If you win the attack round, you may do damage to your opponent. If your opponent defends successfully, there is no damage to either, but your **FITNESS** will decrease by 1 due to the wasted effort.

If you manage to damage your opponent, then now work out how much **ENDURANCE (EN)** they will lose. To do this, you must compare the **STRENGTH** of both you and your enemy. Roll 1d10 for each of you and add to your respective **STRENGTHs**.

Damage may not just be **ENDURANCE** points, but also other attributes like **FITNESS, AGILITY** and **FIGHTING SKILL**, as the more injured a combatant is, the more this will affect other attributes.

SCORE	RESULT	DAMAGE
Opponents score is higher	NO DAMAGE You hit opponent but you are not strong enough to hurt them (this time!)	No DAMAGE to opponent; You lose 1 FITNESS point for the wasted effort.
Opponent score is level	NOMINAL DAMAGE to your opponent	Opponent loses 1 ENDURANCE. Opponent loses 1 FITNESS point
Your score is 1-3 higher	MEDIUM DAMAGE to your opponent	Opponent loses 2 ENDURANCE Opponent loses 1 FITNESS points
Your score is 4-6 higher	SERIOUS DAMAGE to your opponent	Opponent loses 3 ENDURANCE Opponent loses 2 FITNESS points Opponent loses 1 AGILITY point
Your score is 7+ higher	CATATROPHIC DAMAGE to your opponent	Opponent loses 4 ENDURANCE Opponent loses 1 AGILITY point Opponent loses 1 FIGHTING SKILL as your attack has seriously harmed them
Your score if 10+	MORTAL WOUND	Regardless of their current ENDURANCE score, you have managed to kill them with this blow

3. Your opponent attacks: It is now your opponent's turn, assuming they are still alive (if they were ever). Now roll again to work out your **DA**, and then work out your opponents **AS**. Whichever is highest wins. If your **DA** is higher, you have defended successfully and receive no damage, but your opponent loses 1 from their **FITNESS** due to the waste of energy. If their AS is higher, then you may receive an injury, and lose other attributes.

Now you need to work out the **ENDURANCE (EN)** you may lose. To do this, you must compare the **STRENGTH** of both you and your enemy. Roll 1d10 for each of you and add to your respective **STRENGTHs**.

SCORE	RESULT	DAMAGE
Your score is higher	NO DAMAGE Your opponent hit you but they are not strong enough to hurt you (this time!)	No DAMAGE to you; They lose 1 FITNESS point for the wasted effort.
Scores are level	NOMINAL DAMAGE to you	You lose 1 ENDURANCE You lose 1 FITNESS point
Their score is 1-3 higher	MEDIUM DAMAGE to you	You lose 2 ENDURANCE You lose 1 FITNESS point
Their score is 4-6 higher	SERIOUS DAMAGE to you	You lose 3 ENDURANCE You lose 2 FITNESS point You lose 1 AGILITY point
Their score is 7+ higher	CATATROPHIC DAMAGE to YOU	You lose 4 ENDURANCE You lose 1 AGILITY point You loses 1 FIGHTING SKILL as their attack has seriously harmed you
Their score if 10+	MORTAL WOUND	Regardless of your current ENDURANCE score, your opponent has struck you with a mighty blow that kills you outright.

Obviously, if your opponent wins the **FIRST ATTACK** roll, then points 2 and 3 are reversed.

COMBAT is designed so that the longer it goes on, then potentially the harder it is to fight. If you lose **FITNESS** points, then this affects your **ATTACK STRENGTH** and your **DEFENCE ABILITY**. If you get hit with different types of damage, then you may lose **FIGHTING SKILL** points, which affects your **AS**, or **AGILITY** points, which affect your **DA**.

Once the fight is over, if you are still alive, then your body will recover its **FITNESS** level at 1 point per paragraph, back up to a maximum of your starting value (unless told otherwise). Damage obtained in **ENDURANCE**, **AGILITY** and **FIGHTING SKILL** can only be improved by the use of potions, magic or food – unless you are told otherwise.

$\mathcal{P}$*ursuit*

There may be times when you are being pursued by enemies that you would rather not catch up to you. If you get into such a race, then the rules are simple. Firstly make sure you note all your current scores for **AGILITY, ENDURANCE** and **FITNESS**.

YOUR LEAD: Now throw 2d6 for your pursuer. This is how far ahead of him you are at the start of the race. So if you roll 7 – you are 7 seconds ahead.

EACH ROUND: each round you must throw 1d20 for yourself and any adversary chasing you. You add this to your combined **AGILITY** and **FITNESS** score (this is your ability to travel fast over unsteady areas and how long you can run for).

You then compare scores. If you win, you increase your lead over your adversary. If you lose, they close the distance. You also use your **ENDURANCE** score. For each turn this contest goes on for, you get tired, and so you lose 2 **ENDURANCE** points. If you get down to 0, you pass into unconsciousness. You do not die, and will start to recover all your stamina by the next reference – and so it's not a permanent injury.

For example:

Daemon A   AGILITY 11   ENDURANCE 11   FITNESS 8

SPEED SCORE: You start 8 seconds ahead of Daemon A. You have AG 10 and FIT 10 and roll 8. You score 28. This is your **SPEED** score of 28 for this turn.

Daemon A rolls 10 and has AG 11 and FIT 8. A **SPEED** score of 29– so he gains a second on you. You are now 7 seconds ahead of him.

TO WIN: If you get to plus 20 on your pursuer, you have lost them. If you are pursued by more than one creature, you must continue until you have lost all of them.

ENDURANCE: After this turn, you all lose 2 stamina points. Daemon A is down to 9.

Equipment

You are armed with your Greatsword Devilsbane. This sword is one of the holiest relics of your Faith and is only awarded to the one Knight in a generation who deserves to wield it. It is a massive weapon, fully half as big again as a standard broadsword, but enchantments laid on it by Holy Magician-Priests centuries ago make it light to wield. In addition, it has power over the dead and undead and can injure magical creatures and spirits. If you lose this sword, you must reduce your **FIGHTING SKILL** by 2.

Provisions

You start off with trail rations enough for 3 meals, and a skin of water. The rations can increase your **ENDURANCE** by 2 when eaten (although not above your initial level) but you can only eat one at a time – so you couldn't eat all 3 and recover 6 **ENDURANCE** points. You cannot eat during a battle either, or just before one.

Prologue

You are Kommandant Ulrac De-Villiers. You have been a seasoned crusader for 20 years, feared for both your strength in arms and in your beliefs. You are a Soldier of the One True God, and you have campaigned all your life to defend the One True Church. There is nothing you will not do to protect your church, and you have committed any number of atrocities in God's name. However, you see them as a necessity, and prayer and your belief absolve you of any blame.

Now God's voice on this earth, the Most Holy Zacatecas herself, has sent you on a crucial mission to defend the church.

This has taken you to a remote part of the eighth continent, along with a small force under your command. This matter threatens not just the world, but potentially the cosmos, and even Heaven itself. For aeons, the battle between good and evil has always taken place through agents.

No direct confrontation between Heaven and Hell has occurred since the 4th uprising, over 100,000 years ago, and that threatened to tear the reality apart. Since then, Heaven and Hell have tried to work through mortal agents to gain the upper hand on this reality, and you are one of the key agents of the One True God.

However, something has happened to change all this. Somehow a portal has opened on the 8th continent that links your world with the Hellscape below – the home of hundreds and thousands of devils and demons, as well as uncountable numbers of the damned. If this portal remains open, then the whole of this reality could be pulled into the Hellscape, and all of your world will fall to the cruel dominion of The Dark Ones.

In order to do this, you were sent by boat across the Sea of Dreams to the dark continent in the northern hemisphere. You land with your forces in the northern deserts, barely seeing the sun. Both the days and nights are brutally cold. For days you trek across this hostile landscape, losing 10% of your small force on the way.

On the 13th day, the sun appears for the first time as you emerge at the top of a large fertile valley, with green shrubs and tall, lean trees all around. You gratefully camp and find fresh game to hunt and water to drink, a welcome change to hard trail rations. You allow your troops to rest and send out scouts to try to find the portal.

Of the five that you send out, only one returns and he is in a terrible state. He looks tired and drained, with multiple injuries and contusions. But worst of all are his eyes, which are wide and almost unblinking, and portray a madness that has overtaken him. You can get little sense from the poor wretch, but you know the direction he was sent, and so you decide to set off with your host along that route.

You give short orders to break camp and assemble, and order one of your most eager Lieutenants to kill the scout. A madman will be a drain on your small army's resources. You watch intrigued as Lieutenant Celdron takes his time, slowly running the poor man through whilst staring deep into his face. He smiles cruelly as he sees the pain register on the scout's face. Then he is dead.

Celdron removes his sword and wipes it down on the dead scout's clothes and sheathes it, smiling. You make note of Celdron. You are not alarmed or surprised at his actions. He is relatively new to your command, but any man who can be ruthless when needed, and enjoy his work, has a place by your side. He is a man to be cultivated but also one to be watched in case he has designs on subverting your position.

You head into the forest and travel for several days. In place of the cold, the heat becomes oppressive, and your armour feels like a furnace and the sweat seemingly leaks out of your body. Then you arrive at a deep and fertile oasis in the centre of the forest.

Turn to 1

You descend down into the bowl-like oasis. Once more, the temperature rises until you feel like you will boil in your armour. In the very centre of the natural amphitheatre is a giant machine. It rises up above the tree line, and as you and your men creep closer, you see the full structure.

It's tall; fully 100 yards into the air and pyramid-shaped. But instead of a solid stone pyramid, this is an open structure with three tripod-like legs. Atop the pyramid is a multi-faceted jewel that is spinning at speed, sending out arcs of multi-coloured light.

Around the structure, men in black cowls and robes work, manipulating the crystal either by some magik or technological means you cannot even begin to understand. There are no more than 20 of these figures visible at work on the structure. The light and colour from the jewel is dizzying. You tear your eyes away from it and follow a solid beam of light from the base of the jewel down to the forest floor; or rather what was the forest floor.

In its place between the tripod-like structure's three legs is a whirling vortex that seems to descend down into the soil forming almost a cone of a hurricane going down through the earth. However, on closer inspection, the vortex is overlaying the forest floor that you can vaguely see through the almost semi-transparent maelstrom. It's as if two types of reality are occupying the same space.

This must be the Hellportal, and you need to destroy it. And quickly, as with horror, you spot nightmarish creatures emerging from the portal. Daemons from the depths of the Hellscape are about to set foot on this reality for the first time in millennia. You must act!

Will you: order your army to attack the structure with the hope of disabling it, turn to **549**, or try to take the crystal out with bow fire from cover, turn to **190**

Taking in the vessel, you can't seem to pick out a potential weak spot, and so you resolve just to strike at the same place repeatedly. You swing Devilsbane, but even this mighty sword may take more than one stroke to rupture the vat. Roll 1d6+2. This is how many strokes it will take to breach the vessel.

Now **TEST YOUR STRENGTH** and **FIGHTING SKILL**. Add both together and then roll 4d6. If the roll is higher than your combined **STRENGTH** and **FIGHTING SKILL** in any of the rolls needed, then you fail to breach the container, and your pursuers are now upon you.

You have no choice but to fight - and so turn to **377**. If you manage to make all the rolls, then turn to **448**

This bottle is plain and looks like in the true world that it would just be used to store vinegar or oil. You take out the cheap cork and sniff it. The aroma alone lifts your spirits. You drink the opaque red liquid, and you feel full of boundless energy. You feel like you could run or fight all day with no ill effects.

You have drunk a **POTION OF VIGOUR**. Its effect is that your **FITNESS** has now permanently increased by 3 points.

However, because you are able to move for longer and faster with no ill effects, you fail to notice as much in the environment, and so your **INTELLIGENCE** is reduced by 2 points permanently. In the Hellscape, you get nought for nought.

Turn to the previous reference.

4

Fully 100 yards in, the jump to the last step is the longest yet, and you fail to make the distance. You try to grab at the lip of the stair, but your hands just flail and grasp thin air. For a few moments, time seems to stop, and you are almost suspended in mid-air, as you take in your fate.

The hard floor, fully 100 yards below, then starts to rush towards you as gravity takes hold. You fall, gathering speed, your arms and legs flailing as if trying to swim in the air, but the ground rushes ever closer. You are falling towards the spiral in the middle of the floor that leads to a dark hole. You hit at the top of the spiral with bone-shattering impact and bounce down a couple of levels until you are close to the hole.

You look up, vaguely conscious, and see your arms and legs are laying at unnatural angles, obviously broken by the fall. The pain is intense and unceasing. Then you see a giant vat is manhandled towards the spiral by the giant sub-daemons. They tilt it at the edge of the spiral, and the liquid remnants of souls from the giant vats are poured in. The liquid catches up with you, and your mouth is filled with foul putrescence. You are aware of body parts flowing past you, and you get struck in the face by a still-wriggling arm.

Then the tide takes you, carrying you down the spiral, faster and faster until you drop into the dark abyss of the hole. You drop some way, but then are dumped into a sluice and through a pipe, being washed along with the damned of humanity. The journey seems to last forever, as, still alive, you try to keep your head above the foul liquid but to no avail.

You are dragged under and start to drown as the liquid fills your lungs. Then you are thrown out of the pipe into another giant vat and, unable to move your smashed arms and fractured legs, you drop like a stone to the bottom, with all the sludge of humanity. You lose consciousness and thankfully die, only to awaken as a damned soul, doomed forever to be boiled, strained and turned into their evil liquor.

Your mission has failed, and soon the mortal realms will fall.

Turn to **616**

5

The short route takes you quickly into a clearing with a circular grassy hillock. You rush to the top in the hope that it is cooler.

You take time to rest and can regain 1 **ENDURANCE** point. After resting, you can now choose to go left and turn to **295** or plod straight and turn to **595**

6

You hurry from the passageway, grateful that you survived. You can now either turn left and turn to **418** or go straight on and turn to **422**

7

If the Devil is six

"Ah indeed my master, I will make it so that thou can breathe these fumes like a native"

He places his large 6-fingered hand on your head, you hear a surge of his will and the power jolts down his arm into your body. Your whole body is afire, and the tunnel seems to grow larger and larger around you. Then you realise with horror that it is not the room that is growing - you are shrinking.

You look down and see that your armour is becoming too big for your body and the greaves and gloves slip from you, as does your sword belt. You look at your hands and see that your fingers are fusing together, the first to the second, and the third to the fourth until you have one thumb and two thick fingers - each with a small talon at the end.

The skin of your hand changes, becoming more like scales and taking on a crimson hue. You feel your face elongate, and your ears seem to grow upwards into a point and take over most of the side of your head. Then you start to forget who you are. Your name and memories slip away from you like a dream in the night, and you start to talk in a staccato gibbering dialect.

The Djinn has taken you literally and turned you into an imp, the residents of this chamber, who tend to the pool in the pulsating centre. Imps are almost mindless, but the Djinn knows that it will be a simple job to get you now to make two further wishes on matters of no import, and so he will be freed from his enslavement.

You are doomed to spend eternity in this foul place, tending the acrid pool in the chamber below. Such is the risk of trusting a Djinn.

Your mission has failed. Turn to **616**

9

Climbing a ladder in armour and carrying a greatsword and a shield is no easy feat. You must either leave your sword and shield at the bottom of the ladder or climb it with both and lose 2 **ENDURANCE** points. If you leave your equipment and get into a fight, you must deduct 1 from your **FIGHTING SKILL** and 1 from your **DEFENCE ABILITY**.

You get to the top and climb onto the wooden platform. You crouch down below the lip of the vat so that you are not seen, and then peer over the sides and wish you hadn't.

Turn to **339**

10

Despite your best attempts, you cannot solve the riddle and the time reduces to nothing.

"Ah, a task too far, we fear" says Astaroth almost sadly. *"We had hoped your mind would be more nimble, but we should be used to being disappointed in mortals. Still, thy time will not be wasted".*

He gestures at the mighty dragon, which slowly rises to its feet and stretches. Then it advances on you, its head down and teeth bared; its huge tail thrashing against the walls of the cave. You draw your weapon, but the dragon just slaps it out of your hand with a swipe of its ginormous paw. You back up, trying to find space, but there is nowhere to run, and soon you are pressed against the chamber wall.

The beast lashes out with its claws and rakes its talons across your breastplate. Three long rends appear, and with another swipe, your breastplate is cut from you. It drops to the floor with a clank. The dragon advances and places one paw on your chest and pushes you to the ground. It lowers down a head larger than a coach and sniffs at you.

Then it opens its jaws, and you expect a quick death, but instead, it picks you up and shakes its head, and you are like a rag doll in its mouth. Then it shifts to one side and lets you go, your body skidding across the floor. The dragon bounds over like an oversized hound, clearly enjoying itself, and then flicks you to the other side of the chamber with its claws.

Astaroth laughs and shouts out encouragement to the dragon, who plays like a newborn pup. You will not die for many days until the dragon finally tires of its new toy.

But your mission is failed, and the world above can count its time in mere days as well. Turn to **616**

11

You are a dog of war, at home on the battlefield. As the strong hand of the One True Church, you have been involved in some of the most bloody and vicious battles over the last 20 years. You thought nothing could disturb you, having seen up close the suffering that mankind can inflict on their fellows, often over something as simple as the interpretation of a passage in a book. But this is something new. The mixture of the laughing Daemons, the hacked up and cooked bodies still moving and the stench of cooked man-flesh staggers you. You feel like you are going to be sick, but then with a huge effort, you manage to calm yourself. You determine to try to edge around the hall to the archway, which presumably leads to the kitchens.

TEST YOUR FORTUNE. If you are fortunate, turn to **645**. If you are not so, turn to **386**

12

The Daemons are too busy gorging themselves with succulent human flesh. You waste no time running back into the kitchen to explore further, and head for the back door, making it successfully. Turn to **131**

13

Faithless, you drop to your knees. Your **FAITH** has been the cornerstone of your life and losing it cripples you, physically and emotionally. Having lost all **FAITH** in the One True God, and the One True Church, you curse them under your breath. Tears stream from your eyes as you realise the lie you have been serving for all your life.

All the terrible things you have done for the Faith flash across your mind. The screams of children echo in your mind, from when you have put whole towns to sword and fire for being ungodly. The scenes of roasted bodies and mutilated corpses from when you have carried out the Faiths work. The endless bloody conquest and conflict all over the 12 continents, where you have made the soil red, green and yellow with blood.

The executions of those seen as unholy by being hanged, drawn and quartered, for which you keenly participated as you felt you were freeing their souls from their ungodly bodies. The years of abstinence, where you have forbidden yourself love for anyone, except the church. You realise it was all a lie.

You stay there on the ground, rocking backwards and forwards and sobbing. In between the flow of tears, you strip off your armour and cast it aside. Soon you sit in nothing but a soiled loincloth. You reach for your sword belt, discarded on the floor next to you, with a trembling hand.

You draw Devilsbane for the final time and reverse the blade. The sword is so long your hands cannot reach the hilt, which is pointing away from you. Instead, you wrap both your bare hands around its razor-sharp blade. The steel cuts into your palm and rivulets of blood pour to the ground. You ignore them.

You place the point of Devilsbane at your naval, and remember the countless souls you have sent to everlasting torment on the tip of this great blade. Then you take one final breath and pull the sword toward you. It effortlessly enters your torso, and, while arching your body, you use your legs to throw yourself forward.

The pommel strikes the ground with your bodyweight behind it, and the long blade slides further into your flesh. You slide down the edge until you are caught on the crossguard. Blood flows freely as your life drains away, and the tears continue to flow from your eyes.

You die, alone, unloved and unmourned, far from home. If you ever truly had a home. But your spirit remains in the Hellscape, doomed to torment.

You have failed in your mission and humanity will suffer because of this. Turn to **616**

14

You recognise this is a portrayal of Gremory, a Daemon Lord who often takes the shape of a crowned woman. Gremory is known to reveal secrets and hidden treasures.

Turn to **507**

15

You seem entranced in the music and are unable to stop playing. As you do, you watch your hands move over the instrument, and you see tendrils of flesh starting to extend out of the holes above the keyboard, and soon they are covering your hands and creeping up inside and over your armour. You almost absently watch this happening but have no will to stop it or stop playing.

Soon the tendrils, which are red, purple and blue in colour, entwine themselves around your body. They pulse like they have a heartbeat, and you realise that this is the flesh of some of those whose bodies were used to make this vile instrument. This knowledge does not seem to alarm you.

The tendrils of flesh have now almost cocooned you, and then they reach your head. They move towards your eyes, ears, nose and mouth, and start to slide under eyeballs, up nostrils and into your mouth. They are soon entangled around your brain (not that you are aware) and have extended all the way down into your stomach. You cannot move except to carry on playing.

The Hellsicorde has found a new pianist after it finally consumed the previous one over several millennia. You will now play this machine for the rest of your extended life, as the instrument feeds of you.

Your mission has failed. Turn to **616**

16

After spending some time examining the various pieces of armour, three in particular interest you.

There is a helm seemingly made out of an inhuman skull. The creature's skin is still on the bone, and it had silver scales, seemingly harder than steel, and obsidian horns with a sigil in the centre of its forehead.

Next to this is a shield, seemingly made of gold, with a sigil in the centre. It seems lighter and stronger than any gold you have ever seen.

Finally, there is a surcoat of white, with a sigil emblazoned on the front. Decide which item you would like to examine further.

 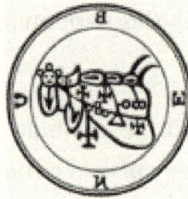 

Shield	Helm	Surcoat
Turn to 40	Turn to 234	Turn to 663

17

You can try to drink either one or both of the bottles. If you decide to drink both, remember this reference. If you are still able to after drinking the first bottle, return to this reference and choose to drink the second you have picked.

To drink green (**125**), red (**3**), amber (**661**), black (**288**), purple (**225**), blue (**426**) and clear (**382**).

After having drunken those that you selected, then turn back to **48** and choose a door you haven't opened yet.

18

Reaching down, you pick up a small crystal bottle and unscrew the stopper. You reach over towards the foul-smelling pool and place your hand over the side. The level of the water is so high it's almost overflowing.

You lower the bottle into the pool, being careful not to let your hand come into contact with the liquid.

TEST YOUR FORTUNE. If you are lucky, turn to **269**. If you are unlucky, turn to **625**

19

Cerberus is indeed the name. If you passed the **INTELLIGENCE** test when you entered this realm, turn to **311**. If you failed, turn to **259**

20

You drop your flask into the crystal clear water and fill it up. You take a long drink. Add 2 to your current **ENDURANCE** as the water refreshes you. However, it is drawn from the corpse trees, and so it is also cursed as the souls are who suffer eternally.

Roll 1d8.

The results are: 1. Strength, 2. Fighting Skill, 3. Agility, 4. Endurance, 5. Fitness, 6. Intelligence, 7. Fortune and 8. Faith.

Now roll 1d4. If the number is odd, you lose 1 point from whichever attribute came up when you rolled the d8. If it's even, you lose 2 points.

As with many things in the Hellscape, there are risks in taking its gifts.

Now turn back to your previous reference.

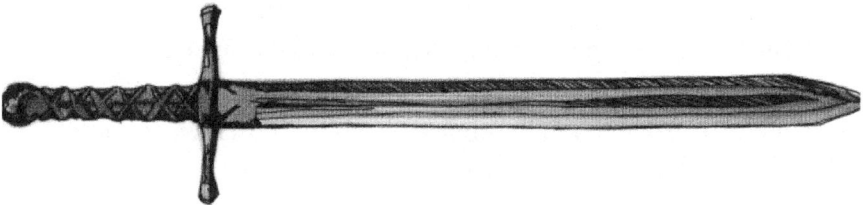

21

Whispering into his ear, you say:

"Most Holy, I am the arm of Zacatecas, the Most Holy on Earth in my time. I am stuck in this place, and I need to get back to Earth to stop a Daemon plot to conquer the world. Will you help?"

TEST YOUR FORTUNE. IF you are fortunate turn to **651**. Otherwise, turn to **580**

22

You recognise the name as Astaroth, one of the great Lords of the Hellscape; part of the main trinity. He is a power to be feared, but also one who enjoys challenging the wits of mortals.

He is known to have power over snakes and other beasts and is said to ride a giant dragon while holding a snake in his right hand. Turn to **431**

23

You turn the key 23 times in the lock and hear a click. You reach down and take hold of the handle, next to the cruel and leering face. As you reach out and pull the door open, the face smiles. There is nothing human in that smile, and then the face says:

"You choose.......unwisely".

The mouth has asked you to combine the numbers, not add them.

You try in vain to stop the door from opening, but it is too late, as a force behind it compels it open, one that is much stronger than you. You try to move, but you are rooted to the spot as if all your muscles have been locked in place and are unable to move.

The space behind the door is dark, until after a few moments you see a speck of orange light in the centre. This speck slowly becomes larger and larger, until you can see it is a streak of flame, but extending from where you do not know. Frantically you try to move, but all you can do is make your body slightly tremble.

Sweat pours down your brow, and you know that you are seeing your impending doom. Then the flame seems to reach the doorway, and it swirls around in a circle within the portal, moving so fast it becomes a single ring of fire. Then, the flame gusts out of the doorway and envelops you.

The heat is so intense it sucks the breath from your lungs and burns your throat. Your hair singes and burns and your skin blisters and blackens. You are being roasted alive inside your iron coffin. Fortunately, this doesn't take long, and soon, as the infernal heat starts to melt the iron of your armour, it starts to buckle, and your dead form crashes to the floor.

You look down, your ethereal soul now free of its mortal remains, and see that the doorway has once more closed, and the face of the Daemon leers at you:

"Excellent. Another soul, another servant, I have need of you. I doubt very much you will enjoy the next ten thousand years."

You are now a soul doomed to service and torment in the Hellscape. Your main regret is that you fear that the mortal world is similarly doomed.

Your mission has failed. Your enslavement, however, is just starting. Turn to **616**

Slowly, your body is being pulled further into the swamp of humankind that you have fallen into. All around you are half or full bodies of humans of all ages. They all writhe in torment, moaning helplessly as arms, some disembodied, grab at you. You are already knee-deep in the mixture of human excrement, blood, mud and worse.

Slowly, as if you are in the sinking swamps of Hbrath, you can feel your legs being inexorably sucked into the mire. You struggle, scrambling at the side of the ridge with hands like claws, but to no avail. You are pulled away by unseen hands and are now in the middle of a sea of corpses; though they are living corpses.

The wailing around you continues, and you try to drag yourself over their bodies, but their flesh is so weak that all you end up doing is pulling away fragments of tissue, or arms and hands. You are now waist-deep, and the more you struggle, the quicker you seem to sink. Your armour weighs you down, and soon your arms are pulled under.

Unable to leverage yourself, your fate is now sealed. You try to tilt your head backwards, as the surface of the meat soup closes in on your head, but soon all that can be seen of you is your face as you vainly try to keep above the line of the filthy liquid.

Soon, however, you are pulled under the surface. You try to hold your breath, but the liquid is up to your nose, in your ears and when you run short of breath, you involuntarily gulp in a mouthful of the gross cocktail.

Your mortal form will soon drown in this putrescent filth, but your spirit will then be stranded in this realm of gluttony. Your mission has failed, and you have doomed the mortal world to torment.

Turn to **616**

You move down onto the floating step that helps you into the corridor below. As you do, the step tilts down until it hits the floor. As soon as it does this, you feel a tingling and then a massive surge of power. Sparks fly along the copper corridor, and then travel up your metal studded boots, into your armour, until your whole body convulses wildly.

Sparks fly around your body and your armour, and the air is alive with the power of lightning. Within seconds, the temperature inside your armour has risen up so high that every area of your body that touches metal starts to smoulder, blister and blacken. You can smell yourself being roasted alive, and feel your hair vaporising where the lightning has leapt into the back of your helm.

The skin of your face splits, and blood flows out, only to be congealed and dried quickly due to the heat of the lightning. Still, your body involuntarily convulses, shaking uncontrollably. Eventually, your armour starts to melt and your legs buckle, and you drop to the floor with a loud crash.

But by now, your eyes have evaporated, your tongue flops and fries on the floor as you have bitten it off, and your brains are boiling in your skull. Your mortal remains continue to cook for some time, as your soul form watches. You are doomed to remain in this land, not damned but stuck in the Hellscape forevermore. Your mission has failed, and your world will burn as your corporeal form has. Turn to **616**

26

After entering the clearing, you are stopped dead by a wondrous sight. Ahead of you is a hart, fully 15 hands high. Its coat is a snowy white, pure and untouched by any of the filth of this forest. Atop its head are a set of antlers that must be at least 13 points, but black like obsidian. Emerging from its back are a pair of wings, also white, but feathered.

The creature is startled and moves to run, but you stop still. Its eyes gaze at you, seemingly full of love and peace. You wonder how such a divine creature could end up in this realm.

TEST YOUR INTELLIGENCE. If you roll lower or equal to your current intelligence, turn to **531**. If you roll higher, turn to **313**

27

Deciding to head for the nearer green door, you edge a few feet around the kitchen.

TEST YOUR FORTUNE. If you are fortunate, turn to **402**. If you are unfortunate, turn to **72**

28

You resolve to go straight on and set off walking at a brisk pace. The ground, if it can be called that, of this strange realm, feels almost spongy and it saps your strength as you walk.

There is still no horizon to walk towards, and so it's impossible to tell how long you have been walking. Then you see something on the ground ahead of you, and your heart skips a beat as it could be proof of life, or at least matter, in this grey place. You walk towards it and bend to examine it.

It's the remnants of a soldiers trail pack, the same type that you ate a few hours (or minutes) ago. You pick it up and recognise the marks on the wrapper - it is the exact same pack that you ate. You have somehow arrived back where you started. Increasingly frustrated, you throw it to the ground in disgust and decide you must try another "direction".

You can now choose to go left, turn to **649**, or right, turn to **89**

29

As you fight the loathsome creature, each hit on the tail seems to distress the beast more than you would have thought possible. Your blade slices into the thinner layers of fat where the thick body tapers down. In the body, you see what appears to be a large white nerve ganglion.

You hope the organ is something akin to a brain, and you resolve to thrust your steel into it. The blade slides in, and the beast rears once again, but even higher until almost all of its huge body is off the ground, except for the 6-foot tail section.

Then the creature starts to thrash around and convulses once, dropping lifeless to the ground.

TEST YOUR AGILITY. If you succeed, turn to **388**. If you fail, turn to **445**

30

The passage through the corpse trees soon ends at what appears to be a large burrowed hole angling down into the ground. There is no other way for you to go and so steeling yourself, you enter.

It turns into a tunnel, and you can vaguely see light at the end, but aside from that, there is almost total darkness. You hurry through, but the tunnel is hot, humid and airless. You are soon gasping to catch your breath.

Lose 2 **ENDURANCE** points.

You get to the end and mercifully make it out into the open air, arriving into a grassless muddy clearing. You can leave this place either by bearing left, turn to **303**, or go straight on and turn to **157**

31

As you enter the corridor, there is a whistling sound and all of a sudden, too fast for you to react, a large bone horn scythes down from the roof. Its point is wickedly sharp as it arcs through the air and pierces your chest, passing through your plate and mail as if they were made of nothing but silk.

The force picks you up off your feet and drives you backwards, and then the horn stops swinging, and you are thrown from its point. You have been impaled on the Horn of Bamphonet, a remnant of a Daemon from millennia past who had a single curved horn in the centre of his forehead. Baalberith tore it from his rival during combat to rule this realm and consigned Bamphonet to an eternity of servitude.

The jagged layers of the horn rip out flesh, organs and even bone as they exit your body. Your lifeless form crashes to the floor in the antechamber. Your soul leaves your body, and you are left watching as the blood pumps from the gaping wound, sliding down what's left of your breastplate, and seeping out between the gaps in your plate armour.

Soon the uneven puddle of blood covers half the floor and, in the dark light, it looks like a pool of tar. You are now a soul stuck in the Hellscape in perpetuity.

You will now need to use your wits to try to find some position in this grim realm, or risk being tormented. Your mission has failed.

Turn to **616**

32

Panicked in a way you are not used to, you manage to scrabble on the surface and regain your footing. You take a moment to compose yourself and then set off in another direction. Either turn to **28** or turn to **568**

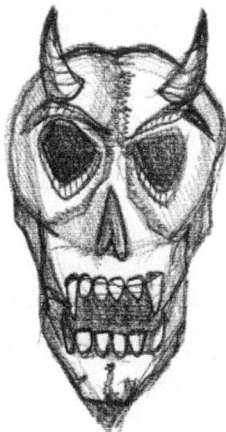

33

In the centre of the glade is a red onyx statue of a beautiful woman wearing a crown. Her shapely arms are held aloft with a shimmering sword in her right hand and a shield on her left arm. She is staring up at the sky, and long curled tresses flow down her back in a cascade. She is clad in what looks to be a breastplate and skirt, with greaves around her shapely calves and tied sandals on her feet.

The statue is incongruous, as it's a thing of beauty in a world of pain, and it jars seeing it against the backdrop of the carcass trees.

TEST YOUR INTELLIGENCE. If you roll less than or equal to your current intelligence, turn to **14**. If you roll higher, turn to **276**

34

With agility that belies your age, you jump and twist in mid-air and grasp onto the first step in the next stair. However, the ledge of the first step remains tantalisingly out of reach. Realising you are not going to make it, you push on the riser of the step so that you fall backwards - as if you were to fall straight down that would be the end of you.

TEST YOUR FORTUNE. If you are fortunate, turn to **76**. If you are not so fortunate, turn to **187**

35

Relieved and almost shaking, you leave the room and once again enter the decrepit courtyard. If you wish to go through the archway into the walls of the castle, then turn to **485**.

Otherwise, you can take the steps down into the bowels of the castle.

Turn to **233**

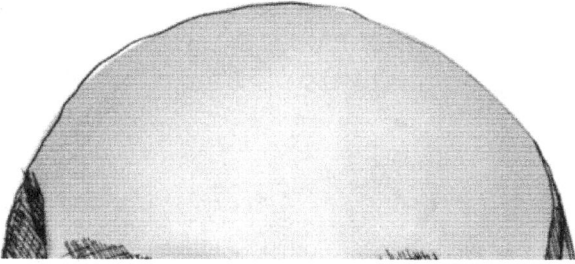

36

TEST YOUR INTELLIGENCE. If you succeed, you manage to pick the lock and open the drawer, then turn to **253**. Otherwise, you fail and get bored of searching the room and leave. If you go, you can try the other door on the left, turn to **535**, or the door on the right, turn to **333**

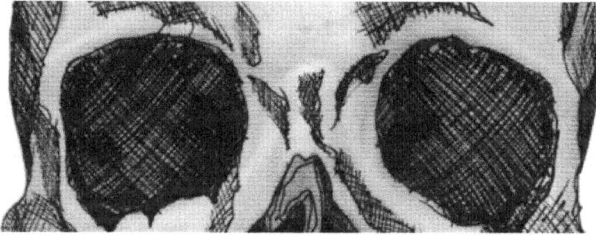

37

The effort and the air is killing you as you climb, but you must continue, or you will certainly perish on this stair. Add your **STRENGTH** to your **FITNESS**. Now roll 4d6.

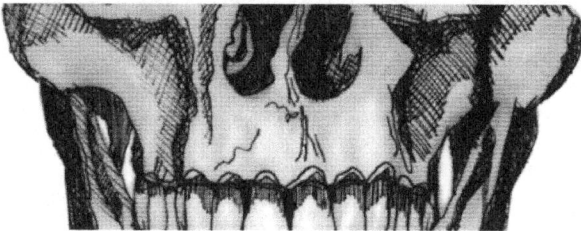

If you roll less than or equal to your sum, turn to **132**. If you roll higher, subtract the difference from your **ENDURANCE**. If you are still alive, turn to **665**. If your **ENDURANCE** is 0, turn to **335**

38

Having decided on your intended victim, you sneak across the plain, towards the incline. The Daemons are too busy arguing amongst themselves to see you as they also have their backs turned. You then break into a run and aim a vicious swing of Devilsbane at the neck of your intended victim.

Work out your current **FIGHTING STRENGTH**, now roll 4d6. If you roll less than or equal to your **FIGHTING STRENGTH**, your stroke is true, and the Daemon's head flies from his shoulders, the body slumping to the ground. If you fail this roll, read to the end of this paragraph.

If you have killed one of the Daemons, which one did you decide to kill? If it was the Ape Daemon, turn to **68**. If it was the Thin Daemon, turn to **481**. If you fail the **FIGHTING STRENGTH** roll, you must fight both Daemons at the same time.

THIN DAEMON has **FS 8, EN 10**

{ADVANCED - Initial AS: 16, Initial DA: 16; FIT 8, AG 8, ST 7}

APE DAEMON has **FS 9, EN 9**

{ADVANCED - Initial AS: 16, Initial DA: 14; FIT 7, AG 7, ST 8}

If you win, turn to **589**

39

"My good Professor," you say. *"My blade is forged against Daemons and their magik. I may be able to sever your tie and free you. If you are willing to let me try, as I know not the risk".*

He simply nods. You draw Devilsbane and slide the point inside the loop around Hancox's ankle. Then you swipe it to one side to try to cut the loop.

TEST YOUR FAITH 3 TIMES. If you pass all three, turn to **211**. If you fail any of them, turn to **391**

40

You pick up the golden shield. It is light, weighing less than half the weight of your current shield, and yet seems stronger than the most tempered steel you have ever seen. Unlike the traditional almond shape of your own shield, it is perfectly round and embossed with the sigil of its previous owner, the Daemon Lord Beleth.

The surface is also highly mirrored and may give you an advantage in dazzling foes. You decide to leave your shield behind and take this one. While you have it, you can, if playing advanced combat, increase your **DEFENCE ABILITY** by 2. If you are playing simple combat, it will reduce your enemy's **FIGHTING SKILL** by 1.

Turn to **553**

41

You find yourself in another clearing with more options on which way to go. Lose 1 **ENDURANCE** point due to your exertions. There is nothing of note in this area, and you leave it quickly.

You either go left and turn to **443**, or straight and turn to **350**

42

You do not fancy your chances against this giant beast, and so you try to distract it by hurling your blade at the giant conical flask with the hope of breaking it.

TEST YOUR FIGHTING SKILL. If you pass, turn to **141**. If you fail, turn to **289**

43

You look down and realise that the green ichor is corrosive and is eating away at the steel and leather of your armour. Fortunately nearby is a small stream and so you are able to quickly strip off your armour and wash it clean before any damage is done.

GAIN 1 FAITH point for escaping the previous realm - the realm of Lust.

Now you must determine which new Hellscape you are in.

TEST YOUR INTELLIGENCE. If you succeed, turn to **320**. If you fail, turn to **427**

44

Desperately short of options, you decide not to wait and approach the wynch. You take hold of the rusty handle and turn it with all your strength. It groans in protest but starts to turn, and the moaning bodies dangling above you start to descend. Within a few moments, their feet are touching the ground. Then you hear a noise outside and realise that someone is at the door.

Quickly you unhook all the moaning souls, and they start to shamble around the small room like the undead you have seen following the death plague in Certarsys. The door begins to open.

TEST YOUR FORTUNE AND YOUR FAITH. Add the two values together and then roll 4d6. If the total is greater than your combined score, turn to **186**. If it is less, turn to **208**

45

The hart's eyes melt your soul, and you are tempted to trust this divine animal.

TEST YOUR FAITH. If your **FAITH** is strong, you realise it's a trap, and you run from the clearing. You can either go straight on and turn to **376**, or head right and turn to **524**.

If you fail, then you stand there hypnotised as the hart lowers its head and charges. The razor-sharp points of the antlers pierce your armour and thrust into your body, impaling you. The hart raises its head in victory, and you slide down further onto the creature's antlers. Blood pools on the floor in front of you. Then the giant hart flicks its head back and forwards, and you are flung off its antlers into the corpse trees with bone-crushing force. Tendrils try to grab hold of you, but the hart bellows,

'Leave him, he is mine'

and they shrink back. You drop back to the floor, and lie in the clearing face down in the sodden earth, as blood oozes from your many punctures. The hart clops over and stands in front of you.

You stare up at it, but then it shimmers and in place of the hart is a beautiful youth, clad in white. His eyes are the same golden colour as the hart, and even as your life ebbs away, they captivate you. He is naked except for a loincloth, and white wings rise gracefully out of his back. Atop his head are swept-back obsidian horns, which protrude from his pale, almost white, straight hair that flows down his back. A golden glow almost surrounds him, and the youthful form of Furfur smiles lovingly at you and then kneels down by your side. He holds your head and cleans the blood and grime from your face.

'Ah, maybe you should not have trusted me, my child, as I can be a bit of a scoundrel. Still, all is not lost, as I, Furfur, am in need of a new servant, and your mortal form withers as we speak. Your shade will aide me for the coming millennia'

He holds your head and strokes your face lovingly as your strength leaves you. With that you die, only to be reborn as a doomed soul joined to Furfur in servitude for eternity. Your mission has failed, and the world will burn.

Turn to 616

46

The passage twists and turns until you have almost lost all sense of direction. Fortunately, you get to the end and find yourself in a clearing with a grassy hillock. You rush to the top to get some fresh air and rest.

Regain 1 **ENDURANCE** point as you cool down. Now you must leave, and so you can either go straight on and turn to **588** or go the right way and turn to **295**

47

Her pleading makes you stop your advance, and you tilt your head in agreement. She continues, croaking,

"You must go to the Daemon door at the end of the hallway. If you speak my name as the door instructs, then it will gain you passage to the next realm. Now go, and leave me to suffer".

You look down in pity at the wretched form of the Daemon, sheathing your sword as you turn and leave the room. You go back to the corridor and head towards the door at the end.

Turn to **94**

48

You dash through the door in order to try to stop the fleeing Sabine. Beyond is a long corridor with two doors leading off it on the left, one on the right and a larger, more ornate door at the end.

You can either choose to go through the first door on the left (turn to **231**), the second left (**521**), the door on the right (**196**) or the large door at the end (**554**)

49

You finish your apology, saying:

"Again I apologies My Lady, I was overcome by your beauty".

The figure smiles and then shakes its head sadly. The large sword runs you through before you have a chance to react.

"You call me my lady? You cur. How dare you. I am Gremory, Lord Duke of Ginnestan, and Lord over 26 legions of Daemons."

He twists the blade, and you scream, his beautiful face now a snarl. He now smells of charnel and death. He raises up his feminine leg and pushes your body off his blade onto the ground.

"You think me a lady, then, My Lord, I must return the compliment."

He reaches down into your groin and emasculates you, tearing away your male flesh with one talon-like hand. You shriek like a child. He glances down at the maimed contents of his hand and tosses it with contempt to the ground. The pain is unbearable but short-lived as the blood flows freely from your two wounds.

Death is almost a release, until you wake again in your soul state, with Gremory staring down at you and laughing. You fear the worst is yet to come. Your mission has failed, and the world will soon fall. Turn to **616**

50

Have you fought and killed Sabine? If so, turn to **392**. If she is still not dead, turn to **415**

51

"My Lord Furfur of the 5th Circle sent me to beg for your aide, oh mighty Lord".

Turn to **626** to see if Baalberith believes you.

52

You make a heroic attempt, and your hand brushes the ledge leading to the door, but do you have the strength to grab it and hold on? Roll 2d6 and compare it to your current **STRENGTH** score.

If you roll less than or equal, then turn to **183**. If you roll greater, then turn to **476**

53

"*Hmm, you ask for my arms. But you judged me right and so I will honour you. Take them and pray, if you still pray, that they aide you in coming days, as I see many challenges ahead of you. Now go, and leave me to my machinations*"

If you had reduced **FIGHTING SKILL** due to losing your sword and shield, you can return them to your normal level.

You thank the Lord and leave the glade. You can either go left and turn to **433**, or head right and turn to **105**

You head back towards the entrance tunnel. However, as you walk, the incline seems to get steeper and steeper, to the point where you almost have to use your hands as well as legs to move upwards.

The walk down was in no way this steep. The atmosphere continues to get hotter and hotter, despite you moving upwards. The air gets more acrid and burns your face and throat as you gasp for air. You start to breathe in rapid shallow breaths, the air like fire in your throat, burning your lungs. You realise that your human body is dying.

If you have a blue potion you think may help, write down the reference **312** and turn to **647**. Or if you happened to bottle some of the Daemons-wine, turn to **600**. If you have neither of these things, turn to **608**

You hurl the last imp's almost dead body into the vat of fluid and momentarily get a rush of satisfaction as you see it is still conscious enough to flail around in the liquid. It is finally pulled under by the other occupants, keen to get a small measure of revenge against one of their tormenters.

You quickly transverse the ladder back to the ground. Remember to pick up your shield and sword if you left them there.

You can now either investigate the other section of the building, then turn to **290**. Otherwise, you can leave and check the larger domed building, then turn to **193**; or go and enter the smaller domed building, turn to **122**

56

You decide to take what you perceive to be a left turn and head along this route. However, in this strange realm, normal rules do not seem to apply. You carry on walking for some time until all of a sudden, the ethereal ground starts to open up under your feet. You nearly panic as you begin to slide inexorably into the nothingness beneath. You can only assume that to fall through this surface would be an even worse fate than walking around this bleak land.

TEST YOUR AGILITY. If you roll equal to or less than, then turn to **32**. Otherwise, turn to **79**

57

Using all your stealth, you try to skirt around the pair of Daemons. But just as you are nearly passed, your foot is grabbed by a hand from the pit below. You trip and land on the floor with a crash of armour. The Daemons turn and are on you in an instant. You draw your sword and try to fight, but all you can do is deflect the first blow from the Thin Daemon's talons. The Ape Daemon is armed with a curved, serrated scimitar which screams through the air towards you.

You try to raise your sword again but are too late, and the force of the impact shatters your arm, which falls useless to your side. The Thin Daemon quickly takes advantage and starts to lacerate your body with his wickedly sharp talons, producing sprays of blood. Then the Ape Daemon finishes it all with an almost casual backhand swipe with his blade, which sends your head flying, bouncing about until it is met and swallowed by a Gorger Wyrm which has just emerged from the human plains.

Your mission has failed, and humanity will not survive the year.

Turn to **616**

58

You decide against bottling the foul liquid and instead choose to leave the chamber.

Turn to **54**

As you regain your feet, you look around in shock. As bleak as the last domain was, this is anything but. All around you are tall buildings, houses with balconies and high wooden roofs, or castles with towering battlements. On the woodwork of the doors, pillars and windows are rich gold insets and filigree work. There seems to be one long, endless street, with imperious buildings on each side. However, only the first building on each side is clearly in focus.

The house on the left is gaudily painted with a clash of colours that cause your eyes to ache. As well as the sights, there are the sounds. Sounds of people; male, female and possibly others, shouting, screaming and shrieking. As well as that, there is also laughter in the air, but not that made by any human voice, but cruel laughter emanating from each building.

It looks like a highly expensive bordello. As a man of The Faith, you have never frequented such places, but have been ordered to set them alight in the past and watched as they have burned - and pushed those trying to leave in panic back into the flames. Even children who worked in the scullery, or old women who cleaned the premises. All burnt under your watch.

On your right side rise the battlements of a tall, imposing castle. Cages hang on chains from the bulwarks, and sooty torches are in sconces around the lower walls.

As you stand at what seems to be the start of the street, which stretches endlessly into the horizon, you need to make a decision.

You can either continue on down the street, turn to **610**. Alternatively, you can try the bordello on your left, turn to **283**, or the castle on your right, and turn to **273**

60

"THAT NAME, I KNOW THAT NAME. BUT HE IS NOT A LORD OF THE 5TH CIRCLE. HE IS BARELY MORE THAN A PISSING IMP, AND NOT WORTH MY TIME. I WOULD RATHER EAT SHIT FOR ETERNITY THAN HELP THAT FOOL. YOU LIE, STRANGER, AND MUST SUFFER"

He leaps up from his throne, holding his sword aloft and leaps down the stairs to land in front of you. He is fully 10 feet tall, and almost that wide, with a huge head and torso. His green eyes gleam malevolently, and he licks his lips with a purple postulated tongue in anticipation. You have no choice but to fight him.

Turn to **371**

61

Entering another clearing, there are two exits. You can go right and turn to **433**. To your left is what appears to be a dark clearing just through the trees. To investigate this, turn to **33**

62

Walking over, in a sign of respect, you remove your gauntlets and tuck them into your belt. You take his right hand with your naked hand. Then you recoil, as out of nowhere a snake appears and strikes. Its sharp fangs pierce your skin and pump in venom. Lose 2 **ENDURANCE** points. You move back, holding your hand.

"Ah," says the beautiful being. *"You choose to fight. A shame, as we had thought this would be a more peaceful outcome. But the challenge is set!"*

Then he drops his hand to his side, and the small green snake slips off his wrist, now fully visible, and onto the floor. You draw your blade, thinking this should be easy. But then, before your eyes, the snake grows and expands. It gets longer and longer, and thicker and thicker until it is a full 8 feet long. It sits atop its coils and hisses, bearing its teeth, displaying fangs 6 inches in length.

You now have to fight this beast. Turn to **605**

63

You quickly close the short yards to the imp, who is slow to react. With no sword, you decide to go for a more direct route, and you just barge into the much smaller imp and knock it over. Then swiftly, you pick it up and hurl the wriggling body into the now empty vat with all your strength. The imp plummets towards the floor many yards below and hits it with a bone-crushing thud.

You decide it's time to leave and move towards the nearest ladder.

Turn to **252**

64

You make it back to the floor of the dome and decide it's time to leave. If you left Devilsbane and your shield at the bottom of the steps, then **TEST YOUR FORTUNE**. If you are fortunate, turn to **562**. If you are not, turn to **206**.

If you kept Devilsbane with you, then you leave the dome. You can either check the smaller dome, and turn to **122**, or head back to the crossroads, and turn to **483**

65

A mounted opponent is too much for you. Try as you might, landing a blow on the rider is too difficult as the skeletal horse often dances aside with surprising agility. It's as if the horse and rider are linked, or as one; their movements are so fluid.

Eligos doesn't need to get close either, as his lance gives him an advantage of range. You tire, bleeding from several wounds, and the horse and rider continue to charge at you. Realising that you won't survive much longer, desperate measures are required.

As the horse charges one more time, you try to dodge the tip of the lance by diving and rolling underneath it. However, fortune, or your tiring body, is not on your side as you badly misjudge the manoeuvre. You dive too soon and roll, coming up when the lance is about to pass overhead. With snake-like speed, Eligos lowers his aim in time for the broad head of the lance to take you fully in the chest. The razor-sharp point pierces your armour and flesh, and the springy ash lance's length flexes, picking you up and throwing you with tremendous force against the cavern wall.

It just so happens that your head hits the wall where a heavy war mace is hung. The spikes of the mace, which are several long inches of hardened steel, pierce the rear of your helm and strike deep into your skull. You hang there, impaled on the mace, blood pouring from your chest. Life leaves you quickly, and you are now doomed to remain as a soul in this realm. Your mission has failed, and your world will soon be subject to pain and abject suffering.

Turn to **616**

66

Just as you place the book in your pack, the figure stops his work and turns toward you and ceases moving, staring at you. He is a tall, gangly figure, and distinctly not a Daemon. He looks human. He has grey balding hair, what remains of it sticking up in spikes, and wears a long white coat, buttoned up. On his long, hawk-like nose, rests a pair of pince-nez with thick lens that make his eyes appear huge and staring. He looks at you quizzically and says,

"Well, you are no Daemon, what brings you here?"

Do you want to reply, then turn to **623**? If you would rather just attack, turn to **348**

67

The Daemons show no sign of going anywhere. You must now either try to attack, turn to **214**, or try to sneak past them, turn to **397**

68

As the Ape Daemon's body slumps to the ground, green bile-like blood pumping from its gaping neck, the Thin Daemon shrieks and attacks.

THIN DAEMON has **FS 9, EN 9**

{ADVANCED - Initial AS: 16, Initial DA: 14; FIT 7, AG 7, ST 8}

If you win, turn to **509**

69

You shout up,

"My Lord, I am Kommandant Ulrac De-Villiers, and I just seek to travel through this realm. I have no wish to remain or fight".

All is silent for a long moment, and then Baalberith leaps to his feet.

"THAT NAME, I KNOW THAT NAME. YOU ARE ONE OF THE ACCURSED MINIONS OF THE ONE HOW KEEPS US DOWN HERE. I WOULD RATHER EAT SHIT FOR ETERNITY THAN HELP YOU - APART FROM MAYBE TO HELP YOU INTO THE NEXT LIFE."

Having said that, he leaps up from his throne, holding his sword aloft and clearing the stairs to land in front of you. He is fully 10 feet tall, and almost that wide, with a huge head and torso. His green eyes gleam malevolently, and he licks his lips with a purple postulated tongue in anticipation.

You have no choice but to fight him.

Turn to **371**

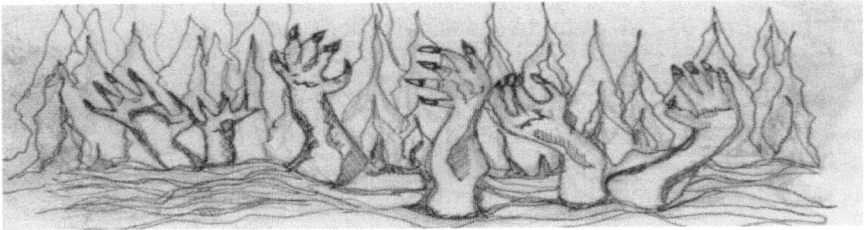

70

You seem to reach the edge of the wood, but the oppressive temperature is still weakening you. Lose 1 **ENDURANCE** point.

To your right is an impenetrable barrier of trees, all intertwined. You can only go left, then turn to **491**, or go straight ahead, turn to **477**

71

"Oh Mighty one, a thousand apologies, but I am from the 5th Circle, come as an envoy, to ask a favour of you from my Lord, as he is in need of your counsel".

Baalberith stops cold, looking down on you in shock.

"THE 5TH CIRCLE?" he rumbles *"WHICH OF THE LORDS IN THAT FOUL REALM NEED THE HELP OF BAALBERITH, AND WHY SHOULD I GIVE IT?"*

Do you know the names of any Lords of Hellscape that you could use to convince Baalberith?

If you think Furfur is a Lord of the 5th circle, turn to **51**. Otherwise, turn to **468**

72

As you edge around the short distance to the door, you hear a hiss. You turn around, and all the imps are standing and staring at you, their small hands raised and their sharp claws gleaming in the firelight. Without waiting, they swarm over you.

Roll 1d10, as this is how many imps are currently working in the kitchen that you will have to fight. You must beat them all.

Each IMP is FS 4, EN 3

If you succeed turn to **544**. If you fail, turn to **334**

73

Again and again, you bash your sword against your shield. The behemoth rears up each time and screams, a horrid, gurgling kind of scream as its mouth is still full of human meat. But each time you beat your shield, it backs away. You glance around the plain and see other wyrms nearby also rearing up and backing off. You realise that these creatures are almost blind, and hunt primarily by sound.

The noise of your sword against your shield must just be at the right pitch to unsettle their incredibly sensitive hearing. Soon the wyrm dives back below the writhing surface, and you can see ripples in the liquid as it moves away.

Add 1 **FORTUNE** point for seeing off the wyrm.

Turn to **101**

74

You were expecting the Monk to be an easy opponent to beat, but he has a sword arm like lightning and moves fluidly, so it's hard to lay your sword on him. You fight on valiantly using all your knowledge and skill earned in 20 years as a fighter. You are fast, but as fast as you are, the Monk seems faster. He has a sword arm as quick as a striking snake. You seem unable to lay a telling blow on him, and he turns most of your attacks aside with contemptuous ease.

Your sword arm is aching from trying to keep up with his lightning blade, and you realise you must do something risky. You try to duck inside his next blow, and he falls for this old trick, his scimitar whistling harmlessly past your head. You grab his sword arm with your free hand so that he cannot recover from the missed blow, and bring Devilsbane round in a swipe, the heavy blade effortlessly cutting through his robes and basic leather armour, and deep into his side. You have almost split him in two horizontally.

You twist his sword arm around so that he spins about in front of you, and with contemptuous ease, you kick his body off your blade. He slumps to the ground dead.

Turn to **161**

75

You fear little on earth, but you are not on earth, and a casual glance indicates that this room is just a dead-end, and any encounter with a servant or underling will not aide you. You decide to leave, but as you do the hinge of the old door shrieks with complaint as you try to close it. The creature snorts and then comes awake, its small yellow eyes looking at you with hatred. You have disturbed his sleep, and he does not care if you are a servant or intruder - he is going to make you pay.

He stands to his feet, a full 2 feet taller than you, and pulls an evil looking serrated dagger from his belt. You must fight this beast, a Bar Egara, a lesser Daemon known to attack men and often used as soldiers by the Lords.

BAR EGARA has **FS 6, EN 7**

{ADVANCED - Initial AS: 12, Initial DA: 12; FIT 6, AG 6, ST 6}

If you win, turn to **370**

76

You have enough strength in your arms to push yourself back onto the top of the previous stair. You land heavily. Roll 1d4 and reduce this from your **ENDURANCE**.

Your fingers sting, and you look down; they are bleeding slightly, and your arms burn from your exertion. You realise that each leap is going to take more strength out of your arms, as well as making your hands slicker with blood as they get caught on the rough, granite-like stone. Temporarily, lose 1 **STRENGTH** point. When, or if, you get to the top, your strength will return.

You must now try to leap again, using your new combined **STRENGTH** and **AGILITY** scores. If you fail that test, then you must **TEST YOUR FORTUNE**. If you are fortunate, you again end up on the top of the step and lose 1d4 in **ENDURANCE**. If you are unfortunate, turn to **187**. If you run out of **ENDURANCE** points, turn to **479**.

You must keep rolling until you make the leap, or die. Your sand dust will give you enough traction and grip to give you one extra point of **STRENGTH** for a single jump. But you only have two portions, so use it when you need it most. If you succeed and make the leap, turn to **298**.

77

And God is seven, and God is seven

78

You speak the name "Baalberith" and the eyes on the carved face open. They stare at you and glow with a malevolent green.

" *YESSS*" rumbles the voice " *WHAT DO YOU SEEK*".

You reply,

"To leave this place and travel to the next circle of the Hellscape."

The eyes bore into you, chilling you to the bone.

"TO LEAVE YOU MUST HAVE A KEY, AND TURN THAT KEY THE SAME NUMBER OF TIMES AS THERE ARE CIRCLES OF THE HELLSCAPE. IF YOU KNOW THE NUMBER OF THE KEY, AND THE NUMBER OF CIRCLES OF THE HELLSCAPE, THEN COMBINE THESE NUMBERS. HOW IS UP TO YOU. BUT IF YOU ARE WRONG, A TERRIBLE FATE AWAITS. CHOOSE WISELY"

If you have the numbers required, then turn to the reference matching the product of these numbers.

If you do not have a key, or cannot work out the riddle, then turn to **646**

79

Your armour slows you down, and you cannot react quickly enough. You slip between the nebulous surface, clawing vainly at it as you fall. You feel like you are falling upwards, downwards and sideways as there is no true sense of direction. The surface starts to thin and soon you are just falling or floating, through a grey void, that's seemingly featureless and infinite.

You continue to fall. Time is impossible to measure as there are no reference points, but soon your body starts to hunger, and then crave nourishment. Your body starts to cannibalise itself, destroying your fat and muscle in order to try to keep your vital functions active. The pain is unbearable.

You are now little more than a skeleton covered in thin, paper-like skin, yet still you live. And still, it hurts. You continue to fall until the end of days - which may not be too long as you have failed in your mission to save humanity. Your mission has failed, but your suffering continues. Turn to **616**

80

Taking in the vessel, you think you notice a potential weak spot in the join between the wood and a pipe that drains out at the base. You swing Devilsbane, but even this mighty sword may take more than one stroke to rupture the vat. Roll 1d4. This is how many strokes it will take to breach the vessel.

TEST YOUR STRENGTH and **FIGHTING SKILL**. Add both together and then roll 4d6. If the roll is higher than your combined **STRENGTH** and **FIGHTING SKILL** in any of the rolls needed, then you fail to breach the container; your pursuers are now upon you, and you have no choice but to fight - in this case, turn to **377**.

If you manage to make all the rolls, then turn to **448**

81

"Ah indeed my master, I will make it so that thou can breathe these fumes like a native"

He places his large 6-fingered hand on your head, you hear a surge of his will and the power jolts down his arm into your body. Your whole body is afire, and the tunnel seems to grow larger and larger around you. Then you realise with horror that it is not the room that is growing - you are shrinking.

You look down and see that your armour is becoming too big for your body and the greaves and gloves slip from you, as does your sword belt. You look at your hands and see that your fingers are fusing together, the first to the second, and the third to the fourth until you have one thumb and two thick fingers - each with a small talon at the end.

The skin of your hand changes, becoming more like scales and taking on a crimson hue. You feel your face elongate, and your ears seem to grow upwards into a point and take over most of the side of your head. Then you start to forget who you are. Your name and memories slip away from you like a dream in the night, and you start to talk in a staccato gibbering dialect.

The Djinn has taken you literally and turned you into an imp, the residents of this chamber, who tend to the pool in the pulsating centre. Imps are almost mindless, but the Djinn knows that it will be a simple job to get you now to make two further wishes on matters of no import, and so he will be freed from his enslavement.

You are doomed to spend eternity in this foul place, tending the acrid pool in the chamber below. Such is the risk of trusting a Djinn.

Your mission has failed. Turn to **616**

82

The Espirits are too fast, and you only have your belt knife to try to hit them. They keep swooping in and out, scoring hits on you using their long talons. Soon your face and arms are a mess of bloodied scratches. As hard as you try, you are unable to kill them all, and you see that reinforcements have just appeared up three of the ladders - several full-sized Daemons.

You try to fight down the panic, as you know that if they close on you before you can defeat the Espirits, then you are in trouble. One of the irritating creatures dives down to attack you, but with options running out, you formulate a risky plan. Instead of defending yourself, as it swoops down, you jump up to try to grab hold of it.

TEST YOUR AGILITY. If you succeed, turn to **637**. If you fail, turn to **393**

83

Almost without thinking, you choose the right ladder that takes you back down to recover your sword and shield. Taking a moment to strap Devilsbane back around your waist, you give thanks.

GAIN 1 FAITH point.

Now turn to **597**

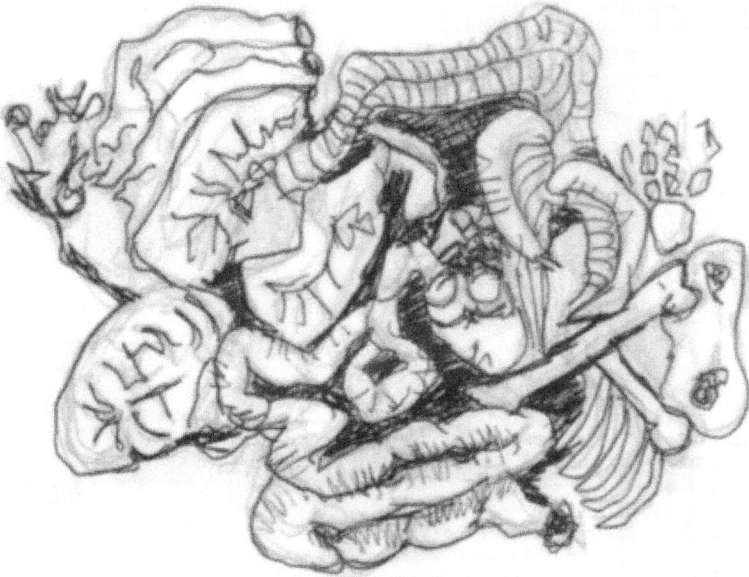

84

Looking around, you see a switch to your left. You flick it down, and a whirring noise starts below you. You look down and see that a platform is rising from the floor, up towards you. This must be how the Professor escaped.

You wait a few moments, and when it appears, you step onto it. Flipping the switch, you start to descend. Turn to **64**

As you exit a path, you come into a larger clearing that is more open, and the heat is less oppressive. The corpse trees are thinner and more spread out and light filters down from whatever source of illumination there is in this gross realm. Dominating the centre of the clearing is a large obsidian obelisk that towers up past the tree line.

You walk up and examine the obelisk. It is four-sided, and each side faces one of the four routes from the clearing, including the one you have just entered by. On each side is a sigil. You ignore the side you came in by and look at the other three. You can choose:

Go left on,
turn to 604

Go straight on,
turn to 235

Go right,
turn to 301

86

You are still half asleep and half awake, and these desperate faces still assail your thoughts, but you cannot make out what they want. Eventually, you wake fully, and the memories of these sad faces leave you completely. You have slept poorly.

Roll 1d6. This is how many **ENDURANCE** points you have lost.

Turn to **381**

87

You look into the haunted face of Aceada and deciding he has little love left for his Church, you choose to approach the Daemon Lord directly.

Turn to **69**

88

As a soldier of honour, you know an unprovoked attack goes against every theory of honourable conduct in battle. But honour in war is contradictory - as in war the mightiest win! Sometimes you have to forsake honour as the ends justify the means. You slowly unsheathe Devilsbane, and before the man can turn, you take a great swing at him.

Your sword passes through the figure as though he wasn't there and the lack of resistance to your blade spins you around, causing you to fall to the floor. Still, the figure ignores you. You clamber up from the strange surface and walk around. The figure is looking at something on the ground, and you squat down to his level. Then you see his face - it's your face! And your other self is looking at a discarded trail ration pack in disgust.

Then the figure gets up and walks off into the distance and disappears - just as you did. You seem to have once again come full circle back to where you were previously - while you were still there.

Lose **1 FAITH** point.

Turn to **343**

After thinking for a moment (or an hour, or a day, or 10,000 years - it's impossible to know), you take what you believe is a right turn, but directions seem meaningless. However, your soldier's mind refuses to accept that this world seems to have no logical or physical attributes. You even try using your lodestone, a heavy rock on a chain that always points north. However, when you try this here, the stone just spins around randomly and eventually shatters the chain and drops straight to the ground.

Being a pragmatist at heart, you make your decision and start walking. You walk for a few hours without seeing anything and so you soldier on. After a couple more hours, your shield starts to feel heavy, and you are struggling to carry it.

Then your armour seems to weigh you down more and more. Your helmet appears to be crushing your skull, and you feel liquid running down your face. You raise a gauntleted hand to your face and touch it to the area, and look down at it. Streaks of blood cover your fingers.

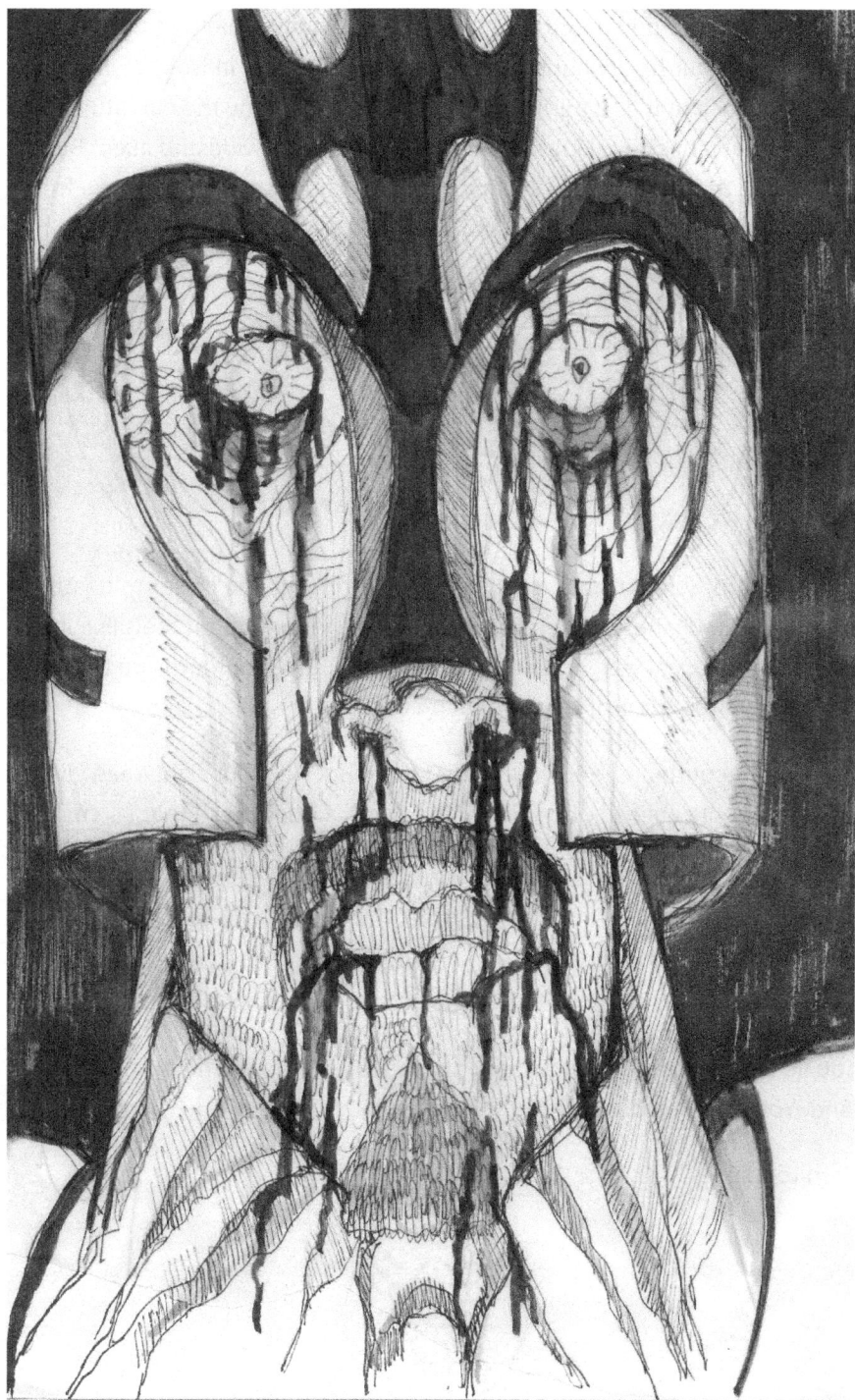

You stop and put down, or more like drop, the heavy shield to the ground. You pull off your highly burnished gauntlet and raise it in front of you, using the back of it as a mirror. Your face is distorted by the curvature of the gauntlet's back, making your face look strangely wide and alien. But you ignore that and instead see in horror that blood is pouring down from your nose, your ears and even your eyes.

The weight of your armour is crushing you, bringing you closer to death; if you can even die here. You try to remove the helmet, but it feels like it is 100 times its usual weight, and you can hardly raise your arms up to your head anymore - it's as if they are made of lead.

The weight continues, and your legs start to buckle. Your right knee gives, and you topple over to one side, landing with a huge crash that seems to echo in your mind but not in this world. You try to move forwards, crawling, but the weight is unbearable.

The very armour that saved you uncountable times is now becoming an iron tomb. You try to move but cannot.

You lie there, unable to move, but also unable to die, in this accursed land. Your mission has failed.

Turn to **616**

The stoppered bottle is in your bag, and you reach in quickly and remove it. The glass stopper is tight but comes off with a slight complaint. Not knowing the effect this will have on you, you raise the bottle to your lips and take a good swig. It seems to both burn and freeze your throat as you swallow the viscous fluid. Then miraculously, you stop choking on the toxic fumes. The Daemon's wine seems to counteract them as you breathe them in.

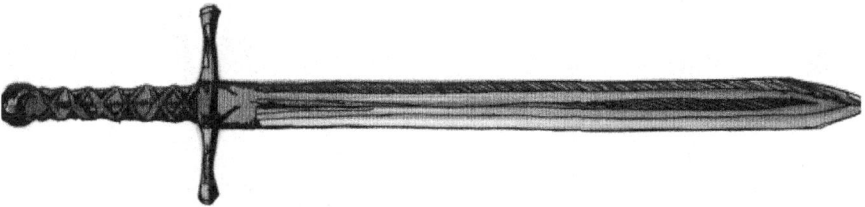

Gain **1 FAITH** point as you believe the help must be divine. You carry on up the corridor and find yourself back in the castle's courtyard. Turn to **454** and choose a route you have not previously taken

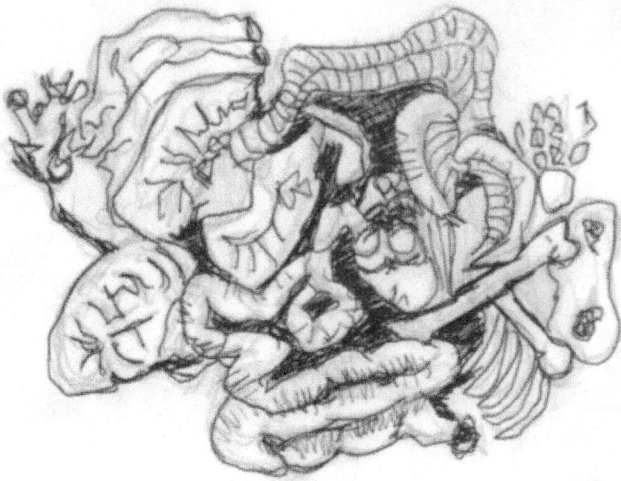

91

As fast as you can run, you have no chance against the giant steps of the sub-daemon. It finally catches up with you and reaches down and picks you up in one of its giant paws. You scream as its foot-long talons pierce your mail and flesh. It raises you up to its face level and stares at you with small, glaring eyes. There are no rational thoughts behind those eyes; just instinct. It reaches up with its other hand, and plucks your helm off your head and drops it to the ground. It lands with a clatter.

Then its free hand takes hold of your head and just pulls. Like a farmer butchering a quail, your head pops off. The beast throws your head into the air, and bending back its neck, opens its ginormous jaw. Your head spins in the air and, reaching its zenith, drops back down into the reeking maw of the sub-daemon. It chews a couple of times and then swallows. Then it continues on its way, stripping armour from your lifeless body and chewing on your naked flesh like a king on a chicken bone.

Your mission has failed, and your spirit is doomed to remain in this realm for all time, and the world will suffer because of your failure. Turn to **616**

92

You stumble into another clearing. On the left, there is a route out, and you can take this and turn to **506**. Otherwise, continue straight on and turn to **70**

As you exit a path, you come into a larger clearing that is more open, and the heat is less oppressive. The corpse trees are thinner and more spread out and light filters down from whatever source of illumination there is in this gross realm. Dominating the centre of the clearing is a large obsidian obelisk that towers up past the tree line. You walk up and examine the obelisk.

It is four-sided, and each side faces one of the four routes from the clearing, including the one you have just entered by. On each side is a sigil. You ignore the side you came in by and look at the other three.

You can choose:

Go left on, turn to 41	Go straight on, turn to 46	Go right, turn to 513

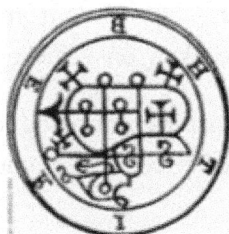

You approach the door, which is shaped like an obscene mouth with needle-like teeth and a forked tongue. Whether this is in homage to Sabine or some other so far unseen terror, you wouldn't like to guess. As you move closer, the tongue of the door starts to thrash from side to side, and what initially appeared to be the wood of the door all moves like some giant mouth; opening and closing and leering suggestively at you.

Then the mouth speaks, its voice is sibilant, almost reptilian, similar to how the Lizard Princes of Drwn of the 12th continent talks. However, the voice speaks in the common tongue, or else your ears recognise it as the common tongue as the movement of the foul mouth does not seem to match the words.

"Whooo isssss thisssss, so you seekkkk to leavee this planeeee? Yes? But you can only get passssage if you have undersssstanding and can reckon the number"

To try to work out the number of which it speaks, turn to **221**

95

Despite fighting hard, you can feel your sanity slipping. The source of this light is unknown, but you can feel a desperate probing will behind it. Or possibly wills. You struggle to keep your thoughts rational, as the pressure mounts in your brain, becoming not just psychological but also manifesting as physical pain. You put your gauntleted hands to your heads as you feel like the internal pressure is going to make your skull go pop.

You then put one of your hands up in front of your face and realise your gauntlets are stained with blood. You can see a reflection of your face in the burnished steel of the back of the gauntlet. Your eyes are red-rimmed and wild, snot is streaming from your nose and drool from your mouth. Intermingled with this are rivulets of blood that are also flowing from every facial orifice.

You are crying blood.

The force of the psychological attack gets even fiercer, and you can hear voices first murmuring, then speaking, and finally shouting, in your head. The voices are cruel and harsh and speak in the tongue of the Hellscape.

Despite not being able to comprehend what they are saying, images flash across your mind; images of horror like you have never seen. They flicker faster and faster through your mind like a living nightmare; one you can never wake from. Interspersed with these images of horror is the likeness of an angel, or more likely a fallen angel.

He is tall and powerful and naked, with a well-muscled body and no visible genitalia. Large feathered wings rise from his back. His head is bald, except for a pair of long curved horns protruding from his ears, and a second, shorter set on top of his forehead. Black markings cover his body in swirls. You hear his voice and his name echoing through your head, for this is Bael, the King of Hell.

Irrationally you know you have to remove these images from your head and so your hand fumbles at your sword belt, and from there you draw your knife. The images are so intense they are causing you pain, and so you feel nothing when the blade slides into your left eye socket. Your eye pops, and you feel a vague sense of its aqueous fluid flowing down your cheek.

You withdraw the blade and target your right eye, and again the liquid flows. Blinded, you hope you have stopped the images, but if anything they have become more intense.

The knife slips from your bloody fingers, and you lean back and howl in pain at the wills tormenting you. Then you drop to your knees and weep blood, as you have no tears left. Your mind has now completely snapped and is incapable of rational thought.

All you see and hear are the dreadful sights and sounds in your skull. Your mortal will is slowly wasting away from hunger and thirst, but your eternal soul will remain in torment.

Your mission has failed, and the sons and daughters of your world will soon experience horror unbridled.

Turn to **616**

96

Without Devilsbane, a sword consecrated to fight Daemons and their magik, it is going to be far more difficult to break the spell.

TEST YOUR FAITH 5 times. If you pass on all 5 counts, turn to **211**. If you fail at any of them, turn to **391**

97

You tell the Duke that you were stumped by the last challenge and it was only luck that got you through it. He seems pleased and smiles.

"Ha, thou thinkest that thou can fool us. And thou speak with a silver tongue."

Then he sneers in contempt.

"Know this, De-Villiers, strength and cunning are respected in the Hellscape far more than aimless flattery".

Lose **1 FAITH** point

Turn to **557**

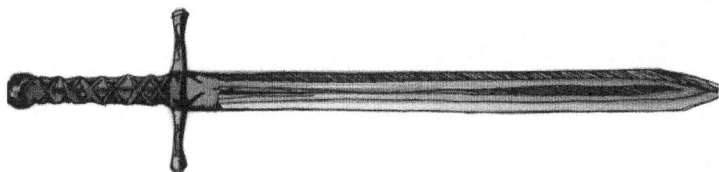

98

Fortune favours you, as the imps are too busy with their foul work to prevent you from getting to the green door. Not wishing to waste any time or risk discovery, you quickly open the door and slip through it. Turn to **402**

99

You jump back and draw your blade in one movement. The animal rears up, and its hooves thrash the air. It roars,

"What? you do not trust me, my child? when all I did was seek to help? In that case then feel the wrath of Furfur."

Then you remember. Furfur is a Lord of the Hellscape who often takes the form of a winged pure white hart. Now you must fight this Daemon Lord.

FURFUR has FS 11, EN 16

{ADVANCED - Initial AS: 20, Initial DA: 17; FIT 9, AG 8, ST 11}

If you win, you exit the clearing as quickly as you can and must either go straight on and turn to **376**, or head right and turn to **524**. If you die, turn to **170**

100

You are not quick enough, and you hear an excited chattering. You look up and see the imps attending the vessel are all staring and moving towards you, armed with their long wooden paddles. Throw 1d6+2 - that is how many imps you must fight.

Each **IMP** is **FS 4, EN 3**

{ADVANCED - Initial AS: 9, Initial DA: 13; AG 8, FIT 5, ST 1}

If you succeed, turn to **55**. If you fail, turn to **658**

101

Continuing along the ridge, you are just high enough from the mire at either side that you are immune to the hands grasping up at you as you pass. You approach the hall that you can see ahead. It looks to your mind like a meeting hall that is commonplace in the centre of larger towns - places where the nobles and common folk alike meet to talk, trade, dine and drink. It is a long low building, with double doors at the front, which stand open.

Chimneys are visible poking up on three sides, billowing out thick, greasy smoke. There is also one very large chimney in the centre of the roof, and the black smoke rises in a column into the still air for hundreds of yards, seemingly to the top of the sky.

The need for heating puzzles you, as the plain is close and clammy, and sweat glistens on your face and runs into your eyes, making them sting. You pause outside the doors.

Are you going to go straight through the doors, turn to **492**? If you would rather look around first, turn to **629**

102

You haul yourself onto the bottom of the final stair. You clamber to your feet and look up. The doorway is another jump away, but even further; this will be your most difficult attempt yet.

If you have provisions, you can use one to help your **ENDURANCE**, but it will not help replenish your strength. The process has really affected your fitness as well, and so you will, this time, need to combine your current **STRENGTH, AGILITY** and **FITNESS**.

Now throw 6d6. If the score you roll is lower or equal to your combined attributes, then turn to **158**. If it's greater, then turn to **52**

103

You make your way around the room, trying to stay close to the walls, and moving around so that most of the imps are on the other side of the conical flask, busy filling the bottles. The only creature on your side is a sub-daemon, carrying a stack of crates.

You are so busy intently watching the movements of the servants of the dome that you catch your foot. You half trip, landing on your hands and knees with a clatter. You look up quickly and see a giant sub-daemon staring at you. It's fully 20 feet tall, but almost brainless. It puts the crates on the floor and roars in anger as it moves towards you, its giant paws reaching towards you with foot-long talons glistening.

You can either try to fight this monster and turn to **442**, try to run and escape, turn to **148**, or try to break the large conical flask behind it to distract it, turn to **42**

104

After seemingly fighting through endless trees, you reach what appears to be the corner of the forest.

You have two choices. You can go left and turn to **565**, or go the right way and turn to **166**

105

You exit the tree line into a sandy hollow. The heat is even more intense, and you lose 2 **ENDURANCE** points. You hurry to exit this hollow and either go left, and turn to **478**, or go straight ahead and turn to **633**

106

Which question do you want to ask? If you want to ask a guard directly, which door leads to death, turn to **277**. If you want to ask a guard who the other guard would say leads to death, turn to **205**

107

After deciding that it may be worth checking to see where the exit at the other side of the vessel leads to, you head towards it. The exit is, in fact, a tunnel that drops down into the ground and is only about 10 yards wide. You start down it, but when you are halfway, a sub-daemon appears, heading the opposite way. It is so giant it has to duck as it makes its way up the tunnel back to the dome.

TEST YOUR FORTUNE. If you are fortunate, turn to **483**, if you are not, turn to **592**

108

Using all your stealth, you managed to skirt past where the Daemons are waiting, and are soon around the corner and away. You arrive back at your entry point to this cursed realm. You now have no option but to take the right turn. Turn to **483**

109

You reach out and grasp the hand of the bone door, which appears to be the balled joint of a hip bone. You pull, and it slowly creaks open, the whole door shaking alarmingly as its base drags along the floor.

You open it and see a dark, empty passageway. Do you want to explore this passage? If so, turn to **31**. If you would rather leave and choose another door, turn to **209**

110

In horror, you realise that where the wound is, something is growing. Out of the gash comes what at first seems to be two tentacles. Then the tentacles start to widen, and at each end, a slit appears. The girth of the protrusions expands quickly, and as it does, so does the slit.

Soon the new growths are both the same giant width as the main body of the wyrm, and then the slits open up wide to reveal rows of needle-sharp teeth. The beast has grown two new heads. Realising that attacks to the head are foolish, you must now try to strike either at the main body, turn to **632**; or the tail, turn to **430**

111

You enter through the portal, and your whole world seems to be turned upside down, as you seem to spin endlessly and uncontrollably through a pitch-black netherspace.

Eventually, you see a bright light ahead, and you hurtle towards it and are thrown through a doorway onto the ground of the new realm. **TEST YOUR AGILITY**. If you succeed, you manage to roll as you land and are unhurt. If you fail, you land awkwardly and lose 2 **ENDURANCE**.

Turn to **59**

112

Against all the odds, you strike a killing blow against the giant beast which topples over into the large conical vessel. You expect the multi-coloured liquid to flood the floor, but instead, the different coloured forms seem to float out of the broken flask. They are all roughly human-shaped, but more like formless coloured shades of humanity. These are the souls used to make the soul spirit - a delicacy in these realms. Each is a doomed soul freed for the first time in an eternity.

The souls float around the room, at roughly head height, while the imps jump up and down panicking. Then the souls start to swoop down and pass through the bodies of the imps. Each screams every time a soul passes through their body, as the spirits take revenge on their captors.

Deciding you have seen enough, you resolve to leave the dome. If you lost your blade, you can recover it on the way out. If you want you can grab up to 1d4 of the bottles at the side of the room.

If you do and you decide to try drinking one of them, write down the reference you are on and turn to **226**.

You leave the dome.

If you haven't checked the large dome, then you can do this instead and turn to **193**. If you would rather just head back to the crossroads, turn to **483**

113

You walk over to the infernal instrument and sit down on the stool - which is in fact made of a human body bent over backwards so that the arms and legs form the legs of the seat. You sit down gingerly and examine the instrument. Up close, it is even more loathsome, but you are compelled to play it. Its keys are made from finger bones, and the pedals on the floor are human feet. Above the keyboard are a series of irregularly arranged and shaped holes that seem to serve no purpose.

As a knight, you are highly educated in many ways and learned the harpsichord as a child. You grimace as your fingers touch the evil keyboard and start to play, haltingly at first. But as you limber up, your fingers remember something old, a Hymn to the One True God.

However, as you play the hymn, *"We Die for He Who is Above Us"*, the music changes. Instead of notes coming out of the pipes of the organ, human voices come out in screams and wails, each set to a key, and so the hymn is played out in the cries of dead souls. However try as you might, you cannot stop playing. **TEST YOUR FAITH**. If your **FAITH** is strong, turn to **494**. If it is weak, turn to **15**

114

You come to an open clearing, and you fancy you can almost see the sky above. You must stop and rest, and as you do so, a gust of air heads through the glade. It cools you down, and you can regain **1 ENDURANCE** point. But then the wind dies, and the temperature starts to rise. You must leave now. Your options are to head in the right direction and turn to **552**. If you go straight on, turn to **379**

115

You fail to notice that the green ichor is not just foul-smelling, but also corrosive. Before you know it, it has eaten through the leather and steel of your armour, and therefore will not give you as much protection. If you are playing the simple combat rules, reduce your **FIGHTING SKILL** by 1 permanently.

If you are playing the advanced combat rules, you must reduce any calculated **DEFENCE ABILITY** by 2 permanently. Now you must determine which new Hellscape you are in. **TEST YOUR INTELLIGENCE**. If you pass, turn to **320**. If you fail, turn to **427**

116

Fortune smiles on you, and you are able to approach the crates unnoticed. You remove a bottle and stare at it. The bottle is clear but in the shape of a human female and inside it, a blue liquid swirls. You check several other containers, all in the shape of a different human form, and each containing a different coloured swirling fluid.

There are purple, blue and red colours, green and yellow and pink, and other colours you can't even describe, all ever-moving around inside their bottles. Then you realise that each of these coloured moving shapes is a distorted human form, with hollows for eyes and a black hole for a mouth. They move round in their tiny bottle ceaselessly. You are both disturbed and intrigued. If you want to uncork a bottle and take a drink, turn to **447**.

If you would rather just stow it away in your pack, then roll 1d4. This is the number of bottles you can fit into your backpack. Write this down on your **ADVENTURE SHEET**. If you ever decide to drink a bottle, write down the reference you were on, turn to **226** and follow the instructions. You can now either go and investigate the exit from the dome, turn to **107**, or leave the dome by the way you came in, turn to **655**

117

You rack your brains for names of the Lords of the Hellscape and eventually mention one, Bael, as you believe that he is one of the mightiest of Daemons in the Hellscape, and this Lord must rank most highly.

"Ah, thou cannot even name thy host, we find that rude and impertinent. We had hoped that you would be more accomplished and educated, but it seems like you are just fit to be our pet's toy".

He gestures at the mighty dragon, which slowly rises to its feet and stretches. Then it advances on you, its head down and teeth bared; its huge tail thrashing against the walls of the cave. You draw your weapon, but the dragon just slaps it out of your hand with a swipe of its ginormous paw. You back up, trying to find space, but there is nowhere to run, and soon you are pressed against the chamber wall.

The beast lashes out with its claws and rakes its talons across your breastplate. Three long rends appear, and with another swipe, your breastplate is cut from you. It drops to the floor with a clank. The dragon advances and places one paw on your chest and pushes you to the ground. It lowers down a head larger than a coach and sniffs at you.

Then it opens its jaws, and you expect a quick death, but instead, it picks you up and shakes its head, and you are like a rag doll in its mouth. Then it shifts to one side and lets you go, your body skidding across the floor. The dragon bounds over like an oversized hound, clearly enjoying itself, and then flicks you to the other side of the chamber with its claws.

Its owner, in the meantime, laughs and shouts out encouragement to the dragon, who plays like a newborn pup. You will not die for many days until the dragon finally tires of its new toy. But your mission is failed, and the world above can count its time in mere days as well. Turn to **616**

118

Deciding quickly that it would be ill-advised to fight, and having no wish to flee, you draw your sword and run towards the nearest vat. Quickly you scan the vessel, looking for a weak spot. Thinking you have found one, you swing Devilsbane. This is no ordinary sword and should make quick work of the wooden vats. However, your first strike bounces off. You stop and think feverishly.

TEST YOUR INTELLIGENCE. If you succeed, turn to **80**. If you fail, turn to **2**

119

"Thank you, comrades," you say *"You were the bravest and truest of men in life. And how can I escape this dread realm, wherever I am?"*

Hatton replies, his voice like dried parchment,

"What good are thanks to the dead. Do you not know? I am disappointed in you Kommandant. You are in Limbo, the realm between Heaven and Hell. The One True God has forsaken us and we are doomed to roam here for eternity - not fit to serve in Heaven, and not doomed to suffer in Hell. The living should not be here and so you must leave. And the only exit is to somewhere far worse"

"Where?" you ask.

Turn to **266**

120

You have only gone up a handful of steps, but maybe you have become overconfident as when you jump for the next step, your boot catches the lip of the stair and you slip. **TEST YOUR FORTUNE**. If you are fortunate, turn to **260**. If you are not, turn to **601**

121

After bowing to your host, you head towards the portal and prepare to walk through it. Turn to **571**

122

Deciding to enter the smaller domed building, you edge towards it and peer through the open doorway. Inside, a huge glass tube enters via the roof and then separates into dozens of smaller tubes that descend. These tubes then each submerge into a large ice bath and exit the other side. Under each cylinder is a funnel, and from these fall drops of liquid, which are collected in an open channel.

The fluid then flows into a large conical vessel with taps coming off it all the way around the circumference of the base. Inside the flask, drops of liquid fall from the pipes that leave the ice bath, and join with a multi-coloured liquid that swirls around unceasingly in the flask, which is about three-quarters full.

The imps busy themselves filling bottles from the taps, corking them and placing them in crates. Giant and almost mindless sub-daemons move the filled crates, carrying them out of a door at the far side. Turn to **519**

123

You ignore the swinging bodies suspended above, and a thorough search of the room finds that there is no other way out. The floors and wall are solid stone and cannot be dug into, and there is no mortar to try to tease bricks apart. The whole room seems to have been made out of one solid block of stone.

You try chipping away at the stone wall in desperation, but it is not of the human world and seems stronger than iron - and soon all you have to show for your efforts are blistered hands and a blunt belt-knife. You try praying, but the words seem to fade instantly before you even say them out loud. Lose 1 **FAITH** point. You resolve that all you can do is sit, and wait.

Turn to **352**

Despite pulling with all your might to try to dislodge your blade, it is caught deep in the blubber of the giant wyrm. You continue to struggle, but it's stuck fast. The reek from the creature is disgusting. It stinks of a charnel house and rotting flesh. You are almost choking on the smell, as it is so cloying, it fills your nose and mouth, distracting you from the movement of the wyrm.

Sensing the injury you have caused it, it tries to turn and snap at you but is unable to. Instead, it rolls is ginormous body onto its side and moves towards you. Your legs get trapped under its dreadful weight, and it continues to roll over, crushing you.

You lose hold of your weapon and can only hammer at its blubbery flanks with your mailed fists, which does nothing except infuriate the creature more. It continues to move, and you feel your legs snap under the weight, and soon its massive body rolls onto your pelvis, which shatters like glass under pressure as it continues to crush your body into the ground.

You feel the bone cage of your chest snap like twigs, and try to scream as the broken ribs pierce your lungs. However, as your chest fills with internal liquids, all you can do is vomit out blood and phlegm, and your scream is more like a wet gurgle. Pinioned under the vast body, you cannot move and just lie there hopelessly as the life is crushed out of your body.

Your soul will now live on in this dread plain, to be consumed over and over by Cerberus. Your mission has failed, and the mortal world will soon fall.

Turn to **616**

125

The green bottle is tall and slender and delicate, something you did not expect to see in the Hellscape. It is stoppered with a small crystal top, which you slowly twist and remove.

The smell from the bottle fills the room. It is a sweet and enticing aroma, and you raise the bottle to your lips and drink. The liquor is sweet, almost to the point of sickly, but it makes your body tingle.

You have drunken a **POTION OF ENDURANCE**. For the next battle you face, the potion will stop you losing any **ENDURANCE** points, unless your advisory rolls a double 6 - and then you will be hurt as normal.

However, as with most things in the Hellscape, a deal with a devil gives with one hand and takes with the other. The potion also reduces your **AGILITY** by **2** until you have fought that battle. Turn to the previous reference.

126

Despite trying your best to catch yourself on the step with your fingertips, you are not able to hold on. You once again plummet to the ground, fully 20 yards below and land with your right arm out in front of you to brace your fall. Your right-hand hits first and is bent back and you feel a stabbing pain. When you recover you realise you have badly sprained your wrist and are lucky not to have broken it.

Lose **4 ENDURANCE** points. Reduce your **AGILITY** and **STRENGTH** both by **1** for the remainder of your time in this realm while your injury heals. Now turn to **487**

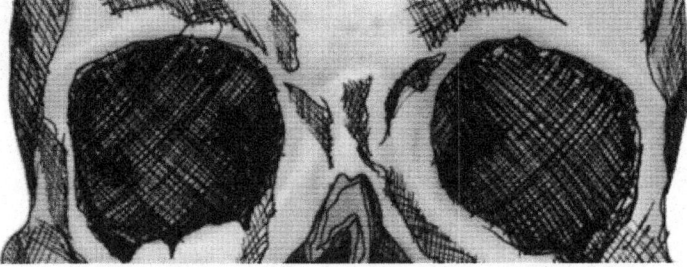

127

You are not nimble enough, and your blade does not target the tail but instead plunges into the beast's body. You panic as the edge catches in the blubbery flesh and you struggle to remove it. You are pressed against the stinking flesh of the beast, and if you cannot retrieve your blade, you are doomed.

TEST YOUR STRENGTH. If you succeed, turn to **489**. If you fail, turn to **124**

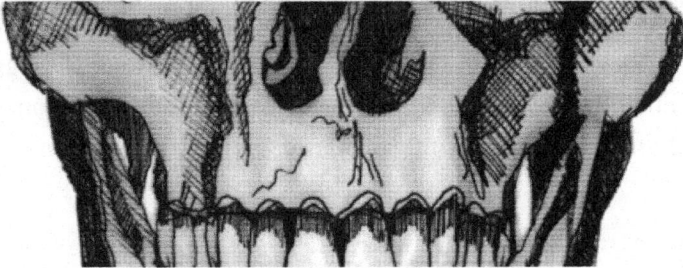

128

Throw 1d6. This is how many imps you must fight as the others continue to tend to the pool. Individually they are not that fearsome, despite their sharp teeth and talons, but due to the fumes of the room, you will lose **1 FIGHTING SKILL** for every 3 rounds you fight.

Each **IMP** is **FS 4, EN 3**

{ADVANCED - Initial AS: 9, Initial DA: 13; AG 8, FIT 5, ST 1}

If you win, turn to **563**

129

When you were last in the kitchen, did you fight anyone? If so, turn to **355**. If you did not, turn to **455**

130

It takes seemingly forever for you to turn the key 130 times. When you finally do, the face in the door smiles, but there is no humour in the smile. Then it opens its mouth, which continues to open, wider and wider. The tongue advances towards you and then lies on the floor in front of you, almost making a carpet for you to walk along past the teeth and into the stinking maw. You steel yourself before putting one foot on the hideous tongue and beginning to walk towards the passage beyond.

Turn to **384**, but before you do write the name **BAALBERITH** on your **ADVENTURE SHEET.**

131

You decide enough is enough and flee through the kitchen. Fortunately, you encounter no enemies, and soon you are out of the rear door, and at the back of the building. You stop for a moment, panting as you lean against the back of the building.

Did you find a map of the 11th circle? If you did, turn to **270**. If you did not, turn to **365**

132

You are about halfway up the stairs, but the ascent is taking its toll. Once again, combine your **STRENGTH** and **AGILITY** and roll 4d6. If the result is less than or equal to your combined score, then turn to **665**. If the result is higher, then deduct the difference from your **ENDURANCE**.

If you are still alive, turn to **665**. If you are not, turn to **335**

133

As the beast is mere feet from you, you resolve to remain as still as possible. You know from your time as a hunter that a lot of a predator's vision does not look for prey, but their movement. You hope that by standing stock-still, it's vision will not differentiate you from the world around you.

Close up the wyrm is even grosser. It is standing almost vertically out of the morass of flesh, swaying from side to side. Its flesh is covered in folds, and in each fold is an off white ichor that runs down its hide, lubricating the body. Thick hairs about a foot long, and wider than a tooth of a wyvern, protrude from the body at regular intervals. This, you surmise, is how it propels itself through the swamp below.

You dare not move but take in as much as you can for future reference. Then you realise that there is nothing around the mouth that equates to eyes; instead, the mouth is ringed by a series of small holes, which seem to reverberate and push out a light green puss type liquid. These, you realise in horror, are its nostrils.

Turn to **319**

134

Wasting no time, you return to the courtyard. If you haven't already you can try to go up to the battlements and turn to **485**.

Otherwise, you decide to approach the double doors. They are similar yet smaller than the external doors, except they are covered in polished silver that makes them mirror-like. But as you approach you do not see the desolation of the courtyard, but instead reflected in the mirrored doors is a courtyard of opulence and wealth, with men and women of high birth walking together, talking and laughing.

The women wear elegant dresses of silk and satin, and the men are wearing tailored uniforms of varying rank and insignia. Being well trained in military uniforms, you recognise the crests and sigils of various historical empires. Here you see a Conjuror-Major dressed in the uniform of the Emperor of Terainh.

Walking past him, arm in arm with a tall, beautiful lady in a yellow silk dress, is a Knight-Lieutenant of the King of Vitroliz. You know that 200 years past before the Rightful Order took over, the kingdoms of Terainh and Vitroliz were mortal enemies, and these two soldiers would never share the same courtyard without violence.

As well as this, the courtyard has elegant sculptures, clever fountains and beautiful trees. It's like the doors are reflecting images of times gone by - or maybe places gone by. Steeling yourself, you seize the handles of the doors and open them. Turn to **307**

135

Just as you are about to enter the corridor, you notice a couple of odd things. Directly after the doorway is a ring of what looks like the sap from the rubar tree, which grows in the Ayatic continent. Your keen eyesight picks out that the doorway at the far end also has a similar ring of the same material.

Then you look down and see that upon the floating step that leads into the corridor a wire is attached to the side, almost unnoticeable. You gently push the step with your foot and realise that it is designed to hinge with pressure so that it will tilt down and hit the copper floor. You reason that when this happens, then it will complete a circuit.

Bottled lightning is a new almost magical invention on earth - but you have seen it in operation and know that it travels along copper. Assuming this is a trap designed to fry unwanted guests, you jump over the step and wait nervously. Nothing happens. You continue along the corridor and find a similar step at the far end. You step forward to open the door but are careful to climb up, avoiding the step.

Turn to **643**

136

Mentally preparing yourself for any horror or threat, you turn the handle and slowly pull the door open. You slip through the gap and close it gently behind you.

Turn to **174**

137

The beast rears up. This is Cerberus, and he guards this route from all. None may pass, mortal or Daemon. He is fully twice as large as any previous Gorger wyrms you have seen or encountered, and you are unable to run. You must fight. Armed only with your belt knife, you will struggle to do any real damage against such a monster. Reduce any damage you do to Cerberus by half.

Where are you going to target? If you want to target its huge gaping maw at the head of its body, turn to **373**. If you would rather try to plunge your weapon into its blubbery body, turn to **609**. If you want to dodge aside and hack at its tail, turn to **511**

138

The door across the room means you need to try to negotiate around the area past all the busy imps. Fortunately, they are concentrating on their grim work, although they seem to delight in it, chirping happily to themselves as they work. Occasionally they will raise a gobbet of flesh to their small mouths and nibble at it with razor-sharp teeth.

TEST YOUR FORTUNE. If you are fortunate, turn to **500**. If you are not, turn to **620**

139

Disgusted, you cannot see any point in staying in this place. You move back towards the ladder to climb down.

TEST YOUR AGILITY. If you succeed, you successfully climb the ladder back down without alerting anyone. Don't forget to pick up your sword and shield if you left them there, turn to **150**. If you fail, turn to **100**

140

You lie in a state between sleep and wakefulness. You can sense the world around you, or what little there is to sense, but you can still see and almost hear the voices of the grey people. Then you realise - these are the denizens of this world and they are trying to communicate with you. You stop fighting the draw of these faces and try to relax your mind. Now you can hear a myriad of voices all saying,

"Go stranger, this world is not for the living, leave us in our suffering, to see you alive upsets us and it reminds us of our everlasting doom".

You ask back in your head

"How can I leave? There are no roads, no doors, and no portals out of here. I seem doomed to roam this eternal greyscape".

There is silence and then they say in unison

"Wake up and look for us. It pains us that you are here, and we would show you how to leave, even though this option is withheld from us".

Turn to **247**

141

Having been seen, you decide combat is a bad option and hope to create a distraction instead. You draw your blade and hurl it towards the giant conical flask. It strikes the flask point first, and the glass shatters. You expect the multi-coloured liquid to flood the floor, but instead, the different coloured forms seem to float out of the broken flask.

They are all roughly human-shaped, but more like formless coloured shades of humanity. These are the souls used to make the soul spirit - a delicacy in these realms. Each is a doomed soul freed for the first time in an eternity.

The souls float around the room, at roughly head height, while the imps jump up and down panicking. Then the souls start to swoop down and pass through the bodies of the imps and the sub-daemons. Each screams every time a soul passes through their body, as the spirits take revenge on their captors.

Deciding you have seen enough, you recover your blade and resolve to leave the dome. If you want you can grab up to 1d4 of the bottles at the side of the room. If you do and you decide to try drinking one of them, write down the reference you are on and turn to **226**. You leave the dome.

If you haven't checked the large dome, then you can do this instead and turn to **193**. If you would rather just head back to the crossroads, turn to **483**

142

You slip as you jump, and so don't manage to gain the distance needed to clear it.

TEST YOUR FORTUNE. If you are fortunate, turn to **657**. If you are less so, turn to **4**

143

Your third hit rends a huge gaping wound on the wyrm's flesh, just below the mouth. You feel like the tide of the fight is turning, and that luck is finally on your side. Then the wyrm's huge body starts to convulse, and you watch in fascination. You hope that it is in its death throws.

Turn to **572**

144

You walk into a much smaller clearing, and there appears to be only one other exit - a route to the right. However, ahead of you is what appears to be a dimly lit corpse of trees, forming a circle just beyond what appears to be almost a doorway.

If you have not investigated this area before, you can do so by turning to **26**. Otherwise, you must take the right passage and turn to **376**

145

Fortunately, you used your right hand to lower the bottle into the pool. Lose 2 **ENDURANCE** points and turn to **416**

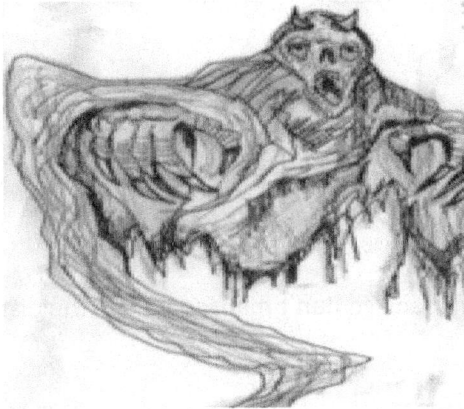

146

The Hellscape uses a mixture of your spoken tongue and Infernal, the language of Daemons. Both are written right to left.

For Infernal, there are also some letters used as substitutes for others. Other conventions are that there are no spaces between words in infernal, no capital letters and no punctuation. It also uses a stacked vowel system in that the vowel is above the letter after it. There are never any double letters used in Infernal

A	B	C	D	E	F
G	H	I	J	K	L
M	N	O	P	Q	R
S	T	U	V	W	X
Y	Z	Ch	Th		

Write this reference down in case you need to refer to it in the future.
Now turn back to the reference you were told to.

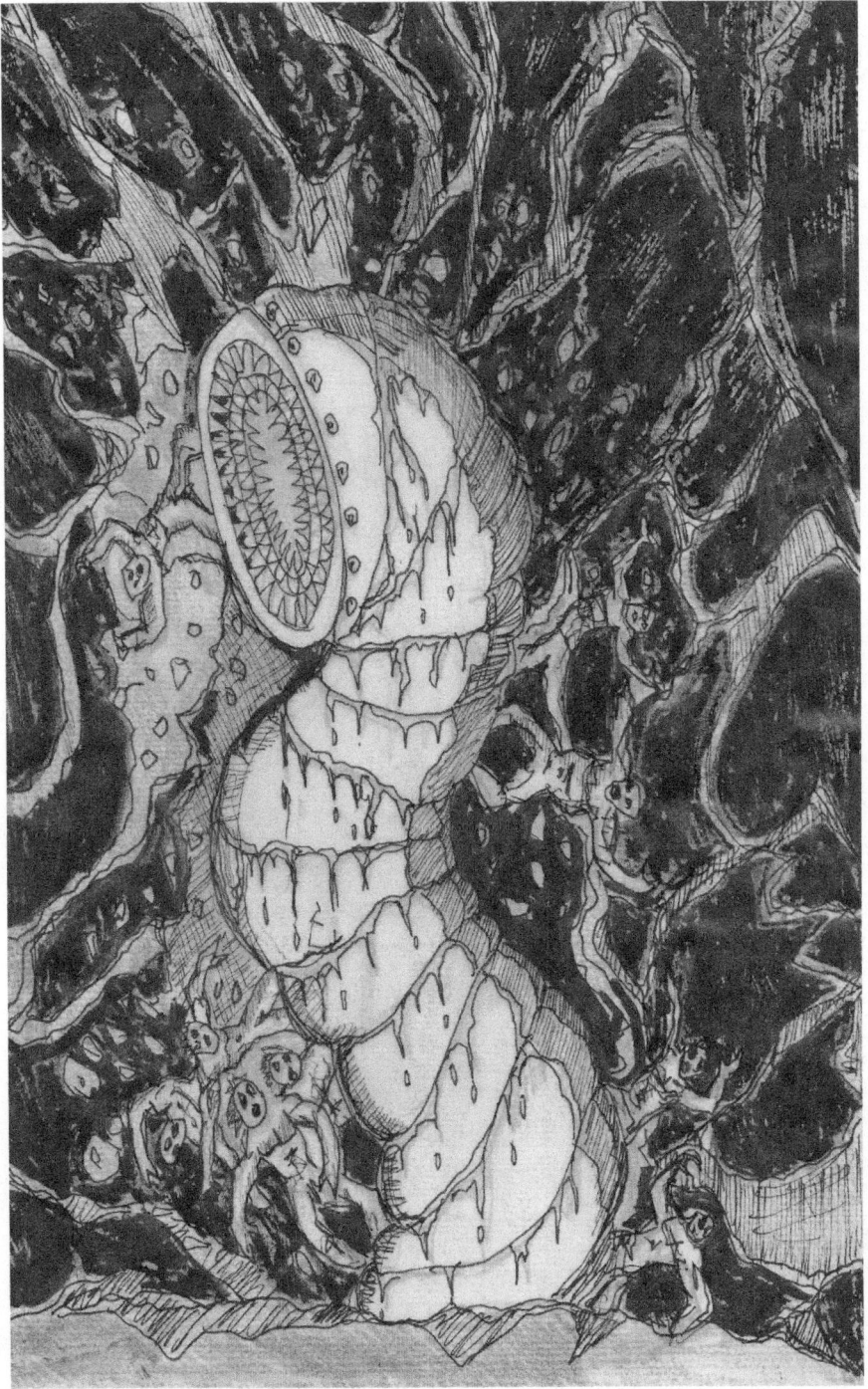

147

The beast rears up. This is Cerberus, and he guards this route from all. None may pass, mortal or Daemon. He is fully twice as large as any previous Gorger wyrms you have seen or encountered, and you are unable to run. You must fight, using Devilsbane. Where are you going to target?

If you want to target its huge gaping maw at the head of its body, turn to **373**. If you would rather try to plunge your weapon into its blubbery body, turn to **609**. If you want to dodge aside and hack at its tail, turn to **511**.

CERBERUS has FS 8, EN 20

{ADVANCED - Initial AS: 13, Initial DA: 10; FIT 5, AG 5, ST 11}

If you fail to kill the beast and your **ENDURANCE** falls to 0 at any point, turn to **644**

148

Fighting this behemoth seems to be a reckless task, and so you decide to run, but the sub-daemon runs after you. Its legs are twice the length of yours, and so it covers the ground in giant strides, but you can move your legs faster. Add up your current **AGILITY**, **ENDURANCE** and **FITNESS**. This is your **SPEED**. Now do the same for the sub-daemons

SUB-DAEMON has AG 3, EN 20 and FIT 7.

Now roll 2d6 for yourself and the sub-daemon. If your combined score is higher than the sub-daemon's, then you are faster and stay ahead of it. If you can beat it three times in a row, then you outrun it and are free, and you leave the dome but have no option but to head back towards the crossroads - in case the sub-daemon alerts anything else. Turn to **483**. If you fail one of those rolls, turn to **91**

149

The Daemons show no sign of moving and keep their vigil on top of the ridge. You weigh up your options. You could choose to wait and hope that they leave. If you choose this turn to **452**. Alternatively, you can try to sneak up and attack, turn to **214**, or you can try to sneak past them and head back to the original fork on the road.

Turn to **397**

150

With speed made from desperation, you climb back down the ladder unnoticed. You can now choose to investigate the other section of the building, then turn to **290**. Otherwise, you can leave and check the larger domed building, then turn to **193**; or go and enter the smaller domed building, turn to **122**

151

You spend a few moments examining the compelling font. When you look back up, you see that the professor has already left. Part of you curses him for leaving you when he obviously would have been a useful travelling companion. But the other part wishes him luck. Mayhap your paths will cross again. Finding nothing more of interest to look at in the room, you resolve to leave.

Turn to **484**

152

You run the last imp through, and then with a flick of your sword, the small body flies off your blade. **TEST YOUR FORTUNE**. If you are fortunate, it hits the Daemon full in the chest and does 2 **ENDURANCE** damage.

If you are not so fortunate, it just hits the wall with a crash and drops to the floor unmoving. The Daemon bellows, drawing two long, slim filleting knives from his belt and attacks. You must now defeat this beast.

KNIFE DAEMON has FS 7, EN 8

{ADVANCED - Initial AS: 12, Initial DA: 11; FIT 5, AG 6, ST 6}

If you win, turn to **446**

153

The passage through the corpse trees ends at what appears to be a large burrowed hole angling down into the ground. There is no other way for you to go and so steeling yourself, you enter. It turns into a tunnel, and you can vaguely see light at the end, but aside from that, it is almost total darkness. You hurry through, but the tunnel is hot, humid and airless. You are soon gasping to catch your breath.

Lose 2 **ENDURANCE** points.

You get to the end and mercifully make it out into the open air. You can go straight ahead and turn to **144**, or go right and turn to **358**

154

Vainly, you try to hold onto your **FAITH**, but it is crushed out of you by the will of this foul mind. You wish for a foe of blood and skin that you can fight instead of this mental challenge. But you are not done yet.

TEST YOUR INTELLIGENCE. If your mind stays strong against such an attack, then lose **1 FAITH** point, but you can escape the terrible light and turn to **6**. If you fail again, turn to **95**

155

You settle down on the strange surface and, adjusting your backpack to rest on, you try to close your eyes. A good soldier learns how to take their rest even in the most inhospitable locations. You are exhausted by the trials of the day, and soon you are drifting off into sleep - despite the world still being grey around you. You sleep fitfully, and strange dreams fill your mind. Your head is filled with indistinct faces, who are all seemingly trying to talk to you at once. Their faces and clothes are all grey, and try as you might you cannot hear what they say, but they are very insistent.

TEST YOUR INTELLIGENCE. If you roll more than your current **INTELLIGENCE** score, turn to **86**. If you roll less than or equal, then turn to **140**

156

As you feel your legs getting dragged into the swamp of humankind, your rising panic gives you a boost of desperation and strength. You scramble against the side of the ridge and manage to pull yourself back up to the top. You sit there panting while breathing in more fumes. Thinking quickly, you reach into your backpack and find a piece of material. Using your water bottle, you wet it until it is damp, and then tie it around your mouth and nose.

This simple mask helps and seems to filter out most of the noxious gases. You continue to walk along the ridge. As you walk, you see the horrid white wyrms appearing from the swamp of bodies, and almost like the giant Feasting Whayles in the Black Ocean, they seem to suck up the bodies around them. You carry on, as on the horizon you can see a building. Then all of a sudden, the surface of the mire below is broken.

Turn to **275**

157

Due to the heat, you continue to weaken, and you lose **1 ENDURANCE** point as you make your way through the foul trees. You soon emerge into a clearing that's rich with grass, which is so unlike the rest of this forest of the damned. You notice that all around you poking up through the grass are mushrooms. They are tall, with broad heads mottled with red and white.

If you are in need of food, you can try to eat some of the mushrooms. If you want to, note down this reference and then turn to **444**. After trying the mushrooms, or if you didn't try them, you can exit the clearing either by going left, turn to **497**, or you can go straight and turn to **104**

158

You leap and catch the ledge of the door with both hands. Heaving yourself up, you roll through the rough stone doorway and lie there for a few moments in the cold darkness. You shake your hands and feel the strength slowly returning to your arms. You can sense no danger where you are, and so you rest long enough for your full strength to recover.

Turn to **183**

159

"Very well, my master, I am bound to your will, although I do think both you and I will regret this course".

He places his large hand over your head, and the room shimmers. You find yourself in a grey featureless place, floating.

" I regret, my master, that even I cannot take you out of the Hellscape back to your world" you hear the disembodied voice of the Djinn say *"my powers are reduced here, but I have taken you as far as I can. This is the realm between the worlds, a void where nothing lives, nothing dies, nothing ages and nothing is born. Once here, you can never escape. This is your new home, my master, for all eternity"*

The voice slowly fades and finishes saying,

"I must return to the Hellscape and wait another millennia for one such as yourself to free me, as my power will not work here, and you cannot wish if you cannot speak."

You try to open your mouth to make a further wish, but you realise you cannot move a muscle

"I thank thee not for this, my MASTER" the voice says sarcastically, and then you hear no more. You are doomed to remain here, never ageing, never dying, never moving, but always thinking, until the end of time or the end of your sanity - whichever comes first. Your mission has failed. Turn to 616.

160

TEST YOUR ENDURANCE. If you pass, turn to **11**. If you fail, turn to **466**

Your combatant dead, you take stock. The rest of your force has almost finished off the Death Monks, but there are still a couple of Daemons that are causing considerable problems - ripping your dwindling forces apart limb from limb and often eating the remnants of the dead (or sometimes, not quite dead). You see Celdron overwhelmed by two Daemons and wish him a swift death.

But with the tower unprotected, now is your chance. You care not if the rest of your men will survive, as either they will by the Grace of God, or they will end in this life and be welcomed as Defenders of the Faith in the next. You rush to the tower, and there is a ladder on the outside that takes you to a platform that surrounds the crystal jewel.

Not even thinking of your own safety, you swiftly climb the ladder taking care to stay clear of the beam of concentrated power coming down vertically from the jewel and into the vortex. The power in that beam would turn you into atoms in a heartbeat. The noise of the machine is like a deep "*THRUM*" that gets louder and louder as you climb.

Eventually, after what seems like hours of climbing, but is in fact only a few minutes, you end up on the platform. The jewel almost blinds you as you stand by it, and you realise you don't have much time. You draw Devilsbane for one final time and thrust the blade deep into the crystal.

There is a massive detonation of light, all the more eerie as it is completely silent. You are blown from the tower top and fall, but as you do so, the swirling force from the vortex pulls you towards it. You see the mouth of the vortex is closing as the power from the stone is lost. Down you fall for an eternity until you remember no more.

Turn to **560**

162

Despite the heat and its effects on your body, you jump to your feet and spring to the wall where the door is.

TEST YOUR INTELLIGENCE. If you succeed, turn to **197**. If you fail, turn to **195**

163

Thinking back on your knowledge of the Hellscape, you recall that in the ring of gluttony, there was a forest of addicts, where those who were killed by their addictions are doomed to reside. They are rooted in the earth, unable to move, undergoing eternal withdrawal from their substance of choice. Occasionally, the occupants of the realm come along and harvest the human trees, bleeding them of sap that the Daemons use to make their own pleasure enhancing narcotics.

Whatever you do, you remember that the substances expelled by the soul trees can cause addiction into those coming into contact with them. You must not touch the trees.

Turn to **237**

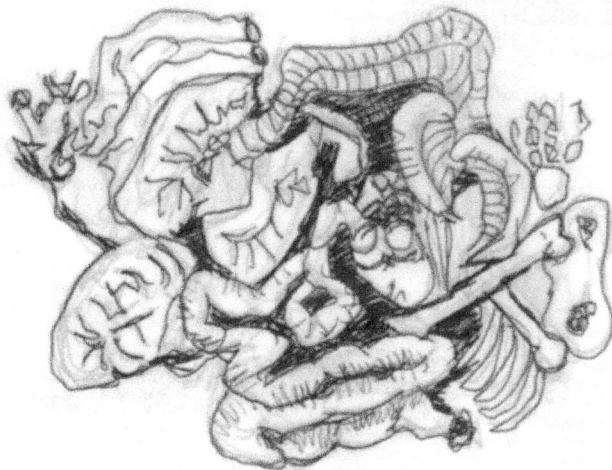

164

If you haven't already you can check the larger domed building, then turn to **193**, or head back to the crossroads, turn to **483**

165

The venom in your veins takes its toll. You are almost delirious, half-blind, and sweating profusely. You stagger around like a drunken man, flailing left and right, but the snake is too fast. But then as it strikes once more, you swing your blade and feel it bite into flesh. You hear a hiss of pain and leap backwards, as the giant body flops to the floor and convulses in its death throes. You rub the tears out of your eyes and see your vanquished foe now lying still, apart from the very tip of its tail that continues to thrash from side to side for minutes afterwards.

"Ah, you killed our companion for the last 1000 years" says the beautiful voice, then it pauses and says *"But no matter. We have plenty more companions. Thou hast done well. Come here and take our hand and receive thy reward."*

Not wishing to cause offence, and having no desire to fight a fully grown dragon in your state, you stagger over and take his right hand. Instantly you feel restored, and the pain from the venom ceases. You can restore your **FIGHTING SKILL** to its original value. You can also recover up to 4 points of **ENDURANCE**

"Well" says your host *"what are we to do with you now?"*

If you ask for forgiveness, turn to **212**. If you ask just to leave this realm, turn to **557**

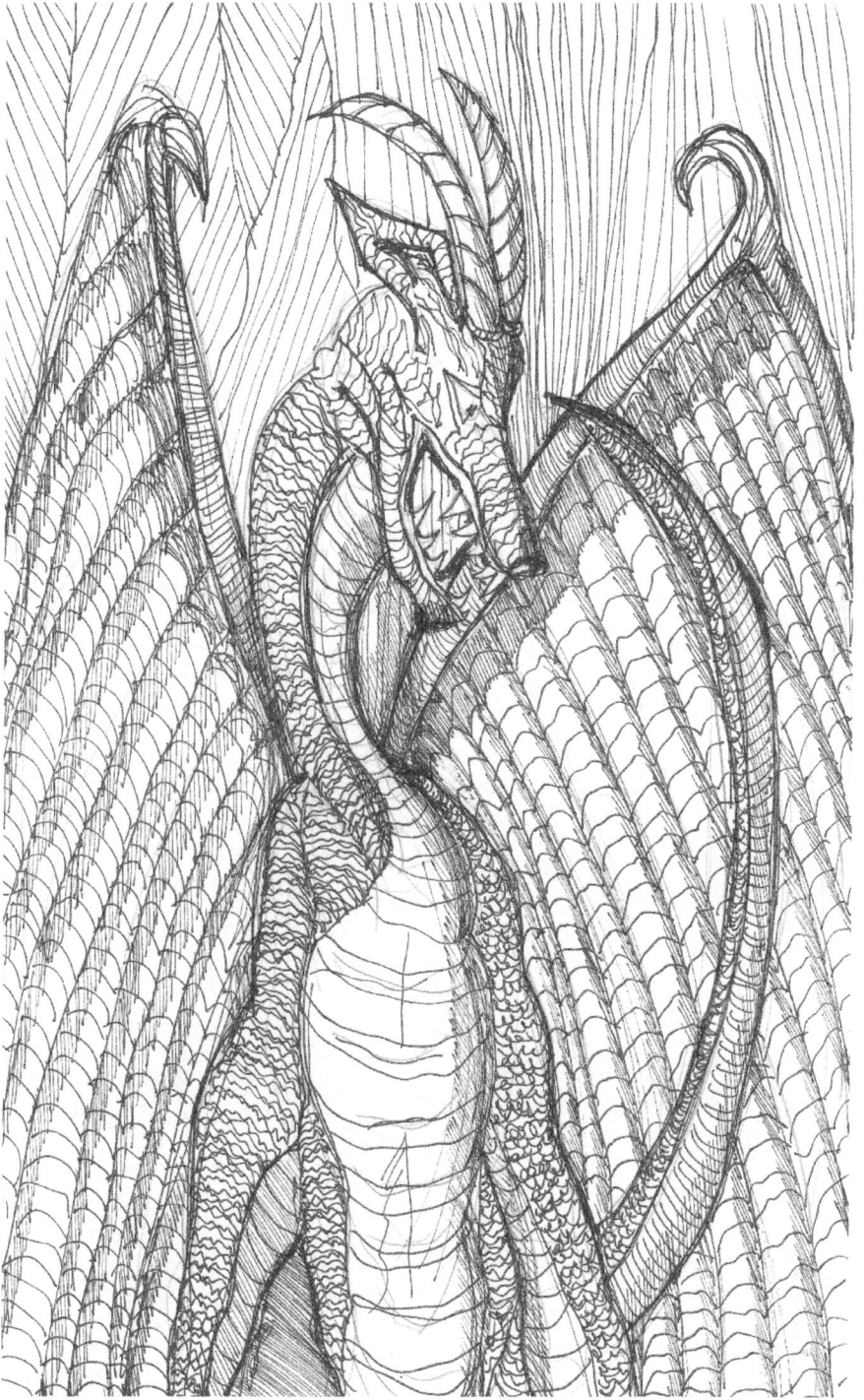

166

You walk down this path into this dead wood, and the forest starts to thin, almost imperceptibly at first. Then the cadaver trees noticeably become more spaced out, and the temperature drops.

You have left the forest of addiction and are now on a small plateau with a sheer wall climbing up in front of you. Cut into the cliff is a staircase. This appears to be the only exit - as there is no way you want to negotiate the infernal forest again.

Turn to **577**

167

The Daemons strength is immense, but time and again Devilsbane stays true to its name and turns the black blade of the Herald of Hell. You are close to exhaustion when finally you see an opening. Baalberith's rage increases each time you catch and turn away his sword, and now he is almost mindless. He overextends a thrust, and you step to one side and in towards the horrific beast, and Devilsbane smoothly slides into his torso.

You angle the strike upward to try to pierce his black heart. His glowing green eyes open wide in surprise, and black blood pours from his bellowing mouth. Before you, his mighty body starts to shrink and wither, and soon all that is left is a tiny Daemon form, no more than 6 inches high.

No mortal man can truly kill a Daemon, but you have returned him to his initial state from when he was created uncounted millennia ago. He is now just an impling, and for him to regain any power in hell will take centuries of torment. The small pathetic form looks around, not realising what has happened, and then looks up to see you towering above him.

He then sees the ragged kings and queens that have been subjected to an eternity of torment turning on him. He screams, a pathetic little sound like a child whistling with a blade of grass, and turns to run as the grey forms surround him. On the floor is a key. It looks to be made of bone and sinew and is twisted and gnarled. You pick it up and examine it.

Stamped on it is the number **10** and a green eye. Note this on your **ADVENTURE SHEET** along with the name **BAALBERITH**. You leave the throne room as sounds of conflict fill the air, as having obviously resolved their issues with Baalberith, the faded rulers now fight for supremacy to see who will take his throne. Such is the eternal lust for power.

Turn to **35**

168

You exit the tree line into a sandy hollow. The heat is even more intense, and you lose 2 **ENDURANCE** points. You hurry to exit this hollow and either go right and turn to **478** or go straight ahead and turn to **61**

169

Knowing not what the strange words mean, you decide to try stepping into the portal. You first raise your hand and press, and the surface is fluid but resists you. You push harder, and the surface seems to push back. Then you feel a presence in the room.

You turn around and seemingly out of nowhere a massive figure has appeared. It's a mighty dragon, crimson red with glowing yellow eyes. However, your eyes are drawn to the figure astride its long, snake-like neck. The figure is humanoid but clearly not human. He looks like the statues in the Holy City that represent the greatest of the seraphs who service the One God.

He is dressed simply in a white pleated robe, and his body is slim but well-muscled. His hair is golden and curls around his face, which has high cheekbones, ice-blue eyes and he is impossibly beautiful. From his back grow a pair of graceful swan-like wings. He puts his hand on the dragon's head, communicating with it silently, and the dragon brings its ginormous head down to the ground. The figure gracefully leaps off the neck of the beast and lands silently. He stares at you with curiosity, but no hostility, in his eyes. Then he speaks.

Turn to **630**

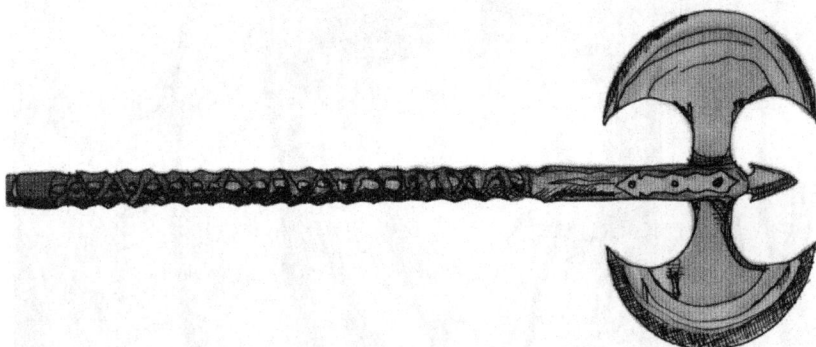

170

The creature is large and powerful, and the obsidian antlers are sharp as spears. You fight your best but are too weak. You stand back panting, and the hart lowers its head and charges. The razor-sharp points of the antlers pierce your armour and thrust into your body, impaling you. Furfur raises his head in victory, and you slide down further onto the Daemons antlers.

Blood pools on the floor in front of you. Then the giant hart flicks its head back and forwards, and you are flung off its antlers into the corpse trees with bone-crushing force.

Tendrils try to grab hold of you, but the hart bellows, *Leave him, he is mine!* and they shrink back. You drop back to the floor, and lie in the clearing face down in the sodden earth, as blood oozes from your many punctures.

The hart walks over and stands in front of you. You stare up at it, and then it shimmers and in place of the hart is a beautiful youth,. His eyes are the same golden colour as the hart, and even as your life ebbs from you, they captivate you. He is naked except for a loincloth, and white wings rise gracefully out of his back. Atop his head are swept back obsidian horns, which protrude from his pale, almost white, straight hair that flows down his back. A golden glow almost surrounds the youthful form of Furfur, and he smiles lovingly at you and then kneels down by your side.

He holds your head and cleans the blood and grime from your face.

If only you had trusted me, my child, I could have helped you. Instead you forced me to spill blood and your mortal form withers as we speak. But no mind, I am in need of a new servant, and your shade will aide me for the coming millennia'.

He holds your head, and strokes your face lovingly as your strength leaves you. With that you die, only to be reborn as a doomed soul joined to Furfur in servitude for eternity. Your mission has failed, and the world will burn. Turn to **616**

171

You walk up to the figure which has its back to you. Once again, you try to speak. The figure ignores you. You put your hand on his shoulder, and it passes through this seemingly solid man. Again he ignores you. He is looking at something on the ground, and so you walk around and squat down to his level. Then you see his face - it's your face! And your other self is looking at a discarded trail ration pack in disgust.

Then the figure gets up and walks off into the distance and disappears - just as you did. You seem to have once again come full circle back to where you were previously - while you were still there.

Turn to **567**

172

Seeing no obvious alternative, you start the precarious way back down. **TEST YOUR AGILITY** 3 times. If you fail at any time, turn to **281**. If you pass, you safely jump your way back to the floor of the dome. Turn to **64**

173

"The lord of this realm is the Lord Astaroth. His sigil is a 5 sided star and he lives in the mountain at the ends of this forest. He is mighty and so seek not to provoke him. If he asks you to take his hand, then avoid the one that is the least sinister. Now that is all I will reveal. Begone and leave me to my contemplations".

You thank the Lord and leave the glade. You can either go left and turn to **433**, or head right and turn to **105**

174

You flatten yourself against the wall while you take in the scene in front of you. You are in a large hall. Stone tables and benches form a square around the perimeter of the room, and every space is taken by a Daemon. The Daemons are too busy laughing, drinking and eating to notice you. In each of the fireplaces around the perimeter are large spits, and human forms slowly roast, the spits being slowly turned by fire imps.

Each human wails quietly as their flesh is slowly roasted to juicy perfection. Many of these human figures are obese, and the fire sizzles and flares as fat drips onto it. However, this being hell, the victims never die even as their organs are roasted, and their brains are boiled. When they are ready, the imps take the spits out of the fire and cut the still-living bodies off their mounts and into wheeled barrows.

The separate body parts are still moving and writhing in agony. The imps then wheel the barrows around to the far end of the hall and tip them onto a wide moving belt, which is driven by a wheel constantly turned by minor Daemons. The wide belt conveys them up over the diners and drops them into a large fire pit in the centre of the tables.

The assembled Daemons then reach over and grab whatever delicacy they desire, be it a haunch of man, a head to suck the brain juices out of, or a torso of a woman. Buzzing around the hall are numerous imps, each holding a serving dish which contains another human delicacy. These are loaded onto the Daemons' plates, or sometimes a Daemon just seizes a dish from the imps and tips it down their gullet, to the hilarity of all watching.

The Daemons laugh as they tear the meat apart with their cruel talons and eat it in big ravenous bites. They wash the flesh down with cups of human blood and fat. Every few minutes, when a Daemon fills themselves to capacity, they get up and stagger to one of several bowls in the walls of the room, and vomit up all that they have eaten.

The foul liquid of those they have consumed then drains away into a centre bath, where the pieces of flesh slowly reconstitute themselves back into human form, and they are dragged out of the bath with vicious hooks and then taken away either to the spits or to elsewhere, to begin the cooking process all over again. The gruesome feast continues ad nausea.

Turn to **160**

175

Although more accustomed to brave assaults on military positions, you have come to realise in your time in this grim domain that stealth will serve you best. And so using the experience you have gained over many campaigns, and time served as a scout in your formative days, you move quietly but steadily.

You know that quick movements attract the eye, and so instead you take your time. It's hell on your nerves as you cross the floor to one of the gantries, but it works. You arrive underneath a gantry and look up. The wood construction is fairly archaic compared to the rest of the building, but the boards of the gantry are solid, and you can only just see shadows moving above.

Confident no one can see you, you resolve to look around. Soon you get to a ladder. If you want to climb this ladder to see where it leads, turn to 9. If you would rather forgo this, you can move to the next section of the building, turn to **290**

As you try to cross back towards the wooden vats near the door, you hear a shout behind you in a harsh non-human tongue. You realise you have been spotted. You speed up and head towards the wooden vats as the shout came from behind. You stop briefly when you get to the vats to check behind you.

Sure enough, you soon see a number of imps and Daemons running across the floor, some on two legs, some ape-like on all fours. You have three options.

You can stop and fight by turning to **377**. If you want to flee the building, turn to **559**. Or if you want to draw your sword and try to breach one of the nearby vats, turn to **118**

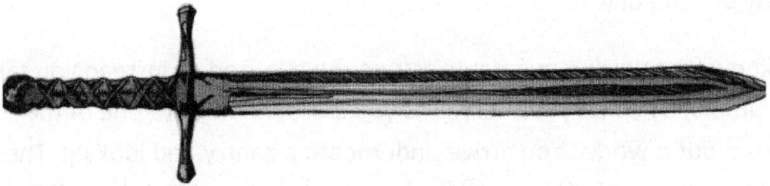

The path winds through the trees, and you make every effort not to touch them. The heat is oppressive under the canopy of the humanoid trees, and you are sweating freely. Lose 1 **ENDURANCE** point.

Soon, you appear in another clearing. The human trees here seem to be wailing even louder than at other locations. Keen to escape the disconcerting noise, you quickly choose a route and decide to head left, but as you do, the trees seem to close in and block the route. You now only have two choices.

You can bravely head straight on by turning to **85**, or risk going right, turn to **593**

178

Despite your advancing years, you manage to dodge past the tree limbs without needing to touch them or interfere with them. You find yourself in a clearing. While you assess the route, you hear a noise behind you and turn around quickly, your hand flying to your weapon. The corpse trees behind you seem to have moved so that the passageway you fought your way in through has now disappeared.

You must now continue onward and try to find your way through this dread forest of the doomed. You have three options. To turn left, turn to **368**. To turn right, turn to **538**. To go straight on, turn to **579**

179

Inside is a huge throne room. At the end is a long set of marble steps ending in a dais, on top of which sits a throne. As with the rest of the castle, the throne room is in a state of terrible repair. Piles of stone cover the floor, where the rocks have fallen in from the huge vaulted ceiling. The marble steps are grey and chipped, not white and vibrant, and the throne itself is of brass turned green by age.

All around the room are tall mirrors that show the throne room in all its former opulence. Constantly going up the stairs are smaller figures in ragged clothing, carrying items up to the throne's occupant, a huge Daemon. He wears a soldier's uniform with a large broadsword resting over his knees, and a tarnished gold crown on his head.

Every time one of the smaller figures reaches the top, the Daemon raises a foot or a fist, and pushes them back, tumbling them down the stairs. Sometimes he raises his huge broadsword and cuts them down, only for them to pick themselves up after they reach the bottom and start the climb again. You notice that in the mirrors reflecting the scene, the ragged figures are all dressed in opulent clothing with crowns upon their heads. You recognise the faces and colours of various monarchs from the past; great conquerors each and all, with a lust for power.

Carrying up a cask of ale is King Xaersos of Cembadia, a ruler feared and hated by his subjects for his bloodlust, cruelty and desire for power, who died over 500 years ago - hacked down by his own subjects. Next to him, carrying a haunch of venison, is Prince King Heria, of the Empire of Sarbria, who ruled in a reign of terror for 30 years but has long since been dead. Numerous other queens, empresses, kings and pontiffs, all known for their lust for power, and their love of cruelty, also endlessly climb the steps with offerings to their Daemon Lord, only to be cast down.

You realise that the mirrors placed around the room show them how they looked in the height of their pomp when they believed they were immortal. This is eternal torment for those with a lust for power - to be cast down as a powerless victim abused by their ruler while seeing their reflections of when they were on the throne abusing their own subjects.

Turn to **304**

180

Regardless of how hard you run, the devils remain on your tail. Soon they overtake you, and you stand there panting, with barely enough breath left to fight. You vainly go to draw Devilsbane, but as soon as it is clear of its scabbard, it is knocked from your hand by the clawed hand of the Thin Daemon. Tired and unarmed, you try to fight, but the beasts are far too strong for you. The Thin Daemon wraps its wiry arms around your shoulders, and soon your arms are unable to move.

You try kicking out with your legs at the Ape Daemon, but it just dances out of the way with surprising agility for a beast that size and laughs at you. Next time you kick, he catches your foot and then moves in and manages to grab the other. You can hear the Thin Daemon laughing into your ear as he holds you in a head-lock, your arms waving powerlessly above your head.

The Ape Daemon pulls so that your feet move away from your body and you are now dead straight, held in the iron-like grip of these two fiends. Then, in a harsh voice, the Ape Daemon says:

"So, this fellow wants to see how we brew down here. Mayhap we should show him how we crush the spirit out of puny humans to make our wine?"

The Thin Daemon laughs, a horrible high pitched sound, and then the Ape Daemon starts to turn your feet. There is terrible strength in his arms. As he turns, your legs also start to turn, followed by your body, whilst your shoulders stay static. The pain is incredible as he slowly wrings your body like a human would a damp cloth. Muscles tear, ligaments snap, and bones fracture as he continues to turn your lower half. Slowly and deliberately, he is wringing the life out of you.

You try not to scream, but the pain is too much, and you cannot help but let out a shriek, half from pain and half of rage. Then your vertebrae finally crumble under pressure, your legs go dead, and you mercifully can no longer feel anything from your shoulders down.

You are still barely alive, but delirious with pain, when the Ape Daemon throws your mangled legs to the ground. He gestures to the Thin Daemon, who lets go of you and your body falls limply to the ground. Then the Ape Daemon picks you up as if he was lifting a damp towel, and throws you over his shoulder. The two Daemons trudge back towards the factory.

The Thin Daemon snickers, and says,

"This will be a fine addition to our latest brew. Mortal flesh should add a bit of spice to the flavour".

The Ape Daemon adds *"and a bit of body"*, and they both laugh uproariously.

You are doomed to be part of their next brew, and your soul will remain here for all time. Your mission has failed. Your once green world will soon be scorched earth. Turn to **616**

181

As you grab onto the limb, vines creep around your hand and under your mailed gauntlet. You panic and pull off the gauntlet as quickly as you can. The vines have not spread far, and you pull them off quickly, cursing silently as the barbs that were digging into your flesh are pulled away. Lose 1 **ENDURANCE**.

Turn to **178**

182

There are rows of crates with full bottles less than 10 yards from you. You sneak over to them, taking care to keep an eye on where the imps and sub-daemons are positioned as you do so.

TEST YOUR FORTUNE. If you are fortunate, turn to **116**. If you are not, turn to **292**

183

Having rested and regained your strength, you take in your surroundings. You are in a corridor that has been cut through the cliff face. At the end, you can see light, and there appears to be no option but to head towards it. You soon emerge into a circular chamber, with one exit, a shimmering portal ahead of you. Seeing nothing to worry about you cross the chamber to the portal.

Turn to **326**

184

You cannot remember what befell these poor souls. Their torment is clear in their eyes for each one you pass. You try to stop and converse, but they seem beyond rational thought and the ability to communicate. Instead, each soul tree just fixes you with a glare of hatred and envy. Frustrated, you carry on along the tree-lined route.

Turn to **237**

185

The path winds through the foliage, and you make every effort not to touch anything. The heat is oppressive under the canopy of the humanoid trees, and you are sweating freely. Lose 1 **ENDURANCE** point. Soon, you appear in another clearing. The human trees here seem to be wailing even louder than at other locations.

Keen to escape the disconcerting noise, you quickly choose a route and decide to head right, but as you do, the trees seem to close in and block the route. You now only have two choices.

You can bravely head left by turning to **593**, or risk going straight ahead, turn to **255**

186

The almost mindless bodies of the tormented are hungry. They have not been fed for centuries or even millennia. All they can dream of in their minds is the feasts they experienced as mortals, where they ate the finest food, feasted on the rarest flesh and never knew the pangs of hunger. Now, however, they are starving.

Ignoring the noise outside, they turn almost as one and stare at you. Their eyes focus on the fresh flesh visible and the promise of more once you have been peeled out of your iron shell. They lick their lips with dried out tongues and start to drool freely. Their arms come up, and they move towards you. You do not have space to draw Devilsbane, and so you try stabbing with your belt knife, but to no avail.

The mass of bodies is too great for you to fight against, and hands clamour at you and pull you down. When you are on the floor, they fall upon you, ripping armour and chain from your body.

Their rotting teeth dig into your now bare skin and take out huge chunks of flesh, which they devour with relish. Mercifully you soon pass out in pain as the blood spurts from you like fountains and is lapped up by the dead souls. Your soul is now stuck in this realm and will likely become like those who even now feed upon you.

Your mission has failed. The human world will fall to horrors such as this. Turn to **616**

187

Realising you have missed the jump, you try to throw yourself backwards onto the step below, but you only manage to hit it with the small of your back. Even with armour, the blow is painful, and you gasp. You try to reach around and get purchase on the step, but your hand just scrapes the surface, and gravity then takes over. You start to fall, tumbling in the air. Your arms and legs flailing, you vainly try to stop yourself. As you turn, you can see the ground hurtling towards you.

Time seems to both pass in an instant and last forever, as you take in every detail of your onrushing doom. Then you hit, with full force. You are almost in a standing position when you land, and your legs hit first and take the brunt of the impact, as your lower legs splinter. But your thigh bones remain strong, and so they are pushed up into your body. Your hips shatter as the strong thick bones force their way into your abdomen and pierce first your guts and then your vitals.

Blood spurts out of your mouth in a gush. Then your mangled body topples to the floor. Your six-foot height has been reduced to almost half of that. You try to scream in pain, but your mouth is filled with iron-rich blood, and you can only manage a wet gurgle. You don't die from your injuries, but instead, feel your lungs filling further with liquid, and you realise as you gasp for breath that you are drowning in your own blood.

Your tortured breaths become weaker and weaker as more thick, viscous blood floods into your chest cavity. Your body, starved of air, starts to shut down and your eyes see strange visions as you begin to hallucinate due to oxygen deprivation. A strange, almost euphoric feeling, takes over momentarily and then your head drops to the ground for one final time, and your eyes stare blankly out.

You have failed in your mission, and the world will surely burn.

Turn to **616**

188

Sometimes discretion is the better part of valour. You manage to leave the terrible house without being noticed. You can now either choose to go left, turn to **610**, or try the house over the road, turn to **273**

When you recover from the lightning attack, you evaluate your situation and decide to take a risk and trust this other apparent mortal. You announce,

"Apologies, Sir that was in haste. I assumed you were a Daemon. I am Kommandant Ulrac De-Villiers"

You give a brief overview of how you were dragged alive into the Hellscape. The lanky figure nods along, stroking his thin wispy beard as he does so. When you stop talking, which doesn't take long as you deliver your adventure to date like a military report, he replies,

"No harm done my boy, it is best to assume most will mean you ill will in this sorry realm. Hmmm. Yes, a mortal trapped in the Hellscape would find the only way to leave would be to make your way to the final circle. That will be quite a journey to survive, one worthy of an epic tale".

You ask him who he is.

"Ah, a pertinent question, my boy. I am Professor Erlic Hancox. I, like you, am a mortal trapped here."

You ask how long and he replies

"Time is hard to figure in this world, where night is like day and day is like night. An age may pass in the mortal land, and it may only be a few moments here. Or millennia may pass here, but be only a day in the living realms. Time is not......constant. It fluctuates. You see......"

And then he launches into a long rambling discourse on his theory of time in the Hellscape. You listen for as long as you can, but the theory is beyond your comprehension. You hold up your hand, and Hancox stops and apologises.

"I am sorry, my boy, I do like the sound of my own voice and it's so long since I had another sentient mortal to talk to"

Again you ask how long he has been there and Hancox says,

"I estimate that when I left our plane, it was 2502AN."

You gasp, as when you were sent on your mission, it was 1742AN, nearly 750 years before Hancox. You tell him, and he replies, shaking his head.

"Yes, my lad, as I said. Time is not consistent"

Turn to **631**

190

You order your men to unlimber their bows and use their heaviest arrowheads to try to hit the spinning jewel. They all take aim and wait for the signal. You nod once to Celdron, who brings down his arm, and a volley of arrows arc towards the crystal. Almost as one they hit or would have done, but instead, they seemingly are stopped by an invisible barrier surrounding the stone.

The arrows drop harmlessly to the floor. One of the Death Monks, who is on a platform just beneath the jewel, shouts to his men,

"Protect the machine!" and they form in ranks.

A monk with a red sash around his waist talks in a hideous guttural language to the Daemons, who also form up and wait as a barrier. You have no option but to charge. Turn to **475**

191

The beast is too powerful for you and eventually knocks you almost lifeless to the floor with a flick of its foot-long talons. It bounds over with speed surprising for its size and picks up your barely living body.

You scream as its talons pierce your mail and flesh. It raises you up to its face level and stares at you with small, glaring eyes. There are no rational thoughts behind those eyes, just instinct.

It reaches up with its other hand, and plucks your helm off your head and drops it to the ground causing it to land with a clatter. Then its free hand takes hold of your head and pulls. Like a farmer butchering a quail, your head pops off. The beast tosses your head into the air, and throws back its head, opening its ginormous jaw. Your head continues to spin through the air, and, upon reaching its zenith, drops back down into the reeking maw of the sub-daemon. It chews a couple of times and then swallows.

Then it continues on its way, stripping armour from your lifeless body and chewing on your naked flesh like a king on a chicken bone.

Your mission has failed, and your spirit is doomed to remain in this realm for all time, and the world will suffer because of your failure.

Turn to **616**

192

By running along the sides of the ridges that make the roads across the plain, you are able to get far enough ahead of your pursuers to hide. You look for a good spot and see an area where most of the bodies appear to be still. You slide down the side of the ridge and lie on the ground, pulling a naked torso of an obese woman over you.

You wait. You hear the Daemons pass this way, speaking in their harsh guttural tongue. Daring to look, you see them standing on the ridge not 20 yards from you. You stay still.

TEST YOUR FORTUNE. If you are fortunate, turn to **456**. If you are not, turn to **149**

193

As you approach the large building, the heat becomes even more intense. Sweat streams down your face, and soon you are panting for liquid. If you have some provisions, drink now, or lose 2 **ENDURANCE** points.

You walk around the building and find one single entrance, a small, seemingly insignificant doorway. You peer inside and see a short corridor that seems to take you through the twin copper walls of the building. You edge down the corridor and look inside.

Turn to **244**

194

Again you get about a quarter of the way up before slipping and missing the next step.

TEST YOUR FORTUNE. if you are fortunate, turn to **260**. If you are unfortunate, turn to **126**

195

In your haste, you forgot on which side the door was hinged. It swings open into the room, and you find yourself face to face with two imps and a giant Daemon.

For a moment, you all just stand there not reacting, and then the Daemon yells at the imps,

"Intruder, and mortal so it seems. Take him, you snivelling scum" and he kicks both the imps forward with his clawed hoof. You must now fight both imps.

Each **IMP** is **FS 4, EN 3**

{ADVANCED - Initial AS: 9, Initial DA: 13; AG 8, FIT 5, ST 1}

If you win, turn to **152**

196

The door is small and plain, compared to the others in the corridor. You grasp the handle and turn, yanking the door open, causing it to wail in protest.

There is nothing but a dark passageway beyond. Do you want to enter? If so, turn to **375**. Alternatively, you can return to **48** and choose another option.

197

Fortunately, you noticed that the door opened inwards and that the door was hinged on the left-hand side. You leap behind the door as it opens. With the space limitations, you choose not to draw Devilsbane and instead draw your belt knife. However, as it was partially blunted on the wall earlier and as it's a shorter weapon, lose 2 **DAMAGE** if you strike a foe. You wait with your arm raised, ready to strike.

Two imps come into view, and behind them, you hear a voice saying,

"C'mon you scum, the Lords want more smoked meat for their table. Wynch these poor wretches down and bring them to the carving bench"

You realise you are in a smoking room where meat is being smoked for the table. Then you hear the footsteps of a large creature echoing down the hall as it leaves. You now only have to face 2 imps. You wait until their backs are turned as they are busy trying to wynch down the bodies above, and as they are heaving on the rusty wheel, you strike.

Each **IMP** is **FS 4, EN 3**

{**ADVANCED** - Initial AS: 9, Initial DA: 13; AG 8, FIT 5, ST 1}

But you can throw 1d4 and remove that from one of the imps **ENDURANCE** as you were able to strike from behind. If you win, turn to **446**

198

Before setting off, you get out the map that you found in the feast hall. On it is the path that you are about to go up. The path seems to cut across a part of the plains named on the map as:

surebrecfodleifeht

If you can make a name out of these words, then convert these letters into numbers, and add these numbers up – but don't forget the convention of how everything is written in the Hellscape. Now turn to this reference. If it says the name is correct, continue, if not, turn back here. If you cannot find a name, turn to **346**

199

The hall is immense, not tall, but fully 200 yards on the longest sides. It is built of a red brick that seems to gleam like freshly spilt blood in the ruddy light. You walk around and try to see if there is anything as commonplace as a window so that you can spy what's inside.

The walls are too thick for you to hear what is happening. You reach the rear of the building, and next to one of the 20-yard-wide chimneys is a small door.

If you choose to enter the building via this door, then turn to **439**. Alternatively, you can ignore the building and head on across the plain, turn to **603**

200

You remember from your schooling in the One True God that there are 13 circles of torment in the Hellscape. The first is Limbo, which you realise must be where you are now. You feel a pang of guilt for your fallen comrades, who despite fighting at the command of the Most Holy, have been left in this everlasting torment; not of pain or torture, but of boredom. You cannot believe that the One True God would let them suffer so. Lose 1 **FAITH** point.

Steeling yourself, you realise that if you can escape Limbo you still have 12 circles to get through, and if you remember correctly the next one is Lust, which will test the willpower of a knight who has pledged their body and soul to the Church. Your quest seems impossible.

Now turn to **215**

201

You say the name and the figure smiles.

"Ah, good, good, Yes, we are the Duke Astaroth, and thou are most welcome here, Ulrac De-Villiers. Mayhap that was too simple to test your mighty intellect. Let us think of more of a challenge".

He pauses for a moment and then says,

"Thou art obviously an educated man of breeding, then let us test this"

He waves almost negligently, and a flaming square appears. In it are the 9 squares with runes in 3 of them. You have to complete the other squares. If you solve the problem, turn to the number that is the solution.

"However, haste is required, De-Villiers, and so one will only give you until this number reduces to nothing to complete it. Fail, and my pet gets a new plaything"

Again, Astaroth gestures and the figure 3:00 appears in human numbers. Set a timer to countdown from 3:00 minutes. If you fail to solve the problem in time, or cannot answer it, turn to **10**. If you solve it, turn to the reference you have identified.

Don't forget the convention of written language in the Hellscape.

202

You race through the woods towards the Hellish machine. The men working on it shout and stop their work, leaping down from the scaffold and drawing swords.

"Protect the machine, protect the machine!" you hear one of them shout. As well as that, the Daemons who have already come through take a look at your charging force and seem to smile with relish - if a Daemon can indeed smile. They also head towards your force. About 10 yards from the device you clash.

The black-robed men you recognise as part of a Death Cult, who work towards uniting this reality and their patron devil, Bael. They are indifferent fighters but will fight to the death. The Daemons are a different proposition. They are fully 7 to 8 feet tall, with clawed feet and sharp talons on their hands.

TEST YOUR FORTUNE to see if you will fight a DEATH MONK or a DAEMON. In order to do this, roll 1d10. Make a note of this number. Now roll a 1d10 again. If the second number is greater than the first, turn to **213**. If it is lower or equal, turn to **556**

203

Successfully you make it across the floor without being seen. Turn to **309**

204

Your third hit rends a huge gaping wound on the wyrm's flesh, just below the mouth. You feel like the tide of the fight is turning, and that luck is finally on your side. Then the wyrm's huge body starts to convulse, and you watch on in fascination. If your strike was a **MORTAL BLOW**, turn to **110**. You assume you have dealt a fatal blow, and that it is in its death throws. Turn to **572**

205

If you want to ask the left-hand side "guard" who has just spoken to you, then turn to **399**. To ask the right side "guard" who is staring at you now, turn to **299**

206

In your haste to leave, you have completely forgotten to recover Devilsbane and your shield. You are about to venture back inside to retrieve them when you hear a shout from inside the dome. You peek around the doorway, and your heart falls as you see a couple of imps gathered around Devilsbane.

More Daemons are coming over to see what has been found - too many for you to fight without a sword. Lose 1 **FIGHTING SKILL** and 1 **FORTUNE** for being so foolish. Now you can either check the smaller dome and turn to **122**, or head back to the crossroads, turn to **483**

207

You stand patiently and wait, the shapes getting closer, your hands on the hilt of Devilsbane, its point standing in the ground. The figures appear to be 10 in total, and they continue to grow in number until there are roughly 50 of them.

They are all clad in grey robes with grey cowls covering their faces. They approach and circle you, each drawing a sword, so that soon 50 grey blades, which look like they are made of smoke, are pointed at your throat. Your nerve breaks, and you raise Devilsbane and swipe at the swords.

Your great blade passes through them as if they did not exist, and the shapes laugh as you flail around. The laughs are as dry and dusty as a desert. Then one of them stabs you in the shoulder, and the ethereal blade slips into your body but does not pierce your flesh. Instead, it sucks 1d6 in **FAITH** points out of your body. If your **FAITH** points are 0, turn to 13.

A figure then steps forward and makes a sign, and the figures lower their unearthly blades. He laughs and then says in the same dry voice,

"We owed you that, My Kommandant, for deserting us in the valley. Some leader of men".

Then, as one, the 50 figures throw their cowls back. In horror, you recognise a lot of the faces. They are the men of your small force that you were leading to destroy the Hellscape machine. But their faces are old and haggard and drawn, as if they are millennia old corpses, not freshly dead.

"How can this be? You are my men. I fought with you but a day or so ago - and led you in a holy battle. How can you be here? There hasn't been the time"

The lead figure, who you now recognise as one of your sergeants, Hatton, laughs.

"Time, what is time to the dead. It has been 10,000 years since that day, and we have been here all that time, suffering in this limbo and yet you still live"

"How can this be?" you ask again

"How do we know, we are just the dead, trapped on this plane for eternity"

"Then I will find a way to free you," you say rashly. *"Show me how to leave this realm, and I will do all that I can to return and save you."*

Hatton laughs once more, a dry, dusty sound like the wind blowing dried leaves

"There is no saving us, and you betrayed us, and so why should we aide you?"

Turn to **357**

208

Fortune or the One True God is with you. The shambling figures ignore you as they hear the noise at the door. They approach and wait, ravening, with drool falling to the ground to form puddles.

Then the door opens, and two imps and a huge Daemon enter. The dead waste no time and fall upon them. The imps do not last long as they are ripped limb from limb. Their soon clean bones are thrown aside as a king would a chicken drumstick. But the Daemon is a tougher foe. He fights back, with tooth and claw, but even he cannot stop the many hands.

Soon he is pulled to the floor, and the tormented should get a measure of revenge by eating him alive. He screams in pain in a very high pitched cry resembling a child, and of someone who has never experience suffering. You wait at the back of the room for your chance.

When the Daemon is almost down to a pile of bones, you dart past the feasting souls and run. You manage to escape the building via the rear door unmolested.

Turn to **131**

209

You decide to head along the corridor. The dusty corridor opens up into a room, and you enter from what you perceive to be the south, although perceptions are not to be trusted in this hellish plane. The room is almost perfectly square. In the centre of each wall is a door. The door in the north wall appears to be made of bone. The door in the east wall is made of shimmering emerald. The door in the western wall is made of onyx.

Which door will you try, or would you prefer to go back and try a route you haven't taken? If you want to try the bone door, go to **257**. For the emerald, it's **429**. For the onyx, it's **548**. If you would rather leave, turn to **134**

210

Looking around desperately, you plan a route to a ladder that takes you past several of the vats. You sprint to the first one, which is still full of boiling liquid. At the controls is one imp, whom you simply body check into, knocking it over the edge of the gantry to the floor below. You look at the controls, and quickly ascertain which two buttons you need to press. Doing so, you then move on and do the same at 3 more vats. In sequence, lights start to flash and then for each one, the valve at the bottom opens where no pipe is connected.

Boiling liquid floods out of the vats and swamp the Daemons below, washing them away. Next, the side door in each vat is released, and the human ingredients shamble out of the doorways and fall upon their tormentors. There is chaos below, and you simply wait for a few minutes until the Daemons are too busy fending off the remnants of humankind. You jump onto a nearby ladder and slide down to the bottom.

Turn to **294**

211

Using your blade, you try to break the ring of fire around the Professors ankle. You saw away at the circle of flame, and it seems like strands are starting to break. You carry on, moving your razor-sharp blade up and down as it cuts into the seemingly almost indestructible filament. Then all of a sudden, it snaps, and the Professor's ankle is free. The flaming strand, now cut, flares briefly and them seems to fizzle out into nothingness. Your **FAITH** has held strong and broken the bind. **RESTORE 1 FAITH** point.

The professor pulls it away and leaps around in celebration like a man possessed. You sheath your blade, smiling at his antics whilst he cavorts, free for the first moment since time unknown. He dances towards you and takes your gauntleted fist in both of his hands and shakes it again and again until you feel the need to pull free. He is smiling from ear to ear.

"Oh thank you, my boy. Words cannot convey how this feels to be free. Now how can I reward you?"

Do you want to ask him how to escape this realm, then turn to **327**? If you want to ask him if he has anything that can aide you, turn to **344**

212

Feeling nervous in spite of yourself in front of this angelic figure, you stutter an apology.

"Oh, thou must not apologise for your actions, thou has done well. In Hellscape we admire strength, but despise weakness"

Lose **1 FAITH** point for apologising. Now turn to **557**

213

You find yourself in front of a Daemon from the higher realms of hell. This Daemon, whilst strong in human terms, is nothing compared to the major Daemons that will come out of the vortex if you fail. Your main hope is that this Daemon is taking time to acclimatise to this reality, and this has affected his fitness.

SCOUT DAEMON has **FS 7, EN 8**

{ADVANCED - Initial AS: 12, Initial DA: 11; FIT 5, AG 6, ST 6}

If you win, turn to **220**. If your **ENDURANCE** gets below 1, turn to **498**

Drawing your sword slowly, you wait until both have turned away, and measure the distance between you and them. It's about 20 feet, but you will have to dash up the side of the incline up the ridge. You think you have a good chance of an attack that will kill one of the Daemons outright, leaving you just one to fight.

Will you try to kill the Thin Daemon or the Ape Daemon? You know they have **FITNESS 8** and **7** respectively. Make your decision now and turn to **38**

215

"You must go soon, Kommandant. Your presence pains us".

You reply that you will, but you notice that there is one amongst your men who you cannot recall seeing in this dreary realm. You ask what happened to Celdron. Hatton sighs and says,

"None of us knows, or those that think they know saw a different fate for Celdron. Some say that he was consumed by Daemons, others that he was pulled into the Hellportal, and others that he turned and fled in fear and panic. None here know his fate".

You nod, and then ask how you can escape this realm. Hatton gestures with an almost incorporeal arm over your shoulder, and you turn and see that from nowhere, seemingly a swirling black circle has appeared, about 6 foot in diameter.

"That is where you must go, and now, or else risk being stuck in here for all eternity."

You swiftly thank Hatton and your men, who seem non-plussed by your thanks and head towards the portal. Surely nothing can be worse than this pale realm of desperation and tediousness. Turn to **111**

216

The face on the door opens its eyes, glaring at you with undisguised malevolence. The mouth turns into a cruel grin, yet the face says nothing. Do you want to try to walk up and open the door? If you do, turn to **316**. If you decide against it, then return to **209** and choose another door.

217

As you edge around the kitchen, you accidentally catch the leg of a tripod that supports a black cauldron over a small fire. As you kick the leg away, the cauldron wobbles and then, seemingly after being about to right itself, tips to the floor with a crash. The contents, a soup of brains and eyes, spill onto the floor.

The imps stop stone-still and then turn and glare at you. They hiss, their small sharp teeth glistening in the firelight. Then they launch themselves at you. Roll 1d10+2, as this is how many imps are currently working in the kitchen that you will have to fight

Each **IMP** is **FS 4, EN 3**

{ADVANCED - Initial AS: 9, Initial DA: 13; AG 8, FIT 5, ST 1}

But you must beat them all in turn. If you succeed turn to **544**. If you fail, turn to **334**

218

With practised ease, you draw your greatsword. The wyrm has noticed you and rears up to its full height, and then dives down towards you. Despite its giant size, the wyrm is not well-armoured and not used to its prey being armed - but you will still need to kill it.

GORGER WYRM has FS 5, EN 7

{ADVANCED - Initial AS: 9, Initial DA: 9; FIT 4, AG 5, ST 7}

If you take more than 5 attack rounds to defeat the beast, then throw 1d4. This is how many more Gorger Wyrms are attracted by the noise, and you must now also fight them in turn. If you win, turn to **413**. If you killed more than one wyrm, turn to **423**. If you lose, turn to **286**

219

The door swings open, and behind you there is a short passageway, and at the end is another door. Everything feels safe. If you want to head towards the door, turn to **607**. If you would rather leave, and try another door, then turn to **209** and choose again.

220

The Daemon is large and ponderous compared to you, and so using your speed and agility, you are able to dodge his most devastating blows. The fight is short, savage and ugly. The Daemon has tremendous strength, but your superior skill eventually wins through. The final thrust of your sword takes your opponent in the chest and pierces the creatures hide-like skin, finding its way to what may be its heart; if Daemons have such a thing.

Foul stinking yellow liquid, which you assume is the blood of the creature, erupts from the wound and the Daemon staggers and falls with an earth-shaking thud. Turn to **161**

221

Can you remember the name of the owner of this house? If so, work out their name in number form (A=1, B=2, ...Z=26) and add all these numbers together. Then turn to that reference. If you don't know, turn to **48** and try another option.

222

Your grip on sanity remains true, and you resolve to carry on and ignore your past selves. Turn to **424**

223

Unable to think of a name, you stand there, your poise deserting you. As quick as a flash Baalberith leaps from his throne, swinging his mighty sword above his head. He lands in front of you, and as he does so, his sword swings down with such power that it cuts through your armour and cleaves you in two from neck to groin. Your mortal body falls to the ground, one part to the left, and the other to the right. Blood, guts and worse cover the floor.

"HAH" says the Daemon Lord *"YOU THINK TO FOOL ME WITH THAT LITTLE CHARADE? I AM BAALBERRITH, HERALD OF THE KING OF HELL, AND WILL NOT BE FOOLED BY A MORTAL WORM. BUT NOW, I HAVE A NEW SERVANT"* he continues, looking at your spirit form which stands over your mortal remains.

His taloned hand shoots out and grabs you, pain shooting through your ethereal form.

"COME, WORM, YOU WILL JOIN MY LEGIONS OF QUEENS AND EMPERORS AND SERVE ME NOW, FOR ALL TIME".

He throws you across the ground and towards the bottom of the steps. He then returns to his throne and gestures for you to bring him a side of rotten beef. You hoist the stinking carcass on your shoulders, and start the long climb up to the throne, for the first time. You will be fated to continue this climb for all eternity. Your mission has failed.

Turn to **616**

224

Panting with exertion, you haul yourself off the ground and dry off your hands. Lose 1 **STRENGTH** point and roll again to try to make the jump, using your new **STRENGTH** and **AGILITY** scores. If you have sand dust left, you can use it to negate the loss of **STRENGTH**. You must keep trying to make the jump. If you succeed, turn to **102**. If you fail, **TEST YOUR FORTUNE**. If you are fortunate, you miss the leap but land safely back on the top of the third stair. You again lose 1 **STRENGTH** point and must try to make the jump again. If you are unfortunate, turn to **187**. Your only options are to jump or die.

225

You open this bottle, and the aroma is purple, thick and pungent, with seemingly small particles in it. You drink, and the liquor is hot and fiery as it passes down your throat. Immediately, your body seems to tremble, and your muscles begin to bulge.

You have drunk a potion of **DAEMON'S BLOOD** that has the effect of increasing your **STRENGTH** by two for your next 3 combats. However, gifts in the HellScape are a double-edged sword. Daemons are not renowned for their brains, and this newfound strength dulls your intellect, so you lose 2 from your **INTELLIGENCE** for the same period. Turn to the previous reference.

226

Nervously, you uncork a bottle and first take a sniff. The aroma is heady and alluring. You raise the bottle to your lips and drink. You feel as though another soul has entered your body as you swallow the piquant liquid.

Then an extraordinary thing happens. You feel like your body is filled with energy. You look down and see a bloody scratch on your wrist, between your mail coat and gauntlets, knit itself together until it is no more than a scar, which then fades away as though it was never there.

You have drunk a bottle of soul-spirit, a highly prized drink in the Hellscape, and only made in this one place. It heals all your wounds and injuries, and so you can restore your **ENDURANCE** to its original level. However, it is a two-bladed knife. As well as helping, it hurts. As you are using other human souls to heal yourself, you lose 1 **FAITH** point each time you drink a bottle. Now turn to your previous reference.

227

After seemingly fighting through endless trees, you reach what appears to be the corner of the forest. You have two choices. You can go straight on and turn to **166**, or veer right and turn to **590**

228

It's too risky to return back up this route, so you carry on down the path back to the fork in the road. The only option open is the right-hand path, Turn to **483**

229

Whilst you stop and refresh yourself, you notice that the ground to your right is rippling, as if something huge is moving along just under the surface. You ready yourself for action just in time, as a huge gorger wyrm breaks through the surface and heads towards you.

Do you still have Devilsbane? If so, turn to **147**. If you do not, turn to **137**

230

The throw was true and heading towards the crystal, but then it starts to slow down and lose momentum. The greatsword dips below the jewel and into the beam of light never to be seen again. You let out a sigh. The Daemons and monks have stopped staring in horror at the tower, and now move towards you. You draw your belt knife.

A Daemon reaches you first with great strides, grabbing you by the neck and lifting you effortlessly off the ground. You stab with your knife, which pierces its torso, but it just laughs. At least you can only assume it's a laugh. Then it brings your face close to its gaping maw, and it slowly, almost lovingly, closes its razor-sharp teeth around your face and bites.

Your mission has failed. Turn to **616**

231

The door leads to a small room that has floor-to-ceiling shelves on all three sides. On these shelves are an array of glass bottles, each a different colour. There are labels on the bottles and written on them in red ink are words you cannot read. They are in HellGlyphs, a language you recognise from teachings, but none in your Church are ever given instruction in it. You realise in disgust that the ink is in fact, blood. You can choose to take two bottles.

The colours are: green, red, amber, black, purple and blue. You may add any two of them onto your **ADVENTURE SHEET** and go back into the corridor (reference **48**) to pick another door you haven't tried. If you keep the bottles, you can drink them at any time (except in battle) by turning to the reference next to the colour: green (**125**), red (**3**), amber (**661**), black (**288**), purple (**225**), blue (**426**) and clear (**382**).

Note these down on your **ADVENTURE SHEET**, but remember when you drink the contents and turn to the relevant section, you will be instructed to return to the reference where you were previously. If you want to drink them now, turn to **17**

232

You return back to the main corridor. Choose a route you haven't taken before; the corridor with two doors leading off it on the left, the one on the right or the larger, more ornate door at the end. You can either choose to go through the first door on the left (turn to **231**), the second left (**521**) or the large door at the end (**554**)

233

The steps descend down into a spiral staircase. It's dark and unpleasantly warm, with a dank, musty odour. You feel like you are going endlessly in circles that seem to get tighter and tighter. The mixture of the atmosphere, the warmth and the downward circles make you feel dizzy. You stumble and start to fall forward.

TEST YOUR AGILITY. If you pass, turn to **533**. If you fail, turn to **473**

Removing your own helm, you drop it to the floor. You place the new helm on your head, and it fits well. Then you start to feel an agonising pain in your head. You look around and see your reflection in the burnished steel of a shield still hanging on the wall. The horns on the top of the helm have started to turn and pierce inwards, their wicked points embedding themselves in your skull. Quickly you yank the helm off and throw it across the room, where it lands with a loud clatter.

You check your scalp in the mirror of the shield. Two rivulets of blood flow, one on each side. Throw 1d4 and lose the result in **ENDURANCE**.

Little did you know that it is a helm made out of one of the Great Duke Bune's heads - for he had three heads: a silver dragon, a golden griffin and an obsidian man. You pick up your own helm and place it back on your head.

Turn to **351**

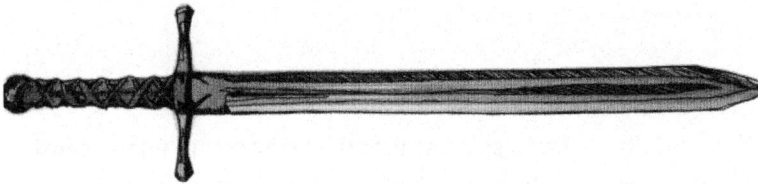

You emerge into a very small clearing - although it's not exactly clear. The corpse trees here seem taller and thicker and reach up many yards into what little sky there is here. They then converge so that they blot out almost any light. Keen to get out of this place, you must quickly choose an exit.

You can either go left and turn to **92** or take the right route and turn to **227**

236

Foolishly, you used your left hand to try to fill the bottle. This is your sword arm, and although you can fight with your right hand, it will reduce your **FIGHTING SKILL** permanently by 1. Make this change on your adventurer's profile, and turn to **654**

237

The pathway narrows and you struggle to get through as a mass of tree limbs bar the way. You can choose to push back the branches of these sad trees. If you decide to do this, turn to **407**. Or you can just try to dodge through, turn to **250**

238

As you exit a path, you come into a larger clearing that is more open, and the heat is less oppressive. The corpse trees are thinner and more spread out, and light filters down from whatever source of illumination there is in this gross realm. Dominating the centre of the clearing is a large obsidian obelisk that towers up past the tree line.

You walk up and examine the obelisk. It is four-sided, and each side faces one of the four routes from the clearing, including the one you have just entered by. On each side is a sigil. You ignore the side you came in by and look at the other three. You can choose:

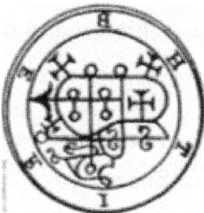

| Go left on, turn to 5 | Go straight on, turn to 177 | Go right, turn to 291 |

239

You find yourself in another clearing with more options on which way to go. Lose 1 **ENDURANCE** point due to your exertions. There is nothing of note in this area, and you leave it quickly. You either go right and turn to **443** or straight and turn to **460**

240

Your **FAITH** remains strong, and even the nightmare construction before you cannot shake it. Turn to **638**

241

You arrive into a grassless mud clearing. You can leave this place either by continuing straight on and turn to **153**, or you can go the right route and turn to **303**

242

You look down in disgust at the pathetic creature cowering at your feet, and raise your sword only to bring it back down in a mighty blow. The edge slices through Sabine's brittle form, and she screams and curses, her hands clawing at the blade. Then her body turns to dust. She is not truly dead, but she will take many centuries to find a new form in Hell. For now, she is just a faint spirit.

However, you struck down someone who had surrendered and offered help. Lose 1 **FAITH** point.

Do you want to examine what's left of Sabine? If you do, turn to **546**, If not, leave the room and turn to **48** and select another option.

Despite your internal screams from the rational part of your mind, you remain intoxicated by her. All you know is that she is the most beautiful woman you have ever seen and that your vows of chastity and purity mean nothing now. You would give anything to be with her for all eternity. She continues to walk around you slowly, her fingernails (if that's what they can be called) continue to gently scratch your exposed skin.

"Well, this is a prize indeed for Sabine. One that she will not share. Come with me, my dear, to my private chambers where we can be alone."

She walks off towards a large stair that circles the main room. She walks up the steps, and you follow like an eager puppy. You cannot take your eyes off her as she moves gracefully up the staircase, the silk dress parting to reveal long slim legs as pale as alabaster. You mount the stairs and follow. At the top, she opens a door, which looks more like a mouth filled with needle-like teeth, and enters the room.

Lost, you follow. You vaguely notice the decor of the room, which is all red and black and dominated by a giant bed. She motions you over before putting her arms around you and kissing you. As she does so, she starts to loosen the straps on your armour.

TEST YOUR FORTUNE. If luck is on your side, turn to **540**. If not, turn to **398**

244

As you approach the large copper dome, you see that there is a small door in the side of it made of riveted copper. You edge over to have a closer look. The surface is warm to the touch. You look up and see that huge glass pipes are reaching up to the sky. They are opaque, and you cannot see what's going on inside, but you sense rather than see that gas is rising up through these tubes until it reaches the upper heights.

Then they merge into a single, smaller tube that heads back down from the atmosphere and into the roof of the small domed building. Again, this tube is opaque, but you can see it quivering as if a high volume of liquid is passing through it. Curious despite yourself, you reach for the door and open it to head inside.

Turn to **534**

245

Carefully, so as to not alert the busy figure, you creep towards the desk on cat feet. You reach out and take the book and without wasting time stow it in your pack. **TEST YOUR FORTUNE**. If you are fortunate, turn to **66**. If you are not, turn to **596**

246

Stopping to check the map you found earlier, you find that there is a wooded area indicated along the right-hand path, past the plain you have to traverse. You look closely at the spindly writing which appears to say,

"stciddafotserofehT"

The wooded area seems to be extensive with many paths, but you cannot pick a route through from the confused depiction of the area. At the end, however, there is a Hellsign.

You take this as a possible exit from this terrible realm. Encouraged, you carry on.

Turn to **237**

247

You wake up fully, not sure if what you heard and saw was real. Then you look up, and in the distance, you can see shapes that seem to be moving. Human shapes. Your spirits lift at the potential sight of other people in this dreadful domain. You resolve to wait for them to approach you.

Turn to **207**

248

You stand rooted to the spot. You have never felt better in your life, and you realise you no longer need the trappings of war. You let your weapons drop to the floor, and you raise your arms up to the sky in exaltation. Fire seems to course through your veins, and you stand there, staring upwards and smiling widely. You have no idea how long you have been like this, but then the feeling wears off.

You start to feel pain instead of pleasure; agony, not ecstasy. The pain is so intense you double over. Or at least you try to, and then you realise that you can no longer move. You look up with your eyes and see your arms extending far about you. But they are no longer arms, they are elongated limbs that reach for the sky, wrapped in vines and tendrils and covered in moss.

You try to look down but can only move your eyes. You can just see that your bottom limbs, as they are now, extend to the forest floor. Instead of toes, you have tendrils and roots growing out of your feet and into the earth. Your armour has buckled and split as your shape has changed, and now half-hangs off your elongated form. Unable to move, you feel the unending pain of withdrawal. You open your mouth, now shaped like an elongated oval, and wail in despair. You have become part of the forest and will remain rooted to this spot for eternity, whilst feeling the sweet pain of withdrawal.

Your mission has failed, and the earth will soon fall. Turn to **616**

249

Resolving to stay still, the wyrm continues to sway around mere feet in front of you. The holes around its mouth continue to twitch, and in fact seem to quicken, in time to something. Slowly it dawns on you. The holes are quivering to the rhythm of your breath. It can hear you! You jump into action to draw your sword and fight, but alas, it's a split second too late. As you try to draw your sword, the wyrm rears up even higher, right above your head, as it has keyed in on your exact location. Then when it's directly above you, its mouth turns down towards you, and it dives , its mouth fully open.

The needle-like teeth pierce both armour and flesh with ease, and the wyrm tastes its first mortal flesh for aeons. Delighting in the delicacy, it takes its time sucking the flesh from your bones and digesting you slowly. Your armour stays stuck on its teeth, as its digestive juices work on your flesh. It's like being slowly and excrutiatingly burned to death. You try to scream but realise that the wyrm has digested your vocal cords, and all you can do is gurgle pathetically. Slowly you are pulled into the immense body where you are fed on until the wyrm excretes your spirit form back into the sludge of humankind surrounding it. You will remain here to be fed on, digested and excreted again and again for eternity.

Your mission ends here, and you likely have doomed the mortal realm, Turn to **616**

250

It will be tough to get through, but using your agility you think you would rather dodge around these grey forms, rather than come into contact with them.

TEST YOUR AGILITY. If you succeed, turn to **178**. If you fail, turn to **367**

251

Deciding that these souls deserve their damnation, you turn away from the human ice bath. You can now either try to steal some of the bottles of liquid, then turn to **182**, or try to go and see where the exit leads at the other side of the building, turn to **107**

252

The immediate route to the ladder you climbed is being cut off by other enemies. Below on the factory floor, you glance over and see that numerous Daemons are now pointing up at you. Even if you climb down a ladder, you will be met by too large a force for you to possibly overcome.

TEST YOUR INTELLIGENCE. If you succeed, turn to **210**. If you fail, turn to **613**

253

The lock gives way easily under your touch. You hear a click as the locking mechanism releases. Nervous of the trap at the door, you stand to one side and slowly pull the drawer open. Your care is rewarded, as there's a *"pfft"* sound and a small dart thuds into the leather back of the chair. Using a pair of tweezers from your kit, you pluck the dart from the seat and look closely at it. The point still glistens with a pale milky white liquid. You look under the desk and find a hidden slot in towards the rear. You stick the end of your belt knife into it, and you hear a *"clunk"* as the mechanism is deactivated.

You open the drawer with more confidence, and inside is a sheaf of papers. You rifle through them and stop suddenly, not believing your luck. One of the papers is folded up but is sealed with a wax circle with the number 11 imprinted in the centre. You try not to think about the source of the wax as you cut the seal with your finger.

You open it out, and it is as you'd hoped; a map of the 11th circle listing a safe way through the realm and the exits from it. Smiling briefly, you stow the map in your tunic, replace all the other papers and close the drawer. Finally, you retrieve your knife and hear a *"tek"* as the mechanism resets. Record the map on your **ADVENTURE SHEET** and gain 1 **FORTUNE** point for such a good find.

You leave the room. You can either choose one of the other doors or leave the building entirely. To try the other left-hand door, turn to **535**; to try the right door, turn to **333**. If you decide to leave the building, turn to **270**

254

You select the left path and move along a high ridge across the plain. On either side of you, bodies, complete and not, roll around in the muck and filth. As you descend down from the portal, the stench gets increasingly cloying and foul.

TEST YOUR ENDURANCE. Throw 4d6, and if the number is above your current **ENDURANCE**, then turn to **558**. If it is below or equal, turn to **302**

255

As you exit the path, you come into a larger clearing that is more open, and the heat is less oppressive. The corpse trees are thinner and more spread out, light filtering down from whatever source of illumination there is in this gross realm. Dominating the centre of the clearing is a large obsidian obelisk that towers up past the tree line. You walk up and examine the obelisk. It is four-sided, and each side faces one of the four routes from the clearing, including the one you have just entered by. On each side is a sigil. You ignore the side you came in by and look at the other three. You can choose:

| Go left, | Go straight on, | Go right, |
| turn to 291 | turn to 653 | turn to 5 |

256

This bottle is short and squat, containing a viscous black liquid that coats the side of the bottle as you swill it around. The liquid seems to cling to the inside of your throat as you try to swallow, and it's bitter beyond belief. However, as soon as you have swallowed it, you feel that you can do no wrong. You realise that you have drunken a **POTION OF FORTUNE**. Roll 1d6. This is how many **FORTUNE** rolls you will next win. If you roll 3 or less, roll again until you get a score of 4 or more. However, all this good fortune has to be balanced. What you gain in luck you lose elsewhere. Roll 1d6, and whichever number you roll, you lose 2 from that characteristic for the same length of time: 1 (**STRENGTH**), 2 (**FIGHTING SKILL**), 3 (**AGILITY**), 4 (**ENDURANCE**), 5 (**FITNESS**), 6 (**INTELLIGENCE**). Such is Madame Fortune; she gives with one hand and takes with the other. Turn to the reference you were told to write down.

257

Walking over to the bone door, you notice there are numbers etched on it. The numbers are:

20-5-14-15-8-16-13-1-2-6-15-14-18-15-8

Can you interpret these numbers? If so, then it may give you an idea as to whether to open this dread door. If you decide to open it, then turn to **109**. If you decide against it, return to **209** and choose another door.

258

You are unable to catch hold of the step. You fall, plummeting to the ground 50 yards beneath you. You land with a crash onto the packed earth floor, gasping in pain. Rolling over, your belt knife has somehow come loose and pierced the mail of your left arm.

Lose 6 **ENDURANCE**. In addition, as this is your sword arm, lose 2 **FIGHTING SKILL** and 2 **STRENGTH** until you get to the end of this realm, as you will have to fight with your right hand. The noise has also attracted the attention of the workers, and so you run towards the door. If you left Devilsbane on the platform.

TEST YOUR INTELLIGENCE. If you pass, turn to **409**, if you fail, turn to **387**. If you did not leave Devilsbane, turn to **467**

259

Somewhere in the back of your mind, you can remember the name Cerberus and that there is something significant about it. You rack your brain but still cannot come up with anything. Disappointed in your lack of recall, you head off down the road, none the wiser.

Turn to **346**

260

As you start to fall past the step, you manage to catch it with your fingertips.

TEST YOUR STRENGTH. If you succeed, turn to **432**. If you fail, turn to **601**

261

After struggling on for several minutes, you come to a fork in the path. Lose 1 **ENDURANCE** due to the heat sapping your strength. In the centre of the fork is a single body tree that grows high up into the air. The strangely elongated face stares at you as it moans. The face is that of a young woman, and in her eyes, you can see a terrible longing. The wail then changes and you can hear words in that terrible cry.

"Please please make it stop, the pains to great" it says over and over *"give me what I crave, please, I can't take the pain any more"*.

Then the voice starts to wail again. You try to ignore the pleading face and walk past. If you want to turn left, turn to **238**. If you prefer to continue straight on, turn to **322**

262

It dawns on you that you have seen this whole process before, albeit on a much smaller scale. The vats of hot liquid are the mash tun. You guess that further over in the building will be large metal vessels filled with boiling liquid extracted from this vat. Then the cooled liquid is taken to the copper-domed building and heated again. The whole area seems to function as a brewery and distillery. But instead of malted barley, the raw ingredients are humans.

The Daemons are brewing their own drink out of the damned, and you suspect that the victims are those that were alcoholics or dipsomaniacs in their past life. Now they must suffer for eternity being turned into the thing that ruined their lives - drink!

Turn to **139**

263

You attempt to dodge and strike, but fail and mistakenly attack the head. If you are playing the simple combat rules and this happens for the third time, turn to **143**. If you are playing advanced combat, and the resulting wound is **MEDIUM DAMAGE** or higher, turn to **204**

264

With agility that belies your age, you jump and twist in mid-air and grasp onto the first step in the next stair. With considerable difficulty, due to your armour, you haul yourself up and sit with your back to the cliff, panting. Your fingers sting, and so you look down. They are bleeding slightly, and your arms burn from exertion.

Temporarily lose 1 **STRENGTH** point. When, or if, you get to the top, your strength will return. You realise that each leap is going to take more strength out of your arms, as well as making your hands slicker with blood as they get caught on the rough, granite-like stone. However, your sand dust will give you enough traction and grip to provide you with one extra point of **STRENGTH** for a single jump. But you only have two portions, so use it when you need it most.

Turn to **298**

265

You were expecting the Monk to be an easy opponent to beat, but he has a sword arm like lightning and moves fluidly, so it's hard to lay your sword on him. You fight on valiantly using all your knowledge and skill earned in 20 years as a fighter. You are fast, but as quick as you are, the Monk seems faster. He has a sword arm as quick as a striking snake. You seem unable to lay a telling blow on him, and he turns most of your attacks aside with contemptuous ease.

Your sword arm is aching from trying to keep up with his lightning blade, and you realise you must do something risky. You try to duck inside his next blow, but you are too slow, and the Monk anticipates this old trick and steps aside, delivering a viper-like slash across your throat. It's not a fatal wound, but blood starts to stream from the wound, and the Monk watches you with a wicked smile on his face.

The blood is everywhere, and you drop to your knees and onto your face, drowning in your own vital fluid. He walks around to the other side and then stands above you. He reaches down and turns you onto your back, and you splutter and take a deep, racking breath. He kicks your sword, still clutched in your left hand, away and slowly runs you through.

Your mission has failed. Turn to **616**

266

"Why, is it not obvious, mine Kommandant. You must go to Hell"

Turn to **530**

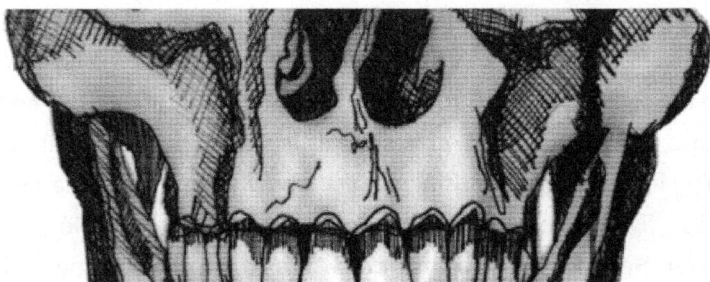

267

You head back towards the stairs. However, as you climb, the incline seems to get steeper and steeper and the atmosphere hotter and hotter... the air burns your throat as you gasp. You start to breathe in rapid shallow breaths, and the air is like fire in your throat and burns your lungs. You are not sure if you will make it to the top of the stairs alive.

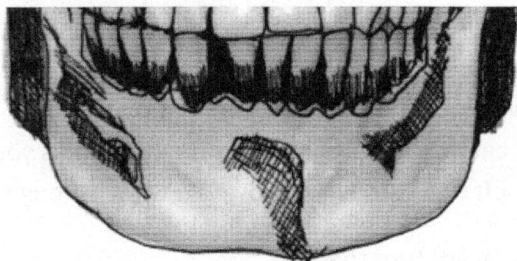

If you have a bottle of Daemons-wine, turn to **624**. If you have a blue potion and wish to use it, turn to **337**. If you do not have either of these things, turn to **37**

268

The steps are each a couple of feet apart, a distance which seems to increase as the stair spirals around the copper vessel. If you are still in possession of Devilsbane and your shield, you will have to leave them here or face a -2 to your **AGILITY**.

Now turn to **551**

269

You carefully lower the bottle and half submerge it in the thick red liquid. It gloops into the bottle quickly, filling it, and you remove it from the pool. You stopper it and place it carefully in your backpack. You have time to fill a second bottle. Add them to your **ADVENTURE SHEET**.

Now turn to **654**

270

Having escaped the building uneaten and mostly intact, you take time to hunker down in the shadow of the building. If you need to, and you still have some, eat some provisions to boost your **ENDURANCE**. Otherwise, you just rest and think. You take the map out of your backpack and slit the seal with a long thumbnail. You open out the map, and it clearly shows the route you are on, and the hall you are currently sheltering behind. On the map, it is listed as:

You trace the route and see that the path merges with the central route that you could have initially taken. This path eventually merges with the right route as well, and at the end, there is a circle with the number 10 in it.

You can either continue on this path or merge with the central path. If you do this, turn to 480. Alternatively, you can trace your route back to the start and try the right-hand side route - which may be more direct. If you want to do this turn to 483

271

You take a bite out of the wyrm blubber and feel refreshed, but it loses its nutritional value over time. Roll 1d4. Whatever number you roll is how many **ENDURANCE** points you can recover.

Now return to your previous reference.

272

Foolishly, you used your left hand to try to fill the bottle. This is your sword arm, and although you can fight with your right hand, it will reduce your **FIGHTING SKILL** permanently by 1.

Make this change on your **ADVENTURE SHEET** and turn to **416**

273

The house on the immediate right is more of a castle, with tall, imposing grey battlements and towers. Hanging from the battlements at irregular intervals are short metal cages. In each is a human form, inside a cage that is both too small to stand in, yet too narrow to sit in, and so the encumbered souls are forced to continually change their positions in an everlasting agony of cramped muscles, stretched tendons and aching bones.

The floor of the cage is solid but noticeably covered in pieces of glass and metal spikes that are embedded in the floor, constantly piercing their naked feet. Although these men and women are dead, in the Hellscape, your soul feels all the torment of the body. You fear little in life (or the afterlife), but it is with trepidation that you walk up the road towards the large copper-covered gates.

On the ground next to the gates are huge braziers, filled with red hot coals and burning hardwoods.

The ruddy colour of the fires and the flicker of flame are reflected into the large gates. This gives the appearance of walking towards the very fires of hell. This is aided by the fact that above each brazier hangs a human form, dangled on a chain so that their feet are touched by the flames, and the forms constantly writhe in an air dance macabre. You approach the door. At one side is a bell pull.

Do you want to try pulling the bell pull, then turn to **383**, or do you just want to open the gates and walk in unannounced? If so turn to **324**

274

You decide against bottling the foul liquid and choose to leave the chamber. Turn to **416**

275

Just below you, a wyrm breaks the surface of the mass of bodies. People are drawn into the mouth and impaled on the rows of teeth that then pull the victims in. The screams are horrendous. The wyrm continues to feast, and you are unsure what to do. If you move, will it attack you? You run through strategies in your head with the speed of a practice combatant. You could draw your sword and attack. If you choose to do this turn to **218**. Otherwise, turn to **332** for other options.

276

The figure smiles and says,

"Well done, thou art courteous. Maybe Gremory can grant you a boon?"

What would you like to know? You can ask either how to escape the forest, then turn to **512**. If you would rather ask how to escape this plane, then turn to **173**. If you have lost your sword and shield then you can ask to borrow Gremory's, then turn to **53**

277

You need to ask which of the doors leads to death. If you want to ask the left-hand side "guard" who has just spoken to you, then turn to **308**. To ask the right side "guard" who is staring at you now, turn to **280**

278

As you exit the path, you come into a larger clearing that is more open, and the heat is less oppressive. The corpse trees are thinner and more spread out and light filters down from whatever source of illumination there is in this gross realm.

Dominating the centre of the clearing is a large obsidian obelisk that towers up past the tree line. You walk up and examine the obelisk. It is four-sided, and each side faces one of the four routes from the clearing, including the one you have just entered by. On each side is a sigil. You ignore the side you came in by and look at the other three. You can choose:

| Go left, | Go straight on, | Go right, |
| turn to 301 | turn to 185 | turn to 604 |

279

The Djinn looks down at you with its three red eyes, half-dead in the dark tunnel, a half-smile playing on its lips. Again the voice echoes,

"I see thou art in dire need, young master, make your wish and I will aide thee".

Will you wish to be taken out of the Hellscape altogether, then turn to **159**; if you ask the Djinn to get you out of this room, turn to **501**; or if you ask the Djinn to take you to the exit of this realm, turn to **331**

280

Turning, you ask the right-hand side guard, who also looks insane, which door she would tell you to take. She replies, in a harsh voice burned red-raw by smoke,

"The left, oh Great Warrior. Only the left will see you safe"

If you want to believe her and open the left door, turn to **465**. If you think she lies, then open the right door and turn to **517**

You try to jump down to the next stair, but your foot slips on the edge. For a few moments, time seems to stop, and you are almost suspended in mid-air as you take in your fate. The hard floor then starts to rush towards you as gravity takes hold. You fall, gathering speed, your arms and legs flailing as you try to swim in the air, but the ground rushes ever closer. You hit with bone-shattering impact and bounce down a couple of levels until you are close to the hole in the centre of the dome's floor. You look up, vaguely conscious, and see your arms and legs are laying at unnatural angles, obviously broken by the fall.

The pain is intense and unceasing. Then you see a giant vat being manhandled towards the spiral by the giant sub-daemons. They tilt it at the edge of the spiral, and the liquid remnants of souls from the giant vats are poured in. The liquid catches up with you, and your mouth is filled with foul putrescence. You are aware of body parts flowing past you, and you get struck in the face by a still-wriggling arm. Then the tide takes you, and you are carried down the spiral, faster and faster until you drop into the dark abyss of the hole. You drop some way, but then are dumped into a sluice and through a pipe, being washed along with the damned of humanity.

The journey seems to last forever, as, still alive, you try to keep your head above the foul liquid but to no avail. You are dragged under and start to drown as the liquid fills your lungs. Then you are thrown out of the pipe into another giant vat and, unable to move your smashed arms and fractured legs, you drop like a stone to the bottom along with all the sludge of humanity. You lose consciousness and thankfully die, only to be stuck here as a damned soul, forever to be boiled and strained, turned into their evil liquor.

Your mission has failed, and soon the mortal realms will fall. Turn to **616**

You thought you were quick, but the Thin Daemon is lightning fast across the plains with an agility that almost puts you to shame. Despite your best efforts, you are unable to shake him off, and he is soon breathing down your neck. He tap-tackles you, causing you to sprawl to the ground.

TEST YOUR AGILITY. If you are successful, you are up in time to fight the first combat round. If you are unsuccessful, you are too slow to get up, and you are raked by the long talons of the Thin Daemon. Lose 2 **ENDURANCE**. Now you must fight the Thin Daemon using the current stamina scores you both have.

THIN DAEMON has **FS 8, EN 10**

{ADVANCED - Initial AS: 16, Initial DA: 16; FIT 8, AG 8, ST 7}

If you haven't already lost the Ape Daemon, then note down how many seconds behind he is. The fighting is fast and furious, and each combat round only lasts a second – but each round brings the Ape Daemon a second closer.

If he catches up to you before you have killed the Thin Daemon, turn to **582**. If you win before the Ape Daemon catches up, then you must continue your chase with him still behind you. His new starting distance will be however far behind he was when the final round of conflict was resolved.

If you win, turn to **300**

283

You walk towards the double saloon-style doors of the house on your left. Its exterior paintwork is a riot of bright, almost luminescent colours, and inlaid into almost every surface are depictions of the most gratuitous sorts of physical pleasure between humans. Above the door is a brightly painted sign saying:

"niapdnaerusaelpfoesuohsenibas"

Did you pass the **INTELLIGENCE** test on **530**? If yes, turn to **318**. If not, turn to **576**

284

Cautiously, you approach the door, wondering what further devilments you may chance upon. Your push the door open and it protests with a creak that seems as loud as the cry of a baby. Inside you find a small room. Cowering at the back of the room is the once more corporal form of Sabine. You reach for and draw your sword in one fluid movement and advance on her. She is no longer a beauty, as the fight with her has revealed her true form. She is still tall, but stick-thin with her bones protruding out against her wrinkled, sagging skin.

Her dress, once silk and luxurious, is just rags that fall from her spindly frame as she cowers. Her hair is thin and wispy, and her lips, once so full, are now thin and cracked. Her eyes look at you with fear, the flames no longer dancing around her slitted iris. She holds out a clawed hand in front of her to ward you off, and creaks,

"No, you dare not, you will not, leave me be, mortal man, and I will tell you how to get off this plane"

Do you want to accept her help, if so turn to **47**? Or would you rather finish her off, turn to **242**

285

The portal seems to be made of pure light and blinds you as you step into it. You feel rather than see your way along as the light is so bright you are almost blinded. You close your eyes and force yourself to carry on. Eventually, after what seems like miles but may well have been just yards, your armoured boot touches onto a hard surface with a clink. You try to open your eyes, and the portal has disappeared into nothingness, but your vision is still too blurred to make much out, and you are still half-blind. You blink and try to recover your vision, but everything still swims before your eyes. You sense you are standing in a room on a hard stone floor.

Torches flair in sconces at the side of the room, making it even more challenging to see. However, slowly your eyes start to refocus and in front of you appears a figure, but it is just a blurred shape. It seems to be too small to be a Daemon, and too large to be an imp or other servant race. You guess it is approximately human-sized. Light seems to glance off the figure in places, seemingly reflecting from metal. You squint again to try to focus your eyes, and slowly the figure becomes more defined.

It appears to be a human, roughly your height, dressed in a dark cloak with an iron helm, a cruciformed peak on his head. At his side, you can see a sheathed sword, and on his arm a silver shield. An insignia is half-hidden on the breastplate of his armour, but it is one that is both compelling and immediately familiar. It's the same insignia you bear proudly on your chest. The figure walks forward, removing his helm and furling his iron-grey hair. It is a face you know all too well. A rich, deep voice, a voice used to command, says,

"Welcome Kommandant. I have been expecting you"

He smiles, a smile you know all too well. Years of training allows you to mask your surprise and your reply,

"And to you sir. I must admit you are the last person I expected to see here......." Turn to **666**

286

A wyrm rears up above you, its mouth turning towards you, and it dives, its mouth fully open. The needle-like teeth pierce both armour and flesh with ease, and the wyrm tastes its first mortal flesh for aeons. Delighting in the delicacy, it takes its time sucking the flesh from your bones and digesting you slowly. Your armour stays stuck on its teeth, as its digestive juices work on your flesh.

It's like being slowly and excrutiatingly burned to death. You try to scream but realise that the wyrm has digested your vocal cords, and all you can do is gurgle pathetically. Slowly you are pulled into the immense body where you are fed on until the wyrm excretes your spirit form back into the sludge of humankind surrounding it. You will remain here to be fed on, digested and excreted again and again for eternity. Your mission ends here, and you likely have doomed the mortal realm.

Turn to **616**

287

After what seems like aeons, but may in fact only be minutes, you watch as the Daemons talk and gesticulate to one another. The Thin Daemon shakes its head and jabs a pointed talon into the chest of the Ape Daemon. The Ape Daemon looks down at this talon poking him in the chest, and with snake-like speed one of his long, ape-like arms shoots out. He grabs the Thin Daemon by its throat and lifts it effortlessly off the ground. You hear the cracking sound of bones breaking as the Ape crushes the larynx and neck of the Thin Daemon.

Then with casual contempt, he throws it aside, and the lifeless body tumbles down the hill to rest in a pile of human organs and brains not 5 yards from you. The Ape Daemon shakes his head in annoyance, and turns around and stomps off back towards the factory building. You move, running back along the path so that you soon return to your entry point to this cursed realm. You now have no option but to take the right turn.

Turn to **483**

288

This bottle is short, squat and contains a viscous black liquid that coats the side of the bottle as you swill it around. You take the chance and pull the cork and drink. The liquid seems to coat the inside of your throat as you swallow, and it's bitter beyond belief. However, as soon as you have swallowed it, you feel that you can do no wrong. You reach inside your backpack and find an old pair of knucklebones. You recall using these to gamble with your men for copper half-pennies around the campfire (even though gambling was seen as a crime by the Church). You throw both and score 7 & 7 - the highest possible score. You do this three times, and each time roll 7 & 7.

You realise that you have drunk a **POTION OF FORTUNE**. Roll 1d6. This is how many **FORTUNE** rolls you will next win. If you roll 3 or less, roll again until you get a score of 4 or more. However, all this good fortune has to be balanced. What you gain in luck you lose elsewhere.

Roll 1d6, and whichever number you roll, you lose 2 from that characteristic for the same length of time: 1 (**STRENGTH**), 2 (**FIGHTING SKILL**), 3 (**AGILITY**), 4 (**ENDURANCE**), 5 (**FITNESS**), 6 (**INTELLIGENCE**). Such is Madame Fortune, she gives with one hand and takes with the other.

Turn to your previous reference.

289

You draw your blade and hurl it end over end towards the giant conical flask. It strikes the flask, but the heavy blade just bounces off the thick glass. You have no option now but to fight the sub-daemon.

If you still had Devilsbane, then you must use your belt knife, as you threw your sword and the sub-daemon is now between you. Deduct 1 **FIGHTING SKILL**.

If you had already lost Devilsbane, then you threw your knife, and have no weapon, and must fight this beast with whatever is around you and so reduce your **FIGHTING SKILL** by 3. If you win, turn to **182**, if you fail to beat it, turn to **191**

290

You move across the floor from the vats to the second section of the room, but this is very open, and it would just take a Daemon or an imp to glance your way and you would be in trouble.

TEST YOUR FORTUNE. If you are fortunate, turn to **203**. If you fail, turn to **529**

291

The heat continues to drain you of strength. Lose 1 **ENDURANCE** point. After travelling down a steep incline, there's a fork in the road. You can forge on and go left and turn to **30**, or veer right and turn to **144**

292

You try to sneak to the crates, but upon reaching half the distance an imp turns and stares at you. It chitters alarmingly, jumping up and down and gesturing. The other imps stop working and all stare at you, making even more noise. One of them cries out to a sub-daemon on the other side of the room. It turns, stares at you and roars. It is fully 20 feet tall, but almost brainless, but it knows anger and that you are a foe; or possibly food. It moves towards you, its giant paws reaching towards you with foot-long talons glistening.

You can either try to fight this monster and turn to **442**, try to run and escape, turn to 148, or try to break the large conical flask to distract it, turn to **42**

293

Seeing no option but violence, you draw your weapon and drop into the corridor at almost exactly the same time the Daemon does. However, the Daemon is so enraged that he has forgotten about the floating step. As he enters the corridor, his heel catches the step, and the weight causes it to pivot to the floor.

TEST YOUR FORTUNE. If you are fortunate, turn to **542**. If you are not, turn to **617**

294

Having had to descend by a different route, **TEST YOUR FORTUNE**. If you are fortunate, turn to **648**. If you are not, turn to **539**

295

The path seems to get ever gloomier, and you struggle to get past the loathsome trees. The heat continues to take its toll, and you lose 1 **ENDURANCE** point. In a very narrow pass between the trees, you are overcome by weakness and dizziness due to the heat and claustrophobic environment.

TEST YOUR FITNESS. If you are fit enough to overcome this fainting spell, then you stop and clear your head and can continue and chose a route. To go left, turn to **261**. If you prefer to stay right, turn to **114**. But if you are overtaken by dizziness, you put your hand out to support yourself, and you catch your hand against a limb or branch.

Turn to **407**

296

You pull open the onyx door. The space behind is dark as night. If you choose to enter, turn to **646**. Otherwise, you can close the door and choose another option you haven't tried, and turn to **209**

297

You carefully lower the bottle and half submerge it in the thick red liquid. It gloops into the bottle quickly, filling it, but just before you remove it, the sphincter overhead opens and gushes a torrent of liquid into the pool. This splashes into the surface and the ripple of liquid surges over your bare hand. It burns into your skin, blistering it and forcing you to cry out in pain. The bottle slips from your grasp and sinks to the bottom of the pool. You nurse your hand and try to strip the remaining liquid from it as quick as possible.

TEST YOUR FORTUNE AGAIN. If you are lucky, turn to **338**. If you are unlucky, turn to **37**

298

Dusting yourself down, you look at the next step. Realising that waiting won't help, as the stiffness in your arms will worsen over time, you leap once more. Again, add up your **STRENGTH** and **AGILITY** and roll 4d6. If you roll less than or equal to your score, turn to **504**. If you fail, **TEST YOUR FORTUNE**. If you are fortunate, turn to **515**. If you are not so, turn to **187**

299

Turning to the right-hand side guard, you ask her,

"Which door would your friend over there tell me to choose?"

"The right door, the right door, or Mighty Warrior. Deaths kisses wait for one even as strong as you beyond that door. If you choose that door, you will surely die, and stay with us for evermore."

Then she cackles and will say no more. If you believe her when she says the other guard would tell you to go right, then turn the handle on the left door and turn to **465**. If you think she lies, open the right door and turn to **517**

300

Finally, you dispatch the Thin Daemon, who slumps to the ground. If the Ape Daemon is still chasing you, resume the chase. If he catches you, turn to **435**. If you lose him, turn to **408**. If you have already lost him prior to this fight, turn to **408**

301

Due to the heat, you continue to weaken, and you lose 1 **ENDURANCE** point as you make your way through the foul trees. You soon emerge into a clearing that's rich with grass unlike the rest of this forest of the damned. You notice that all around you poking up through the grass are mushrooms. They are tall, with broad heads mottled with red and white. If you are in need of food, you can try to eat some of the mushrooms. If you want to, note down this reference and then turn to **444**.

Once you have tried the mushrooms, or if you choose not to try them, you exit the clearing either by going left, turn to **104**, or you can go right and turn to **241**

302

Thinking quickly, you reach into your backpack and find a piece of material. Using your water bottle, you wet the cloth until it is damp before tying it around your mouth and nose. This simple mask helps by seemingly filtering out most of the noxious gases. You continue to walk along the ridge. As you walk, you see the horrid white wyrms appearing from the swamp of bodies, and almost like the giant Feasting Whayles in the Black Ocean, they seem to hoover up the bodies around them. You carry on as upon the horizon you can see a building. Then all of a sudden, the surface of the mire below is broken.

Turn to **275**

303

The path winds through the trees, and you make every effort not to touch them. The heat is oppressive under the canopy of the humanoid trees, and you are sweating freely. Lose 1 **ENDURANCE** point.

Soon, you appear in another clearing. The human trees here seem to be wailing even louder than at other locations. Keen to escape the disconcerting noise, you quickly choose a route and decide to go straight on, but as you do, the trees seem to close in and block the route. You now only have two choices. You can risk heading left, turn to **255**, or bravely go right, turn to **85**

304

As you struggle to take all of this in, you must act. Do you want to approach the throne and speak to the Daemon? If so, turn to **621**. Or do you want to try to talk to one of the ragged kings and queens serving him? If so turn to **585**

305

"Excellent" says the figure *"then the trial of wits starts. First, and just a simple task. Does thou knoweth our name?"*

If you do, convert it to numbers (A=1, B=2 etc.) and then turn to the number you have identified. Remember the conventions of the written word in the Hellscape. If you do not know, or if you have obviously not gone to the right reference, then turn to **10**

306

"Sabine,"

you say strongly. Baalberith roars, the sound almost bringing loose stones and mortar falling down from the ceiling above.

"YES HER, THAT HARLOT, THAT SLATTERN, SHE IS ALWAYS WHISPERING IN THE LORD KINGS EAR, TRYING TO GARNER FAVOUR. SHE WILL DO ANYTHING TO ADVANCE IN THE ROSTER OF HELL, AND I WOULD BELIEVE SHE WOULD WORK WITH THE PAPISTS TO FURTHER HER OWN MEANS. VERY WELL, WORM, I WILL HELP. TAKE THIS KEY"

He gestures, and a key appears in the air in front of you. It looks to be made of bone and sinew and is twisted and gnarled. You take the key out of the air and examine it. Stamped on it is the number 10. Note this on your **ADVENTURE SHEET** along with the name **BAALBERITH**.

Baalberith continues in his deep rumbling voice:

"LEAVE ME NOW, FOR I HAVE MY TORMENTS TO ADMINISTER TO MY LOYAL SUBJECTS" He smiles down callously at the ragged kings and empresses serving his needs.

"LEAVE THIS HALL, NEVER TO RETURN, AND GO INTO THE COURTYARD OF MY MIGHTY CASTLE. TAKE THE DOOR WITH THE EYE OF BAALBERITH ON IT AND LEAVE THIS REALM. I WOULD WISH YOU LUCK, BUT THE LUCK OF A DAEMON IS A CAPACIOUS THING AND MAY LEAD TO YOUR DOWNFALL. NOW GO, MY PETTY SUBJECTS AWAIT ME".

Turn to **35**

307

Inside is a corridor, again in ruins, but with tall mirrors placed every few feet inside alcoves in the walls. Again, as you walk down this desolate passage, the mirrors show bright and shining corridors hung with fine tapestries and paintings, lit by delicate oil lamps. You can almost smell the heady and fragrant smoke from the essential oils used to both light and scent the passage.

But instead, you are aware of an acrid undertone of decay and putridness. At the end of the corridor is a tall arch, half-fallen in on itself, but again the reflection in nearby mirrors shows a different image. It shows an arch of gilded gold, with find carvings surrounding it. You walk through the arch.

Turn to **179**

308

The guard says,

"Stay right mighty lord, as only death will be there to greet you if you go left".

Meanwhile, the other guard shouts,

"Liar, liar, don't believe him oh great Lord. He lies"

If you believe the left-hand guard and open the right door, turn to **517**. If you don't and choose the left door, turn to **465**

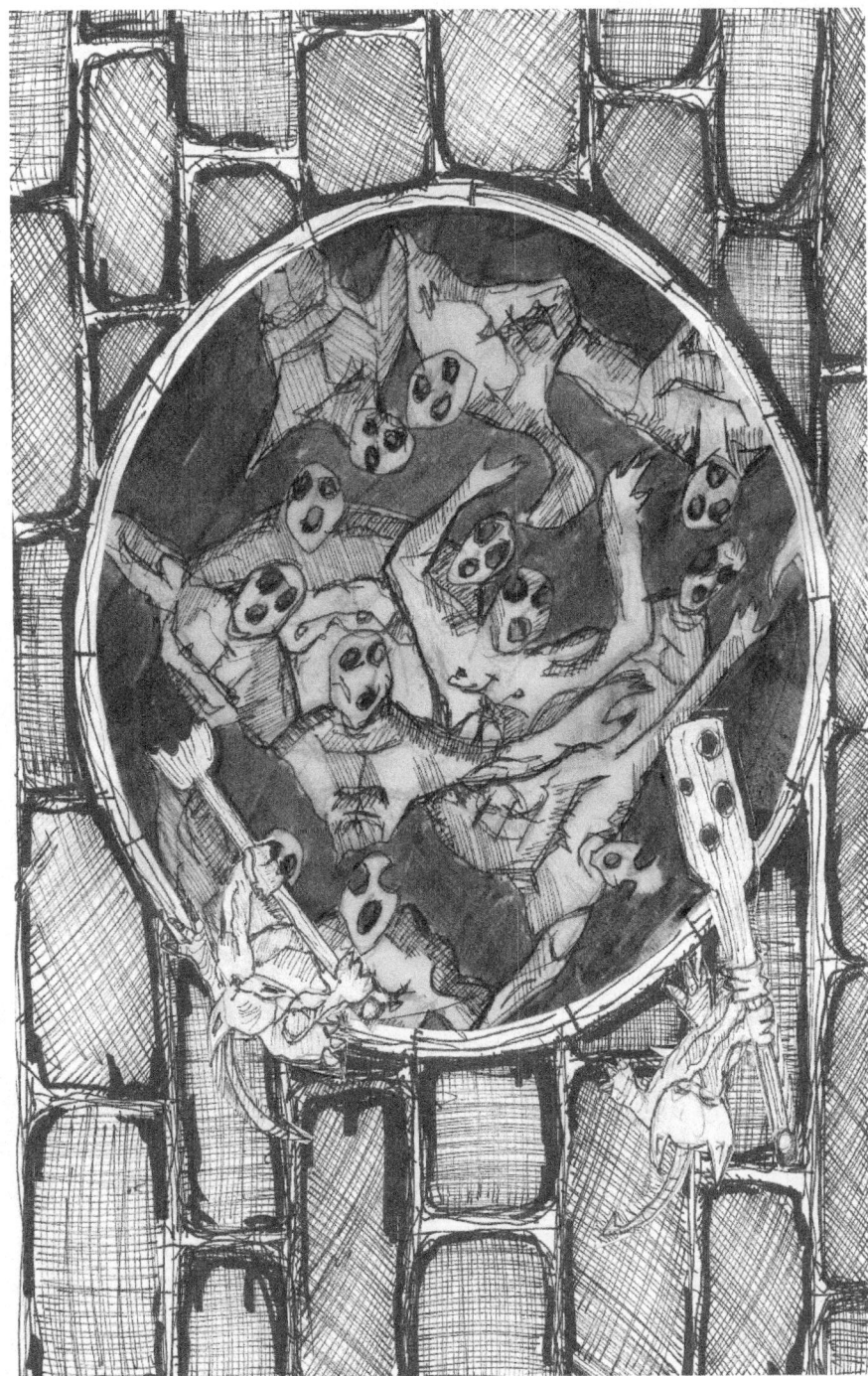

309

Being a curious person by nature, you cannot resist climbing up to investigate what's in the vats. You are forced to leave your sword and shield below, and so if you do get into a physical encounter, you must reduce your **FIGHTING SKILL** by 2.

You take hold of the ladder and start to climb. You make quick work of the climb, and even though you are still in full armour, your breathing hardly increases as you continue up. You get to the top and jump down onto the walkway. The vat rims are about 3 foot from the floor, and so you crouch down for cover. You peak over the top of the vat and look down. In the vat below, there is a soup of blood-red fluid with body parts floating in it.

Somewhere below the liquid is being heated as it is boiling, and acrid iron smoke billows from the vat. The human forms floating in the liquid below raise up their claw-like hands as they try to climb up the inner walls, but to no avail. Instead, the flesh has almost boiled off the bones, leaving the figures as little more than skeletons. Even then, they still moan, despite seemingly having no vocal cords. But this is the Hellscape, and nothing makes sense here. Hovering above the surface of the liquid are some creatures, smaller even than the imps you have encountered. They are less than 2 foot tall, from what you can tell, with bat-like wings protruding from between their shoulder blades. The wings beat quickly as they hover over the vat. They are thin to the point of emancipated and their skin is almost transparent so that their internal organs are visible.

They buzz around, skimming the surface of the liquid, and adding in various herbs from bags draped around their waists. Elsewhere above on

the gantry, each vat has imps standing around a metal panel that seems to have several switches and dials, the function of which you can barely comprehend.

Turn to **486**

For long moments, nothing happens, and then all of a sudden one of the dancing forms on the left speaks to you. Madness burns in his eyes from his near eternal torment. He cackles, the sound like a dry rattle in his parched throat, burned by the dancing flames. He says,

"So you seek to enter the Masters castle, then you must choose which door - The left side door or the right. One will lead to death and eternal torment. The other will lead to, possibly, something worse. You must ask one of us a question before you chose. But beware! From here forth, one of us will answer truthfully, the other will lie. Now who will you ask and what question?"

Turn to **106**

Thinking back, you remember that you learnt in seminary that Cerberus was the largest of the gorger wyrms, and it ruled the wastelands. It was said to be a guard that no one, human or Daemon, mortal or immortal, could creep past. You also remember that its weakness was its tail, and that on no account should you chop at its head.

Now turn to **420**

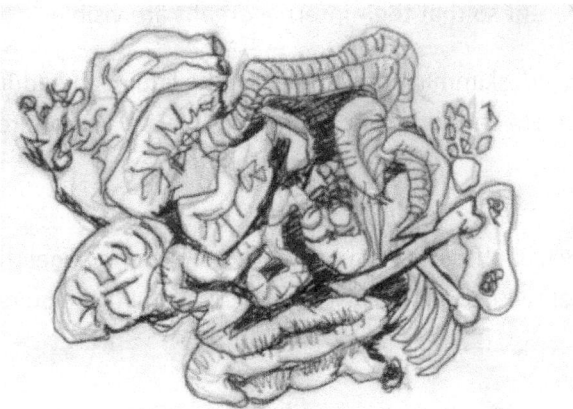

312

The Djinn looks down at you with its three red eyes, half-dead in the dark tunnel, a half-smile playing on its lips, and again the voice echoes,

"I see thou art in dire need, young master, make your wish and I will aide thee"

Will you wish to be immune to the fumes of this place, turn to **8**; to be taken to the door of this realm, turn to **396**; or taken out of this place completely, turn to **619**

313

The hart is almost hypnotic in its beauty. It shakes its head and paws the ground softly and then, its head lowered in a sign of deference, it starts to walk over to you. You carry on staring into the twin pools of its golden eyes that seem to see into your soul. It approaches and lowers its head further, and you reach out and stroke its head.

The wings flap gently in pleasure as you stroke its head and neck. Then its head raises up, towering over you, and it opens its mouth and speaks. The voice is melodious and soothing, the most beautiful voice you have heard, even more so that the choir castratum in the Holy City.

"My child, are you lost? I can help you find your way out of this forsaken wood. Trust in me, my child, for I only seek to help"

If you want to trust the hart, turn to **45**. If you decide not to and want to draw your sword, turn to **99**

314

The whole structure and concept are too much for you. Lose 1 **FAITH** point (remember if you end up with **FAITH** of 0, turn straight away to **13**). If you still have **FAITH** left in your mission, turn to **638**

315

The second Daemon falls, and you stand for a moment panting heavily. The imps who were watching from a few feet away are stood stock-still. They cannot believe you have bested their masters. Then they look down at the two bodies on the floor.

Their eyes widen at the sight of all the blood, and soon they are all licking their pointed teeth with small, forked tongues. Ignoring you, as you are obviously too dangerous to tackle, they fall on the bodies of their dead overseers and start to rip them apart and feast on them.

Deciding it best not to remain, you decide to leave this building. You can choose to investigate the large copper dome, then turn to **193**; if you want to check out the smaller dome, turn to **122**. If you would rather just leave and carry on along the ridge, turn to **510**

316

As you reach out a hand to grasp the handle, which is to the immediate right of the cruel mouth, it opens, and a long purple tongue shoots out and wraps itself around your wrist. The tongue is immensely strong, and it drags your hand towards the now gaping maw.

You struggle in vain, and the mouth closes with terrifying force on your wrist. Lose 1d6 +2 in **ENDURANCE**. Now roll 1d6. If you roll an odd number, it's your left hand (your sword arm), and you must lose 2 points in **FIGHTING SKILL**. If it's even, it's your right hand, and you suffer the **ENDURANCE** damage only. You manage to pull your hand out of the mouth and leave the room hastily. The malevolent face booms with laughter as you leave.

Turn to **209** and choose an option you haven't previously tried.

317

Undaunted, you try again for the third time.

Again **TEST YOUR AGILITY** 3 times. If you pass all 3, turn to **586**. If you fail the first test, turn to **528**. If you fail the second, turn to **401**. If you fail the third test, turn to **142**

318

Before you enter the house, you remember your teachings on the structure of the HellScape. The 12th circle is for those whose life was driven by lust and depravity. Those who die and are sentenced here spend eternity having their immortal souls physically abused and tormented by Daemons - just as they had used their mortal bodies to abuse others for their own gratification in life.

But instead of enjoying this depravity, the Daemons abuse them to the point of torment and pain, so that they can appreciate the pain they bestowed on their victims in their past life. You steel yourself as there are bound to be sights, sounds and smells beyond the depraved thoughts of the most disturbed mortal. You also remember that in the Hellscape, written language is read from right to left.

Turn to **664**

319

Do you want to draw your sword and attack, then turn to **218**? If you prefer to stay standing still, turn to **249**

320

Regaining your composure, you look out on the new landscape in front of you. It's hideous. In front of you is a large plain, and all you can see is mortal remains. Bodies litter the ground, some whole, some not, but all moving or writhing on the ground. Surrounding the bodies are piles of organs; hearts, brains, livers, lungs and many many more. Intestines cover the writhing bodies, spewing out faecal matter at their open ends. The stench is unbelievable.

You have been on many battlefields where blood, guts and shite were commonplace, but this is as if it had been going on for eternity and rotting at the same time. There is an overwhelming sense of purification. Then out from the ground, through some of the writhing bodies, rises up a worm. To say worm is to understate it. The beast must be 10 foot wide and is milk-white.

As it rears up out of the ground, its stubby nose throws up dozens of bodies hundreds of feet into the air. Then as the human parts start to fall, the beast opens its maw - a full 10 foot wide. Hundreds of needle-like teeth ring the inside in rows. As the human remains fall, the beast gorges them down, its teeth piercing the still-living remains as screams fill the air. You feel sick, and have to stop yourself retching.

You prevent yourself from doing so by searching your memory for previous teachings. This must be the 11th circle of Gluttony, and the giant worms are Gorger Wyrms that feed eternally on the bodies of gluttons. The ruler of this realm is reputed to be an even larger 3 headed wyrm. You realise that as a mortal in this realm, your flesh will be a delicacy. You also remember that reputedly, the Gorger Wyrms are almost blind, and have very sensitive hearing by which they can find their prey. Turn to **453**

321

You walk down the passageway and into the light. Suddenly, an overwhelming sense of an evil presence overcomes you. You can sense minds of inhuman making trying to pierce your consciousness. You fight to keep control of your sanity.

TEST YOUR FAITH. If you succeed, you prevail against the will of your unseen foe, as your **FAITH** keeps you sane. You leave straight away, regretting taking this passage. However, gain 1 **FAITH** point for standing strong, and 1 **FORTUNE** point for escaping apparent death. Turn to **6**. If you fail the **FAITH** test, turn to **154**

322

You walk into a much smaller clearing, and there appears to be only one exit - a route to the left. However, ahead of you is what appears to be a dimly lit copse of trees, forming a circle just beyond what appears to be almost a doorway. If you have not investigated this area before, you can do so by turning to **26**. Otherwise, you must take the left passage and turn to **524**

323

Moving quickly, you dash towards the imp who is shocked by your sudden aggression. **TEST YOUR AGILITY**. If you succeed, turn to **63**. If you fail, turn to **520**

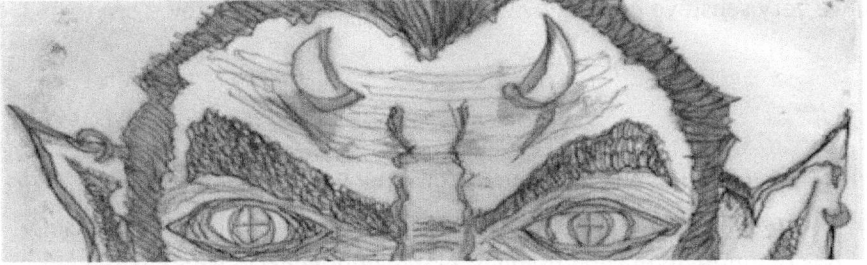

324

Tentatively, you reach out and take hold of the giant handle on one of the doors and pull it down. With a creaking noise that seems to echo around the whole valley, you push the door open and without hesitation, walk inside.

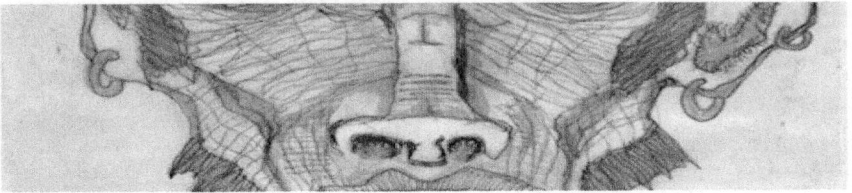

If you opened the left door, turn to **454**. If it was the right door, turn to **517**

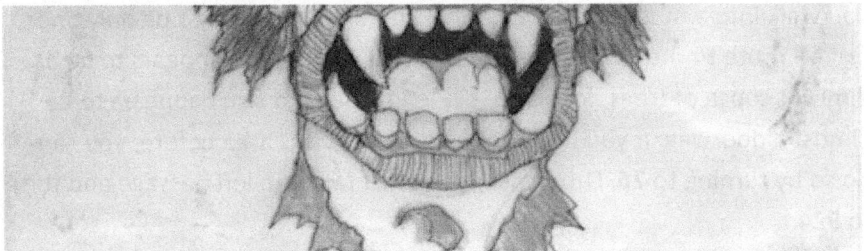

325

'As you wish, my master' the voice echoes.

The Djinn places one large, two-thumbed hand on your head, and you instantly vanish from the corridor. However, you have suffered damage from the fumes; throw 2d6 and subtract this from your **ENDURANCE**. Mark down that you have used one of the Djinns 3 wishes, and if you wish to use him again, you must turn to **404**.

Otherwise, you are moved back into the corridor above. Turn to **554**

326

The portal is about 10 feet high, circular and made up of multi-coloured shimmering light. It's dizzying to watch, and you try to shield your eyes. Above it, written in some bizarre language is the below.

If you have the means to translate this, then turn to **22**. If you do not, turn to **169**

The professor is busy packing things into a backpack; his few possessions he considers valuable enough to take with him when he leaves. But as he packs, he replies,

"The very least I can do for you my lad. The lord of this realm, you may recall, is the Lord Astaroth. To exit his realm you will have to find him and beat his challenge. Look for a sigil with a 5 sided star, as that will help you lead him towards you. As far as I recall, he can be found at the mountain at the end of the Dead Wood, which is to the right of the plains, past the plains of Cerberus. In the forest, do not touch the trees!

Astaroth is mighty and so seek not to provoke him for in conflict he will surely kill you, or give you to his mount as a play thing. If he asks you to take his hand, then avoid the one that is sinister if you prefer to keep your blade in your sheathed.

But he is capricious, and if he takes a liking to you, he may provide you with more aide against his fellow Dukes. If he does not like you, then beware. Now, that's all I can say and I must leave. The Lord may have noticed that his spell has been broken and send his minions to investigate. I recommend you do the same.

I have my own plans, and so will travel alone. In the meantime, take anything else that you wish from this room and leave"

Then with a wave, he turns and leaves via the copper door. Do you want to search around the room, then turn to **366**? If you would rather heed his advice and leave, then turn to **484**

The cauldron is in a large hall, such is the capricious nature of the Djinn - he has literally moved you from the frying pan into the fire. Stone tables and benches form a square around the perimeter of the room, and every space is taken by a Daemon. The Daemons are too busy laughing, drinking and eating to notice you. In each of the fireplaces around the perimeter are large spits, and human forms slowly roast as the spits are turned by fire imps.

Each human wails quietly as their flesh is slowly roasted to juicy perfection. Many of these human figures are obese, and the fire sizzles and flares as fat drips onto it. However, this being Hell, the victims never die even as their organs are roasted and their brains are boiled. When they are ready, the imps take the spits out of the fire and cut the still-living bodies off the rods and into wheeled barrows.

The separate body parts are still moving and writhing in agony. The imps then wheel the barrow around to the far end of the hall and tip them onto a wide moving belt, which is driven by a wheel constantly turned by minor Daemons. The wide belt conveys them up over the diners and drops them into a large fire pit in the centre of the tables.

The assembled Daemons then reach over and grab whatever delicacy they desire, be it a haunch of man, a head to suck the brain juices out of, or a torso of a woman. Buzzing around the hall are numerous imps, each holding a serving dish which contains another human delicacy. They load these onto Daemons' plates, though sometimes the Daemon just seizes a dish from the imp and tips it all down their gullet, to the hilarity of all watching.

The Daemons laugh as they tear the meat apart with their cruel talons and eat it in big ravenous bites. They wash the flesh down with cups of human blood and fat. Every few minutes, when a Daemon fills themselves to capacity, they get up and stagger to one of several bowls in the walls of the room, and vomit up all that they have eaten.

The foul liquid of those they have consumed then drains away into a centre bath, where the pieces of flesh slowly reconstitute themselves back into human form, and they are dragged out of the bath with vicious hooks and then taken away either to the spits or elsewhere, to begin the cooking process all over again.

The gruesome feast continues ad nausea. Your tactical mind considers this in a fraction of a second, despite the pain from the boiling liquid. You have no option but to vault out of the cauldron and face the consequences.

Turn to **636**

329

You are in a kitchen; if a slaughterhouse can be compared to a kitchen. Small imps are everywhere. In the corner lay a pile of bodies, but they squirm on the floor indicating that they are still conscious.

The imps drag bodies over to tall wooden tables that are black with bloodstains, where they are hacked to pieces with large, saw-edged cleavers. Around the rooms are areas where the prepared flesh is taken. Here the flesh is boiled in large vats of Daemon's-wine where a huge pot of meat is also being fried into a spiced curry over a huge fire. Elsewhere, thin slivers of still-wriggling flesh are flambéed with spirits over flames.

The epicures of the Daemons call for human tartare, when the body is just sliced up raw and minced, organs, bones and all, in giant grinders, and molded into patties or sausages, using their own skin as the sausage casing.

When the human feast is ready, it is loaded onto huge platters and taken out through the doorway you have just sneaked in through. Fortunately, you have hidden well enough that the imps do not notice you. You can see two doorways. One on the far side of the kitchen, the other just a few feet away from you.

If you want to try to sneak around to the door at the far side of the room, turn to **138**. If you want to try for the green door which is closer, turn to **27**

330

Feeling pleased to leave the 11th circle and all the foulness and depravity you have seen behind you, as you prepare to step into the portal, you try to recall what you know of the next circle. **TEST YOUR INTELLIGENCE**. If you pass, turn to **573**. If you fail, turn to **380**

331

The Djinn bows once and says in a voice soft and unctuous,

"Yes, my master, at thy command. I shall take you with haste to the doorway of this realm"

Then the room around you shimmers, and you are transported elsewhere. You land feeling exhausted. Turn to **183**

332

Combat is inadvisable against a monster of this scale, and it may attract other wyrms, so you decide upon other options. You can either try to stand still and hope the wyrm cannot see you, turn to **133**; or you can draw your sword and bash it against your shield to try to scare the beast away, turn to **474**

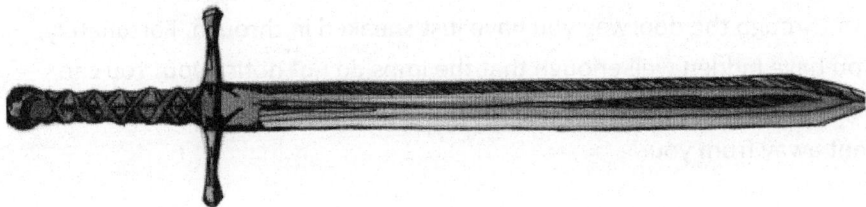

333

You approach the door and open it. The room is dark and appears to be empty, and there is nothing of interest here. Do you want to go in and double-check, if so turn to **550**? If you haven't already, you can try one of the other doors. For the first door on the left, turn to **606**. For the second door on the left, turn to **535**. If you decide you have had enough and want to leave the building, turn to **131**

334

Despite fighting valiantly, you start to get worn down by the small imps. Their teeth and claws do little damage to your mail coat and steel armour, but each of them is armed with a meat cleaver as large as the creatures themselves. The cleavers rise and fall, and there are too many for you to block. Slowly, you start to lose strength, and you are driven to your knees by all the vicious blows from the black cleavers.

You collapse on the floor, and the imps grab you and pull you to a tall table. On it is a wooden block, covered in cut marks and stained dark with blood. They haul you over the table and onto the block, and you are too weak to stop them. They strip off your armour with their small clever claws, and soon you are held naked, arched over the block, two imps to each limb.

An imp wearing a silver collar, seemingly of some rank in the kitchen, stands on a stool next to you. He says something in a harsh guttural language, and all the imps chitter excitedly. Then some more imps, who seem to have appeared from nowhere, wheel over a large machine. You realise in horror what it is.

You try to fight back but are unable, and one of the imps starts to turn the long handle of the machine. There is a hole in the metal casing, about 9 inches wide, and in that hole, you can see two steel blades that are whirling around at an angle. The imps restraining your arm closest to the machine pull the limb towards the aperture. You scream in agony as the hand is pushed into the hole, and the blades rip and grind away at the meat and bones.

At the top is a grated aperture, and you see fresh pink meat oozing out of it in slivers. The imps are grinding your bones and mincing you alive! Then the head imp picks up a long sharp knife, tests the edge of his thumb and squeals when he slices the tip-off. The other imps chitter noisily, seemingly laughing at their superior.

He hisses, and they all go silent. Then he slowly brings the knife to your chest and starts to strip your skin off. It seems they intend to make sausages out of you, using your own skin as the sausage membrane. You die slowly in agony, leaving nothing but your spirit form, which the imps then grab to start the whole grisly process again.

Your mission has failed. The earth is doomed. Turn to **616**

335

It gets harder and harder to walk. You can hardly breathe, and the lack of air saps the strength from your muscles. Each step is agony as you try to make your way up the staircase.

You start to cough, with blood-stained spittle spraying with each retch. You cough harder and it turns into a torrent of blood spurting from your mouth uncontrollably. You mistakenly try to gulp in air, but the toxic gas makes things worse. Your throat is on fire, and you drop to your knees and then all fours, your back arching as you continue to cough, blood now flowing from your mouth in a torrent. Your lungs are burning as you are deprived of fresh air, and your vision starts to swim, making you feel increasingly dizzy.

The strength leaves your legs, and you fall backwards. Your body clatters down the rough stone steps until you end up on the floor of the chamber, your body broken and bruised; but that is of no import, as you have succumbed to the fumes. Your mission has failed, and the world is in peril.

Turn to **616**

336

You decide to go right and head along the corridor. The dusty corridor opens up into a room, and you enter from what you perceive to be the south, though perceptions are not to be trusted in this hellish plane. The room is almost perfectly square. In the centre of each wall is a door. The door in the north wall appears to be made of bone. The door in the east wall is made of shimmering emerald. The door in the western wall is made of onyx. Which door will you try, or would you prefer to go back and try a route you haven't taken?

If you want to try the bone door, go to **257**. For the emerald it's **429**. For the onyx, it's **548**. If you would rather take the other turning into the battlements, turn to **428**. If you want to try somewhere in the courtyard you haven't been, then for the dungeon turn to **233**, or the large doors, turn to **134**

337

You uncork the bottle and immediately a great whoosh of air is released, like a plume of blue smoke. The smoke swirls around you until it starts to solidify and take a corporeal form. The Djinn appears before you, floating in the air. The Djinn looks down at you with its three red eyes, half-dead in the dark tunnel, a half-smile playing upon its lips, and again the voice echoes,

"I see thou art in dire need, young master, make your wish and I will aide thee"

Will you wish to be immune to the fumes of this place, turn to **81**; to be taken to the door of this realm, turn to **607** or taken out of this place completely, turn to **340**

338

Fortunately, you used your right hand to lower the bottle into the pool. Lose 2 **ENDURANCE** points and turn to **654**

339

The vats are full up to a foot from the rim and full of bodies steeped in liquid. The imps use their long paddles to constantly move the liquid around, and push the bodies under the surface. But this being the Hellscape, the bodies aren't dead and struggle to keep their heads above the murky fluid. The imps chatter excitedly as they push a person's head under the surface and wait until they have drowned. But again, death is not permanent, as shown when the drowned body floats unmoving for a few moments before jerking back to life. And the process continues.

The liquid is warm, not enough to boil, but warmer than comfortable for its occupants, their skin blistering on their faces and exposed arms, peeling off in flaps into the liquid. This is gathered by other imps using the paddles and pulled out of the vat. But the blistered skin grows back on the victims and the process starts again.

TEST YOUR INTELLIGENCE. If you pass, turn to **262**. If you fail, turn to **353**

340

"Very well, my master, I am bound to your will, although I do think both you and I will regret this course"

He places his large hand over your head, and the room shimmers. You find yourself in a grey featureless place, floating.

" I regret, my master, that even I cannot take you out of the Hellscape back to your world" you hear the disembodied voice of the Djinn say

"My powers are reduced here, but I have taken you are far as I can. This is the realm between the worlds, a void where nothing lives, nothing dies, nothing ages and nothing is born. Once here, you can never escape. This is your new home, my master, for all eternity"

The voice slowly fades and finishes saying,

"I must return to the Hellscape and wait another millennia for one such as yourself to free me, as my power will not work here, and you cannot wish if you cannot speak.".

You try to open your mouth to make a further wish, but you realise you cannot move a muscle.

"I thank thee not for this, my MASTER"

The voice says sarcastically, and then you hear no more. You are doomed to remain here, never aging, never dying, never moving, but always thinking, until the end of time or the end of your sanity - whichever comes first. Your mission has failed.

Turn to **616**

341

Reflexes honed with many thousands of hours of practice and experience take over your body. You spring to your feet, but sadly the temperature and water loss from your body has caused your calf muscles to cramp. As you try to jump up, your right leg is almost immobile, and you end up tripping over and falling in a heap upon the floor. By now the door is open, and framed in it are two imps and a large fierce-looking Daemon. The Daemon sees you and yells something in a harsh guttural tongue. Other imps arrive, probably from the kitchen, and swarm over you. By themselves, they are weak, but together the mass of them keeps you pinned to the ground.

The Daemon smiles with both his mouths, showing long yellow fangs as he does so. He draws a saw-edged knife, more like a cleaver, from his belt and walks over. The imps have you pinned by arm and leg, and no matter how hard you struggle, you cannot break free.

"*Ah*" says the Daemon "*fresh meat, how sweet. And you will taste all the better after you are well hung. Smoked mortal flesh is indeed a delicacy in this realm, you will fetch a pretty price, my sweet.*"

He bends down towards you and carefully cuts the armour and chain mail from your body. Soon you are lying there naked, your hands and legs bound with strips of cured leather. At least you hope it's leather. The Daemon points at the wynch, and two of the imps struggle to turn it. Slowly the bodies are lowered to the ground.

The Daemon points at one "*ah, that one seems done and ready for the table. Take it away to the kitchen to be skinned, gutted and jointed*".

The imps grab a naked body of a half-conscious woman and drag her away. The Daemon looks up at the now-vacant butchers hook hanging from a rusty iron chain.

"*Ah, this can be your perch, my pretty*" he says to you.

He reaches down and picks you up with one huge claw-like hand, and with a jerk upwards, he raises you above the glistening hook, still slick with the blood and fluids of its previous occupant. He slams your body down onto it, and the hook enters between your shoulder blades with tremendous force. You gasp at the impact, unable even to scream. Then the Daemon stands back and signals to the imps.

The wynch is once again turned and you are hoisted to the roof.

"*Right, you scum, leave this room and close the door, it needs to get back up to temperature.*"

He smiles up at you again and says in parting

"*Well, my sweet, I will see you in a few days when your flesh is good and tender. Enjoy your time here. Please feel free to hang around*"

And then he laughs, an ugly bark of a sound, and leaves. The door shuts, the eerie light comes on, and the smoke starts to fill the room. You hang, unable to even move, and your mortal flesh is slowly smoked to juicy perfection. Your mission has failed, and you have doomed your world to suffering, and yourself as the main course at the Daemon's table. Turn to **616**

342

Without a pause for further thought, you run for the nearest ladder back down. **TEST YOUR INTELLIGENCE**. If you pass, turn to **83**. If you fail, turn to **349**

343

Once more, you carry on. You have no idea how much time has elapsed, whether it is night or day, or when you should stop to eat and rest. You resolve to keep going until you physically have to stop. And so you trudge onwards across this miserable place. Once more, you see something on the horizon. It's two figures, one crouching, and the other standing over him with a sword.

The swordsman swings the weapon, and the blade passes through the supine figure, the swordsman then falling to the cold grey surface. Again you realise you are back at the point you ate, and are witnessing you trying to attack your former self. This is enough to drive a normal man mad.

TEST YOUR FAITH by rolling 1d20. If your roll higher than your current **FAITH** score, turn to **567**. If it is lower or equal, turn to **622**

344

The professor is busy packing things into a backpack; his few possessions he considers valuable enough to take with him when he leaves. But as he packs, he picks up a black book that is on his desk. He stops, about to place it into his bag, but then instead throws it at you,

"You may find this useful, my fellow. I don't really need it after all this time, but it was useful when I got here. It's a dictionary into how to read Infernal, the language of the hierarchy of the Hellscape. You may have noticed that some words are written in a tongue you recognise, but as you get closer to the First Circle, you will increasingly see everything is written in Infernal. As with all written word in this backward world, all writing goes from right to left. But this may aide you".

You stop and flick through the book, drawn to the strange figures. Write down the reference **151** and then turn to **146**

345

You quickly eat the blubber, but then something feels wrong. Within minutes, your stomach is convulsed with pain, and you drop to your knees clutching your guts. They feel like they are about to explode, and cramp-like pain courses through your body.

Then the convulsions get worse and, unable to keep control, your guts explode, soil passing out of your body. At the same time, you start to retch, until you throw up a huge gush of brown liquid. You continue to rock on your knees as your stomach expels the toxic substance from your body in any way it can. The liquid gets up your nose, and you can hardly breathe, and the fire in your belly gets worse and worse.

Soon you topple over to one side, and you continue to retch. Strength leaves you, and through tear-stained eyes you lie there weeping in the soil of humanity, writhing bodies pawing at you. You close your eyes for the final time and are left lying there, your body reeking of vomit and faeces. Your soul will remain in this spot, with the gluttons of society, for aeons to come. Your mission has failed, and humanity will soon be overrun.

Turn to **616**

346

After staring at the map for some time, you still cannot make any sense of it and decide to carry on along the road. Turn to **420**

347

The first set of steps you transverse relatively easily. Then you get to the first cut back. You check the gap, and it appears to be about 2 yards. You will have to jump up and twist in mid-air in order to grab onto the first step in the next set of stairs.

Add your current **STRENGTH** and **AGILITY** together. Now roll 4d6. If your roll is less than or equal to your combined score, turn to **264**. If it is higher, turn to **34**

348

You raise your blade and move to attack the seemingly defenceless figure. He doesn't seem at all perturbed as you cross the distance and seek to strike. But he just shakes his head and tuts to himself in disappointment, and then raises his right hand. On the hand is a kind of metal glove that covers just his fingers and thumb. He brings them together in a point, lightning dancing from the tips of his fingers and into your chest. Your body convulses briefly with pain, and then he lowers his hand, and the lighting disappears.

Lose 2 **ENDURANCE** points and 1 **FAITH** point for attacking a seemingly harmless mortal.

Turn to **414**

349

Swearing under your breath, you realise that you are some way from where you left Devilsbane and your shield. You can hear the angry noises of Daemons and Imps climbing down ladders to intercept you once more, and you realise you will have to abandon your sword and shield if you want to stand any chance of escape.

Make sure you permanently reduce your **FIGHTING SKILL** by 2 and lose 1 **FAITH** point for losing your holy blade. You feel regret but turn to leave, wishing you had never climbed up to investigate the vats.

Turn to **597**

As you exit the path, you come into a larger clearing that is more open, and the heat is less oppressive. The corpse trees are thinner and more spread out, and light filters down from whatever source of illumination there is in this gross realm.

Dominating the centre of the clearing is a large obsidian obelisk that towers up past the tree line. You walk up and examine the obelisk.

It is four-sided, and each side faces one of the four routes from the clearing, including the one you have just entered by. On each side is a sigil. You ignore the side you came in by and look at the other three. You can choose:

| Go left, turn to 449 | Go straight on, turn to 642 | Go right, turn to 618 |

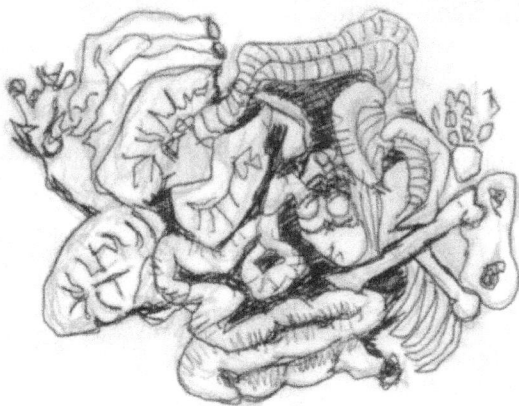

351

Despite your bad experience, if you still want to look at other items then turn to the reference below:

Shield
Turn to 40

Surcoat
Turn to 663

Otherwise, if you have had enough of this chamber, you can leave by turning to **267**

352

As an experienced soldier, you know that when all else fails, rest. There is no immediate danger, and you trust your senses and reflexes to warn you as you cannot do anything else. You sit down against the far wall with your knees to your chest, resting your head on them. You block out the moaning from above while sitting in a half-doze. As you fitfully rest, unbeknownst to you the temperature of the room seems to increase and starts to fill with a reddish smoke. Soon it is uncomfortably hot, and you are started awake and cough as you breathe in the fumes.

Roll 1d4 and lose this in **ENDURANCE** and also lose 1 point in FITNESS. You hear a noise, and the door starts to open. You try to spring to your feet. **TEST YOUR AGILITY**. If you succeed, turn to **162**. If you fail, turn to **341**

353

You rack your brains for an idea of what the vat is being used for, but nothing in this realm makes sense to you. Turn to **139**

354

The men stare at you, clearly unmoved. Then Hatton once again speaks for the group.

"My lord, we have little love of you, as we have suffered more torment than in Hell itself. Thou will not be able to escape this fate and therefore will not be able to aide us. Therefore, regretfully, we decline your offer. We will not help. We would rather see you suffer our fate, even more so as a mortal man in the realm of limbo, than help you."

With that, they, as one, turn their backs on you and leave.

Turn to **436**

355

The kitchen is still devoid of life, as no one has noticed that you have butchered all the butchers. The imps still lie where they fell, and are yet to return to the original spirits they once were. You quickly cross the room and go to the green door.

Turn to **402**

The large brick building looks incongruous in this setting. In a place as old as the Hellscape, to have a modern factory-style building jars with sense and logic. However, it looks like it has been here for millennia. The red bricks are covered in moss and lichen, or the equivalent in this dread realm. The mortar, as blood-red as the bricks, is in places crumbling from between the foundations.

In horror, it dawns on you as you look closely, that the bricks appear to have human features. Here you can see a hand, compressed, but still a hand. There you can see a leg, again flattened but clearly a leg. Then in horror, you notice that some bricks have eyes that are flickering open, mouths that seem to endlessly mumble, and ears that hear the sound of torment. Gingerly you reach out and touch a brick. It is not hard, but spongy and gives as you prod it.

You realise that this building was constructed from the compressed bodies of the damned, and they are still alive and part of this living structure. You pick at a piece of mortar and rub it between your fingers, and then raise it to your nose. The smell is rich and like iron, and you realise the mortar is mixed with human blood. The whole building assaults your sense.

TEST YOUR FAITH. IF you are successful, turn to **240**. If you fail, turn to **314**

357

"My men, I did not betray or sacrifice you. I was pulled into that infernal machine and have just found my way here. Please, as comrades in arms, help me - and I promise that I will do all I can to free you from this dread realm."

TEST YOUR INTELLIGENCE, if you succeed, you have persuaded them and turn to **119**. If you fail, turn to **354**

358

As you exit a path, you come into a larger clearing that is more open, and the heat is less oppressive. The corpse trees are thinner and more spread out, and light filters down from whatever source of illumination there is in this gross realm. Dominating the centre of the clearing is a large obsidian obelisk that towers up past the tree line. You walk up and examine the obelisk.

It is four-sided, and each side faces one of the four routes from the clearing, including the one you have just entered by. On each side is a sigil. You ignore the side you came in by and look at the other three. You can choose:

Go left,
turn to 653

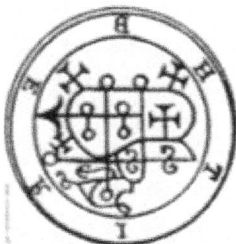

Go straight on,
turn to 5

Go right,
turn to 177

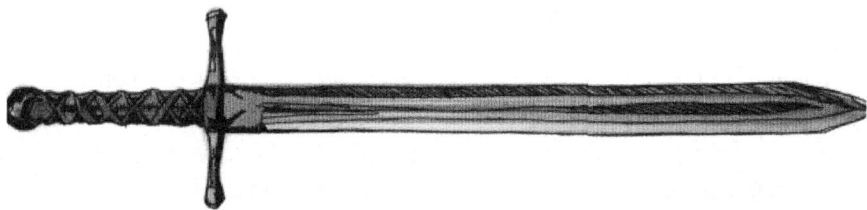

359

As you exit a path, you come into a larger clearing that is more open, and the heat is less oppressive. The corpse trees are thinner and more spread out, and light filters down from whatever source of illumination there is in this gross realm.

Dominating the centre of the clearing is a large obsidian obelisk that towers up past the tree line. You walk up and examine the obelisk. It is four-sided, and each side faces one of the four routes from the clearing, including the one you have just entered by. On each side is a sigil. You ignore the side you came in by and look at the other three. You can choose:

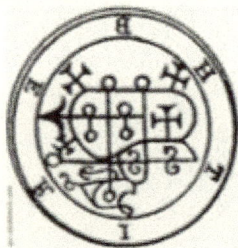

Go left, turn to **235**	Go straight on, turn to **301**	Go right, turn to **185**

360

Stopping at a place where you have a good view, you break out some supplies.

Gain 2 **ENDURANCE** points, as your body was sorely in need of sustenance. Turn to **229**

If you choose to drink a bottle, it will improve one of your attributes, but randomly. After drinking, roll 1d8 and consult the list below. This will be the attribute that will be improved. 1. **STRENGTH**; 2. **FIGHTING SKILL**; 3. **AGILITY**; 4. **ENDURANCE**; 5. **FITNESS**; 6. **INTELLIGENCE**; 7. **FORTUNE**; 8. **FAITH**. Now roll 1d4. This is the amount that attribute will improve by.

However, now roll 1d8 again.

As with most things in the Hellscape, there is always a trade-off. If you gain in one area, you lose in another. So now roll 1d4 and half that amount (rounding down). You must now lose that number of points from the second attribute you rolled. If you roll the same attribute twice, then this attribute will be affected twice - and so you may even lose out. You can go above (or below) your initial level.

Now turn back to the reference you noted down.

362

Despite nearly being killed by the possessed spirit of the previous owner of the surcoat, if you still think it's a good idea to look at other items then turn to the reference shown:

Shield
Turn to 40

Helm
Turn to 234

Otherwise, if you have had enough of this chamber, you can leave by turning to **267**

363

From your observation point, you can see that apart from the numerous vats of liquid souls being boiled and the giant hole in the ground, that there appears to be another doorway into a partitioned section of the dome.

To get to this, you will have to continue up the stairs. These steps are bolted to the inside of the dome, and zig-zag the circumference as they go upwards. There are no rails, just open metal steps. If you want to continue up, turn to **268**. Otherwise, turn back to **419** and make another choice.

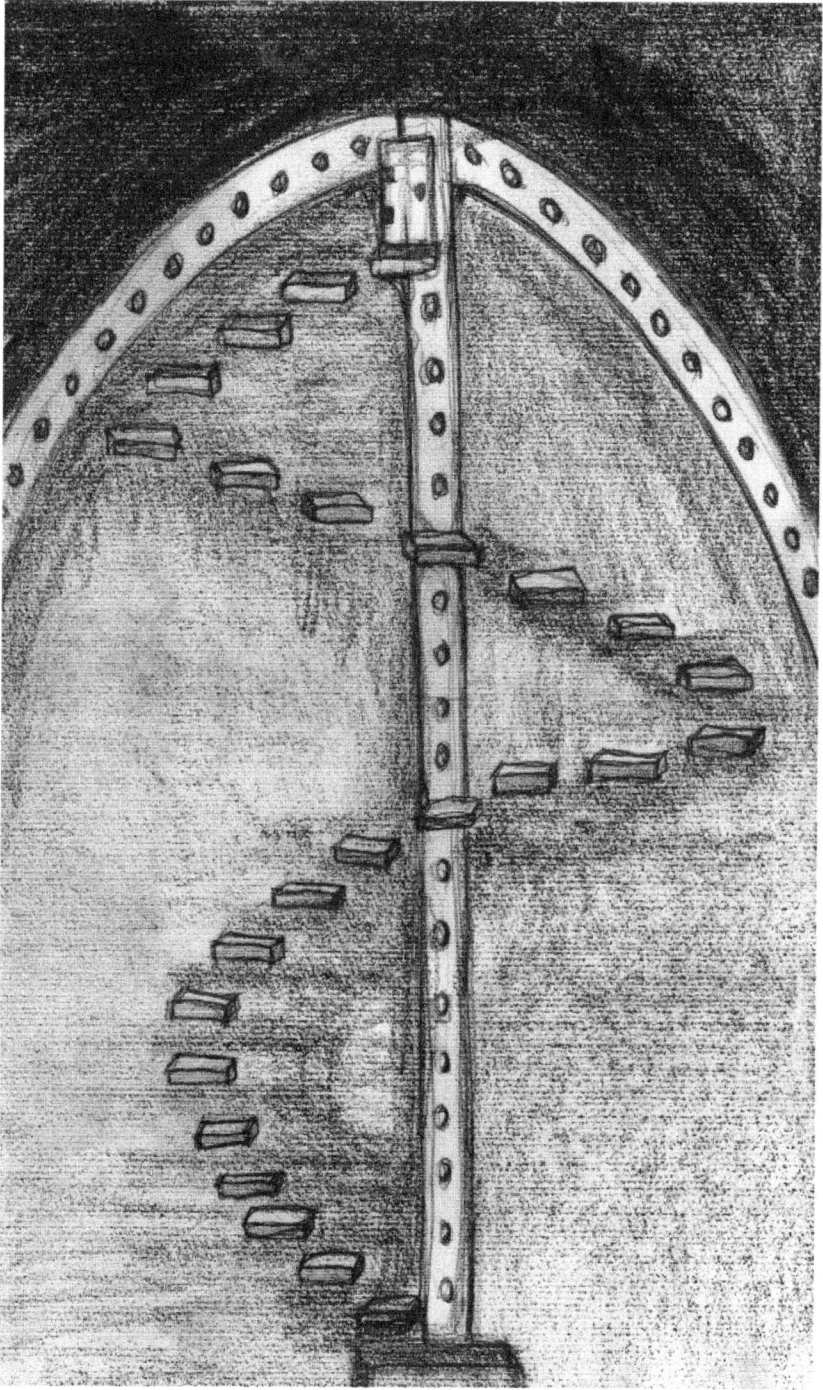

364

Walking over, in a sign of respect, you remove your gauntlets and tuck them into your belt. You take his left hand with your naked hand. You look into the ice blue eyes. The face breaks into a smile, a full, beaming grin of happiness. Then your host says,

"Excellent, a wise choice, for you forgo conflict and instead choose challenge. If thou can answer these challenges, then the portal will open for you, and you may leave with our blessing. If thou does fail, well, then a different fate awaits"

He looks at the giant dragon and smiles. The dragons head moves down and sniffs you, saliva dripping down its broad face in anticipation. Turn to **305**

365

Seeing no other obvious option, and being loathed to retrace your steps, you continue on the path towards the central route. Turn to **480**

366

Realising that time is against you, you scan the room and see nothing of interest except a black book on the desk. You pick it up and flick through it. The strange characters are compelling and next to each is a symbol you recognise - a letter from the common tongue. You realise you have found a dictionary of how to read Infernal, the language of the hierarchy of the Hellscape.

Write down the reference **484** and then turn to **146**

367

You try to dodge your way past the branches, or more appropriately, limbs of the trees. As you duck under a branch, you accidentally trip (or were you tripped?) and stagger as you try to dip under. To halt your dive to the floor, you reach out and grab at a limb. **TEST YOUR FORTUNE**. If you are fortunate, turn to **181**. If you are not, turn to **390**

368

The path winds through the trees, and you make every effort not to touch them. The heat is oppressive under the canopy of the humanoid trees, and you are sweating freely. Lose 1 **ENDURANCE** point. Soon, you appear in another clearing. The human trees here seem to be wailing even louder than at other locations. Keen to escape the disconcerting noise, you quickly choose a route; will you bravely head left, then turn to **85**, risk going straight ahead, turn to **593** or to veer right, turn to **255**

369

You edge into the chamber. The stench is unbelievable and cloying, seemingly sticking in your throat. You carry on, moving cautiously around the rim of the pulsating room. Your steps seem spongy in the material that passes as the floor and seems to stick as you try to walk. This will reduce your **FIGHTING SKILL** by 1 if you need to fight.

You move slowly to try not to disturb the workers. As you get closer, you notice the workers are small, only about 2 feet tall. They stomp around on short stubby legs that curve back like a goat's and end in hooves. Their torso is naked, and the skin is scaled.

Their arms end in talon-like hands with 2 fingers opposite what acts as a thumb. Their heads are thin and pointed, with long upswept ears and gleaming red eyes. Their teeth are short but like a saw blade. At the base of their backs grows a short, prehensile tail that constantly moves from side to side and seems to help them balance. They are fire imps, small and almost mindless, but vicious.

You are too busy watching them to mind your footing, and your foot snags in the strange spongy floor causing you to stagger forward, your sword clashing against your armour. The imps turn around and snarl, their viciously sharp teeth gleaming in the light of the room.

Turn to **128**

370

You quickly leave the room. Fortunately, no one has heard the scuffle, or else has not dared to investigate its cause. You go back to the junction and head down the other passage as quickly as you can. Gain 1 **FAITH** point.

Turn to **209**

371

The enraged Lord **BAALBERITH** has **FS 12, EN 20**

{ADVANCED - Initial AS: 21, Initial DA: 16; FIT 9, AG 7, ST 12}

If you beat this Daemon, turn to **167**

372

You cannot see how there is anything to gain from exploring this room and decide to leave before anyone notices you.

TEST YOUR FORTUNE. If you are lucky, turn to **188**. If not, then turn to **537**

373

As you fight the beast, you aim at its head, hoping to target its brain or nervous system, if it has such a thing. The first time you score a hit on the beast, turn to **503**

374

Powered by your desperate strength, or the Power of the Lord, or both, Devilsbane flies true, and the point flies into the centre of the crystal. There is a massive detonation of light, all the more eerie as it is completely silent. You are blown from your feet, and as you lie on the ground the now chaotic swirling force from the vortex pulls you towards it.

You see the mouth of the vortex is closing as the power from the stone is lost. You try to claw at the ground to pull yourself away from the portal, but inexorably you are still dragged towards it. Everything goes dark, and you remember no more.

Turn to **560**

375

You walk nervously along the corridor. It is dark and unpleasantly warm, with a dank, musty odour. You feel like you are going downwards, although direction can be, like a lot of other things in this realm, merely your point of reference. As you carry on, the odour gets stronger and makes you want to retch. But you steel yourself and carry on.

You come to a round chamber that seems to be made of pulsating flesh. In the ceiling is a throbbing hole like a sphincter, with a tube that goes to the floor of the chamber. Every few seconds the sphincter opens and a gush of liquid flows down the tube, which looks like a giant transparent gizzard. The tubs empty into a bubbling pool that is constantly being tended by some small creatures.

Do you want to explore the foul cavern further, then turn to **369**. Otherwise, you can return back up the corridor, turn to **611**

376

After struggling on for several minutes, you come to a fork in the path. Lose 1 **ENDURANCE** due to the heat sapping your strength. In the centre of the fork is a single body tree that grows high up into the air. The strangely elongated face stares at you as it moans. The face is that of a young woman, and in her eyes you can see a terrible longing. The wail then changes into a voice, and you can hear words in that terrible cry,

"Please forgive me, it hurts it hurts so much"

it says over and over

"please help me, help it stop, please give me what I need, want, crave. Please please please"

Then the voice starts to wail again. You try to ignore the pleading face and walk past. If you prefer to risk going straight, turn to **469**. If you would prefer to turn right, then turn to **238**

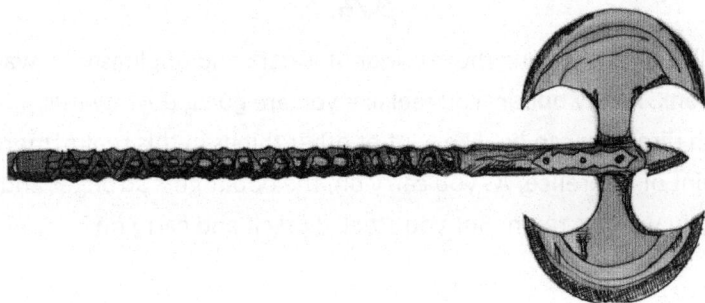

377

There are two Daemons in front of you. One is thin and emaciated, with arms like rope. The other is short, squat and powerful, with huge shoulders and long, well-muscled arms that almost hang to the ground. He walks almost on all fours, using his hands and arms as extra feet. You must fight them both - and it will not be an easy fight

THIN DAEMON has **FS 8, EN 10**

{ADVANCED - Initial AS: 16, Initial DA: 16; FIT 8, AG 8, ST 7}

APE DAEMON has **FS 9, EN 9**

{ADVANCED - Initial AS: 16, Initial DA: 14; FIT 7, AG 7, ST 8}

If you win, turn to **315**

378

The youthful face smiles and moves towards you.

"Take our hands" he commands.

Not daring to upset this mighty lord, you take his hands in yours. Then you see around his wrist, a tattoo of a serpent appears. In astonishment you watch as the tattoo comes to life and takes shape until a real green snake is wrapped around Astaroth's wrist.

He sees the worry in your eyes and says

"Fret not, our servant will aide you not harm you"

The serpent slithers across Astaroth's hands and onto yours, winding itself around your wrist.

Then it starts to become flattened, and the snake becomes a tattoo on your own right wrist.

"Thou now have the power over serpents".

Write **SNAKE CHARM** on your **ADVENTURE SHEET**. If in this or future adventures you encounter any kind of serpent foe, you can calm them and not have to fight them. Now turn to **121**

379

You arrive in what appears to be a corner section. You can only go right. However, before you go, you notice a passageway off to the left, where you can see a light shining down from above, illuminating the passage. If you haven't investigated it, then you can turn to **321**. Otherwise, go right and turn to **418**

380

Feeling tired, your mind cannot recall the nature of the 10th circle, and so you will have to go in blind. Feeling apprehensive, you walk through the portal.

Turn to **285**

381

Shaking off all fatigue, like a true soldier, you stand and pick up all your possessions and set off again. After walking for an age, you look up, and in the distance, you can see shapes that seem to be moving; human shapes. Your spirits lift at the potential sight of other people in this dreadful domain. You resolve to wait for them to approach you.

Turn to **207**

382

The stopper on this bottle almost hisses as you open it and a plume of smoke seems to magically emerge from the clear glass, though you cannot see anything that would have caused it. You take a deep breath and raise it to your lips and drink. You gasp as the seemingly invisible potion seems to coat the inside of your throat, and you struggle to breathe. You spit it out quickly.

Unfortunately, you have drunk a potion of **SOUL-DEATH**. It will not affect your mortal form, but even now it is eating away at your immortal soul. Your quick actions have stopped it from completely devouring your soul; however, you must lose 3 **FAITH** points as your soul has been reduced. It is a rare poison, and one of the few true ways to kill a Daemon.

But there is still a full dose in the bottle, so if you ever get a chance to use it on a Daemon, turn to **461** - write this number on your **ADVENTURE SHEET**. Now turn to your previous reference.

383

You reach up and grasp the rope in your gauntleted fist. In disgust, you realise that it is not actually rope, but sinew and tendons from human bodies woven into a rope. It is slick with blood and difficult to grasp, but you clench your fist around it and pull down.

Turn to **310**

384

You walk along the foul sponge-like and horribly moist carpet and on through the maw. Beyond that is a red-purple corridor, uneven and soft and undulating. It drips with some sort of horrible green slime. Underfoot you struggle to keep your footing, and then the mouth closes around you, and you are in darkness. You seem to fall down the passage, glancing off the walls as you drop into the foul miasma. You continue to fall, bouncing off the wall like a child's toy, until all of a sudden you are expelled from the passageway and onto the ground. You are unharmed as the passage was so soft, but your armour is covered in the green mucus-like substance.

TEST YOUR INTELLIGENCE. If you pass, turn to **43**. If you fail, turn to **115**

385

Having dashed across the gap between the two areas, you drop down to hide and observe. Again you can see rows of towering gleaming metal vats, reaching dozens of feet up.

The vessels are in rows of 6 and are at least 4 deep, and are staggered so that you cannot see through to the other side. You slip quietly between two of them so that you are out of sight. Each vat has a ladder attached which leads to a criss-cross of walkways suspended above you. You can hear a faint click-click-click of clawed feet as they move along the overhead gantries and assume that they are imps, not Daemons, making the noise.

If you decide to climb a ladder up to the gantries, turn to **309**. If you would rather leave the building, turn to **176**

As you edge around the room, you catch your foot on an empty plate that has been cast onto the floor by one of the diners. You trip and end up in a heap, your armour clattering as you fall. One of the Daemons hears you and turns around to glare at you. It stands up quickly, knocking the immense stone table over, to the despair of the other diners as their food falls thrashing to the floor. The Daemon is immense, but more in girth than height, and turns slowly and ponderously and shouts in a gurgling voice,

"Mortal Flesh, Mortal Flesh"

in excitement, saliva dribbling freely over its many chins.

It seizes you with a great taloned hand. You struggle to get free, but other Daemons nearby turn to see what all the commotion is about. They surround you, and soon many clawed hands are pawing at you. Then, the pawing becomes pulling, as the strong hands seize each of your limbs and tug in earnest. Slowly, you are torn apart, still living, and see one Daemon stripping the greaves from one of your legs before ripping away the calf muscle with its cruel teeth. Another has your arm, and rips off your gauntlet, slowly sucking the flesh from your fingers.

Then, you feel your breastplate being torn off, and the claws tear apart your torso, spilling your guts and stomach, which are soon snatched up and consumed. Other hands delve deeper still, pulling out glistening red and purple organs while biting huge chunks out of them.

Mercifully soon, your mortal form has been consumed. Your bones are sucked dry and crunched down into powder to use as seasoning for the next course.

But your immortal soul still remains, and that is dragged off to one of the alcoves where you are tied with cruel metal wire to one of the spits, and slowly roasted. You will still be consumed again and again for all time. Your mission has failed and may have doomed the earth.

Turn to **616**

387

In your haste to leave, you have completely forgotten to recover Devilsbane and your shield. As your fall had alerted the workers inside the dome, you dare not venture back in. Lose 1 **FIGHTING SKILL** and 1 **FORTUNE** for being so foolish. Now you can either check the smaller dome, turn to **122**, or head back to the crossroads, turn to **483**

388

As the lifeless body falls, you pull your blade free and leap to one side. The giant body falls to the ground with a huge crash, and pieces of fat and blubber are thrown everywhere. You manage to avoid the falling beast, and you are not hit by these 50-pound pieces of fat. You watch as the body slowly shrivels and shrinks, until all that is left is a tiny worm, no bigger than your finger, wriggling on the ground.

 Then you watch in amazement as one of the human forms that this beast has sated its appetite on for millennia, reaches over and grasps the pathetic little animal, raising it to his (you think) shredded lips. Broken, uneven teeth bite the worm in two, the human soul swallowing both halves. So it is in the Hellscape, from diner to dinner in but a moment. Gain 2 **FAITH** points, one for triumphing over such a beast, the second for having **FAITH** that the punished themselves deserve punishment.

Write down the name **CERBERUS** on your **ADVENTURE SHEET** and continue on. Turn to **522**

389

You take the stairs three at a time. At the top is only the single door that you saw Sabine's non-corporeal form escape through. The door is large and ornate featuring more hellish scenes of depravity and torture. You barge it open and run through. You vaguely notice the decor of the room, which is all red and black and dominated by a giant bed, but otherwise the room is empty.

There is another door at the far end. You barge through it. Turn to **48**

390

As you grab onto the limb, vines creep around your hand and under your mailed gauntlet. You panic and pull off the gauntlet as quick as you can. The vines have already encircled your wrist and are growing smaller spiked tendrils. These spikes pierce your skin, and you watch in half horror, half amazement, as a green fluid seems to be pumped under your skin and into your hand.

You can feel the liquid coursing through your veins and spreading across your body. Then all of a sudden, you get the most overwhelming sense of wellness. You feel as though everything is right with the world. You stop still and sigh contentedly. What does this matter, your quest? It seems to pale into insignificance compared to how well you now feel.

Turn to **248**

Using your blade, you try to break the ring of fire around the Professor's ankle. You saw away at the circle of flame, and it seems like strands are starting to break. You carry on, moving your razor-sharp blade up and down as it cuts into the seemingly almost indestructible filament. Then all of a sudden, it snaps, and the Professors ankle is free. He pulls it away and leaps around in celebration like a man possessed.

You sheath your blade, smiling at his antics, and don't notice as the cut band of flame, still tethered to an unknown point by a long flaming rope, starts to move towards you. It rears up behind you, not unlike a snake, but you remain unaware. Then you see the grin on Hancox's face disappear and turn into a look of sheer terror.

The flaming strands strike and encircle your neck, re-joining together to form a once more solid bond. The fire starts to burn more brightly, and it begins to burn through your mail coif. Molten steel drips down, sizzling and burning everything it touches. Then the circle of flame wraps around your neck and burns into your flesh. Your skin blisters as the flame bites and streams of tears roll unbidden from your eyes as you gasp in pain.

The flame seems to flare hotter, and the circle constricts, biting even further through the skin of your neck and into the muscle and flesh. Tendons snap as if a hot knife has seared through them, and you are unable to hold your head up as it drops to one side due to the weight of your helm.

Arteries and veins are cut through, but no blood flows as the heat cauterises them immediately. You find it increasingly difficult to breathe and eventually hyperventilate, with short, sharp breaths that do nothing to help as you just breathe in more heat from the flames.

Then with the blood supply to your brain cut, you start to lose consciousness, and you stagger against the console in front of you before sliding to the floor. As your brain dies, the circle continues to constrict, until it has scythed through all the muscle and severs the vertebrae.

Your head falls from your shoulders and rolls across the floor, the metal helm clanking against the copper surface, coming to rest with your eyes staring unseeingly at the Professor. He just shakes his head sadly and then gathers up a few things and leaves the room, a free man. You have failed in your mission, and you are doomed to remain in this realm as a soul dispossessed. Humanity may also perish due to your ineptitude.

Turn to **616**

392

When you killed Sabine, did you find an amulet? If you did, multiply the number of Sabine's name by the number on the amulet, and then turn to that reference.

If you didn't, you have no option but to turn to **415** and hope you survive

393

The agile spirit dives down at you, and you manage to grab hold of one of its legs with one hand. The creature flaps its wings for all its worth, and you are lifted off the ground. You flail around, trying to catch hold of the beast with your second hand so that you have a more secure hold. As you struggle, the creature flies out over the now empty vat. It is clearly struggling to keep its height as your weight pulls it towards the ground.

As it flaps and moves, you feel your grip loosening on the beast's skinny leg. You try to keep hold, but a mixture of sweat, blood and some other foul substance on the translucent skin of the beast causes your hand to slip. You try to swing up your free hand to grasp, but as you do so, the beast lurches to one side. Your grip gives way completely, and time seems to stop momentarily as you flail around in mid-air. Then gravity catches up, and you start to plummet towards the ground. You hit the hard-packed earth floor with bone-shattering impact.

Throw 1d20. This is how much **ENDURANCE** you lose. If you are still alive, turn to **570**. If your **ENDURANCE** is down to 0, then the fall breaks your back and shatters your skull, and you lie there twitching as life leaves your broken body. But your soul will soon be used for the next batch of foul liquid these devils are brewing. Your mission has failed, as is the whole of your reality.

Turn to **616**

394

They may only be small, but the imps are a handful. They nip at you with their small, sharp teeth and slash you with their talons. Eventually, you weaken and drop to the floor. You lay on the floor, close to death. The imps chitter and chortle to themselves, jumping up and down excitedly.

A fierce-looking Daemon, attracted by the noise, enters the room and sees you lying on the floor. The Daemon smiles with both of his mouths, showing long yellow fangs as he does so. He draws a saw-edged knife, more like a cleaver, from his belt and walks over.

"*Ah*" says the Daemon "*fresh meat, how sweet. And you will taste all the better after you are well hung. Smoked mortal flesh is indeed a delicacy in this realm, you will fetch a pretty price, my sweet.*"

He bends down towards you and carefully cuts the armour and chain mail from your body. Soon you are lying there naked, and your hands and legs are bound together with strips of cured leather. At least you hope its leather. The Daemon points at the wynch, and two of the imps struggle to turn it. Slowly the bodies are lowered to the ground.

The Daemon points at one

ah, that one seems done and ready for the table. Take it away to the kitchen to be skinned, gutted and jointed".

The imps grab a naked body of a half-conscious woman and drag her away. The Daemon looks up at the now-vacant butchers hook hanging from a rusty iron chain.

"Ah, this can be your perch, my pretty" he says to you.

He reaches down and picks you up with one huge claw-like hand, then with a jerk upwards, he raises you above the hook, still glistening with the blood and fluids of its previous occupant. He slams your body down onto it, and the hook enters between your shoulder blades with tremendous force. You gasp at the impact, unable even to scream. Then the Daemon stands back and signals to the imps.

The wynch is once again turned, and you are hoisted to the roof.

"Right, you scum, leave this room and close the door, it needs to get back up to temperature."

He smiles up at you again and says in parting,

"Well, my sweet, I will see you in a few days when your flesh is good and tender. Enjoy your time here. Please feel free to hang around"

And then he laughs, an ugly bark of a sound, and leaves. The door shuts, and the eerie light comes on, smoke starting to fill the room. You hang, unable to even move, and your mortal flesh is slowly smoked to juicy perfection. Your mission has failed, and you have doomed your world to suffering, and yourself as the main course at the Daemon's table.

Turn to **616**

395

Deciding against eating the flesh of a dead Daemon wyrm, if you have no provisions, then you are in a terrible situation. Lose 2 further **ENDURANCE** points, and you will need to find sustenance soon, or your decline will continue. Turn to **437**

396

'As you wish, my master' the voice echoes.

The Djinn places one large, two-thumbed hand on your head, and you instantly vanish from the corridor. However, you have suffered damage from the fumes, and so throw 2d6 and subtract this from your **ENDURANCE**. Mark down that you have used one of the Djinns 3 wishes, and if you wish to use him again, you must turn to **404**. You are moved back into the corridor above.

Turn to **554**

397

It would be too risky to attack both Daemons, even with surprise, and so you decide to sneak past them and try to get back to the original fork in the road at the start of this realm. You have created too much chaos to risk returning to investigate the copper-domed buildings.

TEST YOUR AGILITY. If you succeed, turn to **108**. If you fail, turn to **57**

398

Her hands move in a practised manner, and soon she has you down to your loincloth. She smiles a thin, cruel smile, but all you can see is love in that smile. She pushes you back onto the bed and leans on top of you and starts to kiss you. Her hands rake your body, the long talons rend huge cuts in your flesh that Sabine feeds off.

For hours and hours, she torments you in ways you cannot have imagined until you are past exhaustion and the silk sheets of the bed run red with your blood. Realising that she has fed on you to the point of death, she leans over you, and her mouth opens wider and wider, the long canines and incisors seemingly growing impossibly long, doubling in number as her mouth becomes the size her head previously was. The long forked tongue thrashes around inside, and as she leans over, you feel her teeth, like hundreds of small needle-like pricks on either side of your throat.

Then she closes her mouth violently and pulls back, ripping out your throat and swallowing it whole. The blood pours from you like a fountain, and she feeds on it, lapping it up with her forked tongue until her face is as red as her hair. You slowly die as the blood seeps from you. Your eyes flicker and close one last time, and you know no more. That is, however, until you awake looking down on the scene of your death and your mortal remains. Sabine looks up at your immortal soul and says,

"You are mine for eternity now, my brave knight. You will stay as my consort

forever, or until I get bored of you and turn you over to my servants. You will spend all time in my servitude, suffering agony or ecstasy as I decide to bestow on you. Welcome to Hell, Ulrac De-Villiers. You will not be leaving"

Your mission has failed and you are doomed to an eternity of torment in Hell.

Turn to **616**

399

You decide to ask the left guard, as he looks slightly saner than the guard on the right. You ask him,

"Which door would your friend over there tell me to choose?"

The dry voice replies, madness dancing in his eyes

"Oh the right hand side door, oh Great Lord, as she will lie and see you burn in hell with us forevermore. Do not trust her, she means you ill".

Do you believe this guard that the right-hand door leads to death, then turn to **517**? If you chose to ignore this guard and try the left-hand door, turn to **465**

400

It gets harder and harder to walk. You can hardly breathe, and the lack of air saps the strength from your muscles. Each step is agony as you try to make your way up the corridor. You start to cough, and it soon turns into retching, spittle's of blood spurting from your mouth uncontrollably. You mistakenly try to gulp in air, but the toxic gas makes things worse. Your throat is on fire, and you drop to your knees and then all fours, your back arching as you continue to cough, with blood now flowing from your mouth in a torrent. Your lungs are burning as you are deprived of fresh air, and your vision starts to swim with increasing dizziness.

The strength leaves your arms, and you collapse forward into the dirt of the tunnel floor, your face jammed into the mixture of stone and earth. Your eyes flutter and then close, and your breathing becomes increasingly shallow as you inhale mud from the floor. Then your breathing stops, and you topple over onto your side, your eyes now open, staring unseeingly at the roof. Your mission has failed.

Turn to **616**

401

You are progressing well and are about halfway up the stair when you jump for the next step. However, this time you underestimate the distance and your foot completely misses the step. You fall forward and try to catch the step with your body.

TEST YOUR FORTUNE. If you are fortunate, turn to **589**. If you are not so, turn to **258**

402

You reach the green door and slip through it as quick as your armour allows, closing it behind you. You are in a corridor. There are two doors on the left-hand side, and one on the right-hand side further along. If you want to try the first left-hand door, turn to **606**; for the second door, turn to **535**; or if you decide to try the right-hand door, turn to **333**

403

"My lord," you carry on but in vain.

With a roar, Baalberith leaps from his chair with frightening speed and takes the steps down from his throne, five at a time. You have tried to trick and outtalk this monster, but now you must try to outfight him. Turn to **371**

404

You uncork the bottle for a second time, and again there is a great whoosh of air and a plume of blue smoke released. The Djinn appears before you for the second time, floating in the air. In your mind, you hear the Djinn say,

"What is your bidding, my "master"?".

This is your second wish of three, so if you are sure you want to use it now, turn to the reference you were told to write down. Make sure you note this on your **ADVENTURE SHEET**. You now have one wish left

405

Carefully you make your way back to the doorway and quietly open the door. As you do, by happenstance, the door at the other end of the copper corridor also opens. Framed in the doorway is a large Daemon, who looks to be about 7 foot high. He sees you and bellows, and it is only moments until he will charge down the short corridor to engage. Do you want to draw your weapon and run to attack, then turn to **293**.

Remember if you have left Devilsbane behind to deduct the points from your **FIGHTING SKILL**.

Or is there something else you can think to do, then turn to **542**

406

Mistrusting magik, you regret your choice, but you dare not to risk upsetting Astaroth. You pick up the gleaming silver ring and slip it onto your finger.

"Thou hast chosen wisely. This is a ring of communion. Should you need our help, you may call upon it three times in your time in the Hellscape when prompted, and if we can help, we shall".

You thank the Lord Astaroth and realise that you have an ally here, although you are sure that it is purely as it serves the Daemon Lords purpose. He seems to have an interest in you escaping the Hellscape. Still, as a soldier, you realise a tactical advantage when you see one.

Write **RING OF COMMUNION** on your **ADVENTURE SHEET**. Turn to **121**

407

You reach up and grab hold of one of the arms, or branches, of the trees that are barring your passage. As you do so, vines creep around your hand and under your mailed gauntlet. You panic and pull off the gauntlet as quick as you can. The vines have already encircled your wrist and are growing smaller, spiked tendrils. These spikes pierce your skin, and you watch in half horror, half amazement, as a green fluid seems to be pumped into your hand.

You can feel the liquid coursing through your veins and spreading across your body. Then all of a sudden, you get the most overwhelming sense of wellness. You feel as though everything is right with the world. You stop still and sigh contentedly. What does this matter, your quest? It seems to pale into insignificance compared to how well you now feel.

Turn to **248**

408

Finally, you outpace the Ape like Daemon, and you can hear a howl of frustration. You hide and see a shape on the ridge in the distance. It looks like the Ape Daemon, and so you stay still, close to the ground.

Then all of a sudden, the earth next to the Daemon erupts, and a Gorger wyrm appears, throwing up human body parts. It bears down on the Ape Daemon, and its rows of sharp teeth pierce his flesh. He screams just once and is then silent. You have no more pursuers to worry about.

Turn to **228**

409

In your haste to leave, you nearly forget to recover Devilsbane and your shield, but you remember just in time and are able to grab them from the platform as you run by.

You leave the large dome and dare not return. You can either check the smaller dome and turn to **122**, or head back to the crossroads, turn to **483**

410

Years of experience means you recognise the noise instantly; the sound of a tripwire. Without thinking, you move in the way you believe would be the most unpredictable, throwing yourself back against the door.

This saves you as a giant spiked ball on a chain whistles past your nose from one side to the other. If you had remained where you were, it would likely have taken your head off or broken your back. You stop and wait whilst the ball slowly loses momentum and comes to a halt directly in front of you. Clearly, there is something in this room that is worth protecting. You duck under it and continue into the room beyond.

Turn to **412**

411

Having stripped off your gauntlets, you stow one of them away and then hold the other like a bag. You bend down to the ground and find that, as hoped, there is stone dust at the base of the cliff. You fill your gauntlet as best you can, but there is not as much as you would have hoped.

Still, the dust will help keep your hands dry and aide your grip, as you will have to climb most of the way on all fours, the distance between each step being too great just to walk up. This is a trick you learned whilst serving in the desert wilderness of Caylandia. You judge you may have enough to replenish your hands twice. Deciding that there is no time like the present, you dust your hands and head towards the first step.

Turn to **347**

The room is clearly a study, although it seems incongruous to your mind to find something so human in this realm. A large leather-topped desk dominates the room, with an ornate high backbone chair behind it.

The curtains are drawn, and the room is dark. Adorning the walls are various icons and pictures depicting the foulest scenes of gluttony. This is the working office of whomever, or whatever, rules this realm. You head around the side of the desk and look at the desktop. It is almost unscrupulously messy and dirty - the quills made of dried arteries accompanied by bottles of blood-red ink.

Scattered on the desk are numerous documents. You pick one up and shudder when you recognise that it is dried human skin, used as papyrus. Looking down, you see that there are requisitions for goods, souls and servants. Apparently, even in the Hellscape, there is bureaucracy to contend with - which seems quite apt. Record keeping always seemed torturous to you. You try the desk drawer, but it's locked.

Do you want to try to pick the lock? If so, turn to **36**; if you would rather leave and try the other door, turn to **535**; or if you would prefer to try the door on the right, turn to **333**. Otherwise, you can leave the building and turn to **365**

Stabbing the wyrm has little effect due to its layers of fat and blubber, and so you focus your attack on the small holes around its gaping mouth, which you identify as some sort of sensory organ. Each time it rears up to strike, you wait and then jump aside a split second before it attacks. Slashing with your sword, you target these nodules, rending huge gashes in the head of the wyrm. This enrages the wyrm, which was at first hunting for food, but now realises it is fighting for its life.

But each time you successfully target its nodules, its attacks seem to be less sure and less accurate. Eventually, its strength leaving it, with a hissing roar, it puts all its effort into one last strike. As it does so you target a slight bump atop its head. As it strikes, slowly and sluggishly now, you nimbly dance aside and stab at this bump. The sharp point of your great blade effortlessly penetrates the weak skin of the wyrm and slips into what passes for its brain. The creature falls to the ground with a massive thump.

You have slain the gross creature. Award yourself 1 **FORTUNE** point and turn to **101**

414

"Well" the figure says. *"Now that that nonsense is over and done with, maybe we should talk"*.

Turn to **623**

415

You speak the number, although the ungodly language is almost impossible for your human mouth to utter. The door smiles, showing row upon row of razor-sharp teeth.

Then it laughs, a chilling sound with no humour in it. Its tongue, covered in black corpuscles, then shoots out and wraps itself around you, pulling you towards the leering mouth. The smile widens as you are inexorably pulled towards the door. The strength in the foul tongue is horrendous, and as much as you struggle, you cannot stop your advance.

Eventually, you find yourself between the many rows of the glistening yellow teeth of the mouth, and it brings its jaws together. The needle-like teeth easily pierce your armour and stab you in innumerable places again and again. Blood starts to flow from your many wounds, and the tongue, now disengaged from you, seeks out the flow and laps up your life's blood.

Slowly you bleed out as the mouth feeds off you until your physical body is dead. You look down on yourself lying in this hallway, half in and half out the Daemon door, your body almost split in two at the waist by the sawing action of the teeth. You are now another trapped soul, doomed for eternity to reside in this terrible domain. Your mission has failed.

Turn to **616**

416

Without a further word, the horse runs to the end of the chamber and then turns to face you. The rider lowers his lance and the horse charges towards you. Unable to get out of the way, all you can do is draw Devilsbane and fight.

ELIGOS has **FS 10, EN 9**

{ADVANCED - Initial AS: 18, Initial DA: 16, FIT 8, AG 8, ST 8).

If you win, turn to **362**. If you lose, turn to **65**

417

You take a bite out of the wyrm blubber, but now it tastes rancid and rotten. You quickly spit it out of your mouth. Roll 1d4 and lose this many **ENDURANCE** points, as the blubber makes you sick and weak. Now return to your previous reference.

418

The path climbs up steeply here and, added to the temperature, this tests your fitness. Roll 2d6. If you roll more than your current fitness then roll 1d4 - and lose this many **ENDURANCE** points. If you roll less than or equal to your current fitness, you manage to get to the top of the hill with no ill effect.

At the top are two paths. Either pick right and turn to **93**, or go straight and turn to **471**

419

If you want to further investigate this dome, turn to **363**. Alternatively, if you haven't already, you can investigate the factory style building, turn to **356**. If you want to look at the smaller domed building, turn to **122**

If you decide to do none of these, you can return down the path away from the building complex, and back to the fork in the road where you first entered this realm. You take the right-hand fork this time.

Turn to **483**

420

With purpose, you head off down this road, which is more like a valley between the piles of human bodies and organs. You stay alert, aware of any possible attack. At a distance, you can see the gorger wyrms rearing up and consuming the poor souls whose bodies litter the plains, but here is all quiet; apart from the ever-present moaning of the damned.

However, you are so used to this that you almost block it out. You walk for what seems to be hours, and the ground becomes more like sand, and you struggle to get purchase on it. This is sapping your strength.

If you want to stop and have some provisions (if you have any left) turn to **360**. If you decide to plough on regardless, or have no provisions left, turn to **457**

421

You decide there is nothing to gain by pursuing this foul creature, and so you leave this wicked house as fast as you can.

You can either turn left outside, turn to **610**, or go to the building opposite, turn to **273**

422

You come to a clearing that is one of the most open you have found here, and you fancy you can almost see the sky above. You must stop and rest and take some provisions. If you have anything you can eat, then use it now, or you will lose 2 **ENDURANCE** points due to the overwhelming heat.

Any food or liquid that will add more than 2 **ENDURANCE** points, you will benefit from the difference. Then you set off.

Your options are to head left and turn to **552** or go straight on, turn to **459**

423

You make quick work of the last wyrm, having identified that they are vulnerable when you attack the small holes around its gaping mouth, which you realise was some sort of sensory organ. Each time it rears up to strike, you wait and then jump aside a split second before it attacks. Slashing with your sword, you target these nodules, rending huge gashes in the head of the wyrm. This enrages the wyrm, which was at first hunting for food, but now realises it is fighting for its life.

But each time you successfully target its nodules, its attacks seem to be less sure and less accurate. Eventually, its strength leaving it, with a hissing roar it puts all its effort into one last strike. As it does so you target a slight bump atop its head. As it attacks, slowly and sluggishly now, you nimbly dance aside and stab at this bump. The sharp point of your great blade effortlessly penetrates the weak skin of the wyrm and slips into what passes for its brain. The creature falls to the ground with a massive thump. You have triumphed against these gross creatures.

Award yourself 2 **FORTUNE** points and turn to **101**

424

Slowly and almost imperceptively, you almost sense, rather than see, that the landscape is slowly changing. It seems like there is a horizon ahead and you squint to try to see further. On the horizon are shapes that seem to be moving. Human shapes. Your spirits lift at the potential of finding other people in this dreadful domain.

Then you force yourself to stop and think. You have always been a private man, aloof and not requiring company, but your time here has made you realise that human contact is what you crave. But the soldier in you stops you. You do not know if they are human or otherwise, or whether they are friendly or hostile. You must decide how you are going to approach this mass of shapes.

Do you want to: Draw your sword in preparation for battle, turn to **612**; Use some undergarments from your pack to make a white flag to show your peaceful intent, turn to **640**, or wait, as the figures do seem to be heading towards you, turn to **207**. There is no option to hide, as there is nowhere to do so.

425

You speak the number, although the ungodly language is almost impossible for your human mouth to utter. The door half smiles, half grimaces, and then it starts to open, wider and wider.

The tongue advances towards you and then lays on the floor in front of you, almost making a carpet for you to walk along past the teeth and into the stinking maw. You steel yourself and put one foot on the hideous tongue and walk towards the passage beyond.

Turn to **384**

426

You uncork the bottle and immediately a great whoosh of air is released, like a plume of blue smoke. The smoke swirls around you until it starts to solidify and take a corporeal form. The creature before you is floating in the air, with no discernible legs. Instead, it has a tail of smoke. The torso is naked and heavily muscled, and thick gold bands surround its wrists and forearms. Its skin is blue-green, and the head has glowing red eyes that are arranged vertically up its face, and an intricate topknot of long blue-black hair.

You have unleashed a Djinn, a powerful magical creature much coveted by mortals and Daemons alike. The thick gold bands signify it has been bonded into service and is bound to help its owner 3 times - but then it will be released from bondage to return to its own magical realm.

The Djinn speaks to you in the corridors of your mind, telling you that you can call on its service three times. However, you cannot wish yourself out of the Hellscape, as even a creature as powerful as the Djinn are limited in this dark realm.

To use the Djinn, turn to **647** when you first decide to unleash it. Write this number on your **ADVENTURE SHEET**. You have gained a potentially powerful ally - however Djinn are neither creatures of good or evil, but of chaos and chance, and so there is always a risk in asking for their aide. Now return to your previous reference.

427

Regaining your composure, you look out on the new landscape in front of you. It's hideous. Ahead of you is a large stretch of ground, and all you can see are mortal remains. Bodies litter the plain, some whole, some not, but all moving or writhing on the ground.

Surrounded by the bodies are piles of organs; hearts, brains, livers, lungs and worse. Intestines cover the writhing bodies, spewing out faecal matter at their open ends. The stench is unbelievable.

You have been on many battlefields where blood, guts and shite were commonplace, but this was as if it had been going on for eternity and rotting at the same time. There is an overwhelming sense of putrification.

Then out from the ground, through some of the writhing bodies, rises up a worm. To say worm is to understate it. The beast must be 10 foot wide and is the colour of rancid milk. As it rears up out of the ground, its stubby nose throws up dozens of bodies hundreds of feet into the air.

Then as the human parts start to fall, the beast opens its maw - a full 10 foot wide. Hundreds of needle-like teeth ring the inside in rows. As the human remains fall, the beast gorges them down, its teeth piercing the still-living remains as screams fill the air. You feel sick, and have to stop yourself retching. As you stand there, more wyrms burst through and feed on the poor souls littering the plain.

Turn to **453**

428

You take the left turn and come to a solid oak door. You can either try to open the door, turn to **495**, or return to the junction to take the other corridor, turn to **209**

429

Walking over to the emerald door, you inspect it and find numbers etched on it in a crude hand. The numbers are:

Can you interpret these numbers? If so, then it may give you an idea as to whether to open this shimmering portal. If you decide to open it, then turn to **219**. If you decide against it, return to **209** and choose another door.

430

Each head of the beast now has an attack round and will do damage. If you manage to strike the beast's tail, turn to **511**

431

You call out the name, and seemingly out of nowhere a massive figure has appeared. It's a mighty dragon, crimson red with glowing yellow eyes. However, your eyes are drawn to the figure astride its long, snake-like neck. The figure is humanoid but clearly not human. He looks like the statues in the Holy City that represent the greatest of the seraphs who service the One God.

He is wearing a white, pleated robe, and his body is slim but well-muscled. His hair is golden and curls around his face, which has high cheekbones, ice-blue eyes and is impossibly beautiful.

He puts his hand on the dragon's head, communicating with it silently, and the dragon brings its ginormous head down to the ground. Like a cat, the figure gracefully leaps off the neck of the beast and lands silently. He stares at you with curiosity but with no hostility in his blue eyes. Then he speaks.

Turn to **630**

432

Desperation gives you strength, and you hold onto the step with your fingertips. You haul yourself up onto the step and lean back against the wall, panting from the exertion. Lose 1 **STRENGTH** for the duration of this climb due to the wrench it has given your arms when you caught the step.

You can now resume climbing ; start the first of the 3 **AGILITY** tests again.

If you pass all the **AGILITY** tests, turn to **586**. If you fail the first test, turn to **194**. If you fail the second test, turn to **401**. If you fail the third test, turn to **142**

433

You seem to reach the edge of the wood, but the oppressive temperature is still weakening you. Lose 1 **ENDURANCE** point. To your left is an impenetrable barrier of trees, all intertwined.

You can only go right, then turn to **491**, or go straight ahead, turn to **594**

"I am a mortal agent of My Lord, who whilst working under his augers on the human world, I discovered a Papist plot to block the Hellscape off from the human realm forever and stop souls from travelling back here after their mortal bodies wither. Whilst I fought to try to thwart this scheme, some magik unknown to me took me and threw me into Limbo.

"I was too strong for them to destroy, so they seek to banish me into the never-ending fields of limbo for eternity. As a mortal, only by travelling down through the circles of the Hellscape can I hope to escape back to the mortal plane and attempt to stop this plot. Otherwise, Daemonkind will forever be denied the sweet flesh and dark souls of humankind to feast on. Can you help me travel through this circle? My need is dire, as is the Hellscapes'".

Baalberith sits still, his gleaming green eyes boring into your skull as he considers your words. It seems like an eternity.

TEST YOUR INTELLIGENCE to see if you have out-foxed Baalberith. If you succeed, turn to **482**. If you fail, turn to **525**

The Ape Daemon is not as quick as you, but he's got the constitution of a dwarf or a barbarian, and no matter what you do, you cannot shake him. His pursuit is implacable. You are aware that he is getting closer and closer and yet there is nothing you can do. If he catches you, you are no match for him hand-to-hand.

Eventually, a large hand reaches over and grabs you around the neck, and you are sent sprawling to the ground. With unbelievable speed for his size, the Daemon draws a wicked curved sabre from his belt and brings it down on you in a bright arc – and the last thing to go through your mind is its jagged edge. Your mission has failed. Humanity is doomed.

Turn to **616**

436

As they leave, you plead with them, but they ignore you and float off into the horizon and you are left alone in this terrible grey world. You walk endlessly, encountering no one or nothing. Soon your supplies are used up, and your stomach tries to eat itself. Your throat is as dry as the northern wind, and your lips chaff with dehydration.

You continue to stagger on around this world, as your mortal body cannot die here, and yet still you feel all of its pain. Eventually, you are overcome with weakness and fall to the floor. You scramble to keep moving but something in your mind snaps, and you are left bawling and sobbing into the strange ground.

You look up with red-rimmed eyes that show that all sanity has left your mind. You howl and scream as you try to crawl across the ground, driven by a longing need to keep moving. And so you are left in this limbo, alive but insane, in a world of nothing for all eternity.

Your mission has failed, but your suffering will not. Turn to **616**

437

The road, if it can be called that, seems to wind through the peaks and valleys of the plains, with the usual sounds of moaning humans accompanying your every move. You have become so used to this environment you just shut out the sound of the suffering below. Ahead of you, the plain seems to change into a wood. Tall, tree-like objects rise from the ground on both sides, but they are too indistinct for you to make out any details.

You carry on walking, and the shapes slowly move closer as you close the distance. But as you walk on, it looks like what initially was a small copse or wood of trees now seems to be a mighty forest. As you get closer, you can hear the wail of wind passing through the trees, and yet there is no breeze in this godforsaken land. Then the first trees come plainly into view, and all is explained, suddenly, horridly. You stop dead in your tracks, as the horror registers on your face.

Turn to **581**

438

Feeling pleased to leave the 11th Circle and all the foulness and depravity you have seen behind, you prepare to step into the portal, trying to recall what you know of the next circle.

TEST YOUR INTELLIGENCE. If you pass, turn to **573**; if you fail, turn to **380**

439

Reaching out, you take hold of the door handle and twist. It's not locked, and the door opens. You peer inside. The room is a kitchen, if a slaughterhouse can be compared to a kitchen. Small imps are everywhere. In the corner lay a pile of bodies which squirm on the floor, indicating that they are still conscious.

The imps drag bodies over to tall wooden tables that are black with bloodstains, where they are hacked to pieces with large, saw-edged cleavers. Around the room are areas where the then prepared flesh is taken. Here the flesh is boiled in large vats of Daemon's-wine while a huge pot of flesh is being fried over a fire into a spiced curry.

Elsewhere, thin slivers of still-wriggling flesh are flambéed with spirits over a hot fire. The epicures of the Daemons call for human tartare, when the body is just sliced up raw and minced, organs, bones and all, in giant grinders, and moulded into patties or sausages, using their own skin as the sausage casing. When the human feast is ready, it is loaded onto huge platters and taken out through a door, presumably to the main area of the hall.

Turn to **514**

440

The chamber around you is octagonal and built using large stones. On the walls in sconces are torches that burn with a dirty, smoky light. Between them on the walls are a variety of arms and armaments. There are hooked bastard swords, long pikes, vicious halberds, double-edge battle axes, spiked maces, cruel flails and a variety of bows.

Also, there are shields and helms of various sizes, all with different sigils on them. You approach and look at the assembled weapons. You see no value in exchanging Devilsbane for one of the weapons, but you are intrigued by the armour.

Turn to **16**

441

You raise your blade and move to attack the seemingly defenceless figure, seeking to stab him in the back. Much quicker than you expected, he turns and sees you. He doesn't seem at all perturbed as you cross the distance and seek to strike. But then he just shakes his head and tuts to himself in disappointment, and then raises his right hand.

On the hand is a kind of metal glove that covers just his fingers and thumb. He brings them together in a point and lightning dances from the tips of his fingers into your chest. Your body convulses briefly with pain, and then he lowers his hand, and the lightning disappears.

Lose 4 **ENDURANCE** points and 2 **FAITH** points for attacking a seemingly harmless mortal. Turn to **414**

442

You have no choice now but to fight for your life, and more importantly, your soul.

SUB-DAEMON has FS 7, EN 20

{ADVANCED - Initial AS: 12, Initial DA: 10; FIT 7, AG 3, ST 12}

If you win, turn to **112**. If you are beaten, turn to **191**

443

The path leads out into a clearing and in the centre is a large pool, filled with clear blue water. If you want to refill your flask with the clear water, then remember this reference and turn to **20**.

If you decide not to, or already have tried the water, then you must leave either by going left, turn to **652**, or go right and turn to **168**

444

You pick a handful of the mushrooms. They smell earthy and good, and so you quickly eat them. Roll 1d6 and add this to your current **ENDURANCE** as they replenish you. However, the mushrooms grow feeding on the despair leached into the earth from the cadaver trees. Roll 1d8. The results are: 1. **STRENGTH**, 2. **FIGHTING SKILL**, 3. **AGILITY**, 4. **ENDURANCE**, 5. **FITNESS**, 6. **INTELLIGENCE**, 7. **FORTUNE** and 8. **FAITH**.

Now roll 1d4, and lose that number from whichever attribute you rolled just now. If you reap the bounty of the Hellscape, then you must be prepared for all consequences.

Now turn back to your previous reference

445

As the lifeless body falls, you pull free your blade and leap to one side, but you are too slow. The giant body falls to the ground with a huge crash, and pieces of fat and blubber are thrown everywhere. You manage to avoid the falling beast but not a 50-pound piece of fat that is thrown from its body. It hits you in the head with the velocity of a cannonball.

The impact snaps your neck, ripping the flesh open. Your helmet wheels away, turning and bouncing end over end until it comes to rest a full 100 yards from your body. Your head, still in the helmet, looks up at the sky through unseeing, but still blinking, eyes. Your body drops to the floor in a heap, and then the dead are on it, ripping it apart and gorging themselves with your still-warm flesh.

Your soul is now doomed to join this human soup and remain in this realm until the end of days.

Your mission has failed, and humanity will also soon fall. Turn to **616**

446

Having escaped the smoking room, you close the door behind you to hide the evidence of the dead bodies. Back in the corridor, if you haven't already, you can choose one of the two doors on the left-hand side.

If you want to try the first left-hand door, turn to **606**; for the second door, turn to **535**; or if you have had enough of this foul building, then you can leave, turn to **131**

447

Nervously, you uncork a bottle and take a sniff. The aroma is heady and alluring. You raise the bottle to your lips and drink. You feel as though another soul has entered your body as you swallow the piquant liquid. Then an extraordinary thing happens.

You feel like your body is filled with energy. You look down and see a bloody scratch, located on your wrist between your mail coat and gauntlets, knit itself together until it's just a scar, and then fade away as though it was never there.

You have drunk a bottle of **SOUL SPIRIT**, a highly prized drink in the Hellscape, and only made in this one place. It heals all your wounds and injuries, and so you can restore your **ENDURANCE** to its original level.

However, it is a two-bladed knife. As well as helping, it hurts. As you are using other human souls to heal yourself, you lose 1 **FAITH** point each time you drink a bottle.

Roll 1d4, as this is the number of bottles you can fit into your backpack. You can now either go and investigate the exit from the dome, turn to **107**, or leave the dome by the way you came in, turn to **655**

448

With one final mighty stroke, Devilsbane cleaves through the wood and metal bindings of the keg, and liquid starts to gush out. The force of the many hundredweight of water quickly expands the hole, and what was a leak soon becomes a torrent. You jump back to avoid the foul liquid, and see that not just fluid is escaping.

Wretched human forms are also being washed from the vessel. They stagger in the force of the water, but a few find their feet, and then a few more, and then even more. Soon more than 100 souls stand, and the chasing imps and Daemons stop still.

You watch in fascination as the human wretches see their torturers, and their eyes light up with a terrible glee. With surprising speed, the host of undead souls shamble across the floor and fall on the imps and Daemons. The imps they make short work of, ripping limb from limb with the strength given only to the desperate.

The Daemons, who are each as strong as 5 healthy men, take more effort to subdue. But the sheer weight of numbers is sufficient. For every soul cut down by a Daemon, two more appear having just escaped the vat. The screams, for once, are from the non-human throats of the Daemons who have now become the victims. Sickened by the carnage, although you cannot blame the damned for getting their terrible revenge, you leave the building.

You can now either try the larger domed building, then turn to **193**; or go and enter the smaller domed building, turn to **122**

449

You exit the tree line into a sandy hollow. The heat is even more intense, and you lose 2 **ENDURANCE** points.

You hurry to exit this hollow and either go left, turn to **633**, or go right and turn to **61**

450

Visibly weakened, Sabine backs away, cowering in fear as her eyes dart to you before returning to your sword. You advance and prepare to deliver a "coup de grâce", and she backs up against the stairway.

As you prepare to swing, she hisses *"you think you can defeat me so easily. Think again brave Knight, but it's hard to kill what does not live"*.

Then with a cackle, she starts to stretch and becomes almost transparent until her physical form breaks up into smoke, which streams towards the stairway and through a door at the top of the stairs. The laugh echoes through the room as the non-corporal form of Sabine makes good her escape.

You can either try to catch her and finish her off by going up the stairs, turn to **389**, or leave the room and this dreadful house of pain. Turn to **421**

451

"Well done, thou art the most gifted of mortals, as you answered our challenges. Thou has made us look foolish, mortal".

He looks sad. If you flatter Astaroth on the excellence of his puzzles to try to cheer him up, turn to **97**. If you decide to press home your advantage and ask to leave this realm, turn to **557**

452

You decide patience is the best option and decide to wait.

TEST YOUR FORTUNE. If you are fortunate turn to **67**. If you fail, turn to **287**

453

You look out over the plain and, trying to put aside your overwhelming sense of disgust, you try to think like a tactician. There are seemingly three distinct paths across the plain.

You can try taking the left path, then turn to **254**. Otherwise, you can try the middle path, turn to **480**, or head along the right path, turn to **483**

454

In front of you is a vast courtyard, which is both deserted and derelict. Dust, dirt and filth cover the floor; the detritus of millennia of decay and corrosion, as are the broken piles of rubble from the battlements that have fallen in on themselves. This once-mighty castle seems a shell of itself. Ahead of you is an inner keep, once again with double doors flanked by flaming braziers. To your left is an archway seemingly into the walls of the castle. To your right, there are steps going down, presumably into the dungeons.

Do you want to approach the doorway (turn to **641**), go left into the battlements (turn to **485**) or go down the stone stairs (turn to **233**)

455

The imps keep too busy with their foul butchery as you further survey the room. You resolve to edge yourself around the room to the green door.

TEST YOUR FORTUNE. If you are fortunate, turn to **98**. If you are not so, turn to **217**

456

As the Daemons scour the horizon for you, they are clearly not looking behind them. All of a sudden, a huge gorger wyrm rears up from their flank and strikes. The huge maw bears down on the Daemons and swallows them in one movement. The wyrms are not picky; meat is meat to them. The wyrm dives back into the ground, and all is silent, aside from the moaning of the doomed.

Turn to **228**

457

Lose 2 **ENDURANCE** points for not eating or drinking, due to the increased exertion. Turn to **627**

458

The route is steep, and the surface is uneven so that every step is a risk.

TEST YOUR AGILITY. Roll 2d6 and if you roll higher than your current agility, you trip over a stone on the path and tumble to the floor, rolling down the hill a few yards.

Role 1d4 and take that from your current **ENDURANCE**. If you roll less or equal to your **AGILITY**, you get to the top of the climb unscathed and find yourself in a clearing. You can either turn left and turn to **541** or head right and turn to **471**

459

The path seems to get ever gloomier, and you struggle to get past the loathsome trees. The heat continues to take its toll, and you lose 1 **ENDURANCE** point. In a very narrow pass between the trees, you stumble due to weakness and fall forward. **TEST YOUR AGILITY**. If you are agile enough, then you catch yourself and can continue and choose a route, looking for the least sinister-looking way out. To go left, turn to **526**. If you prefer to go straight, turn to **261**. But if you are clumsy, you stagger forward, and you put your hand out to break your fall, catching your hand against a branch or limb.

Turn to **407**

As you exit the path, you come into a larger clearing that is more open, and the heat is less oppressive. The corpse trees are thinner and more spread out, light filtering down from whatever source of illumination there is in this gross realm.

Dominating the centre of the clearing is a large obsidian obelisk that towers up past the tree line. You walk up and examine the obelisk. It is four-sided, and each side faces one of the four routes from the clearing, including the one you have just entered by. On each side is a sigil. You ignore the side you came in by and look at the other three. You can choose:

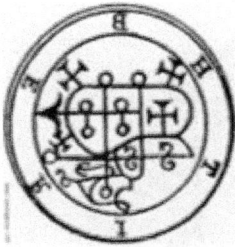

| Go left, turn to 46 | Go straight on, turn to 513 | Go right, turn to 458 |

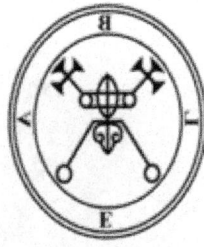

461

A potion of soul death is one of the few things that can totally destroy a Daemon. If you can pour this liquid into a vessel and make a Daemon drink it, then the effect will be swift. It is colourless, odourless, tasteless and in fact not visible to the mortal eye. If you are in a position to use this, then pour this into a drinking vessel, then make a roll of **FORTUNE**. If you are successful, then the Daemon drinks the draft and is obliterated from all reality. If you are unsuccessful, then the Daemon fails to drink the potion. Now turn back to your previous reference.

462

The face on the door opens its eyes, and they glare at you with undisguised malevolence. The mouth turns into a cruel grin, yet the face says nothing. Do you want to try to walk up and open the door? If you do, turn to **316**. If you decide against it, then you turn round and take the passageway leading away from the door. Turn to **209**

463

There are simply too many of them to fight off, and they start to tear chunks out of your exposed skin. Then some bite into your armour and begin to chew through as if it were made of linen. You feel the teeth inside your armour, boring into your body. As they do, the flesh and bone they consume disappear as if nourishing another being elsewhere.

These are the Fangs of Chrononzon, a Daemon made of a thousand mouths. These teeth were ripped from him two at a time by Baalberith as he overthrew Chrononzon as the ruler of this realm. Each morsel is now nourishing the shade of Chrononzon as he slowly tries to regain his strength over hundreds of years. Baalberith knows he is growing in strength again and relishes the day that Chrononzon will try to regain his crown. Such is the way of Daemons.

Bit by bit, the teeth gorge themselves on your mortal form, until all that is left is your soul. You are now just another doomed soul stuck in this Hellscape for eternity. But perhaps with wit and strength, you can be a power in the Hellscape. It would be better to rule in the Hellscape than suffer in it. But your mission has failed.

Turn to **616**

464

In your haste to leave, you have completely forgotten to recover Devilsbane and your shield. You are about to venture back in to retrieve them when you hear a shout from inside the dome. You peek around the doorway, and your heart falls as you see a couple of imps gathered around your arms. More Daemons are coming over to see what has been found - too many for you to fight without a sword.

Lose 1 **FIGHTING SKILL** and 1 **FORTUNE** for being so foolish. Now you can either check the smaller dome or turn to **122**, or head back to the crossroads, turn to **483**

465

Grasping the left-hand door handle, you push it down to open it. You have chosen wisely as there is nothing behind it but a courtyard, which is both deserted and derelict. Dust, dirt and filth cover the floor; the detritus of millennia of decay and corrosion, as are the broken piles of rubble from the battlements that have fallen in on themselves. This once-mighty castle seems a shell of itself. Ahead of you is an inner keep, once again with double doors flanked by flaming braziers.

To your left is an archway seemingly into the walls of the castle. To your right, there are steps going down, presumably into the dungeons. Do you want to approach the doorway (turn to **641**), go left into the battlements (turn to **485**) or go down the stone stairs (turn to **233**)

You are a dog of war, at home on the battlefield. As the strong hand of the One Church, you have been involved in some of the most bloody and vicious battles over the last 20 years. You thought nothing could disturb you, having seen up close the suffering that mankind can inflict on their fellows, often over something as simple as the interpretation of a passage in a book. But this is something new. The mixture of the laughing Daemons, the hacked up and cooked bodies still moving and the stench of cooked man-flesh staggers you.

You fall back against the wall and release the contents of your stomach onto the floor. One of the Daemons hears you retching, despite the cacophony in the hall, and turns around to glare at you.

It stands up quickly, knocking the immense stone table over, to the despair of the other diners as their food falls thrashing to the floor. The Daemon is immense, but more in girth than height, and turns slowly and ponderously and shouts in a gurgling voice,

"*Mortal flesh, Mortal flesh*" in excitement, saliva dribbling freely over its many chins.

It seizes you with a great taloned hand. You struggle to get free, but other Daemons nearby turn to see what all the commotion is about. They surround you, and soon many clawed hands are pawing at you. Then, the pawing becomes pulling, as the strong hands seize each of your limbs and tug in earnest. Slowly, you are torn apart, still living, and see one Daemon stripping the greaves from one of your legs before ripping away the calf muscle with their cruel teeth. Another has your arm, and rips off your gauntlet, slowly sucking the flesh from your fingers.

Then, you feel your breastplate being torn off, and the claws tear apart your torso, spilling your guts and stomach, which are soon snatched up and consumed. Other hands delve deeper still, pulling out glistening red and purple organs while biting huge chunks out of them.

Mercifully soon, your mortal form has been consumed. Your bones are sucked dry and crunched down into powder to use as seasoning for the next course. But your immortal soul still remains, and that is dragged off to one of the alcoves where you are tied with cruel metal wire to one of the spits, and slowly roasted. You will still be consumed again and again for all time. Your mission has failed and may have doomed the earth.

Turn to **616**

467

The large dome has lost your interest. You can now either check the smaller dome or turn to **122**, or head back to the crossroads, turn to **483**

468

You search your mind and come up with a name of a Daemon from your previous studies in Daemonology. **TEST YOUR FORTUNE**. IF you are fortunate, turn to **626**. If you are not so lucky, turn to **60**.

Or, if you have a black potion and you first want to try to drink it, write down reference this reference and turn to **256**

469

The path seems to get ever gloomier, and you struggle to get past the loathsome trees. The heat continues to take its toll, and you lose 1 **ENDURANCE** point. In a very narrow pass between the trees, you stumble due to weakness and fall forward. **TEST YOUR FORTUNE**. If you are fortunate, then you catch yourself and can continue and choose a route. To go straight on, turn to **114**. If you prefer right, turn to **526**. But if you are not fortunate, you stagger forward, and you put your hand out to break your fall, catching it against a branch or limb.

Turn to **407**

470

Previously Daemon's-wine helped you breathe the toxic atmosphere in parts of the Hellscape, but it also has other properties. If you choose to drink a bottle, it will improve one of your attributes, but randomly. After drinking, roll 1d8 and consult the list below. This will be the attribute that will be improved. 1. **STRENGTH**; 2. **FIGHTING SKILL**; 3. **AGILITY**; 4. **ENDURANCE**; 5. **FITNESS**; 6. **INTELLIGENCE**; 7. **FORTUNE**; 8. **FAITH**. Now roll 1d4. This is the amount that attribute will improve by. However, now roll 1d8 again. As with most things in the Hellscape, there is always a trade-off. If you gain in one area, you lose in another.

So now roll 1d4 and half that amount (rounding down). You must now lose that number of points from the second attribute you rolled. If you roll the same attribute twice, then this attribute will be affected twice - and so you may even lose out. You can go above your initial level. Now turn back to the reference you noted down.

471

The path leads out into a clearing in the centre of which is a large pool filled with clear blue water. If you want to refill your flask with the clear water, then remember this reference and turn to **20**.

If you decide not to, or have already tried the water, then you must leave either by going right, turn to **635**, or straight on, turn to **168**

472

You emerge into a very small clearing - although it's not exactly clear. The corpse trees here seem taller and thicker and reach up many yards into whatever sky is visible. They then converge so that they blot out almost any light.

Keen to get out of this place, you quickly choose an exit. You can either go straight on and turn to **227**, or turn right and go to **278**

473

The world seems to spin, and you lose your balance completely. You fall, tumbling down the last 10 or so steps, crashing into the wall and bashing against the roughly hewn steps. Roll 1d4 and lose the result in **ENDURANCE** points.

You are at the bottom of the stair, and now have no choice but to search the area, as you feel like you need time to recover before risking the stair again. Lose 1 **FIGHTING SKILL** whilst you are in this chamber due to your dizziness.

Turn to **440**

474

Resolving to try to frighten the monster off, you draw your sword and bash it powerfully against your shield. A metallic ring pierces the air, and the wyrm stops feeding, rearing up as it screams.

Do you want to continue, then turn to **73**. Otherwise, you can try to stand still and hope the wyrm leaves, turn to **133**

475

As you have lost the element of surprise, the Monks have had time to form a defensive line, and even manage to get the Daemons to do the same. They form up in a circle surrounding the machine, and every few moments their ranks are swelled by more arrivals from the netherworld. Your men fight valiantly, but eventually, your enemies whittle your force down until you are outnumbered.

You think you see Celdron dying, his throat ripped out by a Daemon, and soon you are alone. You look up exhausted and see the line of remaining Monks as well as the now numerous Daemons. Knowing you are as good as dead, you drop your shield and take Devilsbane in both hands and raise it over your head. But instead of bringing it down on an advancing foe, you hurl it in the air towards the jewel. Your desperation gives you strength, and the great blade turns end over end as it whirls up towards the jewel. You mutter a prayer under your breath as time seems to slow down.

Roll 1D20. If the number is less than or equal to your **FAITH** score, turn to **374**. If it is more, turn to **230**

476

Momentarily, you hang by one hand from the ledge. You try to pull yourself up, but you do not have the strength. Your hand is on the far edge of the ledge, and your other arm is pinioned against the rock face. Your arm and chest are burning, and then your first finger slips off the ledge, then the next, until you are hanging just by two fingers and your thumb. You try to heave yourself up one more time, but all strength deserts you. Your fingers slip with the movement, and for a moment, you feel suspended in the air.

But then the infernal gravity of this place takes effect. You start to fall, tumbling in the air, arms and legs flailing as you vainly try to stop yourself. As you turn, you can see the ground hurtling towards you. Time seems to both pass in an instant and last forever, as you take in every detail of your onrushing doom. Then you hit, with full force. You have spun into an almost standing position when you land, and your legs hit first and take the brunt of the impact, as your lower legs splinter. But your thigh bones remain strong, and so they are pushed up into your body. Your hips shatter as the strong thick bones force their way into your abdomen and pierce first your guts and then your vitals.

Blood spurts out of your mouth in a gush. Then your mangled body topples to the floor. Your six-foot frame has been reduced to almost half of that. You try to scream in pain, but your mouth is filled with iron-rich blood, and you just manage a wet gurgle. You don't die from your injuries, but instead, feel your lungs filling further with liquid, and you realise as you gasp for breath that you are drowning in your own blood. Your tortured breaths become weaker and weaker as more and more of the thick, viscous fluid floods into your chest cavity.

Your body, starved of air, starts to shut down, and your eyes see strange visions as you begin to hallucinate due to oxygen deprivation. A strange, almost euphoric feeling takes over momentarily before your head drops to the ground one final time, and your eyes stare blankly up. You have failed in your mission, and the world will surely burn.

Turn to **616**

477

Entering another clearing, there are two exits. You can go left, turn to **105**. Ahead of you is what appears to be a dark clearing just through the trees. To investigate this, turn to **33**

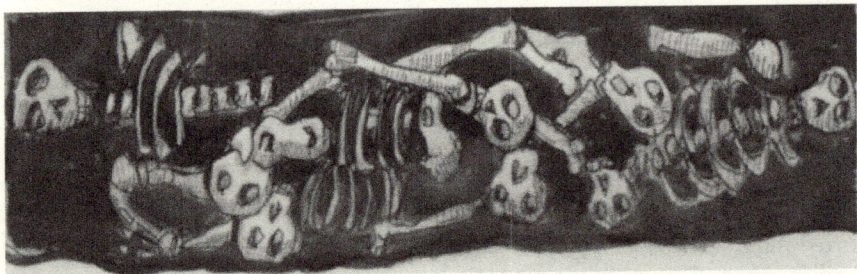

478

As you exit the path, you come into a larger clearing that is more open, and the heat is less oppressive. The corpse trees are thinner and more spread out, and light filters down from whatever source of illumination there is in this gross realm. Dominating the centre of the clearing is a large obsidian obelisk that towers up past the tree line. You walk up and examine the obelisk. It is four-sided, and each side faces one of the four routes from the clearing, including the one you have just entered by. On each side is a sigil. You ignore the side you came in by and look at the other three. You can choose:

Go left,
turn to 642

Go straight on,
turn to 618

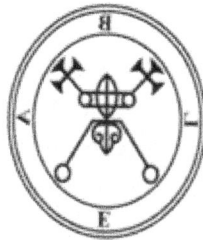

Go right,
turn to 239

479

Weak as you are, you try one last leap, but as you get up from the ground, your much-vaunted strength leaves you. The ordeal has proven too great, and your legs become weak, forcing you to stagger back against the cliff wall and collapse, helpless, upon the step. You lie there for some time, too weak to move but with enough strength to keep breathing. You reflect on a life which you thought was well-lived, but as you reach the mortal curtain, you realise it's all been a lie.

Your great deeds in the name of the One Church were also dreadful deeds, and tens of thousands of innocents have died by your sword or your command. There will be no eternal blessing for you, and you realise that when your mortal form fails, you will instead be doomed to remain as a tortured spirit in the Hellscape. You can feel the end approaching. You die in this horror of a place, alone, unloved and unmourned. You have failed in your mission, and soon the mortal realm will suffer.

Turn to **616**

480

You continue along the ridge path. By now, you have become almost immune to the grasping hands and howling of the damned spirits below. You are also used to the signs of the wyrms emerging from the malaise of writhing bodies and so are able to avoid any more encounters with them. Eventually, after untold minutes or hours of trudging, your path starts to merge with the central route that you could have taken earlier. Slowly, on the horizon, a shimmering set of structures comes into view.

The first building is seemingly built out of red brick if such a thing exists here. It is a squat, square structure very much like a factory in your homeworld. Two tall brick chimneys emerge from the roof and into the air, belching out greasy black smoke. Next to this, but separate, is a building unlike anything you have ever seen. The base is a dome, fully 100 yards across, and made out of burnished copper. Protruding out of the top of this dome is a series of copper pipes, which reach up in the sky a full 1000 yards.

Despite the immense weight of this pipework, they seem to be unsupported. Coming down from the pipes is a final glass tube that goes into the dome of a smaller building. This is the double of the building it's connected to, except that it is only a quarter of the size. As you approach the almost-twin buildings, you can feel the heat from the larger dome, whereas the smaller dome seems to be almost covered in condensation.

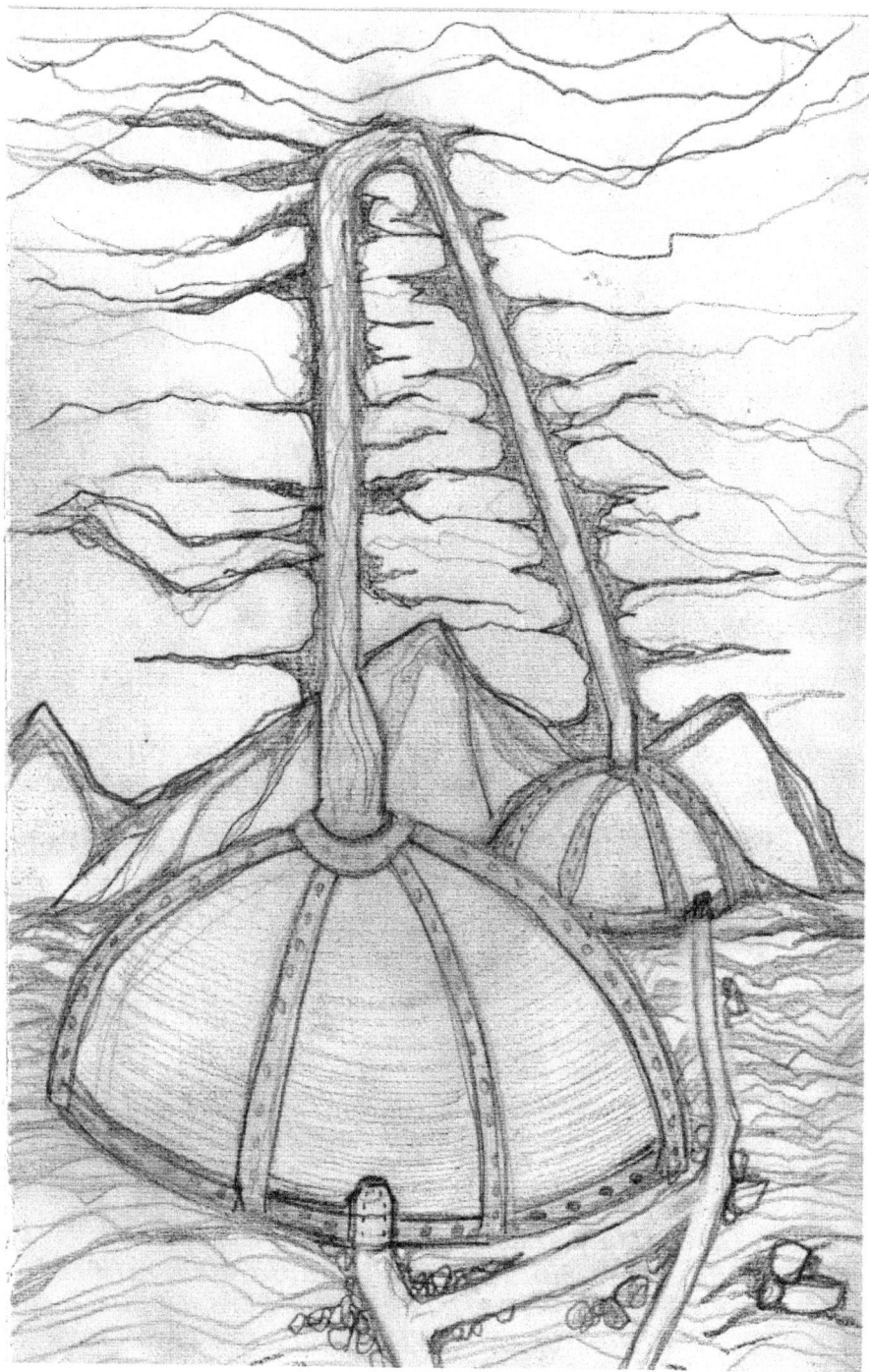

There is a heavy, acrid scent in the air.

Do you want to investigate the factory style building, turn to **356**. If you want to look at the larger domed building, then turn to **193**. Otherwise, you will have to enter the smaller domed building, turn to **122**

481

The Thin Daemon's body drops to the earth, purple blood oozing from his gaping neck. The Ape Daemon turns and bellows in rage, and attacks.

APE DAEMON has **FS 10, EN 11**

{ADVANCED - ST 9, FIT 7, AG 7}

If you win, turn to **509**

482

"HMMM, IT SEEMS OUR PURPOSES ARE ALIGNED FOR NOW. I WILL AIDE YOU. THE QUICKEST WAY FROM MY PLAIN IS TO TAKE THIS KEY".

He gestures, and a key appears in the air in front of you. It looks to be made of bone and sinew and is twisted and gnarled. You take the key out of the air and examine it. Stamped on it is the number 10. Note this on your **ADVENTURE SHEET** along with the name **BAALBERITH**. Baalberith continues in his deep rumbling voice:

"LEAVE ME NOW, FOR I HAVE MY TORMENTS TO ADMINISTER TO MY LOYAL SUBJECTS" He smiles down callously at the ragged kings and empresses serving his needs.

"LEAVE THIS HALL, NEVER TO RETURN, AND GO INTO THE COURTYARD OF MY MIGHTY CASTLE. TAKE THE DOOR WITH THE EYE OF BAALBERITH ON IT AND LEAVE THIS REALM. I WOULD WISH YOU LUCK, BUT THE LUCK OF A DAEMON IS A CAPACIOUS

THING AND MAY LEAD TO YOUR DOWNFALL. NOW GO, MY PETTY SUBJECTS AWAIT ME"

You took an oath as a child of the Church to always be truthful. Lose 1 **FAITH** point for lying, even if it was to a Daemon-Lord. But gain 1 **FORTUNE** point. Turn to **35**

483

Wasting no time, you make your way back to the crossroads and take the right-hand path.

Do you have a map? If so, turn to **198**. If not, turn to **346**

484

Having spent far too long in this room, you leave back down the copper tunnel to return to the stairs around the outside of the dome. Having already transversed them upwards, you have no wish to try going down them, and wonder how the Professor left.

TEST YOUR INTELLIGENCE. If you succeed, turn to **84**. If you fail, turn to **172**

485

Quick as you like, you cross the courtyard of the castle and slip through the archway into the side of the battlement walls. Here you have two choices. Either turn left, and turn to **428**. Otherwise, turn to **209** as you take the right passage.

486

As you watch, a light starts to blink on a panel adjacent to a vat on your left. You watch in fascination as the imps chirp while flicking switches and turning dials. Then there is a whooshing noise, and you see that one of the vats seems to be emptying itself.

Something the imps have done has opened the floor, and the liquid starts to drain away. Soon it becomes apparent that there is a fine mesh that strains out the human remains and keeps the bodies in the vat. You determine that the liquid is being taken by a large pipe attached to a valve at the bottom of the vessel and then transported through a wall into another room or building.

As the vat empties, the immortal remains of the poor victims thrash around on the floor. Then a panel opens in the wall of the vessel, and several medium-sized Daemons enter and shovel up all of the human wretches into barrows, before wheeling the still-moving bodies away. Then all of a sudden, you hear a screach, and you look around and see an imp pointing at you and shouting.

You can either run, turn to **342**; or if you decide to silence the imp, turn to **323**

487

Aware that you were lucky not to have broken your neck, you dust yourself down and reassess the situation.

If you want to try the stair again, turn to **317**. If you decide to leave this building, turn to **634**

Sabine is devilishly strong and quick, evading even your lightning-fast sword arm with a dexterity that is far from human. Each time you miss, she rakes you with talons like steel that rend huge holes into your armour. Soon, blood is flowing from a dozen large cuts in your body. The blood loss makes you weak, and your attempts at attack become increasingly feeble.

Blood flows down onto the handle of your sword, making it slick and difficult to hold, until finally in one desperate parry the sword slips from your feeble grip. Devilsbane flies through the air and impales a Daemon who was busy working on a middle-aged man.

The Daemon screams as the blessed blade sucks the soul out of it. However, you do not notice this as you are too busy trying to stay alive. Sabine stalks you like a cat hunting a mouse. You try to draw your belt knife, but she just slaps it contemptuously from your hand. Unarmed you cower back, knowing fear like you never have.

You are backed against the staircase and have nowhere to run. Sabine smiles a terrible smile and closes on you with her talons extended. She swipes with one hand, and the 6 razor-sharp claws slice through your neck, your head flying from your shoulders. Your body drops to the floor in a heap.

However, this being the Hellscape, your mortal form may be dead, but your immortal soul is released. You find yourself looking down on the hideous scene of your death, and the look of shock on the face of your disembodied head would have been amusing if this wasn't so serious. Sabine looks at your immortal self and smiles thinly, saying,

"You are mine for eternity now, my brave knight. I may not have been able to torment you as I had hoped in life. You deprived me of that, as a living soul is such

a delicacy. I will make you suffer for that.
You will stay as my consort forever, or my
pet, or until I get bored of you and turn
you over to my servants. You will spend all
time in my servitude, suffering agony or
ecstasy as I decide to bestow on you.
Welcome to Hell, Ulrac De-Villiers. You
will not be leaving"

Your mission has failed and you are doomed to an eternity of torment in Hell.

Turn to **616**

489

You place one of your booted feet next to where your blade is stuck in the beast's torso and pull with all your might. Desperation gives you strength, and you pull your blade free.

You resolve not to target the body again. If you haven't done so already, then you can now either target the head, turn to **373**, or attack the tail, turn to **511**

490

The whole ordeal has sapped you of your normal speed. You try to strike at the tail but miss.

Roll 1d4. If you roll odd, turn to **263**, if you roll even, turn to **127**

491

As you exit the path, you come into a larger clearing that is more open, and the heat is less oppressive. The corpse trees are thinner and more spread out, and light filters down from whatever source of illumination there is in this gross realm.

Dominating the centre of the clearing is a large obsidian obelisk that towers up past the tree line. You walk up and examine the obelisk. It is four-sided, and each side faces one of the four routes from the clearing, including the one you have just entered by. On each side is a sigil.

You ignore the side you came in by and look at the other three. You can choose:

 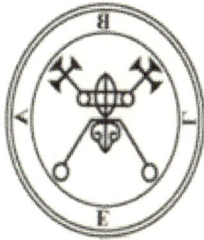 

| Go left, turn to 618 | Go straight on, turn to 239 | Go right, turn to 449 |

492

Not wishing to enter without knowing something of what you may encounter, you sneak up towards the tall, open doors. You edge down alongside them until you reach the door frame before waiting and listening. You can hear muted noises from within - the sounds of a great party or celebration, but there are also less savoury sounds.

You peek around the doorframe and see that inside there are a second set of doors that are closed. You walk on cat feet to the doors and again listen. The sound of music, laughter and carousing fills your ears, but now you can hear distinct cries and moans of pain. You bravely take hold of one of the door handles.

Are you sure you want to continue? If you do, turn to **136**. If you would rather explore the outside of the building, turn to **199**. If you want to ignore the building and carry on across the plains, turn to **603**

493

"Excellent, Kommandant, thou has a quick and nimble mind, but one more challenge we think, and one not so simple"

Again, Astaroth waves his hand, and a new flaming square appears. In it are more figures, but it is more complex. You will need to find the solution and turn to that reference.

"But our time is precious, and so thou must solve this conundrum within a time frame or suffer the consequences"

he says, smiling at his dragon that is currently resting in the corner.

The dragon opens one giant eye and stares at you with longing. Astaroth again waves his hand, and the figure 5:00 appears in flame. Set a timer for 5 minutes.

If you solve the riddle, turn to that reference. If you cannot before the time becomes nothing, then you have failed and must turn to **10**. Don't forget the convention of written language in the Hellscape.

494

You seem entranced by the music and are unable to stop playing. As you do, you watch your hands move over the instrument, and you see tendrils of flesh starting to extend out of the holes above the keyboard, and soon they are covering your hands and creeping up inside your armour.

You pull back in shock and disgust and push yourself away from the instrument. In your haste, you fall backwards over the human stool. Lose 2 **ENDURANCE** points. However, you have escaped the Hellsicorde, and so gain 1 **FAITH** point. You also notice that your playing seems to have opened a passageway to the left of the device.

If you want to examine the passageway, turn to **284**. If you want to leave the room, turn to **48** and choose an option you haven't already tried.

495

You slowly inch the door open and are faced with a huge pair of hobnail boots. They are propped up on a table, and the owner of these boots, along with the feet that are wearing them, is leaning back in a large oak chair. His, or rather it's, head is thrown back and breathing heavily through its maw-like mouth. Cruel yellow tusks jut from the lower jaw of the creature.

TEST YOUR FORTUNE. if you are fortunate, turn to **545**. If you are not so, turn to **75**

496

The noise you make alerts a Daemon nearby, despite the cacophony in the hall, who turns around and glares at you. The Daemon is immense, but more in girth than height, and turns slowly and ponderously and shouts, in a gurgling voice, The Daemon is immense, but more in girth than height, and turns slowly and ponderously and shouts, in a gurgling voice

"Mortal flesh, Mortal flesh"

,in excitement, saliva dribbling freely over its many chins.

It seizes you with a great taloned hand. You struggle to get free, but other Daemons nearby, turn to see what all the commotion is about. They surround you, and soon many clawed hands are pawing at you. Then, the pawing becomes pulling, as the strong hands seize each of your limbs and pull in earnest.

Slowly, you are torn apart, still living, and see one Daemon stripping the greaves from one of your legs, and then ripping away the calf muscle with their cruel teeth. Another has your arm, and rips off your gauntlet, and slowly sucks the flesh from your fingers.

Then, you feel your breastplate being torn off, and the claws tear apart your torso, spilling your guts and stomach, which are soon snatched up and consumed. Other hands delve deeper still, pulling out glistening red and purple organs and bite huge chunks out of them. Mercifully soon, your mortal form has been consumed. Your bones are sucked dry and crunched down into powder to use as seasoning for the next course.

But your immortal soul still remains, and that it dragged off to one of the alcoves where you are tied with cruel metal wire to one of the spits, and slowly roasted. You will still be consumed again and again for all time. Your mission has failed and may have doomed your earth.

Turn to **616**

497

As you exit the path, you come into a larger clearing that is more open, and the heat is less oppressive. The corpse trees are thinner and more spread out, and light filters down from whatever source of illumination there is in this gross realm. Dominating the centre of the clearing is a large obsidian obelisk that towers up past the tree line. You walk up and examine the obelisk. It is four-sided, and each side faces one of the four routes from the clearing, including the one you have just entered by. On each side is a sigil. You ignore the side you came in by and look at the other three. You can choose:

| Go left, turn to **185** | Go straight on, turn to **604** | Go right, turn to **235** |

498

The Daemon's clawed arm whistles down and smashes through your guard one last time, shattering your arm. You scream with abject agony, the impact driving you to your knees. The Daemon grunts and picks you up by a leg, raising your thrashing body up to his horned head.

He opens his mouth, and his breath is that of a charnel house. He licks his lips with his large forked tongue. He rips off your breastplate and opens your jerkin, exposing your bare torso, and almost tenderly pulls you up to his gaping maw. His fangs pierce your skin, burying deep in your chest, and then he swiftly pulls his head back, tearing his teeth from you, taking large chunks of flesh with him. He chews noisily twice and swallows before taking another bite.

Whilst eating, his hands continue to rip you apart, and his claw-like fingers close around your internal organs and pull, like a fisherman gutting a fish. You remain conscious long enough to see him bring your glistening deep red liver to his lips and take a large bite. Then you pass mercifully into unconsciousness never to awaken, as the Daemon continues to devour you and gets his first taste of mortal flesh for millennia.

Your mission has failed. Turn to **616**

499

The venom in your veins takes its toll. You are almost delirious, half-blind, and sweating profusely. You stagger around like a drunken man, flailing left and right, but the snake is too fast and just nips in and strikes you. Each bite injects more venom into your body, your adrenaline and pumping heart only serving to push it more rapidly through your bloodstream.

Then the snake strikes one final time, and it has chosen its place well. The fangs bite into your neck and pierce your artery, and you can feel the fluid being pumped into you from the snake's venom sacs. It withdraws and watches as in your final throws, you flail aimlessly. Your blade slips from fingers that have become weak, and you stagger and lurch and eventually drop to your knees in a heap on the floor.

Your eyes burn, and your tongue is swollen as the venom takes hold. The pain is excruciating and makes you convulse on the floor, whilst it feels like your heart is beating 4 times faster than ever before and feels like it is about to explode out of your chest. You claw at your face in pain, but all you do is pull the flesh from your face, soon causing it to be wet with blood, tears and snot.

Then your body convulses one last time, and all your muscles tense. You arch your back, and your head gazes up unseeingly to the roof of the cave. You scream, but your swollen tongue turns it into a whimper. Then your heart accelerates even further until it cannot take anymore and you feel a detonation in your chest as it bursts. Blood spurts out of your mouth in a torrent and then you topple over to the ground. The last thing you hear is a beautiful voice saying,

"A pity, we had hoped for more, still he is yours now, my pretty"

And then as your brain is starved from oxygen, you can see no more but feel the tread of the giant dragon as it moves towards you. Its head lowers and sniffs your remains, and then it starts to slowly tear strips from your limp but still warm body while lapping up the pooled blood. By now your mortal form has died, but your spirit watches on. Then you hear the beautiful voice say,

"Ah, you are ours now, we have much for you to do, and much we will do to you"

Your mission has failed. Turn to **616**

500

Successfully navigating the packed kitchen, you swiftly open the door and slip through. You are at the rear of the building.

If you think you may have missed something and want to re-enter, turn to **129**. If you decide to leave this foul building far behind and head back to the path, turn to **603**

501

"My master," speaks the Djinn in the very vaults of your mind, *"you ask such a simple task of me, to get you out of a room? Thou hasn't summoned me for such a menial task?"*

Are you sure you want to ask this of the Djinn? If so, turn to **656**. Otherwise, you can return to **279** and choose another option. Without the Djinn's help, it appears you will be stuck in this room, and so the only alternative is to simply wait and turn to **123**

502

On cat-like feet, you steal into the room and manage to avoid the imps, who are too busy working. The giant sub-daemons are almost brainless and so just trudge around. You close in on the centre of the room where the many tubes enter the ice bath before taking a look over the edge. Although by now, you thought you were immune to the horrors of this realm, what you see makes you gasp.

Turn to **659**

503

CERBERUS has FS 8, EN 20

{ADVANCED - Initial AS: 13, Initial DA: 10; FIT 5, AG 5, ST 11}

If you are playing the simple combat rules, after you have hit the creature's head three times turn to **143**. If you are playing the advanced rules, if you hit Cerberus with a medium damage or higher attack, turn to **204**

504

You make it to the third stair and drag yourself up to the top. You have one more jump to make, and then you will be on the final stair, but after that, you still have to reach the doorway. Ever the pragmatist, however, that's to worry about if you get there. You focus on your next leap.

Again add your current **STRENGTH** (minus 1 for the last jump) and **AGILITY**, then roll 4d6. If you roll less than or equal to your combined score, turn to **102**. If you roll more, **TEST YOUR FORTUNE**. If you succeed, turn to **224**. If you fail, turn to **187**

505

You dare not stop and sleep, and so you carry on anyway. Lose 2 **ENDURANCE** points as you are ignoring your body's need for rest. Turn to **381**

506

The endless maze of trees continues, and you chance upon another glade. The heat continues to take its toll. Lose 1 **ENDURANCE** point.

You can either leave by heading left and turn to **359**, or go right and turn to **547**

507

You approach the beautiful statue and stare up at it in wonder. The beautiful face looks down at you and smiles. Her teeth are dazzlingly white against the red skin. She lowers her arms to her side, the blade of her red sword angled at you, though its point is to the ground. Her hair seems to swirl around her perfect face.

She smiles even wider and says, "*Ah,*" in a deep, booming, masculine voice. "*A visitor. To what does Gremory warrant a visitor to disturb me in my glade?*"

You beg forgiveness, saying, **"Forgive me, my..."** but your voice dies as you are unsure as to which title to use to address this figure; a woman who speaks with a man's voice. The figure steps down from its plinth and looks at you, waiting for you to finish your sentence. You are uncertain what to do. The figure, now seemingly flesh, walks around you as you think frantically. Its fingers caress your shoulders lightly, and its long flowing hair tickles your face. Its scent is an intoxicating mix of flowers and spice. Again the creature stops and waits, smiling patiently.

Will you greet the figure as **"My Lord"** and turn to **276**, or **"My Lady"** and turn to **49**

508

"My Lord, all know that you are paramount in the Hellscape, and our Great Lord's strong right arm, but not all can be trusted. I was told to trust no one as all can be a spy. There are others in this realm that are not so trustworthy."

"HMM," ponders Baalberith once more. **"HER, MAYBE HER, SHE SEEKS TO RIVAL MY POWER AND INFLUENCE, AND TAKE OVER THIS CIRCLE AS HER OWN. SHE MUST BE THE SPY. TELL ME, WORM SERVANT OF THE 5TH CIRCLE, DO YOU KNOW OF WHOM I SPEAK?"**

If you know the name of another Daemon in this circle, then change the letters to numbers (A=1, B=2,....., Z=26), add them together and times the number by The Daemonic Number, 6, adding a further 6 onto the result in honour of the King of Hell. Turn to that reference number.

If you do not know this name, turn to **223**

509

The second Daemon joins his associate in the dirt. The two bodies lie quivering as the life leaves them for now. You realise a return back to the factory buildings would be suicide (and there are harsh penalties for suicide in the Hellscape), so you decide to return to the fork in the road and choose the right path.

Turn to **483**

510

A quick reconnaissance of the location makes you decide against climbing up to the metal gantries. You are better off leaving this factory. You resolve to cross the floor back to the wooden vats and then sneak to the door.

TEST YOUR FORTUNE. If you are fortunate, turn to **486**. If you are not, turn to **176**

511

The creature is attacking from the front, so you will need to try to dodge to the side and then strike when you are behind it.

If you win an attack round, you must also **TEST YOUR AGILITY**. If you succeed, turn to **639**. If you fail, turn to **490**

512

"*Ah, this forest is indeed confusing to someone of your feeble skills, but never let it be said that Gremory will not help the needy. You must follow the sigils for the Lord of this Realm; his sign is a 5-sided star. Now go and leave me to my meditations.*"

You thank the Lord and leave the glade. You can either go left and turn to **433**, or head right and turn to **105**

513

You come to a clearing that is one of the most open you have observed so far, and you fancy you can almost see the sky above. But then the trees seem to close in above you and the temperature shoots up alarmingly. Lose 2 **ENDURANCE** points.

You leave as quickly as you can. You can go left, turn to **459**, or right, turn to **379**

514

The imps keep busy in their foul butchery as you further survey the room. As well as the archway that the imps are taking the platters of food through, there is also a door with a green hue at the far side of the room. You resolve to try to edge around the room to this green door.

TEST YOUR FORTUNE. If you are fortunate, turn to **98**. If you are not so, turn to **217**

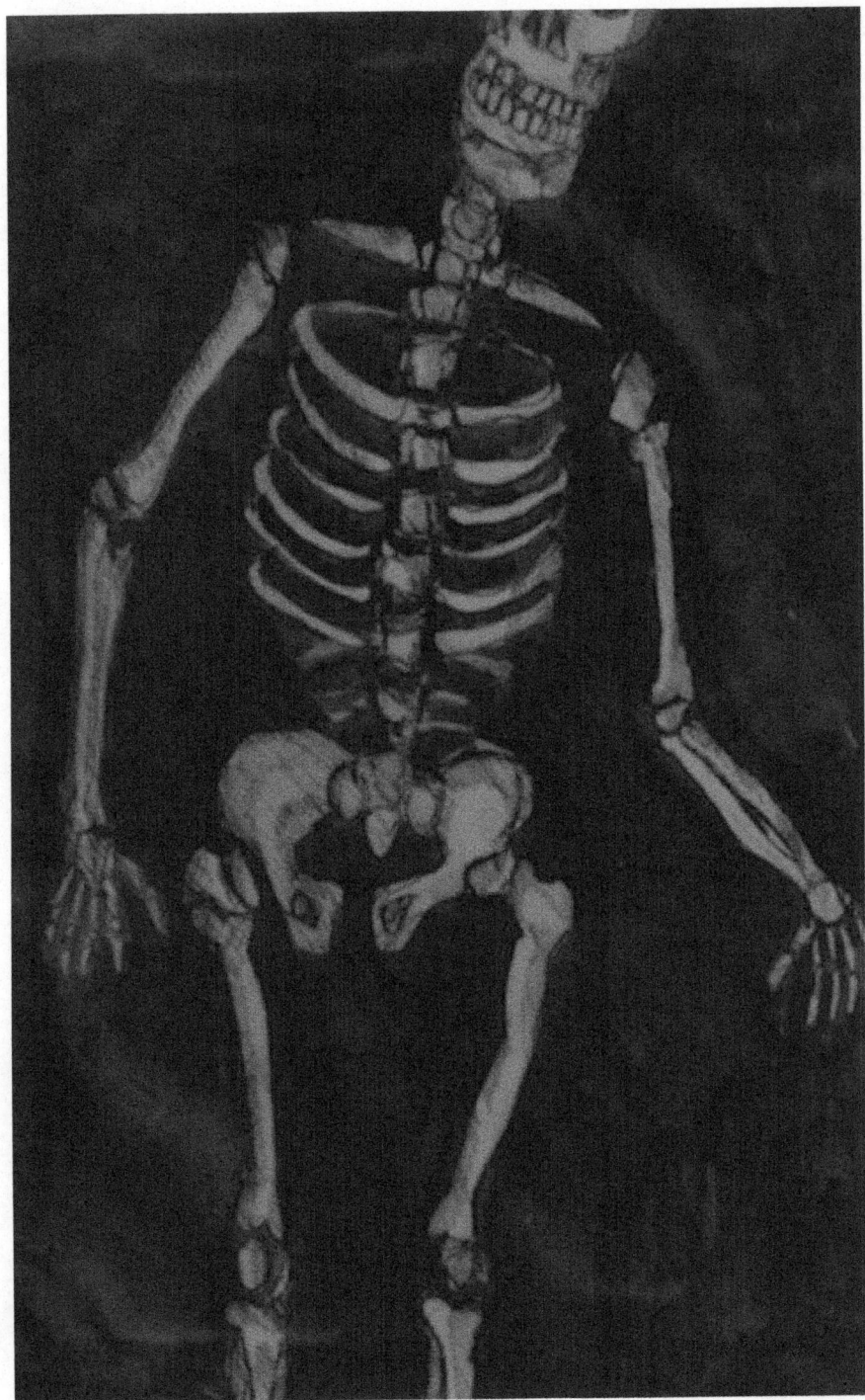

515

You drop back to the previous step and are able to land on your feet. Lose 2 **ENDURANCE** points. Lose 1 **STRENGTH** point temporarily; if you get to the top, you can rest and your **STRENGTH** will return. You must now try to leap again, using your new combined **STRENGTH** and **AGILITY** scores. If you fail, then again **TEST YOUR FORTUNE**. If you succeed, you again end up on the top of the step and lose 1d4 in **ENDURANCE**. If you fail, turn to **187**. If you run out of **ENDURANCE** points, turn to **479**. You must keep rolling until you make the leap or die.

If you want to, you can use sand dust to give you enough traction and grip to give you one extra point of **STRENGTH** for one jump. If you succeed and make the leap, turn to **504**

516

The shimmering clears, and you find yourself waist-deep in liquid that burns you. Throw 1d4 and lose that in **ENDURANCE**. You are in a large cauldron held on chains above a crackling fire. In the cauldron with you are other poor souls who are slowly being boiled alive (so to speak, as they are already dead).

If you have been to the main hall before, turn to **523**. If you have not, turn to **328**

517

As soon as your gloved hand touches the right door handle, a chain drops down from the battlements above, and with frightening speed, too fast for even your reflexes as a warrior, it winds its way around you until you are caught in a vicious embrace.

The chain, still tethered to the battlements, recoils, pulling you off your feet and dragging you up the side of the battlements into the air. Then some unseen will makes it change direction, dropping you back down. In horror, you see you are dropping towards another of the braziers to the right of the door, this one unoccupied but still smoking hot.

The chain pulls taught as it dangles you over the flames which start to lick at your armoured greaves and boots. The pain is intense and makes you scream, sucking the air out of your lungs. You hang there, unable to do more than an air dance yourself, as you try to keep the flames from burning you alive in your metal casement. But, being mortal, you can't do this forever, and soon your mortal body will be consumed by the flames, to leave your immortal soul suffering this torment forever. Your mission has failed.

Turn to **616**

518

With considerable difficulty, due to your armour, you haul yourself up and sit with your back to the cliff, panting. Your fingers sting, and you look down to observe them; they are bleeding slightly, and your arms burn from your exertion.

Temporarily, lose 1 **STRENGTH** point.

When, or if, you get to the top, your strength will return. You realise that each leap is going to take more strength out of your arms, as well as making your hands slicker with blood as they get caught on the rough, granite-like stone. However, your sand dust will give you enough traction and grip to give you one extra point of **STRENGTH** for a single jump. But you only have two portions, so use it when you need it most.

Turn to **298**

519

If you want to further investigate this dome, turn to **583**. If you haven't checked the large dome, then you can do this instead and turn to **193**. If you would rather just head back to the crossroads turn to **483**

520

As fast as you move, the imp is quicker, and it turns and sprints away from you, squealing loudly as it does. You can hear voices from the floor below bellowing orders as Daemons and imps move to cut you off. Then you hear a flapping sound. Almost instantaneously before you can react, you feel a blow to your head. Lose 2 **ENDURANCE** points. You turn to see one of the winged creatures wheeling away from you, and another about to attack. You must fend them off. Without your sword, don't forget to adjust your **FIGHTING SKILL**. Two of the creatures attack you, and you must fight them simultaneously. They are Espirits.

ESPIRITS have FS 4, EN 2

{ADVANCED - Initial AS: 11, Initial DA: 20; FIT 7, AG 13, ST 2}

If you beat them, turn to **252**. If you get hit 3 or more times by them, turn to **82**

521

You turn the handle of the second door on the left and realise as you do that it is made out of human shoulder bone. The door creaks open, and inside is a large high chamber, filled with what seems to be musical instruments. In the centre is a giant pipe organ, with the pipes leading up to the high vaulted ceiling.

You approach and notice with disgust that each of the keys on the instrument is made from a human finger bone, and that the pipes that lead to the ceiling are hollowed-out human leg bones. This is a Hellsicorde, an instrument of the Hellscape made from mortal remains.

Around the room are other examples of instruments crafted from human bodies; a rib cage on a rack that seems to act as a glockenspiel, and two large timpani drums with drum skins or, well, human skin. The faces of the poor souls who willingly (or probably not so) gave their skin to form these drums are stretched across the top of the timpani, their mouths opening and closing in silent screams. The room is seemingly empty of occupants.

You can either try to play the Hellsicorde (turn to **113**), or return back to the corridor (**48**) and choose another door you have yet to try.

522

If you still have provisions left, you can stop and replenish your strength. If you have no provisions left, you have 2 options. You can lose 2 **ENDURANCE** points. Alternatively, scattered around you are pieces of the fat from the giant wyrm. Being an experienced campaigner, you have been used to eating all manner of food in previous campaigns. Horse, goblin, even, a couple of times, human flesh. You recognise food is for survival regardless of its source.

If you want to try to eat a piece, turn to **536**. If you cannot stomach this thought and do not eat any, then lose the **ENDURANCE** points and turn to **395**

523

You are back in the main hall, but this time in a cauldron being cooked alive. Such is the capricious nature of the Djinn. The Daemons are still too busy laughing, drinking and eating to notice you. Your tactical mind registers this in a fraction of a second, despite the pain from the boiling liquid. You have no option but to vault out of the cauldron and face the consequences. Lose 2 **ENDURANCE**

Turn to **636**

524

The heat continues to drain you of strength. Lose 1 **ENDURANCE** point. After travelling down a steep incline, there's a fork in the road. You can choose left and turn to **358**, or choose right and turn to **30**

525

"HMM," muses Baalberith. *"I AM ONE OF THE MOST POWERFUL OF ALL THE DUKES OF THE HELLSCAPE, AND YET I KNOW NOTHING ABOUT THIS PLOT? SURELY THE KING OF HELL WOULD HAVE INFORMED ME.*

IT HAS BEEN MANY MILLENNIA SINCE WE LAST DIRECTLY FOUGHT THE PAPISTS, BUT I WOULD ONCE AGAIN HAVE BEEN HIS STRONG RIGHT ARM. AS WHO IN THE HELLSCAPE HAS MORE LUST FOR POWER AND GLORY THAN I? TELL ME, MORTAL, WHY IS THIS ENTRUSTED TO YOU AND YET I, A DUKE OF THE 12TH CIRCLE, BE UNAWARE?"

You still need to convince Baalberith; otherwise, you may have no recourse but to fight him. **TEST YOUR FORTUNE**. If you are fortunate, turn to **508**. If you are not so, turn to **403**

526

The passage twists and turns until you almost lose all sense of direction. Fortunately, you get to the end and find yourself in a clearing with a grassy hillock. You rush to the top to get some fresh air and rest.

Regain 1 **ENDURANCE** point as you cool down.

Now you must leave. You can either go left and turn to **595** or go on the right route and turn to **588**

527

You react a fraction of a second too late and are smashed in the chest by a huge spiked iron ball that has been released by the tripwire you unfortunately triggered. It thuds into you with tremendous impact, hitting you full in the face as you half-turn to meet it.

You are thrown sideways against the wall, hitting it with bone splintering force before dropping to the ground unmoving. You have failed in your mission, and have doomed the mortal world to infernal slavery.

Turn to **616**

528

Feeling battered and bruised, you decide to try once more to climb the stair. This time you get halfway up successfully and without incident. But after that, the steps get further apart.

TEST YOUR AGILITY twice. If you fail the first test, turn to **401**. If you fail the second test, turn to **142**. If you pass both, turn to **586**

529

A shout goes up as you are halfway across the floor, and you realise you have been spotted. You change direction and run back towards the vats hoping that any pursuers will come from the other side of the large room. Sure enough, you soon see a number of imps and Daemons running across the floor, some on two legs, some ape-like on all fours. You have three options.

You can stop and fight, turn to **377**. If you want to flee the building, turn to **559**. Or if you want to draw your sword and try to breach one of the nearby vats, turn to **118**

530

"Over the millennia we have been here, my lord, some few mortals have visited this plane. Each knows that the only way to escape limbo is either via Heaven or Hell. As Heaven is closed to us, there is only one way open. You must travel through the circles of the Hellscape. The only way for the living to escape Hell is to journey to the bottom of Hellscape and confront the Lord of Hell himself."

TEST YOUR INTELLIGENCE. If you pass, note that you did so at this reference on your **ADVENTURE SHEET** and turn to **200**. If you fail, turn to **591**

531

You remember from seminary training that one of the Lords of the Hellscape, Furfur, often took the form of a large winged hart with obsidian antlers. You decide that a confrontation with this creature is not recommended. You turn quickly and run out of the clearing. Once back on the path, you end up back at a fork in the road.

You can carry straight on, turn to **376**, or head right, turn to **524**

532

Astaroth places his hands on your head, palms down, and you feel a gentle warmth pass through your body.

"Thou hast chosen to be unnoticed""

You ask if this means invisible, and the Lord laughs a pure, joyous sound.

"Oh no, dear Kommandant, that is beyond our gift for mortals. But instead, thou may travel seen but unnoticed to all but the greatest powers"

If you wish to try to sneak past someone or hide and you need a **FORTUNE** roll, then you will no longer need to make the roll to succeed.

However, this power has its limits, and will not work with Lords of the Hellscape.

Now turn to **121**

533

As you start to fall, you are able to grab onto the rough wall and hang on. You stand there for a few moments, swaying and nauseous almost to the point of fainting. However, slowly you recover. If you want to carry on down the stairs, turn to **440**. If you decide that it's not worth the risk to carry on, return to **454** and make another choice.

534

Inside the air is ruddy and you soon see why. To your left is a set of stairs, and so you quickly climb them to get a better view. Vats, presumably from the factory next door, are wheeled in by massive sub-daemons fully 20 feet tall. The entrance seems to be an underground tunnel that leads from the factory direct into the north side, as you reckon it, of the dome.

The huge sub-daemons grunt and swear as they manhandle the vats across the rough ground. Imps gather around and chatter incessantly. Then a vat is placed across another fire roaring with flames, which reflect off the copper surface of the domed roof to make the whole room seem to dance with fire. How apt.

The liquid from the vats, along with the live human remains, boil and bubble. The steam from the boiling pots rises up into the air and is caught by a glass pipe, fully 10 feet wide, suspended over the vat as it narrows to the apex of the dome. There it exits the vessel with numerous other tubes that are from similar vats over roaring fires.

Screams of the tormented fill the air. When the vapour stops rising as frequently from a vat, it is taken off the fire, and taken to a huge spiral in the floor that leads to a hole. There the sub-daemons tip the large vat into the spiral, and the remnants of the liquid, along with the boiled and roasted human souls, flow down into the hole. Presumably, as everything in the Hellscape seems cyclical, this liquid regenerates back into human forms and is transported back to the factory to be used again as ingredients in this devilish brew.

Turn to **419**

535

You warily approach the door, examining the frame and handle. Nothing appears out of the ordinary, and so you turn the handle to open it. The door creaks slightly. In front of you is a storeroom. In it are any number of condiments presumably used by the imps to season their cruel stews and wicked roasts.

You see some bottles of what appears to be wine. If you want to, you can take them. Roll 1d4 to see how many there are and add them to your **ADVENTURE SHEET**. When you want to drink this wine, remember the reference you were on, turn to **660** for information, and then return back to your previous reference.

You leave the room and are back in the hallway. If you haven't already, you can try the first door on the left (turn to **606**) or the door on the right (turn to **333**). If you have tried all of these, or don't want to try any more, turn to **131**

536

Using your knife, you cut a strip of the blubbery fat from one of the large globules nearby from when the wyrm fell. You raise it to your lips and sniff. It smells almost edible, and the stench of the beast does not seem to have carried over.

You take a bite. It's still warm from the body heat of such a giant creature, and it almost melts in your mouth. It's delicious, like the fat of a suckling pig that's been rendered down. Realising you are starving, you wolf down the piece. Regain up to 4 **ENDURANCE** points.

You can choose to take up to 5 portions of this, but it will spoil quickly. After this turn, each time you eat a piece, you will have to roll 1d6. If you roll 1-4, you need to turn to **271** immediately. If you roll 5, turn to **345**. If you roll 6, turn to **417**.

Make sure before eating you note which reference you are on as you will have to turn straight back to it.

Note this on your **ADVENTURE SHEET** and turn to **437**

537

As you turn to leave, a woman stands in front of you. You let out a gasp, as she is, without doubt, the most beautiful thing you have ever seen in your life. She is tall, almost as tall as you, with an athletic but curvaceous body. Her hair is as red as a rose in summer and tumbles over her shoulders in thick, luxurious curls. Her skin is like ivory and as flawless. Her face is almost heart-shaped, with high brows, a long straight nose, high cheekbones and full lips the colour of blood.

But it's her eyes that mesmerise you. They are as yellow as amber with pupils that are vertical black slits like a cat but surrounded by a flickering fire. Her lips part in a smile that reveals pointed white teeth with oversized canines. Her tongue licks her lips salaciously, and you notice that it is forked like a snake's.

"Well" she almost purrs, raising her hand to your face and brushing it with her long sharp nails

"This is interesting. This is new. This is not some old dusty soul doomed to torment. This is a real man. An alive man. And if I am not mistaken, a pure man. Interesting indeed" she says, half to herself, her eyes half hooded but still her gaze is clear.

You cannot move as you are so in thrall to her; your eyes are locked onto hers. Your body is like stone, unable to move as she seems to mesmerise you. She walks around you, the sharp nails of her hand moving across your face and around your neck, sending shivers down your spine. The silk of her gown rustles as she moves around you. Somewhere a small part of your mind screams at you that you are in very real and very deadly danger.

TEST YOUR INTELLIGENCE. If you succeed turn to **614**. If you fail, turn to **243**

538

You find yourself in another clearing with more options on which way to go. Lose 1 **ENDURANCE** point due to your exertions.

There is nothing of note in this area, and you leave it quickly. You either go left and turn to **460**, straight and turn to **443**, or right and turn to **350**

539

Once you are on the ground again, you look around and swear under your breath. You can see Devilsbane and your shield, and there is no way you will be able to retrieve them. Around the ladder where they are stowed is a melee of Daemons, imps and gruesome human bodies fighting and ripping each other apart.

You realise you will have to leave your sword and shield behind if you want to stand any chance of escape. Make sure you permanently reduce your **FIGHTING SKILL** by 2 and lose 1 **FAITH** point for losing your mighty blade.

You feel regret but turn to leave, wishing you had never climbed up to investigate the vats.

Turn to **597**

540

As she moves to disrobe you, her hand happens to brush against the pommel of your greatsword Devilsbane. There is a sudden hissing sound, and Sabine recoils with a cry, holding her hand which is smoking and blackened. An acrid stench fills the air, something you have only experienced once before when you had to transverse a sulfur swamp.

The hilt and pommel of your greatsword are overlaid with delicate filigree work of silver, depicting the 7 virtues of a knight, and silver is a bane to the undead. The fog clears from your mind as you realise this is not a real woman but a Succubus; a creature that feeds on men and their lust. You draw your sword in one smooth movement as you have done a thousand times, and realise you must fight this creature.

Turn to **578**

541

The route takes you downhill, and you arrive in what appears to be a corner section. You can only go left. However, before you go, you notice a passageway off to the right, and you can see a light shining down from above, illuminating that passage.

If you haven't investigated it, then you can turn to **321**. Otherwise, stay left and turn to **422**

542

Fortune is on your side as you had not yet stepped through the doorway into the corridor. At the other end, as soon as the Daemon's heel causes the step to pivot and make contact with the floor, the circuit completes. Immediately the air becomes charged, and you feel a tingling while sensing a massive surge of power. Sparks fly along the copper corridor, travelling up the leg of the Daemon into his thick, scaled body until the whole of his form is convulsing. Sparks fly around his body, which is more a silhouette outlined by lightning sparks.

Within seconds, the temperature inside the corridor rises so that you can smell the fiend being roasted alive. The dark coarse hair on its head melts, as do its horns. Its red skin blackens, and then splits and bursts with blood flowing out, though immediately congealing due to the heat. The giant body involuntarily convulses, shaking uncontrollably. Eventually, his legs buckle, and he drops to the floor with a loud thud. The pressure off the step, it pivots back up into place and breaks the circuit. The lightning

dissipates in seconds, leaving no evidence of its havoc, except for the charred and blistered remains at the other end of the corridor.

From behind you, you hear a human-sounding voice chortle and say, *"Oh my!"* Turn to **566**

543

For each round in the pursuit, roll 2d6 and add them to your **SPEED** (combined **AGILITY, ENDURANCE** and **FITNESS**). Do the same for both Daemons. If your score is greater, then you increase your lead by the difference against each Daemon. If it is less, then that Daemon closes on you by that amount. After each round, whoever rolls highest loses one point of **FITNESS**, as they have run faster and used more of their strength. So for example, if your total was 40, and Thin Daemon was 28, but Ape Daemon 42. You would gain 12 seconds on the Thin Daemon, but the Ape Daemon gets 2 seconds closer. In this case, the Ape Daemon would lose 1 **FITNESS** as he has exerted himself more. If any party gets to a **FITNESS** of 0, they collapse to the floor unable to run. Therefore, you need to outpace your foes before your fitness drops to 0.

If you succeed, turn to **192**.

If you fail and both Daemons catch you, turn to **180**.

If only the Thin Daemon catches you, turn to **282**. If only the Ape Daemon catches you, turn to **435**

544

The last imp launches itself at you from a tabletop, and you dart forward, skewering it on the point of your greatsword. It squeals like a pig as it slides down the thick, razor-sharp blade until it reaches the hilt. Its face is now mere inches from yours, and it hisses at you with hatred in its pale amber eyes before the light goes out of it.

You lower your sword, and the imp's body slides off it onto the floor. If you head for the green door, turn to **645**. If you want to go via the back door, turn to **138**

545

Fortunately, you have not disturbed the sleeping brute. Deciding there is nothing to be gained by searching the small, squalid room, you quietly leave and close the door. You return in the other direction.

Turn to **209**

546

You poke around in the dusty remains of Sabine with the point of your sword. As you move the material of her garments, you see something sparkle. You crouch down and look at it - it's an amulet on a golden chain. You pick it up and examine it.

It's an inverted cross with a blood-red sapphire in the middle. In the centre of the sapphire, in writing like flames, is the number 13. Add this to your **ADVENTURE SHEET**, making sure you note the number down and leave the room.

Turn back to **48** and choose another option

547

As you exit the path, you come into a larger clearing that is more open, and the heat is less oppressive. The corpse trees are thinner and more spread out, and light filters down from whatever source of illumination there is in this gross realm. Dominating the centre of the clearing is a large obsidian obelisk that towers up past the tree line. You walk up and examine the obelisk. It is four-sided, and each side faces one of the four routes from the clearing, including the one you have just entered by. On each side is a sigil. You ignore the side you came in by and look at the other three. You can choose:

| Go left, turn to 239 | Go straight on, turn to 449 | Go right, turn to 642 |

548

This door is solid, black and looks impenetrable. Etched on it are the numbers:

If you can interpret it, you may have a clue as to what's behind the door. If you decide to open the black door, turn to **296**. If not, turn to **209** and choose another door.

549

Your troops are lined up behind you in the cover of the trees. Using military hand signs, you instruct your Lieutenants and tell them to pass your orders down the chain of command. As your force now number no more than 50 souls, this does not take long. You judge the distance. It will take vital minutes to cover the open ground - but you need to do it quickly.

The number of fiends from below increases every moment, and at present, you have the numerical advantage but not for long.

You unsheathe your Greatsword Devilsbane and bring it down. On your order, your men charge.

Turn to **202**

550

There appears to be nothing of note in this room, which worries you. Gingerly you step into the room, and all of a sudden, two things happen almost simultaneously. First, the door slams shut. You spin and draw your sword in one smooth movement. No one is there.

You approach the door and try to open it, but you are thrown backwards by an unseen force. Lose 2 **ENDURANCE** points.

You pick yourself up off the floor and walk back across the room. The door seems to be surrounded by a field of magical energy. You swing Devilsbane, and it just bounces off the field around the door, not even hitting it. You are trapped.

Then the once dark room becomes lit by some mystical source, and you hear a moaning noise from above. You look up, and dangling from the high ceiling are dozens of bodies. They are hung with butcher's hooks in their backs on long chains hanging from the ceiling. They stare down at you with blank eyes, a low moan coming from their mouths. They are above your head and out of reach.

Then you notice that there is a wynch mechanism that also seems to have appeared in the once-blank wall. It is obviously geared to wynch the bodies up to the ceiling. You consider your options. Do you have a blue potion? If you do, then if you have not used it before, turn to **426** and follow the instructions, and at the end turn to **279**. If you have used it before, turn to **404**, and then turn to **279**.

Otherwise, you can try to wynch the moaning bodies down and see if they can help you. Turn to **44**. The only other alternative is to wait. If you decide to do this, turn to **123**

551

In order to get to the top of the stairs without falling, **TEST YOUR AGILITY** three times. If you pass each test, turn to **586**. If you fail the first test, turn to **120**. If you fail the second test, turn to **401**. If you fail the third and final test, turn to **142**

552

As you exit the path, you come into a larger clearing that is more open, and the heat is less oppressive. The corpse trees are thinner and more spread out, and light filters down from whatever source of illumination there is in this gross realm.

Dominating the centre of the clearing is a large obsidian obelisk that towers up past the tree line. You walk up and examine the obelisk. It is four-sided, and each side faces one of the four routes from the clearing, including the one you have just entered by. On each side is a sigil. You ignore the side you came in by and look at the other three. You can choose:

| Go left, turn to **458** | Go straight on, turn to **41** | Go right, turn to **46** |

553

If you want to examine either of the other items, turn to the reference below:

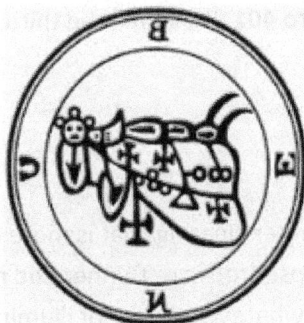 

| Helm Turn to 234 | Surcoat Turn to 663 |

Otherwise you can leave by turning to **267**

554

You approach the door, which is shaped like an obscene mouth with needle-like teeth and a forked tongue. Whether this is in homage to Sabine or some other so-far-unseen terror, you would not like to guess. As you move closer, the tongue of the door starts to thresh from side-to-side, and what initially appeared to be the wood of the door moves like some giant mouth, opening and closing while leering suggestively at you. Then the mouth speaks! Its voice is sibilant, almost reptilian, and similar to how the Lizard Princes of Drwn speak on the 12th continent. However, the voice speaks in the common tongue, or at least you hear it in the common tongue as the movement of the foul mouth does not seem to match the words.

"Whooo isssss thisssss, so you seekkkk to leave this planeeee? Yes? But you can only get passssage if you have underssstanding and can reckon the number"

Do you want to try to work out the number of which it speaks? If so, turn to **221**. If not, turn back to **48** and make another choice.

555

Glad to escape the dark clearing alive, you quickly leave the area. You can either go left and turn to **433**, or veer right and turn to **105**

556

Before you stands a Monk of the Order of Bael. You realise that you cannot reason with this man, as he is a fanatic – a true believer who is willing to die for his cause, as are you. The Monk draws his sword and advances on you, and the battle is joined.

DEATH MONK OF BAEL has **FS 6, EN 5**

{ADVANCED - Initial AS: 14, Initial DA: 12; FIT 6, AG 6, ST 3}

If you manage to defeat the Monk, turn to **74**. Otherwise, turn to **265**

557

"Thou seeks to leave our fair realm? We doubt thou will find much better in the next, but still, thou hast triumphed and passed the test we allocated to you.

Know this, not all in the Hellscape are against you. Many will just enjoy the sport, and watching other Daemon Lords suffer or lose prestige due to your actions. Not all here will hate and hamper you. Most will, but not all."

Then the figure waves. The portal stops shimmering, and a clear path appears. You thank the figure and go to leave, pausing for a moment. You wonder if your host is well disposed to you, and will grant you a boon.

If you want to ask for a boon, turn to **569**. If you do not wish to try his patience by risking it, turn to **121**

558

As you trudge along the ridge, the noxious gases from the plain below rise up, and you cannot help but breathe them in. You start to cough and then retch, struggling to breathe. Your gasps become fast and shallow as the fumes seep into your lungs. You feel dizzy, and spots appear before your eyes. You try to move quicker to escape the fumes, but you are so discombobulated that you trip over a stone on the ridge. Your usual agility fails you, and you fall headfirst down the side of the ridge, and then tumble head-over-tail to the bottom.

Lose 2 **ENDURANCE** points. You come to land in the foul quagmire below, a mixture of writhing human bodies, mud and filth. You scramble to try to escape as your armour starts to pull you into this swamp of humankind.

TEST YOUR FORTUNE. If fortune is on your side, turn to **156**. If you are not so fortunate, turn to **24**

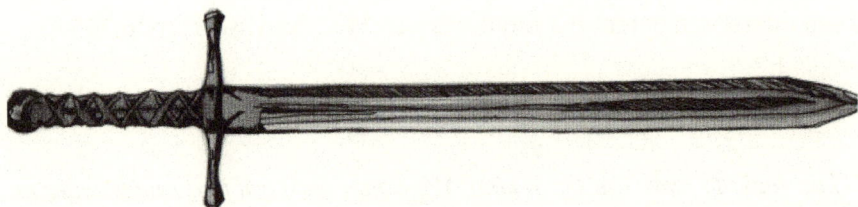

559

You run as if the Devil himself is on your tail, and you are not far from the truth! You exit the building and see behind you that two large Daemons still pursue you. You have now got a race on your hands! You need to outpace them across this terrible plain and hope you can lose them amongst the masses of suffering humanity. For the pursuit, you need to add up your current **AGILITY**, **ENDURANCE** and **FITNESS**. This is your **SPEED**. Now do the same for the Daemons. The first is a thin, almost emaciated beast. The second is a shorter stockier Daemon who runs on all fours like an ape.

Now roll 2d6. This is how far ahead in seconds you are of both of your pursuers. You need to lose them both in order to succeed. If you can get 20 seconds ahead of them, you will have a chance to hide.

THIN DAEMON has an **AG 8, EN 8 and FIT 8**

APE DAEMON has an **AG 7, EN 11 and FIT 11**

Now turn to **543**

The first thing you know is that you hear nothing. The blast from the Hell vortex closing has thrown you to the ground unconscious. How long you have been here, you do not know. Your body is a mass of aches and pains, but you mentally check yourself, and it seems to be nothing more than that. You open your eyes to find a strange world.

All around you is a flat and featureless plain that seems to stretch out from horizon to horizon – although where the horizon starts and ends is hard to say, as there does not appear to be ground or sky; just grey. You have travelled to all 12 continents of the world, and yet nothing ever prepared you for this. Not a sound is audible, and there is no touch of wind on your face. You realise that you feel neither hot nor cold, just a strange numbness.

You stand and check yourself over. You have no serious injuries; just a few cuts and scrapes. You look around and see that you are alone. Inwardly you pray for the souls of your fellow Soldiers of God and hope that if they did meet their fate, they have been rewarded in the next life.

You shout out, in case there are other residents of this strange zone, but the noise just seems to die as soon as it comes out of your mouth. It does not echo, just dies. Your first thought is that you must have perished in that silent explosion and, if so, then you must be in Heaven, as you have devoted your life to the One True God. However, this does not seem like Heaven to you, or if it is, you have been cheated. Lose one **FAITH** point.

You have all your possessions but no horse. Your greatsword, Devilsbane, is on the ground a few feet from you so you pick it up and sheath it. You check your backpack and find you have provisions with you, enough for 5 meals. You eat a quick meal to rebuild your strength. That you can still eat indicates to you that you are still alive, somehow. You leave the remains of the meal on the ground.

Resolving to work out to which strange reality you have been transported, you decide to set off walking. You get your lodestone out of your backpack and place some water in a small bowl. You place the lodestone in the bowl, hoping it will point north. It, however, just spins, first randomly in one direction, and then in another. Clearly, there is no north in this grey realm. You stow it away, against the faint hope it may be of use later. You look up. There are no suns, planets or stars to give you any direction, and no points on the horizon to head towards. All you can do is pick a direction at random.

Do you want to carry straight on? If so, turn to **28**

If you want to try travelling to your left, turn to **56**

If you want to try travelling to your right, turn to **568**

561

You carefully lower the bottle and half submerge it in the thick red liquid. It gloops into the bottle quickly, filling it, before you remove it again from the pool. You stopper it and place it carefully in your backpack.

Add this to your **ADVENTURE SHEET**. Now turn to **654**

562

As you go to leave, you remember Devilsbane and your shield are on the platform. You carefully make your way over and are able to grab them before exiting the dome.

You can either check the smaller dome, and turn to **122**, or head back to the crossroads, and turn to **483**

563

You kill the final imp you face, and the others tending the pool are now too scared to attack you. They back off into the depths of the cavern, cowering. You consider they are inconsequential and ignore them as you approach the foul-smelling pool. Your eyes begin to water, and now that the pool is not being tended, the level of liquid is approaching the rim. This is Daemon's-wine, made from the suffering souls in the rooms above, and it nourishes their corporeal form. At the side of the pool are a number of bottles.

If you want to take some Daemon's-wine, then you can try to bottle a sample. If you try, turn to **18**. Otherwise, turn to **58**

564

Despite wielding Devilsbane, Sabine is too strong for you. Her talons are like steel and are able to rend huge holes in your armour, with each wound feeling like fire. Slowly, she wears you down, fighting in a hunched, almost cat-like stance on all fours. She is quicker and stronger than you expected, and soon blood is flowing from a dozen large cuts in your body.

The blood loss makes you weak, and your attempts at attack become increasingly feeble. Blood flows down onto the handle of your sword, making it slick and difficult to hold. Finally, for one last time, you weakly swing Devilsbane at her, and she catches it between her talons and wrenches it from your weak grip. Devilsbane skittles across the flagstone floor, coming to rest in a corner far away from you.

You try to draw your belt knife, but Sabine is too quick and leaps at you. She flies through the air at a great height and comes down with her talons extended. All 12 of them pierce your neck and shoulders and almost separate your head from your body. You drop to the floor in a heap, dead and knowing no more. That is, however, until you awake looking down on the hideous scene of your death and your mangled mortal remains. Sabine looks at your immortal soul and says,

"You are mine for eternity now, my brave knight. I may not have been able to torment you as I had hoped in life. You deprived me of that, as a living soul is such a delicacy. I will make you suffer for that. You will stay as my consort forever, or my pet, or until I get bored of you and turn you over to my servants. You will spend all of time in my servitude, suffering agony or ecstasy as I decide to bestow on you. Welcome to Hell, Ulrac De-Villiers. You will not be leaving."

Your mission has failed and you are doomed to an eternity of torment in Hell.

Turn to **616**

565

You emerge into a very small clearing - although it is not exactly clear. The corpse trees here seem taller and thicker and reach up many yards into whatever sky there is here. They then converge so that they blot out almost any light. Keen to get out of this place, you quickly choose an exit.

You can either go left, and turn to **278**, or go straight on, and turn to **92**

566

Turning away from the charred remains and looking at the figure before you, you decide to take a risk and trust this other apparent mortal, announcing,

"I am Kommandant Ulrac De-Villiers."

You also give a brief overview of how you were dragged alive into the Hellscape. The lanky figure nods, all along stroking his thin, wispy beard as he does so. When you stop talking, which does not take long as you deliver your adventure to date like a military report, he replies,

"No harm done, my boy. It is best to assume most will mean you ill will in this sorry realm. Hmmm. Yes, a mortal trapped in the Hellscape would find the only way to leave would be to make their way to the Final Circle. That will be quite a journey to survive, and one worthy of an epic tale."

You ask him who he is.

"Ah, a pertinent question, my boy. I am Professor Erlic Hancox. I, like you, am a mortal trapped here."

You ask how long he has been here and he replies,

"Time is hard to figure in this world, where night is like day and vice versa. An age may pass in the mortal land, and it may only be a few moments here. Or millennia may pass here, but be only a day in the realms of the living. Time is not a... constant. It fluctuates. You see..."

It is then that he launches into a long, rambling discourse on his theory of time in the Hellscape. You listen for as long as you can, but the theory is beyond your comprehension.

You hold up your hand, and Hancox stops and apologises.

"I am sorry, my boy. I do like the sound of my own voice and it's been so long since I had another sentient mortal to talk to. Daemons are not the best company one can keep"

Again you ask how long he has been here and Hancox says,

"I estimate that when I left our plane, it was 2502AN."

You gasp, as when you were sent on your mission, it was 1742AN, nearly 750 years before Hancox. You tell him, and he replies, shaking his head,

"Yes, my lad, as I said before, time is not consistent."

Turn to **631**

567

You carry on walking, shaken to your core by what you have seen. **TEST YOUR FAITH**. Roll 2d6. If this is greater than your **FAITH** score, then what you have seen has made you doubt your **FAITH** in God. Lose 1 **FAITH** Point. If you roll less than or equal to your **FAITH** score, you resolve that this is just a trick of the mind. Turn to **343**

568

Your walk seems endless across this barren, grey landscape. You are starting to feel tired, and so you decide to stop and try to get some rest. You feel like you have been walking for days upon days, but it could just be an hour. Time is impossible to judge in this realm if, in fact, time even exists here. There is nowhere to shelter, so you just stop at the spot where you are and sit on the ground.

You must eat now, or throw 1d4 and lose that amount of **ENDURANCE**.

After eating, will you rest and try to sleep? If so, turn to **155**. If you decide to continue on your endless walk, turn to **505**

569

"My Lord" you ask *"I am but a poor mortal trying to find my way home. If you can aide me, then it would be sorely appreciated."*

The handsome youth stares at you in shock, and then smiles a broad, full smile, free of sarcasm and in genuine humour.

"Ah, thou are a rare mortal. We are tempted to keep you here as a plaything. But no, a deal is a deal, even more so here. We can offer you one boon of three. Whilst though have mastery over snakes? Or the ability not to be perceived? Or maybe take this as a token."

He holds out his hand, palm up, and then a plain silver ring appears, seemingly from nowhere. If you decide to choose mastery over snakes, write "**CHARMER**" on your **ADVENTURE SHEET**, along with the number **378**. If you choose the ability not to be perceived, write "**HIDDEN**" on your **SHEET**, along with the number **532**. When you want to use either of these in the future, turn to the reference indicated, and then back to the reference you are on.

If you choose the ring, place it on your finger, and turn immediately to **406**. Bowing to your host, you head towards the portal and walk through it. Turn to **571**

570

You struggle to your feet in considerable pain. You run for the nearest exit, completely forgetting that you have left both your sword and shield behind. Lose 2 **FIGHTING SKILL** for no longer having them, and 1 **FAITH** point for losing your enchanted sword. You leave the building as quickly as you can.

Turn to **597**

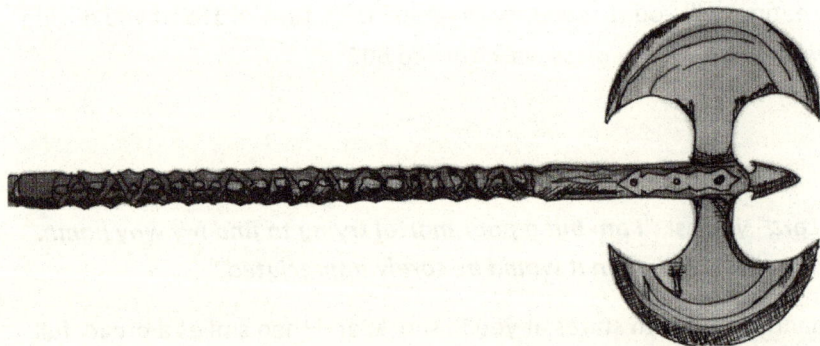

571

Write the word **ASTAROTH** on your **ADVENTURE SHEET**. Now turn to **438**

572

You realise with horror that where the wound is, something is growing. Out of the gash comes what at first seems to be a tentacle. Then the tentacle starts to widen, and at the end, a slit appears. The girth of the protrusion expands quickly, and as it does, so does the slit. Soon the new growth is the same giant width as the main body of the wyrm, the slit opening up wide to reveal rows of needle-sharp teeth. The beast has grown a second head.

Realising that attacks to the head are foolish, you must now try to strike either at the main body (turn to **632**), or the tail (turn to **430**)

573

You recall from your teaching that the 10th Circle of the Hellscape is for those whose arrogance and egotism are their main sin. You cannot remember much else, except that you must keep your enemy close. Deciding that waiting is not an option, you head through the shimmering portal.

Turn to **285**

574

Each hit on the tail seems to distress the beast more than you would have thought possible. Your blade slices into the thinner layers of fat where the thick body tapers down. First, one strike cuts open a gash in the tail, about 6 feet from the end, and the wyrm rears in pain. Your second strike is aimed at the same spot, and as the flesh parts more, you see what appears to be a large, white nerve ganglion. You hope that organ is something akin to its brain, and you resolve on your third hit to thrust your steel into it. The blade slides in, and the beast rears once again, but even higher until almost all of its huge body is off the ground, except for the 6-foot tail section. The creature starts to thrash around, convulses once, and then drops lifeless to the ground.

TEST YOUR AGILITY. If you succeed, turn to **388**. If you fail, turn to **445**

575

"Is this truly your wish, my master?"

If you want to continue, turn to **159**. If not, turn to the previous reference and decide on another option.

576

You walk forward and push both of the swinging doors open before walking through. Before you is a room full of naked or half-naked men and women (and more disturbingly, some children). The room is full of seemingly plush furniture; settees upholstered in rich velvets.

Chaise Longue's covered in the softest leather from the finest cattle. Large iron bedsteads with thick, plumb mattresses stuffed with eider. But what's happening on the furniture is far from comfortable. All human forms are here. Fat, thin. Tall, short. Beautiful, ugly. Old, young. The one thing in common is the look of pain on their faces, and the torment in their eyes as the Daemons perform acts of such brutality on them that it draws all the colour out of your face and makes you stop-still.

Limbs intertwine so that it's hard to see where one body starts and another ends, blood and worse pouring from claw marks and bites to their battered immortal bodies. Cries and groans of agony (or ecstasy) come from the mouths of the once-abusers turned abused. You fancy that you recognise some of those before you, and know from what they did in life they deserve this torment, but it is still hard to stomach such suffering.

You weren't prepared for this, and so **TEST YOUR FAITH.** IF you roll less than or equal to your current **FAITH** score, you are lucky and keep your resolve. If you roll higher, the shock erodes your Faith in your Saviour, and so lose 1 **FAITH** point.

Turn to **372**

577

Glad to leave the forest behind, you can rest here for a moment to recover some **ENDURANCE**. The temperature is noticeably colder, and your body slowly cools accordingly. Gain 1 **ENDURANCE**. If you eat or drink anything, you can also add those **ENDURANCE** points. After resting for a few moments, you stand and head off towards the cliff face. It's not a long journey, and you soon arrive at the foot of it. The exit is a good 200 yards up the sheer cliff face. The stair up, if it can be called that, is hewn out of the rock. Instead of going straight up, it zig-zags up the cliff face, with each step protruding out of the face so that to climb it you will always be facing sideways, and then have to turn to face the other way several times.

Hampered as you are with arms and armour, you must lose 2 **AGILITY** points whilst climbing this stair. If you no longer have your sword and shield, you will lose only 1 **AGILITY** point - as your heavy armour still weighs you down. You spend time studying the route. It appears the stair first heads left, then after about 40 yards, zig-zags right. This happens in reverse after another 40 yards, and in total there are 4 changes in direction. What's even worse is that as well as changing direction, there is also a gap between each set of stairs.

The gap seems to vary in distance, although it is hard to tell from your perspective. So each switchback is going to take strength and agility. When you reach the top, your ordeal will not be over, as the stair stops and there is a leap up to reach the step of the doorway. It will take great strength and grip to pull yourself up.

Turn to **411**

578

Sabine hisses as she backs up, fear showing on her face. She is no longer beautiful, as her face is twisted with hate and her mouth has expanded, showing an expanse of fang-like teeth that seem to have grown longer and sharper. You stalk forward with Devilsbane before you. As you move towards her, her hands (one blackened by the touch of silver) raise up, and her fingernails seem to grow, until they are more than a foot long, and more like talons.

SABINE has FS 10, EN 14

{ADVANCED - Initial AS: 19, Initial DA: 18; FIT 9, AG 9, ST 10}

If you reduce her **ENDURANCE** to 2 or less, turn to **602**. If you lose, turn to **564**

579

Forging straight ahead, you walk down a winding path with corpse trees all around you. They seem to lean in toward you and try to grab hold, forcing you to dodge out of the way. The passage is warm beyond belief, and you are sweating heavily by the time you see a clearing ahead of you. Quickening your pace, eager to get out of this claustrophobic passage, you come out into a circular grassy hillock. You rush to the top in the hope that it is cooler.

You take time to rest and can regain 1 **ENDURANCE** point. After resting, you can now choose to go left and turn to **588**, carry on straight and turn to **295**, or veer off right, and turn to **595**

580

"Help? Help? Help? You ask for help when I unified the Church in the One True Gods name, and what reward do I get for my service? Eternal torment in this foul place. No I will not help. What do I care if the world falls now when my God has forsaken me? My Lord Baalberith"

he shouts up to the immense figure on the throne

"We have a Papist in our midst, a mortal soul who works for the One True God, against the Hellscapes wishes. What shall we do with him?"

The Daemon stares down at you, and then as quick as a flash, Baalberith leaps from his throne some way about, swinging his mighty sword above his head. He lands in front of you, and as he does so, his sword swings down with such power that it cuts through your armour and cleaves you in two from neck to groin. Your mortal body falls to the ground, one part to the left, and the other to the right. Blood and guts and worse cover the floor.

"HAH" says the Daemon Lord *"A PAPIST? YOU SEEK TO INSULT ME AND SNEAK INTO MY CHAMBER? I AM BAALBERRITH, HERALD OF THE KING OF HELL, AND WILL NOT BE FOOLED BY A MORTAL WORM. BUT NOW, I HAVE A NEW SERVANT"*

he continues, looking at your spirit form which stands over your mortal remains.

His taloned hand reaches out and grabs you, pain shooting through your ethereal form.

"COME, WORM, YOU WILL JOIN MY LEGIONS OF QUEENS AND EMPERORS AND SERVE ME NOW, FOR ALL TIME".

He throws you across the ground and towards the bottom of the steps. He then returns to his throne, pointing and gesturing for you to bring him a side of rotten beef. You hoist the stinking carcass on your shoulders, and start the long climb up to the throne, for the first time. You will be fated to continue this climb for all eternity. Your mission has failed, and the world will surely fall.

Turn to **616**

581

Ahead of you is a forest, but not of trees. Instead, they are elongated human forms, naked and rooted into the earth, growing up towards the endless sky. Their arms and legs are massively elongated, and their faces are drawn and stretched. Each one has its mouth open and wails constantly. Their eyes follow you as you move, with hatred in their glance for a being who can still move freely. You pass into the start of the forest, and these human trees tower over and lean in towards you. Unnerved, you continue into this forest of despair as no other route is available to you.

Do you have a map? If you do turn to **246**. If you do not, **TEST YOUR INTELLIGENCE**. If you succeed, turn to **163**. If you fail, turn to **184**

582

The Thin Daemon is proving to be a tough and skilful advisory, and you are unable to dispatch him before the Ape reaches you. Now they have you cornered, one on either side. You raise your sword to your face in a salute, a gesture as time-honoured as the battle between men. The Daemons just laugh and fall upon you. You manage to block the first blow from the Thin Daemon's talons, but the Ape Daemon is armed with a curved, serrated scimitar which screams through the air towards you.

You try to raise your sword but are too late, and the force of the impact shatters your arm, which falls useless to your side. The Thin Daemon takes quick advantage and starts to lacerate your body with his wickedly sharp talons, producing sprays of blood. Then the Ape Daemon finishes it all with an almost casual backhand swipe with his blade, which sends your head bouncing until it is met and swallowed by a Gorger Wyrm which has just emerged from the human plains. Your mission has failed, and humanity will not survive the year.

Turn to **616**

583

Curiosity gets the better of you, and you sneak into the building to get a closer look. It's only a small building, and so you will have to move carefully and be lucky to avoid being seen.

TEST YOUR AGILITY AND FORTUNE. Add them both together and then roll 4d6. If you roll less than or equal to your combined score, turn to **502**. If you roll higher, turn to **103**

Try as you might, you cannot get a foothold on the surface as it starts to dissipate beneath your feet. You drop to the ground and try to grab onto the strange insubstantial surface, but your hand cannot sustain a grip. It's like trying to hold onto a cloud as your hand just seems to close around nothing. Slowly you are dragged towards the nothingness beneath the surface, even though you can feel no force playing on you. No earth-force, no pushing and no pulling. You just seem to be moving towards this yawning gap.

Eventually, maybe minutes but maybe hours later, you slip through the ground into the grey void beneath. You think you are falling, but you have no physical sensation to substantiate this. And so there you remain, in the grey void beneath this terrible world, without means to move or escape. You are doomed to remain in this space, forever falling (or not) for all eternity. Your mission has failed.

Turn to **616**

"Hey, you there," you say to a passing grey form.

The figure turns, and you recognise, with shock, Most Holy Aceada, who was the Pontiff of the One True Church over a millennia ago. He was the pontiff who first unified the church, using his Sorcerer Crusaders to put to the sword and fire tens of thousands of those who objected to a unified church. Statues and portraits of him adorn the Holy City. He is seen as being one of the great leaders of the Church, maybe the greatest; yet here he is, serving a Daemon Lord in the Hellscape. Shock registers on your face.

He scowls at you, and says *"What do you want mortal?"*

Do you ask him to help you as a servant of the One True God? If you do, turn to **21**. If you do not trust him to help, turn to **87**

586

Finally, you reach the top of the stair, to the doorway in the dome that's fully 100 yards from the floor of the bizarre building. You take hold of the handle and slowly open the copper door by a few inches. Inside, you see a copper corridor leading to another door at the end. You see no risk and so decide to enter the corridor and start along it.

Before you do, **TEST YOUR INTELLIGENCE**. If you succeed, turn to **135**. If you fail, turn to **25**

587

You manage, by a combination of luck and skill, to bat away these gnawing menaces, and head back through the door and slam it shut.

Roll 1d6 and this is how much **ENDURANCE** you have lost. Now turn to **209** and choose again.

588

As you exit the path, you come into a larger clearing that is more open, and the heat is less oppressive. The corpse trees are thinner and more spread out, and light filters down from whatever source of illumination there is in this gross realm.

Dominating the centre of the clearing is a large obsidian obelisk that towers up past the tree line. You walk up and examine the obelisk. It is four-sided, and each side faces one of the four routes from the clearing, including the one you have just entered by. On each side is a sigil. You ignore the side you came in by and look at the other three. You can choose:

  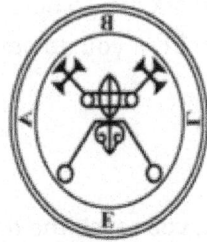

| Go left, turn to 177 | Go straight on, turn to 291 | Go right, turn to 653 |

589

Fortunately, you are able to throw your forearms up and onto the step to catch yourself. You haul yourself onto the step, standing up to continue. You are nearly to the top when you get to the final step.

TEST YOUR AGILITY for the final time. If you pass, turn to **586**. If you fail, turn to **4**

590

Due to the heat, you continue to weaken, and you lose 1 **ENDURANCE** point as you make your way through the foul trees. You soon emerge into a clearing that's rich with grass, so unlike the rest of this forest of the damned.

You notice that all around you poking up through the grass are mushrooms. They are tall, with broad heads mottled with red and white. If you are in need of food, you can try to eat some of the mushrooms. If you want to, note down this reference and then turn to **444**.

After trying the mushrooms, or if you didn't try them, you exit the clearing either by going straight, turn to **241**, or you can go the right way and turn to **497**

591

Though you have always been a man who focused on the teachings of the One True God, you fail to recollect the lectures you were given on the structure of the Hellscape in your seminary years.

If you could just recall the different parts of the Hellscape, it may give you an advantage. However, try as you might, you cannot.

Turn to **215**

592

You try to head back up the tunnel before the beast sees you, but you hear a roar from behind. You turn and see that the sub-daemon has spotted you and is running up the tunnel to attack. To fight this behemoth seems to be a reckless task and so you decide to run, but the sub-daemon runs after you. Its legs are twice the length of yours, and so it covers the ground in giant strides, but you can move your legs faster. Add up your current **AGILITY**, **ENDURANCE** and **FITNESS**. This is your **SPEED**.

Now do the same for the sub-daemon.

SUB-DAEMON has AG 7, EN 30, FIT 78

Now roll 2d6 for yourself and the sub-daemon. If your combined score is higher than the sub-daemon's, then you are faster and stay ahead of it. If you can beat it five times in a row, then you outrun it and are free, and you leave the dome but have no option but to head back towards the crossroads - in case the sub-daemon alerts anything else.

Turn to **483**. If you lose one of those rolls, turn to **91**

593

You arrive into a grassless mud clearing. You can leave this place either by bearing left and turn to **157**, or go right and turn to **153**

594

You stumble into another clearing. On the right, there is a route out, and you can take this and turn to **506**. Otherwise, continue straight on and turn to **472**

595

As you exit the path, you come into a larger clearing that is more open, and the heat is less oppressive. The corpse trees are thinner and more spread out, and light filters down from whatever source of illumination there is in this gross realm.

Dominating the centre of the clearing is a large obsidian obelisk that towers up past the tree line. You walk up and examine the obelisk. It is four-sided, and each side faces one of the four routes from the clearing, including the one you have just entered by. On each side is a sigil. You ignore the side you came in by and look at the other three. You can choose:

Go left, turn to **513**	Go straight on, turn to **458**	Go right, turn to **41**

596

The figure is too busy with his work to notice you. You can now either attack the figure and turn to **348** or leave the room and turn to **405**

597

You leave the factory type building. Do you want to check the larger domed building, then turn to **193**; or go and enter the smaller domed building, turn to **122**. If you decide to do neither, you can return down the path away from the building complex, and back to the fork in the road where you first entered this realm. You take the right-hand fork this time. Turn to **483**

598

The huge wyrm tosses you in the air like a rag doll, but you are able to twist and turn and fall away from the creature's mouth. You land face-down with a thud, and the impact drives the breath out of your body. You gasp, inadvertently taking in a mouthful of a human lung that your face is pressing against. You spit the foul meat out.

Throw 1d6 - and lose this as **ENDURANCE**. If you still have Devilsbane, turn to **147**. If you have lost it, turn to **137**

599

Your heart breaks with the suffering of these poor souls, no matter what they have done in life. You try to break the side of the ice bath so that you can pull them clear. As you struggle, several imps notice and shout to a sub-daemon.

It strides over and picks you up as easily as it would a child. The imps chatter at it and the beast strips away your armour, plucking the pieces off as you would petals from a flower. Then it strips you of your undergarments until you are naked. The imps continue to pull at it and point, and the sub-daemon then lifts your naked body and places it in the ice bath.

Your teeth chatter, and you shiver violently as the cold hits you. Then the sub-daemon, under instruction from the imps, reaches up and grabs a tube hanging down that does not have a host. The glass seems flexible as the sub-daemon pulls it towards your face. You try to clamp your mouth shut, aware of what it is trying to do, but the creature easily levers open your mouth.

It rams the tube into your mouth, and the sharp glass cuts through your tongue and rips the lining from your throat. You try to scream, but you cannot as your mouth is stretched open, filled with the cold glass. You feel your lips start to rip under pressure, but that's nothing compared to the impact the sharp rod makes on your guts, cutting through them until the glass shears through the back of your body and exits.

Warm liquid, just cooled, starts to flow into your now dead body, dripping out below to be caught and bottled. Your soul is now part of this giant ice bath for eternity. Your mission has failed, and humanity will soon be under the cruel yoke of Daemonkind.

Turn to **616**

600

The stoppered bottle is in your bag, and you reach in quickly to remove it. The glass stopper is tight but comes off with a slight complaint. Not knowing the effect this will have on you, you raise the bottle to your lips and take a good swig. It seems to both burn and freeze your throat as you swallow the viscous fluid. Then miraculously, you stop choking on the toxic fumes. The Deamon's-wine seems to counteract them entirely.

Gain 1 **FAITH** point as you believe the help must be divine. You carry on up the corridor back to the main landing.

Turn to **48**

601

Despite trying your best to catch yourself on the step with your fingertips, you are not able to hold on. You fall to the ground, fully 20 yards below and land on your back. The breath is forced out of your lungs, and you feel a sharp pain in your side. Lose 4 **ENDURANCE** points.

You check over your body, realising that when you try to raise your arm that you get a stabbing pain in your side. You have cracked at least one rib. Reduce your **FIGHTING SKILL** and **STRENGTH** both by 1 for the remainder of your time in this realm whilst your injury heals.

Now turn to **487**

602

Visibly weakened, Sabine backs into a corner of the room, near another doorway, cowering as fear fills her face. Her eyes dart back and forth from you to your sword. You advance and prepare to deliver a "coup de grace". As you prepare to swing, she hisses,

"You think you can defeat me so easily. Think again brave Knight, but it's hard to kill what does not live"

Then with a cackle, she begins to stretch while becoming almost transparent, until her physical form breaks up into smoke, which streams towards the gap under the doorway. The laugh echoes through the room, as the non-corporeal form of Sabine makes good her escape.

You can either try to catch her and finish her off by going through the door, turn to **48**, or leave the room and this dreadful house of pain, turn to **421**

603

There is a lot of noise coming from the building. Inhuman voices laughing and shouting, mixed with humans screaming and wailing. You consider your options and decide against entering the building - as this would undoubtedly lead to conflict. You are not scared of a fight, but realise you will have to pick them carefully in a world where you have no allies, and potentially millions upon millions of enemies.

Turn to **480**

604

The endless maze of trees continues, and you chance upon another glade. The heat continues to take its toll. Lose 1 **ENDURANCE** point.

Ahead of you is another path. To choose this turn to **547**. Alternatively, go right and turn to **628**

605

The snake rears up and strikes with lightning speed. The venom from the bite is in your blood, and each round you lose 1 **FIGHTING SKILL** as it takes effect and makes you increasingly disorientated and dizzy. In addition, if the snake successfully attacks you, lose an extra **FIGHTING SKILL** as well as the normal **ENDURANCE** damage - as its strike injects even more venom.

ASTAROTH'S FAMILIAR has **FS 8, EN 6**

{FOR ADVANCED COMBAT ST 8, FIT 7, AG 7}

If you beat the snake, turn to **165**. If you fail, turn to **499**

606

Carefully you walk up to the stout door, which appears to be made out of oak, although it's hard to tell in this unreal place. You try it, and it creaks open. You slip through the door and swiftly and silently close it before turning around, but as you do, you hear a noise like a taught wire snapping.

TEST YOUR FORTUNE. If you are fortunate, turn to **410**. If you are not, turn to **527**

607

You approach the door. Inscribed on it is the face of a Daemon who is the Lord of this Castle. If you know his name, convert it to numbers and turn to the sum of these numbers.

If not, then turn to **216**

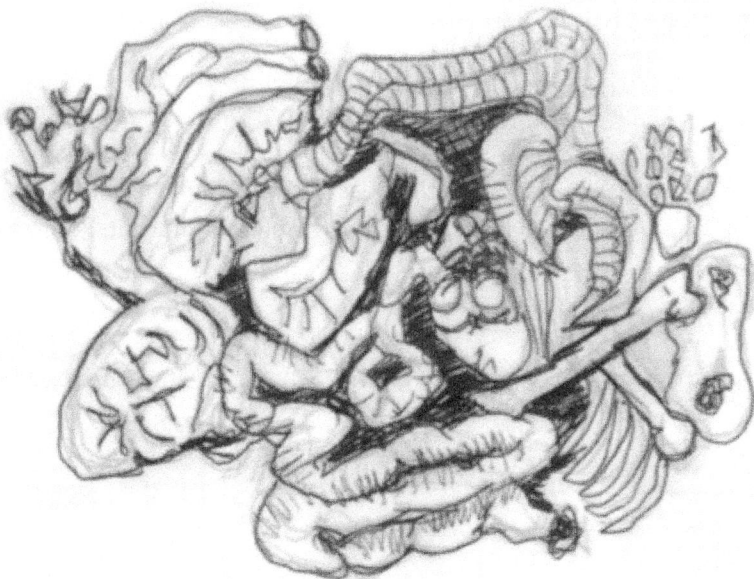

608

It gets harder and harder to walk. You can hardly breathe, and the lack of air saps the strength from your muscles. Each step is agony as you try to make your way up the corridor. You start to cough, with blood-stained spittle spraying with each retch. You cough harder, resulting in a torrent of blood spurting from your mouth uncontrollably. You mistakenly try to gulp in air, but the toxic gas makes things worse. Your throat is on fire, and you drop to your knees and then all fours, your back arching as you continue to cough, blood now flowing from your mouth in a deluge. Your lungs are burning as you are deprived of fresh air, and your vision starts to swim with increased dizziness. The strength leaves your arms, and you collapse forward into the dirt of the tunnel floor, your face jammed into the mixture of stone and earth. Your eyes flutter and then close, your breathing becoming increasingly shallow which forces you to involuntarily inhale mud from the floor. Then your breathing stops, and you topple over onto your side, your eyes now open and staring unseeingly at the roof.

Your mission has failed. Turn to **616**

609

You plunge your weapon deep into the beast's body. You panic as the blade catches in its blubbery flesh and you struggle to remove it. You are pressed against the stinking body of the beast, and if you cannot retrieve your weapon, you are doomed.

TEST YOUR STRENGTH. If you succeed, turn to **489**. If you fail, turn to **124**

610

You decide to ignore the buildings on either side and try to get through this realm as quick as you can. You walk onwards for what seems like hours until you reach what appears to be the end of the road. At either side is a building. You can either try to go into the left building, if so turn to **273**, or you can head for the structure on your right, turn to **283**

611

The room is obviously a dead end with no exit. You decide to leave the room and continue your search for a way out. You turn around and start to walk back up the tunnel. However, as you walk, the incline seems to get steeper and steeper, to the point where you almost have to use your hands as well as legs to move upwards. The walk down was in no way this steep.

The atmosphere continues to get hotter and hotter, despite you moving upwards. The air gets more acrid and burns your face and throat as you gasp for air. You start to breathe in rapid shallow breaths, the air being like fire in your throat and burning your lungs. You realise that your human body is dying.

If you have a blue potion you think may help, write down the reference **312** and turn to **647**. If not, turn to **608**

After all the time alone in this strange land, you are not feeling predisposed to trust, and so you draw Devilsbane and walk purposefully towards the shapes. As you get closer you can see they are roughly humanoid forms, but all in grey with cowls over their faces. Their grey robes are tattered and threadbare, trailing almost to the ground. They do not seem to have legs and feet, and instead appear to float across the grey surface. At present, there are about 10 of them, but each moment more appear in view. You point your sword at them and shout,

"In the name of the One True God, desist and tell me who you are! This I order you!"

You hear what seems to be the sound of wind rustling, although there is not even a touch of a breeze, and then you realise that it is laughter from these creatures. Then one, the closest to you, reaches out a long arm. An emancipated hand is at the end of the limb, pointing at you with one extremely long, almost claw-like, finger.

"You dare to order us? You dare to say that name here? That name deserted us, ignored us and left us here to suffer for all eternity. Now we can get at least a modicum of revenge"

There are about 50 of the floating souls now, and as one they reach up and throw their cowls back. In horror, you recognise a lot of the faces. They are the men of your small force that you were leading to destroy the Hellscape machine. But their faces are old and haggard and drawn, as if they are millennia-old corpses; not freshly dead.

"How can this be? You are my men. I fought with you but a day or so ago - and led you in a holy battle. How can you be here? There hasn't been the time".

Once more, the lead figure, who you now recognise as Hatton, one of your sergeants, laughs.

"Time, what is time to the dead. It has been 10,000 years since that day, and we have been here all that time, suffering in this limbo and yet you still live. This cannot be. This will not be"

Then your ghoulish men and comrades all reach out towards you. You flail with Devilsbane but to no avail, as it has no power in this empty realm. The hands reach out and touch you - or more like they reach into you, and with that, your sanity breaks and you start screaming. You are left to roam this world, alive but insane, in a world of the dead for all eternity.

Your mission has failed.

Turn to **616**

613

In your haste to escape, you have gone down the ladder some way from where you left Devilsbane and your shield. You can hear the angry noises of Daemons and imps climbing down ladders to intercept you once more, and you realise you will have to leave your sword and shield behind if you want to stand any chance of escape.

Make sure you permanently reduce your **FIGHTING SKILL** by 2 and lose 1 **FAITH** point for losing your holy blade. You feel regret, but you turn and leave, wishing you had never climbed up to investigate the vats.

Turn to **597**

Your mind seems to have fallen asleep, but all of a sudden, you jerk yourself back awake. You feel like you have awoken from a dream. You stay stock-still so that the woman, no the creature, before you does not know that your mind is once again alert. You recognise her as a Succubus, a Daemon who preys on men and feeds off sex. The eyes of the Succubus hypnotise their prey so that they are helpless, and the touch of their talons injects a potion into their victim that removes their willpower and makes them pliant. Once the victim is as helpless as a baby, then the Succubus feeds.

You leap into action, realising that not just your life but your eternal soul is at risk. You jump back and unsheathe Devilsbane, readying yourself to fight the creature in front of you. Sabine, the ruler of this evil house, hisses as she backs up, fear showing on her face. She is no longer beautiful, as her face is twisted with hate and her mouth has expanded, showing an expanse of fang-like teeth that seem to have grown longer and sharper.

You stalk forward with Devilsbane before you. As you move towards her, her hands (one blackened by the touch of silver) raise up, and her fingernails seem to grow, until they are more than a foot long; more like talons.

SABINE has **FS 10, EN 14**

{ADVANCED - Initial AS: 19, Initial DA: 18; FIT 9, AG 9, ST 10}

If you reduce her **ENDURANCE** to 2 or less, turn to **450**. If you lose, turn to **488**

615

Faithless, you drop to your knees. Your **FAITH** has been the cornerstone of your life, and losing it cripples you, physically and emotionally. Having lost all **FAITH** in the One True God, and the One True Church, you curse them under your breath. Tears stream from your eyes as you realise the lie you have been serving for all your life.

All the terrible things you have done for the Faith flash across your mind. The screams of children echo in your mind, from when you have put whole towns to sword and fire for being ungodly. The charnel scenes of bodies and mutilated corpses from when you have carried out the Faith's work. The endless bloody conquest and conflict all over the 12 continents, where you have made the soil red, green and yellow with blood. The executions of those seen as unholy by being hanged, drawn and quartered, for which you keenly participated as you felt you were freeing their souls from their ungodly bodies. The years of abstinence, where you have forbidden yourself love for anyone, except the church. You realise it was all a lie.

You stay there on the ground, rocking backwards and forwards and sobbing. In between the flow of tears, you strip off your armour and cast it aside. Soon you sit in nothing but a soiled loincloth. You reach for your sword belt, discarded on the floor next to you, with a trembling hand.

You draw Devilsbane for the final time and reverse the blade. The sword is so long your hands cannot reach the hilt as it points away from you. Instead, you wrap both your bare hands around its razor-sharp blade. The steel cuts into your hand and rivulets of blood pour to the ground. You ignore them. You place the point of Devilsbane at your naval, and remember the countless souls you have sent to everlasting torment on the end of this great blade. Then you take one final breath and pull the sword toward you.

It effortlessly enters your body and, leaning while using your legs, you propel yourself forward. The pommel strikes the ground with your bodyweight behind it, and the long blade slides further into your flesh. You slide down the blade until you are caught on the crossguard.

Blood flows freely as your life drains away, and the tears continue to flow from your eyes. You die, alone, unloved and unmourned, far from home. If you ever truly had a home. But your spirit remains in the Hellscape, doomed to torment.

You have failed in your mission and humanity will suffer because of this. Turn to **616**

616

You were the only chance for the mortal realm. Despite the machine having been destroyed, the Monks of Bael rebuild their forces and re-double their efforts. But they are careful. Knowing that the One Church has tried to disrupt their plans, they move and take them underground, in the pits of Morarkia.

In these icy caverns hundreds of metres below the arctic surface of Ydrit, they rebuild the machine. A new crystal is made from the blood sacrifices of 6 times 6 times 6 of the Monks. The giant blood-red ruby is attached to the top of the machine in a vast crystal cavern. The machine starts to spin and hum, light from the crystal dancing and reflecting on the mirror-like walls of the cavern until it is almost blinding.

Soon a grey portal shimmers next to the crystal's tower. Tentatively at first, the first Daemon steps through the portal, and then bellows in triumph as it sees that they have managed to cross into the mortal realm. The ruby spins ever faster, and the portal expands as more and more Daemons follow. The first thing they do is fall upon the Monks maintaining the machine and rip them limb from limb to devour them. The monks do not cry out but open their arms to the Daemons, as if they are to receive a blessing.

Devout glee fills their eyes even as they are eviscerated and eaten. This is their reward as they are taken into the Hellscape to serve Bael. Soon the minor Daemons, the foot soldiers, are supplemented by the Dukes of the Hellscape. Mammon, Asmodeus and Beelzebub all stand watching as the cavern fills with bloodthirsty Daemons. The main cavern full, the Daemons move into other caves and start to build their army.

Bael delegates command of the forces to Belphegor, with 20 Dukes of Hell, 100 Captains, 2,000 greater Daemons and 8,000 lesser Daemons ready for war against the mortal world. They spread across the globe like a plague, and each death makes their army bigger, as even the just and true have their souls pulled into the Hellscape where they are brought back as lesser Daemons to fight their previous allies. They do not tire, they do not stop, and within a few short weeks, only a few bastions of humanity still stand against the inexorable tide of Hell's army. One of them is the Holy City of Amaldi, where Zacatecas herself leads the defence against the fell. However, that will soon fall, and the sky will be lit with fire, and the earth will be scorched from the flames of the Daemons' breath. The Daemons have taken the earth and soon will consign all mortal souls to their servitude. As soon as their empire on earth is established, they will then turn their thirst for conquest to their ultimate target, the heavenly Golden Citadel in the Silver City.

Your world, and eventually the worlds beyond that, will have a new ruler. And Bael is his name.

Your failure is complete.

617

As soon as the step makes contact with the floor, the circuit is complete. Immediately the air becomes charged, and you feel a tingling sensation followed by a massive surge of power. Sparks fly along the copper corridor before travelling up your metal studded boots, into your armour until your whole body convulses wildly. Although you are unaware, the same happens at the other end as lightning travels up the leg of the Daemon and his body starts to convulse. Sparks fly around both your bodies and the air is alive with electrical power.

Within seconds, the temperature inside your armour has risen up so high that every part of your body that touches metal starts to smoulder, blister and blacken. You can smell yourself being roasted alive, and can feel your hair vaporise where the lightning has leapt into the back of your helm. The skin of your face splits, and blood flows out, only to be congealed and dried quickly. Still, your body involuntarily convulses, shaking uncontrollably. Eventually, your armour starts to melt and your legs buckle, and you drop to the floor.

A few moments later, the Daemon at the other end of the corridor also succumbs to the power of the bottled lightning. But by now, your eyes have evaporated, your tongue flops and fries on the floor as you have bitten it off, and your brains are boiling in your skull. Your mortal remains continue to cook for some time, as your soul form watches.

You are doomed to remain in this land; not damned but stuck in the Hellscape forevermore. Your mission has failed, and your world will burn as your corporeal form has.

Turn to **616**

618

The endless maze of trees continues, and you chance upon another glade. The heat continues to take its toll. Lose 1 **ENDURANCE** point.

You can either leave by heading left and turn to **628**, or go straight on and turn to **359**

619

"Is this truly your wish, my master?" If you want to continue, turn to **159**. If not, turn to the previous reference and decide on another option.

620

As you edge around the kitchen, one of the imps thinks he hears something and turns your way. You duck with lightning speed behind a large cauldron. The imp sees nothing and returns to his grisly task.

As you stand, your sword scabbard swings unexpectedly and catches a shelf of metal trays which spill to the floor with a crash. You try to duck back down, but it's too late. They are all watching you. A collective hiss rises from their lips, and they seem to fly through the air to attack you.

Roll 1d10+2, as this is the number of imps you will have to fight- but you must beat them all.

Each **IMP** is **FS 4, EN 3**

{ADVANCED - Initial AS: 9, Initial DA: 13; AG 8, FIT 5, ST 1}

If you succeed, turn to **544**. If you fail, turn to **334**

621

Ignoring all the ragged monarchs, you push past them to the base of the steps and salute, sword in front of your face. You shout up to the Daemon,

"Oh mighty Lord. I seek thy aide. I am a wanderer lost in your domain, can you aide me to leave?"

The Daemon stops, his large gnarled fist still grasping the faded and tattered silk robe of the ancient King of Perneilsia, and looks down at you with disbelief and contempt.

"WHO DARES, WHO DARES INTERUPT BAALBERITH WHILST HE HOLDS COURT?"

If you want to tell him your name, then turn to **69**. If you would rather bluff, turn to **71**

622

You feel panic starting to catch hold of you. Your heart races, your thoughts become blurred, and you start to breathe quickly and shallow. You are on the edge of losing your mind. You try to relax and breathe normally, praying to the One, and slowly you get some semblance of calm. However, this has frightened you more than any battle you have been in and shaken the foundations of your beliefs to their core.

Lose 1 **FAITH** point. Turn to **424**

623

You decide to take a risk and trust this other apparent mortal, announcing,

"I am Kommandant Ulrac De-Villiers", following with a brief overview of how you were dragged alive into the Hellscape.

The lanky figure nods along stroking his thin wispy beard as he does so. When you stop talking, which doesn't take long as you deliver your adventure to date like a military report, he replies,

"Hmmm. For a mortal trapped in the Hellscape the only way to leave would be to make your way to the final circle. That will be quite a journey to survive, one worthy of an epic tale".

You ask him who he is

"Ah, a pertinent question, my boy. I am Professor Erlic Hancox. I, like you, am a mortal trapped here."

You ask how long and he replies

"Time is hard to figure in this world, where night is like day and day is like night. An age may pass in the mortal land, and it may only be a few moments here. Or millennia may pass here, but be only a day in the living realms. Time is not......constant. It fluctuates. You see......"

And then he launches into a long rambling discourse on his theory of time in the Hellscape. You listen for as long as you can, but the theory is beyond your comprehension.

You hold up your hand, and Hancox stops and apologises.

"I am sorry, my boy, I do like the sound of my own voice and it's so long since I had another sentient mortal to talk to. Daemons are not the best conversationalists one can find".

Again you ask how long he has been there and Hancox says,

"I estimate that when I left our plane, it was 2502AN."

You gasp, as the date of your mission was 1742AN, nearly 750 years before Hancox. You tell him, and he replies, shaking his head,

"Yes, my lad, as I said, time is not consistent"

Turn to **631**

624

The stoppered bottle is in your bag, so you reach in quickly and remove it. The glass stopper is tight but comes off with a slight complaint. Not knowing the effect this will have on you, you raise the bottle to your lips and take a good swig. It seems to both burn and freeze your throat as you swallow the viscous fluid.

Then miraculously, you stop choking on the toxic fumes. The Deamon's-wine seems to counteract them as you breathe them in. Gain 1 **FAITH** point as you believe the help must be divine. You carry on up the steps into the main courtyard.

Turn to **454** and chose another option.

625

You carefully lower the bottle and partially submerge it in the thick red liquid. It gloops into the bottle quickly, filling it, but just before you remove it, the sphincter overhead opens and gushes a torrent of liquid into the pool. This splashes into the surface forcing the ripple of liquid to surge over your naked hand. It burns into your skin, blistering it and causing you to cry out in pain. The bottle slips from your grasp and sinks to the bottom of the pool.

You nurse your hand and try to strip the remaining liquid from it as quick as possible.

TEST YOUR FORTUNE AGAIN. If you are lucky, turn to **338**. If you are unlucky, turn to **236**

626

Baalberith stops stock-still and mutters almost to himself,

"HMM, HE KNOWS HIM. I MUST TREAD CAREFULLY."

He looks back up at you and says *"WELL MY BOY, I DO KNOW YOUR LORD AND WILL HELP YOU ALL I CAN, IN HONOUR OF HIS NAME. WHAT DO YOU ASK?"*

Turn to **434**

627

As you trudge along, you start to feel weak, and your concentration fades for a moment. This could be fatal, as all of a sudden you are cast up in the air by a giant gorger wyrm.

TEST YOUR FORTUNE. If you are fortunate, turn to **598**. If you are not so, turn to **644**

628

You stumble into another clearing. On the left, there is a route out, and you can take this and turn to **70**. Otherwise, take the right path and turn to **472**

629

The hall is immense, not due to its height, but because it is fully 200 foot on its longest sides. It is built of a red brick that seems to gleam like freshly spilt blood in the ruddy light. You walk around and try to see if there is anything as commonplace as a window - so that you can spy what's inside. The walls are too thick for you to hear what's happening. You reach the rear of the building, and next to one of the 20 foot wide chimneys is a small door.

If you choose to enter the building via this door, then turn to **439**. If you would rather enter via the front door, turn to **492**. Alternatively, you can ignore the building, and head on across the plain, turn to **603**

630

"So you are the mortal who is wreaking havoc in our realm? We have heard of you and your antics. What shall we do with you, then, now that you are within our grasp?"

The youthful face looks at you inquiringly, his lips turned up in a sardonic half-smile. You open your mouth to answer, but he raises his hand, and the words die in your throat.

"Hush, mortal, thou doth not need to respond. We shall decide your fate. Let us think."

He wrinkles his brow in mock thought and then exclaims

"We have it. Thou shalt face a test, and if you pass this test you may leave, but if you doth fail, thou shall become a plaything for our mount"

He reaches up and scratches behind the ear of the giant dragon, and a rumbling noise comes from the beast's throat - almost like a cat purring.

"Now" he continues *"to determine the manner of thy test, thou must take one of our hands, and whichever you choose shall determine the challenge".*

Then he holds out both of his hands, open, palms up. Both are empty. Will you choose the left hand and turn to **364**, or the right hand and turn to **62**

631

The man seems likeable, affable and genuinely pleased to talk with you, and so you decide to see if you can help each other. You say that if he can offer any help to escape this realm, then you will try to take him with you.

Hancox smiles sadly and replies,

"Would that you could help me, my fine fellow, but I am afraid I am rather stuck here".

Then he gestures to his right ankle. Looped around it is a thin line of shimmering fire, which then extends like a fine rope to a tether point.

"Astaroth himself placed this ward on me" he explains *"forever tying me to this room. It is a powerful magik that my science cannot break"*.

Do you still have Devilsbane? If you do, turn to **39**. If you do not, turn to **96**

632

Each head of the beast now has an attack round and will do damage. If you manage to strike the beast's body, turn to **609**

633

The path leads out into a clearing where in the centre is a large pool, filled with clear blue water. If you want to refill your flask with the clear water, then remember this reference and turn to **20**. If you decide not to, or already have tried the water, then you must leave either by going left, turn to **635**, or straight on, and turn to **652**

634

Giving up on this climb to the top, you decide to leave the large dome.

If you left Devilsbane on the platform before trying the stair, **TEST YOUR INTELLIGENCE**. If you pass, turn to **662**, if you fail, turn to **464**. If you did not leave Devilsbane, turn to **467**

635

You find yourself in another clearing with more options on which way to go. Lose 1 **ENDURANCE** point due to your exertions. There is nothing of note in this area, and you leave it quickly. You either go left and turn to **350**, or right and turn to **460**

636

TEST YOUR FORTUNE. With all the noise and activity in the room, you may be lucky to not have been noticed.

If you are fortunate, turn to **12**. If you are not, turn to **496**

637

As the Espirit flies down, you leap and grab hold of its legs with your strong arms. The creature squawks in alarm and tries to take off again. You hang on, but the creature has enough strength in its wings to lift you off the ground. As you hoped, it can just about support your weight - and so you manage to shift yourself so that it moves from the gantry to hovering over the edge of the vat. It beats its wings faster than ever, but your weight slowly starts to pull it down. You descend chaotically in half-circles into an empty vat, the ground rushing up to meet you.

But the wings of the Espirit do enough to slow your descent, and you land, albeit a bit heavily. Throw 1d4 and deduct that from your **ENDURANCE**.

Safely on the ground once more, you let go of the winged beast and, relieved, it swiftly flies away from you back up towards the raised walkways. The residents of the ground floor have all climbed various ladders to confront you, and so while you are safely back on the ground, you have little time.

TEST YOUR FORTUNE. If you are lucky, turn to **648**. If you are not, turn to **349**

638

With an effort, you clear your mind of horror and emotion and approach the door to the building. It's a large wooden double door, which stands open. You edge up to it and check around the corner. Inside the building seems to be one large room, but separated into sections or areas. On the left are several huge vats of liquid that are at least 20 feet high, and 20 feet wide. A gantry runs around each, and on each of the gantries stand a lesser Daemons and several imps. Each Daemon seems to be in charge, kicking, hitting and cursing at the imps to get them to obey their commands. Each imp has a long wooden stick, more like a paddle, with a rectangular end. Into each of those ends are set several holes of different sizes. At any given time, the imps have these sticks in the vats, seemingly stirring the contents.

If you want to sneak closer to these vats to find out their contents, turn to **175**. If you would rather move on and look at the next section of the building, turn to **290**

639

Your strike is successful. You target its writhing tail and injure it. Now you must continue to fight the beast.

CERBERUS has **FS 8, EN 20**

{ADVANCED - Initial AS: 13, Initial DA: 10; FIT 5, AG 5, ST 11}

If you are playing simple combat, and you manage to hit the tail three times, then turn to **574**. If you are playing **ADVANCED COMBAT**, then if you manage to score **SERIOUS** damage or higher, turn to **29**

You walk towards the approaching shapes and see they are humanoid in form, but all in grey, with cowls over their faces. Their grey robes are tattered and threadbare, trailing almost to the ground. They do not seem to have legs and feet, and appear to float across the surface. At present, there are about 10 of them, but each moment more appear in view until there are about 50 of the floating souls. The lead figure makes a small sign, and as one they throw their cowls back. In horror, you recognise a lot of the faces. They are the men of your small force that you were leading to destroy the Hellscape machine. But their faces are old, haggard and drawn, as if they are millennia old corpses; not freshly dead.

"How can this be? You are my men. I fought with you but a day or so ago - and led you in a holy battle. How can you be here? There hasn't been the time".

The lead figure, who you now recognise as one of your sergeants Hatton, laughs.

"Time, what is time to the dead. It has been 10,000 years since that day, and we have been here all that time, suffering in this limbo and yet you still live"

"How can this be?" you ask again.

"How do we know, we are just the dead, trapped on this plane for eternity"

"Then", you say rather rashly, "I will find a way to free you. Show me how to leave this realm, and I will do all that I can to return and save you."

Hatton laughs once more, a dry dusty sound like the wind blowing dried leaves.

"There is no saving us, but for the offer and the loyalty we once felt for you, we will aide you"

Turn to **119**

Wasting no time, you quickly cross the courtyard and approach the double doors. They are similar yet smaller than the external doors, except they are covered in polished silver that makes them mirror-like. As you approach, you expect to see a reflection of the desolation of the courtyard, but instead see a courtyard of opulence and wealth, with men and women of high birth walking together; talking and laughing. The women wear elegant dresses of silk and satin, and the men are wearing tailored uniforms of varying rank and insignia. Being well trained in military hosiery, you recognise the crests and sigils of various historical empires.

Here you see a Conjuror-Major dressed in the uniform of the Emperor of Terainh. Walking past him, arm in arm with a tall, beautiful lady in a yellow silk dress, is a Knight-Lieutenant of the King of Vitroliz. You know that 200 years past, before the Rightful Order took over, that the kingdoms of Terainh and Vitroliz were mortal enemies, and these two soldiers would never share the same courtyard without violence. As well as this, the courtyard has elegant sculptures, clever fountains and beautiful trees. It's like the doors are reflecting images of times gone by - or maybe places gone by. Steeling yourself, you seize the handle of the door and open it.

Turn to **307**

You seem to reach the edge of the deadwood, but the oppressive temperature is still weakening you. Lose 1 **ENDURANCE** point.

Ahead of you is an impenetrable barrier of trees, all intertwined. You can either choose to go left, then turn to **477** or go the right route and turn to **594**

643

The door opens into a circular room that seems suspended above the centre of the dome, with glass windows showing the full vessel below. Inside it are various angled desks about waist height that have dials, switches and flashing lights that you cannot understand but you suspect is something to do with lightning power. Standing at one of the desks is a tall, slim figure, his back to you. He busies himself, checking dials and flipping switches.

Below you can see that he seems to be controlling the fires under the vats, and signalling to the sub-daemons which vat is ready to be recycled by setting off a flashing light. You know enough about modern science as any man'o'war, so that you realise this is not mage work. On a desk in the centre are a pile of papers and a black leather-bound book.

If you want to leave the room, turn to **414**. If you want to attack the figure at the raised desk. Turn to **441**. If you want to pick up the black-bound book, turn to **245**

644

The giant wyrm throws you up about 50 feet in the air. You are dazed and confused as you feel like you have been hit by a dragon. Unable to react, you flail in the air as you fly upwards. Then you reach the zenith of your journey, and, spinning around, you start to descend again. You are now face down, falling towards the great wyrm. You can see its huge mouth opening even wider as you fall towards it. Row upon row of needle-like teeth ring its mouth, except these needles are each at least a foot long.

Stuck on the teeth are gobbets of flesh from other victims this behemoth has already consumed, and you are only a matter of moments from being its next meal. But time seems almost to stand still giving you the chance to appreciate the hopelessness of your predicament, and the hugely painful death you are about to suffer. After what seems like aeons, but was only seconds, your body falls into the gaping maw. The teeth effortlessly pierce both armour and flesh, and blood flows from your dozens of wounds. The huge mouth closes, and the teeth bury themselves even deeper into your vitals, and you scream once before your mortal body dies.

The wyrm continues to digest your mortal flesh, a rare treat, but your immortal spirit form is soon excreted out onto the plain, in amongst all the other human remains that feed Cerberus . You will be eaten and excreted over and over again for all time. Your mission has failed, and you pray for your world.

Turn to **616**

645

Having managed to negotiate around the room, you get to the archway and slip through.

Turn to **329**

646

You walk into the dark passage and all of a sudden the air is alive with seemingly small creatures. They fill the air, darting in and attacking you multiple times. You can see that all they appear to be are sets of chattering teeth, but instead of white enamel, they are made of dark ebony bone. There are other differences. The teeth are all long fangs, like a wolf or a dog, with no incisors. They bite at you, and you struggle to protect yourself.

Make a **FIGHTING SKILL** roll. If you fail, turn to **463**. If you succeed, make a **FORTUNE** roll. If you fail, then turn to **463**. If you succeed in both rolls, turn to **587**

647

You uncork the bottle and immediately a great whoosh of air is released, like a plume of blue smoke. The smoke swirls around you until it starts to solidify and take a corporeal form. The Djinn appears before you, floating in the air.

You hear no voice, but in the corridors of your mind the Djinn says *"What is your bidding, my master"*.

This is your first wish, one of three, so if you are sure you want to use it now, turn to the reference you were told to write down. Make sure you note on your **ADVENTURE SHEET**. If not, turn back to your previous reference and take the other option available.

648

Luck is on your side. You can see Devilsbane and your shield, and there is nothing to impede you retrieving both. You sprint to the bottom of the original ladder, and gratefully pick up both, strapping your sword belt back around your waist, and slinging your shield over your back. Turn to **597**

649

You head to the left, once again walking through the grey featureless plain, seemingly for hours. There is no sound as you walk, your boots making no impression on the earth and therefore creating no noise. All you can hear is your own breathing and the clinking of your chainmail. You slog on through the bleak domain until you eventually notice that there is something, or someone, almost visible in the far distance. You shout, but again the sound seems to die as soon as it leaves your mouth. You quicken your pace in anticipation. It's definitely a figure, armoured as you are and of a similar style, but is turned away from you and crouching down.

Do you want to carry on walking and try to engage the strange figure, then turn to **171**. Or do you draw Devilsbane and attack the man, turn to **88**

650

You speak the number, although the ungodly language is almost impossible for your human mouth to utter. The door half smiles, half grimaces, and then it starts to open, wider and wider. The tongue advances, laying itself on the floor in front of you, almost making a carpet for you to walk along past the teeth and into the stinking maw. You steel yourself and put one foot on the hideous tongue before walking towards the passage beyond.

The passage brings you out seemingly into another corridor, but it feels different from where you were. The walls are made of stone. Ahead of you are three doorways. If you want to choose to open one of these doors, then turn to **219**.

If you would rather search the area first, then you leave the corridor and find yourself in the courtyard of a castle. Turn to **454**.

But before you do write the name **SABINE** on your **ADVENTURE SHEET**.

651

Most Holy Aceada stops and turns to look at you. His face is old, drawn and haggard, and regret fills his eyes.

"Tell me, my son, how am I thought of on our world today?"

You feel immense sorrow and compassion for this shade of a man.

"Most Holy, you are seen as one of the greatest, if not the greatest, servants of the One True God. You unified the Church and brought the world under the service of The Almighty. Your name is sacred, and statues and portraits of you are everywhere in the Holy City, and worshippers touch them for luck."

Aceada sighs, and says *"I thought I did all I did for the glory of God, and yet it is here I am in service, not in the Golden Citadel above. For the love that I once had for the church, I can offer this. Wait here".*

He shuffles off and returns quickly. In his hand is a key. It looks to be made of bone and sinew and is twisted and gnarled. You take the key out of the air and examine it. Stamped on it is the number 10 and a green eye. Note this on your **ADVENTURE SHEET** along with the name **ACEADA**.

"Now quickly, my son, leave this room and seek the door the has the eye of Baalberith on it. Go, go quick. There will be, pardon the pun, Hell to pay when he finds out the key is gone."

You nod thanks, your eyes filled with compassion for this once great man, and leave. Turn to **35**

652

The path climbs up steeply here and, added to the temperature, this tests your **ENDURANCE** - literally. Roll 4d6. If you roll more than your current **ENDURANCE**, then roll 1d4 - and lose this many **ENDURANCE** points.

If you roll less than or equal to your current **ENDURANCE**, you manage to get to the top of the hill with no ill effect. At the top are two paths.

You can go left and turn to **93**, or go straight on and turn to **541**

653

After struggling on for several minutes, you come to a fork in the path. Lose 1 **ENDURANCE** due to the heat sapping your strength. In the centre of the fork is a single body tree that grows high up into the air. The strangely elongated face stares at you as it moans. The face is that of a young woman, and in her eyes, you can see a terrible longing. The wail then changes into a cry, and you can hear words within that terrible sound.

"Help me, please"

it says over and over

"give me what I need, the pain is too much and I need it so much"

Then the voice starts to wail again. You steel yourself and walk past. You can either go left, turn to **322**, or to veer right, turn to **469**

654

Now that there are no imps to empty it, the pool is starting to overflow, and the contents are spreading across the sponge-like floor, hissing and burning the floor on contact. It is getting perilously close to your feet, and so you turn and move towards the exit. The fumes that are released upon the liquid hitting the floor of the chamber makes you gag and cough, and burns at your throat.

Turn to **54**

655

If you want to further investigate this dome, turn to **583**. If you haven't checked the large dome, then you can do this instead and turn to **193**. If you would rather just head back to the crossroads, turn to **483**

656

Nodding, you speak again, telling the Djinn that you wish to be taken out of this room.

"Very well" the voice continues in your mind *"If that is your wish, then I must acquiesce to your request. However, young master, I do think that you may regret this course, and you may come to wish you had remained in the skillet".*

The Djinn places his 6 fingered hand on your head, and everything shimmers. Turn to **516**

657

Fortune is with you and has saved you from taking a long fall, likely to your death. You manage to recover and scramble onto the final step. You are at the top of the stair and now can go through the door. Turn to **586**

658

Despite your best efforts, you are overwhelmed by the number of imps. Near-death, they drag you to the edge of the vat and hurl you into it. The shock of the water is terrible, as it is about 70 degrees and you can feel your skin start to blister. You try to swim for the side, but your armour, which has so often saved your life, is now ironically intent on taking it. The weight is too much, and you start to sink. You try vainly to scramble against the other bodies floating in the liquid, but every time you get a handhold, a long wooden paddle pushes you under.

You vaguely see imps wielding these paddles, making sure you cannot grasp the rim of the vat or climb onto other bodies. You start to lose strength, your hand no longer having a grip of iron, and you struggle to hold onto anything. Eventually, the combination of the weight of your armour and the paddles pushing you under is too much, and you start to sink. And sink. And sink. You move down through the vat, past still-animated bodies flailing around in the liquid below the surface. You see faces that are practically just skulls, as the flesh and skin have peeled off them. You hit to bottom with a thud, and you are now struggling to hold your breath.

You draw your belt knife and, with your last strength, crawl along the bottom of the vat, over moving forms, to the edge. You try to prise at the wood with your knifepoint, but the wood is treated and iron-hard, and you only end up breaking your knife. You gasp for breath and take in a mouthful of semi-cooked human sludge. Then soon you are swallowing it by the pint, as you gasp for air that is not there. Your body stops struggling with a twitch, as you drown; but that's not the end for you.

Your mortal form dies, but your soul remains, still stuck at the bottom of this sludge of humanity, breathing in skin and sweat and human fat, whilst you are slowly cooked alive in your armour forevermore. Your mission has failed, and the human world will soon be overrun. Turn to **616**

659

As you look inside, many pairs of eyes look back at you. What you thought was just an ice bath is comprised of dozens of human bodies. They are each frozen to the point of their skin being blue and unable to move as their limbs are frozen stiff by their sides, their bodies bolt upright with their heads tilted back and mouths open. Into each upturned mouth is a tube that drops down from the ceiling.

The tubes are still wide enough so that each person's mouth is filled by their circumference, to the point that the skin is tearing at the corner of the mouths where the tubes enter. You look down and see that each tube seems to travel down the throat of its host and through their bodies before emerging from the host's rectum and out through the bottom of the vessel.

The bodies seem unable to move, except for their eyes, which look at you in horror and with a naked appeal for help. You stare into one young woman's face and struggle to keep your composure as she mutely appeals for mercy.

If you want to try to help the poor souls, then turn to **599**. If you decide that this is their torment and you have no responsibility to help them, then turn to **251**

660

You have found bottles of Daemon's-wine. This is a drink of the Daemons, distilled down from the suffering of human souls. If you have used it before, turn to 470. If not, turn to 361. Once you have done this, turn back to the reference you noted down.

661

This bottle is long, slender and twisted, with an elaborate crystal stopper. Inside is a clear amber liquid that seems to sparkle and effervesce in the bottle. You gently twist the immaculate stopper, and it gives way with a slight hiss. Straight away, you smell a light, herbal essence that seems to fizz while releasing its intoxicating odour.

You sip it, and it seems to form little bubbles on your palette. Once you have imbibed it, it seems like your eyes are seeing more than they ever have. You notice every detail of where you are, almost as if someone has painted portraits in your mind. Any book you read, you realise you will be able to remember word for word.

You have drunken a **POTION of INSIGHT** that allows the user to see and understand the world around them in great detail while also retaining this information. Increase your **INTELLIGENCE** by 2 permanently. However, as your senses are so busy taking in all this new information, it hampers the speed at which you can react - and so you must reduce your **AGILITY** by 1 permanently. Turn to the previous reference.

662

As you go to leave, you remember Devilsbane and your shield are on the platform. Carefully you make your way over and are able to grab them before exiting the dome.

You can either check the smaller dome and turn to **122**, or head back to the crossroads, turn to **483**

663

Taking the surcoat down, you strip off your own cloak and surcoat to try it on. It fits perfectly. But then there is a sudden disturbance in the air in front of you. A swirling vortex appears, and from the vortex charges a semi-skeletal horse ridden by a knight carrying a lance and a sceptre. The horse pulls up, scant feet from you, and the rider looks down at you with disdain.

"Who dares to wear my sigil? I will not suffer this - for it is my mark, and mine alone. Eligos will make you pay dearly for this presumption, mortal."

Turn to **416**

664

You walk forward and push both of the swinging doors open before walking through. In front of you is a room full of naked or half-naked men and women (and more disturbingly, some children). The room is full of seemingly plush furniture; settees upholstered in rich velvets. Chaise Longue's covered in the softest leather from the finest cattle. Large iron bedsteads with thick, plumb mattresses stuffed with eider. But what's happening on the furniture is far from comfortable.

All human forms are here. Fat, thin. Tall, short. Beautiful, ugly. Old, young. The one thing in common is the look of pain on their faces, and the torment in their eyes as the Daemons perform acts of such brutality on them that it draws all the colour out of your face and makes you stop-still. Limbs intertwine so that it's hard to see where one body starts and another ends, blood and worse pouring from claw marks and bites to their battered immortal bodies. Cries and groans of agony (or ecstasy) come from the mouths of the once-abusers turned abused. Fortunately, you were prepared for the worst, even though this is more so, and so you can keep your sanity.

Turn to **372**

665

Finally, you stagger up to the top of the stairs and find yourself back in the courtyard. Turn to **454** and make another choice.

666

"........Kommandant Ulrac De-Villiers"

To be continued in

Hellscape Volume 2

The Devils Right Hand

Straight to Hell

Adventure Sheet

Strength (STR)	1d6 + 6	
Fighting Skill (FS)	1d6 + 6	
Agility (AG)	1d6 + 6	
Fitness (FIT)	1d6 + 6	
Intelligence (INT)	1d6 + 6	
Endurance (END)	4d6 + 12	
Faith (FAI)	2d6 + 12	Turn to Section 13 if your FAITH gets to ZERO

First Attack (FA)	Items	Keywords
FS +1d10		

Attack Strength (AS)

FS + FIT + 1d20

Defence Ability (DA)

AG + FIT + 1d20

Damage (DAM)

STR + 1d10

Notes

Other

Clues

Basic Combat

OPPONENT	S K	ST			S K	ST	
OPPONENT	S K	ST			S K	ST	
OPPONENT	S K	ST			S K	ST	
OPPONENT	S K	ST			S K	ST	
OPPONENT	S K	ST			S K	ST	
OPPONENT	S K	ST			S K	ST	
OPPONENT	S K	ST			S K	ST	
OPPONENT	S K	ST			S K	ST	
OPPONENT	S K	ST			S K	ST	
OPPONENT	S K	ST			S K	ST	
OPPONENT	S K	ST			S K	ST	
OPPONENT	S K	ST			S K	ST	

Advanced Combat

Opponent

STARTING VALUES

STR	FS	AG	END

STR	FS	AG	END

CURRENT VALUES

FA
(FS+1d10)

You	Enemy

ROUND ONE

AS	DA	DIFF	DAM	ADDITIONAL
AS	DA	DIFF	DAM	ADDITIONAL

ROUND TWO

AS	DA	DIFF	DAM	ADDITIONAL
AS	DA	DIFF	DAM	ADDITIONAL

ROUND THREE

AS	DA	DIFF	DAM	ADDITIONAL
AS	DA	DIFF	DAM	ADDITIONAL

ROUND FOUR

AS	DA	DIFF	DAM	ADDITIONAL
AS	DA	DIFF	DAM	ADDITIONAL

ROUND FIVE

AS	DA	DIFF	DAM	ADDITIONAL
AS	DA	DIFF	DAM	ADDITIONAL

ROUND SIX

AS	DA	DIFF	DAM	ADDITIONAL
AS	DA	DIFF	DAM	ADDITIONAL

ROUND SEVEN

AS	DA	DIFF	DAM	ADDITIONAL
AS	DA	DIFF	DAM	ADDITIONAL

ROUND EIGHT

AS	DA	DIFF	DAM	ADDITIONAL
AS	DA	DIFF	DAM	ADDITIONAL

ROUND NINE

AS	DA	DIFF	DAM	ADDITIONAL
AS	DA	DIFF	DAM	ADDITIONAL

ROUND TEN

AS	DA	DIFF	DAM	ADDITIONAL
AS	DA	DIFF	DAM	ADDITIONAL

Acknowledgements

A big thank you to the below who all helped proof read this book – and all for nothing more than generosity of spirit and their name in print below. Thanks to all of you – it made my job so much easier.

Alan Halpin
Allen Klindworth
Clare Goss
Dane Barrett, author of The Mystery of Dracula
David Williams
DeDe Darris
Fenrir Wolfganger, that's who I am online
Gary Dewfield
Greg Allensworth
Hamad Alnajjar
Jam Hirons
Jamie Yardley
Jason Archer
John Savage
Joseph Quinn
Kevin Mullen
Lee Taylor
Louise Lee
Luke Sheridan
Mark Stanley
Oliver Drozd
Samuel Isaacson, author of the Entram series of gamebooks
Simon Scott
TroyAnthony Schermer, author of the Savage Realms series of gamebooks
Victor Cheng

And especially Dane Barrett, who read all 91,310 words (as of writing)

And

James Kail – For re-jigging the advanced fighting system in a way I could never have done

James Spearing of My Gamebook Adventures
Gary Dewfield
for playtesting the whole book

Jason Archer
For link testing it and finding a few orphans

And especially

Rob Hatton, of the Roulette of Death FF play-through fame
Victoria Hancox, author of Nightshift

For play-testing, feedback, support and suffering being messaged grotesque death paragraphs and art attempts at bizarre times of the day

Biography

David Lowrie was an 18th-century philosopher and poet, who fought against the One True Church all his life. He was arrested, excommunicated and then crucified by Most Holy Aceada in 1742AN.

Some years later, this account was found whereby it appears that Lowrie was, in fact, a papist and agent of the One True Church.

Prior to his death, he was tasked by Aceada with sending a small campaign of seasoned troops, headed by the most feared sword arm in the Eastern Realms, across to the 8th continent to stop a plot by the Daemons of the Hellscape to take over the mortal realm.

The record of this campaign was recently found in an excavation of Lowrie's private chateau. In this book, you find the decisions made during the campaign, and you can relive the experience by playing the part of the campaign leader.

Alternatively, Lowrie could just be some bloke who lives in Yorkshire and enjoys making stuff up.

Other great gamebooks from

BLACK DOG GAMEBOOKS

AVAILBLE NOW:

Shadow Thief Book 1:
Jailbreak

COMING SOON:

Shadow Thief Book 2:
Hunted (August 2020)

Psycho Killer
(31st October 2020)

The Hellscape Book 2:
The Devils Right Hand (2021)

Made in the USA
Monee, IL
24 October 2020